"FAST-PACED, ALIVE WITH PLOTS AND SUBPLOTS CHOCKABLOCK WITH CHARACTERS."

—*Publishers Weekly*

You've followed the Lavettes in *The Immigrants, Second Generation, The Establishment,* and *The Legacy.*

Now Barbara Lavette sets off an exciting new chain of events—as Congressional candidate, as foreign correspondent, as a woman rediscovering the meaning of love.

Around the thread of Barbara's life, Howard Fast weaves a tapestry for our times—the vivid, richly embroidered story of the Lavette clan as it enters its fourth generation. It is Barbara Lavette who must fulfill the promise . . .

The Immigrant's Daughter

"BARBARA [IS] CLEARLY ON THE SIDE OF THE ANGELS. . . . THE SUBPLOTS ARE SO COMPLEX ONSTAGE THEIR TANGLED EMOTIONAL LIVES DEMANDING A SIZABLE SHARE OF . . . ATTENTION."

—*Los Angeles Times*

Books by Howard Fast

THE IMMIGRANT'S DAUGHTER
THE OUTSIDER
MAX
TIME AND THE RIDDLE: THIRTY-ONE ZEN STORIES
THE LEGACY
THE ESTABLISHMENT
THE MAGIC DOOR
SECOND GENERATION
THE IMMIGRANTS
THE ART OF ZEN MEDITATION
A TOUCH OF INFINITY
THE HESSIAN
THE CROSSING
THE GENERAL ZAPPED AN ANGEL
THE JEWS: STORY OF A PEOPLE
THE HUNTER AND THE TRAP
TORQUEMADA
THE HILL
AGRIPPA'S DAUGHTER
POWER
THE EDGE OF TOMORROW
APRIL MORNING
THE GOLDEN RIVER
THE WINSTON AFFAIR
MOSES, PRINCE OF EGYPT
THE LAST SUPPER
SILAS TIMBERMAN
THE PASSION OF SACCO AND VANZETTI
SPARTACUS
THE PROUD AND THE FREE
DEPARTURE
MY GLORIOUS BROTHERS
CLARKTON
THE AMERICAN
FREEDOM ROAD
CITIZEN TOM PAINE
THE UNVANQUISHED
THE LAST FRONTIER
CONCEIVED IN LIBERTY
PLACE IN THE CITY
THE CHILDREN
STRANGE YESTERDAY
TWO VALLEYS

The Immigrant's Daughter

HOWARD FAST

A DELL BOOK

Published by
Dell Publishing Co., Inc.
1 Dag Hammarskjold Plaza
New York, New York 10017

Dell ® TM 681510, Dell Publishing Co., Inc.

ISBN: 0-440-13988-0

Reprinted by arrangement with Houghton Mifflin Company.

Printed in the United States of America

February 1987

10 9 8 7 6 5 4 3 2 1

WFH

For you, dear Bette, wife, lover,
companion through all the best and worst
of a full half century

One

She was thinking that it was exactly what she needed, a birthday party. Oh, yes indeed, it was just what she needed to remind herself that she was sixty years old. Thank you, thank you, thank you, I am sixty. That is something to write home about, isn't it? Here's my celebratory verse: It's nifty to be sixty and heavenly to be seventy. Stupid doggerel. Does one still weep at sixty? Or does the brine connote rheumy presenility? All thoughts of irresolute protest, and she was actually saying, "Please, let me be. Not that I don't want you to remind me, because I can't forget for a moment, and I can even face the fact that I am an old woman —yes, in spite of your indignant protests. Old? Since when is sixty old? You're still young and vital and beautiful and all the other assorted bullshit. I am old, and the truth is that I really don't give a damn about parties or any other kind of celebration."

The telephone rang.

Barbara Lavette picked up the telephone and spoke to her son, Sam, more formally Dr. Samuel Thomas Cohen, who kept the name of his father and who put together smashed hands and feet with great skill. In that crisp, knowledgeable tone that doctors assume, he informed his mother that he and Carla would stop by for her at about eleven. Something in Barbara always reacted to Carla and even to the mention of her name. She did not like Carla; howsoever much she tried, howsoever much she looked into herself, she could not bring herself to feel affection for her son's wife. This filled her with guilt. Carla was a Chicana, a Mexican but California born, out of five generations in California, more generations than Barbara could look back at, and, with good reason, proud, defensive and full of walls, safeguards and anticipatory hurts, an unfulfilled actress, who bridled when Barbara referred to her as an actor. "Don't give me that women's lib crap. I'm a Chicana and an actress."

She was a thorny woman, full-figured beautiful, a round face, round breasts, round limbs, yet tall enough to carry it with poise and dignity. But like a porcupine, there were quills of anger and resentment that bristled at a word, a suggestion, an intonation. Barbara prided herself that her relationship with Carla was easy, and that if no affection actually existed, at least a decent pretense of affection was maintained. Perhaps so. She was never entirely certain and never entirely free of the guilt she felt at not caring for her son's wife.

"Sam?" Barbara said.

He knew the tone of voice. "Mother, we want to stop by for you. I know you can drive out there by yourself."

"I wasn't thinking of driving out there by myself. I was thinking of not going. I just can't face it. Don't you understand, Sam, I simply can't face it?"

"Mother, it's seven months since Boyd died," he said, almost harshly. "You can't go on flagellating yourself. These are people who love you and want very much to see you."

She could imagine him looking at his watch while he spoke to her. Sam was always looking at his watch or listening to the tinkle that called him to the telephone. His day was precisely and carefully subdivided. Barbara's brother Joe was also a doctor, but one who lived easily. He might even forget his watch, leave it by his bedside; not Sam.

"I don't whip myself," Barbara said with annoyance. "And I don't enjoy it when you talk to me like that, Sam."

"I'm sorry, Mother. But please, please don't reject everyone. We love you. We've made so many preparations. May I pick you up?"

She sighed and said, "Yes. Very well."

She was aware that she was being childish and petulant. In all truth, she had no intention of avoiding her birthday party. She had never been cruel, and that would have been very cruel indeed, to fail to appear after the entire family had come together. It was a whimper; she admitted that to herself, underlining the fact that she had always despised whimperers, but in this case, a plea to Sam to see her, remember her, beg her. But he would look at her in astonishment if she told him that he had forgotten her. The whole world had forgotten her—or she had forgotten the whole world. That would simply evoke more astonishment. How could she explain what had happened inside herself?

Carla was being sweet. She could be endearing when she put herself to it. She embraced Barbara—unusual—and told Sam, "You drive, Doc. Barbara and I share the back, and I have things to tell her. And you look absolutely beautiful," she told Barbara, who was wearing a jacket of pale gray linen over a white silk blouse—a suit that would have fitted her just as neatly thirty years before. She had kept her figure; she had kept her firmness of body. "You're not going to let your hair go white," Carla added. Barbara wondered whether she was aware of her habit of taking with one hand as she gave with the other. There were pale streaks in Barbara's honey-colored hair, but it was far from white.

In the car, driving across the Golden Gate Bridge on their

way to the Napa Valley, Carla said to Barbara, "I've been holding this because I'm just about ready to explode with it, and I'm not going to pretend to be cool. They've given me the part of Annabella—finally, finally, and it's a special showcase thing, six weeks at the center. Can you imagine, Barbara? Annabella!"

"Back a bit. It's wonderful, of course, but Annabella what?"

"John Ford's play," Sam said from the driver's seat. " 'Tis Pity She's a Whore. Annabella's the lead part—you know, Mother, falls in love with her brother—"

"I know the play," Barbara said. "In fact, we did it a hundred years ago at Sarah Lawrence. Oh, no fear," she assured Carla, "I did not do the role of Annabella. No, I played a nurse or something of the sort. There is a nurse in it, isn't there?"

"There is."

"Carla, I think it's wonderful. Absolutely wonderful. It's what you've been working for, isn't it? And at the center. When? When is the opening?"

Mollified, Carla informed her that there would be six weeks of rehearsal, with an opening just after New Year's. "Of course, nobody does 'Tis Pity the way it was written. Ford was no Shakespeare, you know, and parts of the original script are sheer confusion. Our direction, Stan Lewis, is rewriting and restructuring—" and thus she went, on and on. Barbara listened, trying to nod appropriately and listen and then look past her to the green hills of Marin County. It was about two years since she had been out to the Higate Winery in the Napa Valley, a place bound up and threaded through with the lives and memories of the two families that had their beginnings in the partnership of her father, Dan Lavette, and Mark Levy; and it was disturbing to be without any feeling of anticipation. For most of her adult life, the Napa Valley, and the old winery that Jake Levy had purchased following his discharge from the army after World War I, had been a sort of glowing garden in Barbara's mind. Not that she spent much time there; its existence was enough, a place she could reach for when she was weary or when she had looked too much at the rest of the world. But this had changed. Boyd had died, and everything had changed.

The world turned gray. For three weeks, she left her home only to buy the few things she needed to survive. She had been subject to depression in the past, and, knowing this, her brother Joe had warned her in very careful medical terms that, in a manner, she was committing suicide. "Do you actually want to die?" he had asked her, exercising, as Barbara thought, the physician's right to ask any question, no matter how intimate or demeaning. She was more provoked than such a question demanded.

"Don't be a fool!"

"I think I can guess," Joe said, in that very gentle manner that he took with his patients, "where the guilt comes from. You're so ridden with guilt, Barbara."

"You don't know what you're talking about."

"Maybe."

"Guess! I don't give a damn!" She would forget that he was half Chinese, her brother Joseph, her half brother, actually, born out of their father's second marriage, to a Chinese woman named May Ling, and then he would suddenly look so very Chinese, in spite of his great bulk, two hundred and twenty pounds and six feet two inches tall. It made her smile; anger at Joe Lavette. No one was angry with Joe. How could you be angry with a large, intelligent Saint Bernard dog?

"You've been reading statistics: married men less subject to heart attack. Statistics are a marvelous substitute for mind, but the fact of the matter is that Boyd had been walking around with a bad heart, a very bad heart, for years. If you had married him, nothing would have been different. I didn't recommend the bypass surgery. I didn't think he could take it in his condition, but he insisted. He knew that he was at the end of his rope, and the thought that the surgery might give him five more years with you was worth a tilt with death. He was a good man, and he adored you."

She was crying. "If I had married him," she began, her voice breaking through the tears. "He wanted that so much."

"You were better together than any married people I know. All right, it's good to be sad and tears are a kind of therapy, but not guilty. Guilt kills the appetite. How much weight have you lost?"

"I don't know. I don't weigh myself."

"I'd say too much. You're not the anorexic type. Let me take you home to Napa. Baked ham for dinner."

She had refused the invitation, thinking to herself that her brother could be a very weird, spooky kind of Chinese, but the talk with him helped to shake her loose from the shroud of self-pity she was constructing. Her dear friend Eloise, coming by to see her a day or two later, put it wistfully: "I knew you wouldn't get bogged down with self-pity, Barbara. It's the kind of thing I used to do with these dreadful headaches that no doctor could do anything about, and then when Josh was wounded in Vietnam and came home without a leg, I wept and wallowed in self-pity and guilt until no one could tolerate me except you and poor dear Adam, but then it goes away. The pain goes away."

Barbara had often been tempted to say that nothing very much changed with Eloise, and then a second look would quell the temptation. A great deal changed with Eloise. She had gone through life with a round, lovely face, blue eyes and naturally blond hair and a small, soft voice that deceived people. No one who looked like Eloise and sounded like her could have a brain in her head, except that

Eloise was wise and quick-witted and had lived for years with a very painful incurable disease that she had never allowed to dominate or defeat her. She had been married to Barbara's brother Thomas, unhappily, and then had divorced him to marry Adam Levy, who was the grandson of Mark Levy, Barbara's father's partner. So her thoughts went, loose, disordered, reaching out here and there, while Carla babbled along, spelling out the plot of Ford's play, her own role, and what she planned to do with it. Barbara nodded appropriately, but no longer heard; she was in the well of her own thoughts, unraveling the connections and memories stirred up by the visit to the winery.

It was Boyd's death that had changed everything for Barbara. The solid shape of reality had shimmered and collapsed. Life and death suddenly were no longer separated. When she had wept, she had wept for all the love and beauty that had gone away forever.

"Carla!" Sam said sharply.

Barbara realized that Carla had not broken her account.

"I talk too much," Carla said. "Well, I don't talk too much. But now that I have something to talk about—Did it ever occur to you, Sam, how many hours I sat and listened to you and your smartass doctor friends talk about doing your thing? But that's important. Being an actress is not important. Absolutely not; it only keeps me from getting pregnant and bringing some more Lavettes into the world—"

"Carla, I didn't mean that, I didn't mean that at all. Please, don't make this into another fight."

"Why not? Because Barbara's here?"

The coiled spring of a fight began to tighten. Barbara had been here before, and now she shrank back in dread. Outbursts of fury on the part of her son bewildered and terrified her, and Carla would rise to his anger with a Latin intensity that matched Sam's rage. Barbara sometimes felt that the marriage should never have been, and she surmised that the only force keeping it together was the transformation of the anger into a sexual passion on the same level as the rage. It was an uneasy surmise on her part; son and mother maintained notions of mutual purity that matched each other in unreality.

It was then, at this moment, that she saw the school bus lose its right rear wheel. They had passed Schellville, driving east toward Napa, when Sam found himself behind the school bus. Driving automatically, his attention concentrated on the developing fight with his wife, he made no attempt to pass the bus, which was moving at about forty miles an hour. Actually, he was almost tailgating. Then Barbara saw the school bus lose its wheel, and she screamed, "Sam—for God's sake, look! The bus!"

She saw the rest as if it were being played on a film screen in slow motion. It was an old yellow school bus, half filled with children, eleven or twelve children, for even in those fractions of a second that spelled out the impending tragedy, Barbara was able to estimate the number of children. The wheel rolled off the road, the school bus lurched to the right, and then, seeking to bring it under control, the driver twisted the bus to the left, where it crossed into the opposite lane and crashed head on into an oncoming gardener's truck. Sam's foot on the brakes of his own car brought them to a screeching halt just short of the two wrecked vehicles.

Sam was out of his car the moment he brought it to a halt, telling Carla, "My bag, in the trunk." He threw the keys of the car to her as he ran toward the school bus. Carla got the trunk open; Barbara ran after Sam without waiting for Carla to get the bag and a package of dressings that Sam always carried in the trunk of his car. Sam was shouting to Carla, "Dressings—package next to the bag."

Then he pulled open the back door of the bus and plunged

inside. Barbara followed him, a veritable agony of sound greeting her, cries of terror and pain.

Smoke filled the bus, and Sam shouted, "Get them outside, Mom! Never mind the trauma—just get them outside! The bus is burning!"

She pushed two children who could walk past her. "Outside, darlings!" or something of the sort. "And run from the bus!" not knowing whether they understood. Carla squeezed past her with Sam's bag. A child lay crumpled in her seat, bleeding from a head wound. The children were seven or eight years old. Barbara picked up the unconscious child.

"Don't move her if she's hurt," Carla said.

"Sam wants them out of the bus."

"Up here!" Sam shouted to Carla. "Get up here! I need help!"

Outside the bus, someone screamed in pain. Barbara ran about fifty feet before she laid the child down off the road and then she herded children away from the accident. Carla climbed out of the bus with another child in her arms, and then Sam handed still another bleeding child to Barbara.

A car stopped and the driver came running to help. A black man. He plunged into the burning bus without a word. He came out with a child in his arms, followed by Sam, who carried another child.

"Two more inside." He handed the child to Carla. Barbara was back in the bus. One of two hurt little boys could walk. The other screamed in agony as Barbara tried to pull him out from where he was wedged under a seat.

"Let me," the black man said.

Together they managed to get him loose. Barbara half started toward the driver. Her eyes were burning from the smoke.

"Mother, get out of there!" Sam yelled. "The driver's dead!"

Thick smoke as she felt her way to the exit door. Sam and

Carla fairly plucked her out of the bus, both of them shouting, "Run! Run!"

The bus exploded in a burst of flame as they reached the place where the children were huddled together, and bits of glass and burning bus rained on them. The children were screaming. Barbara tried to soothe them. None of the children was badly injured; cuts and bruises. The child Barbara had first carried out of the bus was conscious now. Sam ran to the pickup truck, where the driver, screaming with pain, resisted efforts to free him. Then the driver fainted. Carla and Sam worked together, smoothly and expertly. The black man threw off his jacket, pulled off his shirt, and tore it into strips. Bandages to hold on their dressings. It took her back forty years to that infamous Bloody Thursday, when the longshoremen on the San Francisco waterfront had clashed with the police and when she had helped man a first-aid station all through the hot and bloody morning. Different but the same, somehow, because, as it came to her in a flash, time is an illusion in any case, and here she was on her knees, holding a weeping, bleeding child to her breast while she wept with her own memories.

Then there were ambulances and fire engines and police cars and tow trucks. The injured truck driver and the children were placed in the ambulances. The police took statements, informed Sam that they would be called upon to attend an inquiry and an inquest, and finally left them alone on the roadside.

The wreckage was dragged away, and the four people, bloodstained from head to foot, were left alone with their two cars.

The black man, in his undershirt but maintaining dignity, introduced himself. "Harvey Lemwax."

"No," Carla said. "Can't be. You're not Harvey Lemwax. Things like that don't happen."

"Oh, absolutely. Harvey Lemwax."

Sam introduced the group. "This is my wife, Carla, my mother, Barbara Lavette. Myself, Dr. Sam Cohen. From Carla's reaction, I realize I should be ashamed not to recognize you. I apologize. Unfortunately, most doctors know little beyond their own medicine."

"Don't apologize, please."

"Then tell us."

"Well—I play trumpet—"

Barbara's knowledge of trumpet players was nonexistent, but on the other hand, Harvey Lemwax gave no indication of ever having heard of Barbara Lavette. Of course, she was by no means the best-known writer in the United States, but neither was she unknown. She had occupied a place in *Who's Who* for the past thirty years, and if her books were not widely enough read, certainly her past had elicited enough nonliterary headlines for her to feel less than apologetic.

"I'm sure you're superb at it," Barbara said. "If you do it the way you stormed into that smoking bus, I take my hat off to you."

"Superb is hardly the word," Carla said.

"About the smoke," Barbara went on, "I've been coughing my head off. Should I worry about it, Sam?"

"Oh no, no. We need a drink."

"Superb, indeed," Carla said. "Only one of the three or four greatest and when I say greatest, I mean greatest, but absolutely. Right there with Dizzy Gillespie and Louis Armstrong and Roy Eldridge."

"Too much, too much!" Lemwax exclaimed. "You are good people. I am glad to have met you, a good meeting, except that we must say God help that poor bus driver and rest his poor soul. Will all them kids be all right, Doc?"

"Cuts, contusions, a broken arm, two or three teeth lost and some blood. Not awful by any means. But don't ride off into the sunset yet, Harvey. Today's Mother's birthday."

"That is your mother?"

He had been told that, Barbara remembered.

"She is too young and too beautiful."

"Bless your heart," Barbara said.

"What I am saying is this," Sam told them. "In the trunk of my car is a cooler containing six bottles of beautiful French champagne. The celebration of Mother's birthday is to take place at the home of family of sorts in the valley north of Napa where they have a winery, which is what they live, talk, and know. They are bigoted peasants who will not drink French wine or even discuss French champagne. But Mother must be toasted properly, so just sit still while I get to it, provided you will drink Dom Perignon out of paper cups."

Barbara listened to him with amazement. They had just witnessed a horrible accident. The driver of the school bus was dead. The driver of the pickup truck, a Mexican gardener, had been taken to the hospital in critical condition. The bloodstains and the oil stains were still plain on the road and the stink of burning gasoline was still in the air.

"We did our best," Sam said, spreading his hands. He saw her expression.

Well, he had. Dried blood marked them all. Carla, dressed in her white silk best, had not hesitated to plunge into the effort, and now the silk was stained with blood and grime.

"I'm sorry, Mrs. Lavette," the black man said, as if compelled to apologize for the others. Barbara realized that he was embarrassed, standing in his undershirt, trying to maintain his original moment of dignity. They didn't know the bus driver. They were under no compulsion to mourn him, or was the whole world under a compulsion to constantly mourn the dead? What do the dead deserve? Barbara clasped her hands and stood stiff and very still for a long moment.

"Are you all right?" Carla asked her.

"Yes," she whispered. "Just shaken."

Sam opened a bottle of champagne. Carla opened a package of plastic cups. The cork popped.

Tenderly, Sam said to his mother, "Drink this. It will help."

She shook her head. She was crying, softly, gently. Even more embarrassed, Harvey Lemwax said that he really had to go.

"One for the road," Sam said, handing him the cup of champagne. He filled a cup for himself and one for Carla, but then offered his cup to Barbara. "Mother?"

She pushed away the tears with the back of her hand and accepted it. Sam poured another for himself, offering a toast: "Life, not death. There were twelve kids in the bus and they'll all be okay. We got them out."

Barbara nodded.

"Then bottoms up!"

The wine was cold and good, and it eased Barbara's throat, and it came to her that if they had not been directly behind the school bus and if Sam had not plunged into it, followed by herself and Carla and Harvey Lemwax—if another two or three minutes had gone by—the children would have died.

"And in this crazy, lunatic country," Carla was telling Lemwax, "my husband could be sued. Can you imagine, for saving lives he could be sued!"

"The hell with that," Sam said. "Once more around."

"I feel a bit strange," Barbara said. "I have to get out of the sun, Sam."

They made an odd group, standing at the side of the road and drinking champagne. Behind them, a billboard proclaimed the merits of Toyotas. Barbara sank into the back seat of the car gratefully. It was hot in the car, but not so hot as out there in the sun. A motorcycle cop pulled up and they offered him champagne. He grinned and shook his head. Probably, Barbara thought, he'd heard about the accident. Sam was a hero. He was questioning them, and writing down the answers on his pad.

The motorcycle cop took off, and Sam opened another bottle of champagne. Their little group was only twenty paces or so away from the car, but through the closed window it appeared to Barbara that she was in one world and they were in another world. It was chokingly hot in the car, parked as it was on the roadside under the noonday sun, but Barbara made no move to open a window or to turn on the motor and use the air conditioning. She was thinking about the driver, and how death could be so summarily dismissed. This was another aspect of her son: death comes, life goes on; and if death comes to someone whose name is not known, a stranger who dies driving a school bus, well, you take a glass of champagne. Sam was open-minded; no sense of the black man being black. The driver of the school bus had had his chest stove in against the wheel and his skull fractured as it crashed against the windshield. Was he married? Did he have children? Did he have life insurance? Was she, Barbara, weeping for him, for herself or for Boyd?

The black man had gone to his car and brought out his trumpet case, and now he took out his shining instrument, put it to his mouth and blew several fanfares into the California air. More champagne. The three of them embraced and then Harvey Lemwax put his trumpet back in its case, took it to his car, came to say goodbye to Barbara, started, stopped when he saw her tears, shook his head and then walked to his car and drove off.

Sam came to the car and threw open the door. "My God, it's so hot in here, Mother, you could choke. Why on earth are you crying?"

"I don't know."

"We finished two bottles of that elixir. Carla and I are

both sloshed, so you'd better drive. Are you all right? I mean, are you settled enough to drive?"

"Of course," Barbara snapped at him. "I had one small sip of champagne."

"I didn't mean—"

"I know what you meant—oh, Sam, I'm sorry. I didn't intend to get so upset and scream at you. That isn't my style, is it? Of course I'll drive."

"About that silly little act we put on? We're not heartless, Mother, but if you bleed for everything—well, how much blood does one have?"

"I know."

Carla was silent. Barbara stepped out of the car and into the driver's seat. Sam held open the back seat door for Carla, but Carla said, "No, I'd like to sit in front with Barbara."

"Sure."

Barbara just glanced at Carla. A few moments after the car began to move, Carla reached out tentatively and touched Barbara's arm. Then Carla burst into tears. Barbara slowed the car and took it off the road onto the shoulder.

"What in hell is this all about?" Sam wanted to know.

"Sam, please shut up," Barbara said. She got out of the car, walked around and opened the door on Carla's side. Carla came out of the car into Barbara's arms, and embracing her, holding her soft, warm body against her own breast, Barbara understood that this was something women could do, a kind of human contact that men had lost long, long ago.

"I only wanted you to love me," Carla whimpered.

"I know. I do, truly."

Back in the car, Barbara drove on again, thinking that this short trip to the Napa Valley could turn into some kind of Voltairean adventure, going on and on, encounters with the hurt, the wise, and the foolish. And what was wrong with her, herself, Barbara Lavette, that here she was at sixty years and supposedly a woman of experience and insight, yet she had never really tried to comprehend this dark, tumultuous woman her son had married? The rich and the poor, always the rich and the poor, something she had wrestled with all her life, the difference being so basic and so deep, like all the apparently unalterable differences this world presented, black and white, Chicano and Anglo.

Sometime around nineteen twenty or nineteen twenty-one, Carla's father, Cándido Truaz, had come to work at Higate Winery, to become foreman, to have Jake Levy build him a house on the property. Carla had been born there on the grounds of Higate, had grown to womanhood there, had played as a child with the children of the Levys and Lavettes in a kind of tangled relationship that she as a child never really understood, except that she did come to realize that the brown-skinned were the disinherited and the white-skinned were the inheritors.

God, help me; Barbara pleaded the thought. Nothing was worse than to face one's own inadequacy and insensitivity. It was too much of being Barbara Lavette. If age did nothing else, it sometimes brought along with the wrinkles a kind of insight.

She sighed and said, "We're almost there, so I imagine we'll have no more adventures. But what shall we tell them about the clothes? We look like we've been through a battle."

"So we shall tell them about the battle," Sam said.

"I wore my best dress," Carla said, mournfully.

"Clothes don't matter. The dress can be cleaned and they have plenty of clothes there." Then she said to Carla, softly, "Forgive me, please."

"For what?"

"Just forgive me."

Sam listened in dubious silence. Emotional outflowing

disturbed him. It gave him a feeling of being naked in a bad dream.

They had done this up brown, and peach and white, which were the colors of the enormous tent they had raised. This was to be only the family to celebrate Barbara's sixtieth birthday, but it was the family in the Western, not in the Eastern sense. A California family, settled there in the last hundred years, was limited; and with this knowledge of limitation and the sense of awayness and loneliness that prevailed before the coming of easy air transport and cheap long-distance telephoning, a family tended to cling to the most fragile relationships. A new family emerged because the Pacific Ocean, only a few miles away, made a barrier to westward wandering, and in this case, the big old winery was a magnet of sorts. It was ruled over by Clair Harvey Levy, Jake's widow, and operationally it was guided by Adam Levy, Jake's son. Eloise was his wife. Freddie Lavette was Eloise's son from her first marriage, to Thomas Lavette, and Freddie and his half brother, Joshua, were totally dedicated to the growing of grapes and the making of wine. Adam's brother, also Joshua, had been killed in the Pacific during World War II, and the third child of Jake and Clair, Sally Levy, had married Barbara's half brother, Joseph Lavette. It went on from there, and Barbara could remember trying to explain the family quilt to Boyd. He never quite got it all straight and sorted out. When Sally's daughter, May Ling, one-quarter Chinese, married Freddie Lavette, no one could comprehend what their previous blood relationship had been. Along the way, other families had interacted and interconnected: the Cassalas, who were a kind of royal Italian clan such as existed only in San Francisco during the first half of the century, and the Devrons, who owned the better part of downtown Los Angeles.

Along with these, there was the Truaz family, Carla's

family, who lived on the place, big, barrel-chested Cándido, his wife, two kids besides Carla; and there were also various and sundry grandchildren and half a dozen other kids whom Barbara could not properly place, and, in the brash, bright pavilion, a five-piece mariachi band. The cooking was Mexican, under the supervision of Cándido's wife, Martha: huge pots of chile beans, stacks of tortillas, wide bowls of mole, succulent chicken immersed in a wonderful bitter chocolate sauce, saffron rice mixed with shrimp, red snapper Vera Cruz, and wine, red wine, which was in tribute to old Jake Levy, who had never considered white wine to be a drink fit for a grown man.

And Barbara, seeing all this, said to herself, ruefully, And I would have missed this and sulked. How awful that would have been.

They loved her, and such expressions of love filled her with guilt, something she had puzzled over all her life.

In Eloise's bedroom, dressed in a clean skirt and blouse that Eloise had provided, Barbara confessed the small agony of being kissed and embraced by so many people.

"Yes, I always feel that way—filled with guilt," Eloise said.

"Do you know why?"

"No, not really. Do you, Barbara?"

"Sort of. You possess deep down the notion of being undeserving of love—or undeserving of anything good, one might say, and then you receive it and it's a mistake, like a package being delivered to the wrong person. I told you about that dreadful accident. The children weren't hurt badly, but the driver of the school bus was killed, and less than a half hour later, Sam was passing around a champagne bottle, and all I could think of was the poor broken body of the man as the firemen dragged him out of the bus, and I was sick with guilt. But why? One moment I say it's the sense of being undeserving of love, and then that doesn't explain it—"

"My parents loved me too much," Eloise said. "I was a pretty little doll—a precious thing, I suppose they felt, but not a person. But today, you and Carla and Sam saved those children's lives. I've never seen Carla like that. It did something to her."

"Yes—to all of us."

"The skirt is perfect on you," Eloise said, and then she sat down and began to cry. Her husband, Adam, knocked, opened the door and waited, his hand on the knob. He was a tall, slender man, with a pleasant freckled face, sunburned arms and orange hair turning white. He stood in the doorway watching his wife for a long moment, and then said, more harshly than Barbara had ever heard him speak to Eloise before, "It's got to stop! The boy is alive and well, and I will not live out my life with a self-pitying bundle of tears."

Surprisingly, at least to Barbara, Eloise snapped, "I am not self-pitying, Adam! I won't have you talk to me like that!"

Adam started to speak—and swallowed his words. He was nervous, distraught.

"In front of Barbara," Eloise said, unhappily.

"I'm sorry." He went to Eloise, but she retreated into herself, her head bent. He looked at Barbara helplessly.

"She'll be all right," Barbara said. "Just leave us together, Adam. Please."

"I don't know," Adam said. "I shouldn't have said that. I'm not myself either. God Almighty," he said to Eloise, "you know how much I love you! We have more damn blessings than ninety-nine percent of the people on this earth!" And with this, he walked out, slamming the door behind him.

Barbara handed Eloise a box of tissues. "We have this in

common," Barbara said. "We're both of us the easiest cry on the Coast. Tears frighten men. It's our old, old weapon, and some men go into an absolute panic with it. Boyd did—just went to pieces—and it appears that your Adam disintegrates just as easily."

"And I don't cry that much. I was so strong all through this agony of Joshua's. Even when I learned that they'd amputated his leg, I managed. I did manage. But two weeks ago, he got his permanent prosthesis, and somehow that—I don't know. It did something to me—"

"I can understand that," Barbara said.

"He became so angry, Joshua did. He was never really against that filthy war. You know, he wouldn't even discuss Vietnam. Oh, he had one awful fight with Freddie, but then when Freddie went to jail for nine months as a conscientious objector, Joshua didn't have a word to say against him. He was in boot camp with the marines then. He just said, His way and my way—they don't mix. But since he came back, his hatred of the war and the government and Johnson—he becomes livid if anyone mentions Johnson. To him, it was Johnson's war. I've never seen anyone change like that—"

"But people do."

"I know. He had to spend those months in the hospital, and that was torment time, but I thought it was easing up. He said to Freddie that he'd never sleep with a girl again," woefully. "Can you imagine, Barbara, that no woman should ever look at his wound? But I thought that would change. I still do, but when this prosthesis was fitted, he just withdrew into himself, and it's been awful. And then Freddie gets the notion of making this huge dance card—you know Freddie adores you—and everyone who wants to dance with you signs it. Josh wouldn't. I know I cry too much."

Barbara found Joshua sitting on a bench outside the old stone aging building, one leg bent, the leg with the prosthesis stretched out in front of him. She had seen him in the hospital, but this was the first time she had seen him since his release and return to Higate. He had changed a great deal from the chubby, cheerful boy she remembered in years past. He was bone-lean, and his face was full of sharp edges and angry knots. He had the same pale blue eyes as her son, Sam; cold eyes. As Barbara approached him, he began to work his way to his feet. She accepted this, feeling that if she told him not to rise, it would have been taken as a direct insult.

"Aunt Barbara."

She was actually Freddie's aunt, but since Freddie was his half brother, he had always called her that. He kissed her cheek, almost absently. Barbara remained silent, and finally Joshua said, "I'm glad to see you."

"Yes, we have something in common," Barbara said flatly. "We lost part of ourselves. You lost a leg. I lost the man I loved better than I ever loved another. He was a part of me, and I lost him. I lost the right to live without endless loneliness. I lost the hope of a warm and decent old age in whatever time I have left. I lost the joy of sleeping with him, yes, of having intercourse with him, which I still need and want; of feeling his good protective warmth. All that—not with fake glory, but with the failure of his poor sick heart." With that, she turned and began to walk away.

She had taken no more than three or four steps before he called after her, "Aunt Barbara!"

She turned and faced him.

"What in hell do you want of me?"

"I want to dance with you."

"What!"

"Exactly. It's my birthday. That's what that big striped tent and all the rest is about over there, and you can hear the music and you can smell the chile beans even down here where you're hiding, and Freddie, I hear, made a dance card, and I want you on it."

"I can't dance!"

"Why not?"

"Because I can't. Look at me."

"That's bullshit, and you know it."

He stared at her in astonishment, and then a long silence, the two of them staring at each other, and then Barbara smiled and then he smiled.

"Do you know what I'll look like, trying to dance?"

"Who cares?"

"I'll probably fall flat on my face."

"I'll pick you up. Now take my arm and escort me back to the party."

Clair Levy, Jake's widow, talked Barbara into staying overnight, and now with the party over and the wine drunk and the food eaten, Clair and Barbara sat in the kitchen of the old stone house that had been Clair's home ever since she and Jake had bought the winery. They were drinking tea and eating ham sandwiches that Clair had put together, neither of them having tasted much food during the course of the party.

"Good party?" Clair asked. Clair was seventy-four years old; her hair, once a marvelous burnished copper color, had turned white, and a lifetime on the farm—this winery being essentially a farm—had turned the skin of her face leathery and wrinkled. Withal, she was a handsome woman, tall, erect when she stood, a woman who worked all day with satisfaction and vigor. Barbara noticed her hands, splotched not with what they called liver spots, but with freckles. Clair ignored the modern warning against women with fair skin exposing themselves to the sun. "I love the warm sun," she would say. "And I'm old. Nothing will change that." But the hands were beautiful, strong, long-fingered.

"Oh, splendid," Barbara assured her. "But such a great, important affair. I am so overwhelmed. It must have cost a fortune."

"We needed a party. Money—oh, for heaven's sake, Barbara, I'm past giving two damns for money. With the new bottling plant in Vallejo, the winery's making more than enough money. But we needed a party. Oh, in any case, I wouldn't have missed your birthday. It's seven months since Boyd passed away. You needed something to shake you up."

"I haven't started to open the presents. Somehow, you reach an age when presents don't mean very much."

"You're not at that age. Not to me. I'm fourteen years older than you—and old? I suppose so. I began to be old when Jake died."

"Do you get over being lonely?" Barbara wondered.

"I'm not sure. Of course, I'm lucky. Here at the winery, there are the children and the grandchildren, and I suppose that makes me luckier than ninety percent of the old women in this country. We're a rotten society on that account. We don't care for the old; we don't want them."

"No, we're not very civilized about that."

"Or about much else," Clair said. "Jake once said an odd thing about that—when he turned seventy. He said that old age is a country you never visit until you come to settle there. Ah, well, I'm not sure I'd want to be younger. I'd go looking for a man like Jake, and I'd never find one. Did I ever tell you how I met him?"

"No, I don't think so," Barbara said.

"I was twelve, one of those impossibly homely, skinny kids. I was already five six, bone-skinny, long legs, freckled everywhere the sun touched me, and hopelessly in love with your father, with old Dan Lavette. He was in the process of buying a big old ship from a man called Swenson—"

"The *Oregon Queen!*"

"Exactly. Pop and I lived on the ship, which was tied up

at the old pier; caretakers—Pop, I mean, when he wasn't drunk, my beautiful, wonderful little-boy father. He captained the last clipper ship to berth in San Francisco. The ship stayed there and rotted until they broke it up, and Pop stayed drunk, on and off, and he had this crummy job of caretaker. Then your daddy brought your mother to see the ship before he bought it, and I saw this glorious, sexy beauty, Jean Lavette, the toast of the town, and it broke my heart. Absolutely."

"I'm so sorry," Barbara said.

"No need. Jake caught me on the rebound. He was fourteen."

"And my daddy bought the ship, didn't he?" Barbara asked. "Of course, that was the *Oregon Queen*. But what happened to your father?"

"You wouldn't remember. You were just in the process of being born. But no one ever told you?"

"No one, I'm afraid."

"Well, you know, Jake's father, Mark Levy, and your daddy were partners then. More like brothers. By the time World War One started, they had a whole fleet of ships. Your father got Pop cleaned up and he stayed sober and then your father made Jack Harvey a captain of one of their cargo ships. I guess Captain Jack Harvey was as happy as any man on earth, but it didn't last. A German U-boat torpedoed him off the British coast, and the ship went down with all hands." She dried her eyes with her napkin. "Why am I crying? That was almost sixty years ago."

"No, no, Clair, dear. Time is an illusion. I think of Bernie. Twenty-six years ago, and the tears are there."

Bernie was her first husband, Sam's father, who had died in Israel in 1948.

"And then I think of Boyd, and at night I reach out to touch him and he isn't there."

Clair said nothing. Barbara rose and said, "I'm a ninny—

this kind of talk. I think I'll go outside and walk a bit. Will you come, Clair?"

Clair shook her head. "Take a sweater. The nights are cold now. There's a whole rack of them in the hall. Just take anything."

Outside, wrapped in a heavy sweater, a sweater sweet with the old smell of a man, Barbara stood still and let her eyes adjust to the darkness. It was cold, with just enough wind to bring her the good smell of hot mesquite out of the burned-down barbecue pits. She looked up and remembered the California sky that she had not seen for so long, the great mantle of twinkling points of light, the endless, unlimited universe that terrified her so when she thought about it. But tonight, she watched it without thought or reflection on anything except an acknowledgment of its cold beauty.

She could still make out the big striped pavilion that Clair had put up for a proper birthday party. What a strange, antique habit it was for man to celebrate each milestone on the road that brought him and all his peers closer and closer to the final end! What else in the darkness? She had given up the contemplation of the heavens, shivering at things beyond thought. She had said to herself, after Boyd died, that she would not fear what he had already passed through, but that did not turn out to be the case. She stared into the dark, her eyes dropping from the hills and the dappled sky. Even the scent of the dying barbecue fires did not make the air less sweet.

Voices came out of the dark on the way to the parking place. Four figures and Freddie's voice, asking, "Is that you, Aunt Barbara?"

Freddie and May Ling, Freddie's slender, dark-haired wife, and with them Sam and Carla; they paused for her to join them.

"What on earth are you doing out here in the cold?" Sam asked.

"Contemplating the universe, I suppose. Then it became too chilly. Not the air. The universe."

"You know, I never kissed you today," Freddie said. "Everyone else did. Hands down, the best-looking woman in the place. I think you were avoiding me."

"Freddie!"

"Can I kiss you now?"

"If you wish."

"Come with us," Carla said impulsively. "We're driving down to Vince's Place in Napa. Nothing very important. We'll have a few beers and listen to some good rock."

"Thank you, darling," Barbara said. "But it's been a long day, and I'm ready for bed. Anyway, I don't love rock."

"We're staying with Freddie," Sam said. "We'll take you back to the city tomorrow, Mother. Unless you want to stay here?"

"No, I'll go back with you."

They went off into the night, their figures becoming more and more shadowy and then engulfed by the darkness. There was a system of floodlights all through the winery, but there was no night shift working, and the velvet darkness, punctured by a lit window here and there in the houses, spread over most of the place.

Barbara heard the cough of a car starting, and then yellow headlights swept out of the winery's big parking place. She followed the progress of the car down the winery's driveway onto the main road. Then she went back into the house to bed.

In the car, driving south toward Napa, May Ling said suddenly, "I don't want to go to Vince's Place. I want to talk. You can't talk with that rock blaring at you. You don't even hear yourself think."

"You can listen," Freddie said.

"I don't want to listen. I want to talk. I want to talk about that whole little act you put on with Aunt Barbara."

"Act! What in hell are you talking about?"

"You know exactly what I'm talking about. That great big flirtation scene you just put on with Aunt Barbara. It's just so charming. Do you really think it makes her feel good or gives you points to tell her she's the most beautiful woman in the party? She's old enough to be your grandmother."

"Oh, come on, come on," Sam said, pulling the car over onto the shoulder of the road. "This is the damn dumbest subject for a fight that I ever heard of. You're talking like Freddie was born yesterday, or as if you met him last week. He's constitutionally unable to avoid coming on to every woman he faces. I've seen him do the same thing with his own mother. It's not his fault. It's just a lovely aberration."

"Oh, great!" Freddie yelled. "Just great!"

"I'm not putting you down. I wish I were that way."

"You don't fight about the things you fight about," Carla said.

"The voice of wisdom."

"She's right," May Ling said. "We're coming apart at the seams, and it gets worse."

"We've been coming apart at the seams since the day we got married," Carla said. "We need a new marriage ceremony—love and cherish for at least three weeks."

"That doesn't help," Sam said.

"Nothing helps, but don't make me the bad guy. She wants a divorce," Freddie said.

"What!" Carla had never thought in terms of divorce. You fought, you screamed, you ripped each other's flesh, and then you fell into bed and made love and wept and made love again, and it was just about as great as it could be. You didn't talk about divorce.

"This is insane and unreal," Sam said. "You're going to tell me that May Ling wants a divorce?"

"That's right."

"Is there a reason?" Sam asked. "Aside from the fact that maybe you hate each other."

"I don't hate him, I love him."

"You hate her?"

"Don't be a fucken idiot, Sam."

"Then why?"

"You know why," May Ling said. "We're first cousins. You saw my baby, Sam. I'll never go through that again. He wants children—then let him find someone else. I'll never have a child again. I won't bring monsters into this world."

"Your baby was an encephalitic. Such babies die in a few hours or a few days. It was not a monster. There are no monsters. It was a poor sick child, and it happened because you were a statistic. I told you that. It has nothing to do with genetics—absolutely nothing—and furthermore, you and Freddie are not first cousins. For you to be first cousins, your father would have to be Mother's whole brother. He's a half brother. And the likelihood is that there's nothing wrong with the kids of first cousins, anyway. Thousands of them are born healthy and normal. It's been going on since the human race started."

"You don't have to bear the baby," May Ling said, stubbornly.

"I'm not divorcing you," Freddie said. "Just get that through your head. I'm not divorcing you."

Carla said, "Let's go to Vince's Place and get drunk and listen to rock and get real spacey and stop all this stupid talk that gets nowhere; except Sam has to drive, and Freddie, if you don't know how to get a woman laid back and cool, you ought to go take lessons somewhere. Except that all you dumb Anglos are all tied up in knots."

"Amen," Sam said, starting the motor, turning on his lights. "It's beautiful when you put me in the driver's seat, and everyone gets potted except Sammy."

"No one gets potted," May Ling said. "It's all talk."

"Ah, drunk with the sound of my own words," Freddie said. "Why don't we stop trying to be clever, hey?" He turned to his wife.

"Yes?"

"Will you dance with me?"

After a long moment, dolefully, "I guess so."

"Bless your heart. No more fights. We just dance until we drop."

It would have spoiled their pleasure if she had gone with them. They would have put a good face on it, but everything would have been properly directed and controlled. What an enormous gap between the generations! Yet a time comes— thinking that there was no gap between herself and Clair. Or was there?

The room had been Sally's, and when she had married Barbara's brother, Clair had hardly changed the room at all. Some of Sally's books were still there, and after Barbara had showered and used the hair dryer, she found a copy of *Pride and Prejudice* and crawled into bed with it. She had always meant to read it and had never found the right moment to begin. The same was true of *Crime and Punishment*. There, too, she had pledged a reading and put it off through all the years. But between Dostoyevsky and Jane Austen, the gap was very wide, and while she had only a literary interest in *Crime and Punishment*, she had often thought of herself as Jane Austen. These were her own private, foolish thoughts —fantasies, if you will—to be shared with no living person, not even Boyd, who certainly would not have laughed at her. She possessed a tiny miniature of Jane Austen, and though only a person of imagination could discover a likeness between Barbara Lavette and Jane Austen, Barbara was certainly not lacking in imagination.

Oddly enough, she had read three of Jane Austen's books

and still missed *Pride and Prejudice,* which was supposedly the best of them. The first acquaintance was made not at her old college, Sarah Lawrence, but in prison, where she had found *Northanger Abbey* in the prison library. Prison. That was an eternity ago and utterly impossible. It had happened, but it remained impossible that for her refusing to name a group of people who had given her money to buy medicine for a Quaker hospital in the south of France, the House Committee on Un-American Activities had sent her to prison for six months—all impossible, all in a time that had never existed. It was the time that Lillian Hellman had so aptly named "scoundrel time," a time of national debasement, without honor or decency. She had met Lillian Hellman on one of her trips to New York, and the cold, almost arrogant stare made a wall around a woman whom Barbara admired so. Never had Barbara been able to erect walls, and her total openness had again and again caused her pain and humiliation. Yet, thinking about it now, as she lay in bed unable to sleep, filled with remembrance, she found no regrets for her openness. She could understand the savage scarring that had driven Hellman into herself. Those who survive have courage, and Barbara had come to believe that courage, real courage that exists without killing or violence, is the best part of the human soul.

Not that she was at all certain that a human soul existed. In the immediate hours and days after the death of Boyd, her friend and protector and lover, she had tried desperately to believe that some part of him survived, that she might touch him again, not with her hands but with some part of her mind or soul, with some vibration, perhaps; but such attempts at a faith she had never dealt with always failed, and her Episcopal instruction at Grace Cathedral, high on the hill in San Francisco, was too long ago, too forgotten and interwoven with the myths of childhood. How she envied religious people who could believe!

Thoughts of prison once more. *Pride and Prejudice* remained unopened. Memories of trial and imprisonment took over. Yet they had given her Boyd—attorney at law. That was how she had met him. He had fallen in love with her. He was the knight in white armor who would defend her in the court, and no prison gate would ever open for her. She smiled at the thought of Boyd, stocky, solid, his sandy hair out in a brush—he could be so fierce and determined—and that way, relaxed suddenly, she closed her eyes and slept.

So ended the day of her sixtieth birthday.

Two

On a day late in August of 1970, more than four years before Barbara's sixtieth birthday, Tony Moretti telephoned Boyd Kimmelman and suggested that they meet for lunch at Gino's Italian restaurant on Jones Street. Boyd Kimmelman, partner in a small but very old and respected San Francisco law firm, knew Tony Moretti, as did a good many citizens of San Francisco; that is, he knew him by reputation and had met him on half a dozen occasions. People will tell you, not only in San Francisco but in most large cities, that the day of the political boss is over and that different forces have taken over the management of American politics; but if that established any kind of a rule, Tony Moretti was an exception.

As chairman of the city's Democratic organization, he pulled a good many strings, most of them successfully, and while lately, as he approached his seventieth birthday, the younger elements in the party looked upon him as an antique and occasionally an embarrassment as well, older politicians still listened to him and learned from him.

Boyd liked him. Within his perimeters, he was honest,

and his word given was an unbreakable contract. He was a heavyset, stooped old man with a shock of white hair and an engaging smile that had won him more rewards than a key to Fort Knox—a smile that greeted Boyd Kimmelman. There was another man at the table, a slender, dark man who was introduced to Boyd as Congressman Al Ruddy. Boyd recalled that Ruddy represented an Oakland district, that he was one of the younger new leaders in the party, one of the bright young men who, typically, would snort in disdain at admiration rendered to Tony Moretti.

"You never ran for office," Ruddy said to Kimmelman.

"No, thank heavens."

The old man, Moretti, watched Kimmelman with interest. Vaguely, in Moretti's encyclopedic memory, where odds and ends of trivia mingled with a detailed and intimate knowledge of San Francisco politics stretching half a century back, there was a reminder that Adam Benchly had run for mayor and had been defeated by the votes of the dead. Boyd had come into Benchly's firm directly after World War II, and Benchly, dead these many years, had had a malignant hatred of politics. Moretti wondered whether Boyd shared it. He needed Boyd's help. Al Ruddy, whom Moretti considered a donkey, had said, "I think it's the worst choice in the world." The object of choice had not yet been mentioned.

"Politics," Moretti said to Boyd now, "is an art, and like all arts, it has its quota of genius, mediocrity, and too often, Boyd, plain goddamn fools. It calls for a combination of charisma, charm, organizational ability and old-fashioned common sense. Trouble is, we live in a land where they equate the politician with the crook. Not good, but it spells out an attitude."

Moretti's language intrigued Boyd. The man was self-educated, with neither high school nor college in his background, and Boyd had the impression that he spoke as the occasion demanded. On North Beach, he'd choose very different words.

"There's no need to plead politics to me," Boyd said. "I've lived without it. I intend to go on living without it."

"Not yourself," Ruddy began, but Tony Moretti cut him off and said, "Let me explain, Al, please. Like this, Boyd—you don't mind me calling you Boyd?"

He would have damn well minded it from Ruddy. Since it was the old man, he simply shrugged.

Ruddy started to speak again, but a glance from Moretti silenced him, and Moretti, exercising his privilege of age, laid a hand on Boyd's arm and said, "Please, hear me out. Don't get upset."

"You haven't said anything yet to upset me."

"I know. Also, you got a reputation. I say Barbara Lavette, and you're likely to stand up and walk out of here."

"It depends on what you say about Miss Lavette."

"Look, Boyd, let me put it on the table. You know me. I don't crap around and I don't bullshit and I don't double-talk. This isn't the world I grew up in, but maybe it's no worse. Different, yes. It's different. Calls for different things. The party wants Barbara Lavette to be a candidate."

"A candidate for what?" Boyd asked suspiciously.

"Congress. We want to run a woman. It's about time," Ruddy put in.

"Ask her," Boyd said. "Why bother me?"

"It's not so simple," Moretti told him. "Not so simple."

"You make it more simple by asking me? If that's what you think, you're out of your mind."

"No, no. It's not that. The party wants her to be our candidate in the Forty-eighth C.D."

"No." Boyd smiled sourly. "You must be kidding."

"There are reasons and there are opportunities."

"Tell me. The Forty-eighth is one of the four most solidly Republican districts in the state. You haven't elected a Democrat there since the district was created. You don't even campaign there. You put a name on the ballot, and that's it. I can't speak for Miss Lavette, but I'll be happy to tell her it's the stupidest idea of the year."

"Maybe not," Moretti said, unperturbed.

"Enlighten me."

"All right," Moretti said, "I'll try to. I knew old Dan Lavette, and I knew his wife and I know his daughter—not like you do," he hastened to add. "You have a different kind of relationship, but I took old Dan and his daughter to dinner right here at Gino's twenty years ago, and we talked pretty good, so it isn't only the public record. I know, too, her time as a correspondent during World War Two, her involvement with the anti-Franco crowd and her stretch in prison. For the past three years, she's been running the peace movement here on the Coast—for my money, the most effective antiwar movement in the country."

"Not running it," Boyd said. "She's only a part of it."

"Come on," Ruddy said, "it wouldn't exist without her."

"I could argue that, but I won't. What in hell's the difference? I haven't seen your goddamn party lifting a finger to stop that rotten bloodbath in Vietnam. It was your man, Johnson, who turned it into an abattoir."

"Some truth," Moretti agreed, unhappily. "But you're pushing it, Boyd. You know by now how badly we want this cursed war over with. That's why we're sitting here, and that's why I'm talking to you. We desperately want a woman candidate. We've been attacked on every hand as male chauvinist pigs, and the Republicans have pulled the rug right out from under us. We need a woman candidate, but not any woman. To just pick a woman out of the grab bag is meaningless. We need a woman like Barbara Lavette, and if you think it was easy to get the party caucus to agree to her—" He shook his big head. "No, not easy. Not easy at all."

"Without asking her."

"Because I know her. She'd be so damn mad at the notion of being used that she'd boot me out of the house. With reason."

"I'm afraid you lost me somewhere," Boyd said. He was thinking that he really didn't give a damn. Too much had happened. The war in Vietnam had snapped him loose from whatever illusions he still cherished, and if he ever troubled to define politics, it was as a pig's game. Ruddy was a skinny pig, and the state houses in fifty states and the Congress in Washington were filled with Ruddys, fat and thin and in between, noses in a long trough that the plain people paid for. Perhaps Moretti sensed what he was thinking and regretted bringing Ruddy, or perhaps not. Moretti's feet were still wet with the mud and dirt of another world, seven thousand miles away, and for him, politics was the song of freedom. Politics was the warm wonder of an enormously extended family, and he contemplated Kimmelman curiously and thoughtfully. He saw before him a man neither short nor tall, stocky, a light complexion, blue eyes and sandy hair. The middle fifties, Moretti decided, a man who had stepped out of uniform into a job at Benchly's office back in 1945. Moretti had known the city the way it was, the city in the hills that the Italians and Jews and Irish built with their own hands, city of wops and yids and micks, their city in spite of the fact that the Wasps owned the banks and the railroads. How much did a Boyd Kimmelman understand? Men like Ruddy understood little or nothing, but Kimmelman—

"I didn't lose you, Boyd," Moretti said gently. "I think you know what I mean. The lady believes. She's not cynical." Which Boyd Kimmelman knew. And Moretti, like so many in the city, knew that Boyd Kimmelman and Barbara Lavette had been living together yet apart for twelve years or so. It was not news anymore, not even gossip.

"She believes," Boyd agreed. "She believes that you can stop war, that you can change history, that the good guys will triumph over the bad guys."

"That's it," Ruddy said. "That's the way we have to look at things."

"God help us," Boyd said.

"What in hell does that mean?"

"Eat your dessert and stop talking," Moretti said to Ruddy. He had a huge piece of chocolate cake on his plate, one of Gino's famous double desserts. For about thirty seconds, Ruddy ignored it, as if to say that he didn't take orders from Tony Moretti. Then he began to eat hungrily. Boyd felt sorry for him, and with that came the kind of guilt he might have felt in mocking the infirmity of a cripple.

"Good, isn't it? I have a sweet tooth, too."

Ruddy smiled with appreciation. His smile said that he held no grudge. He was a congressman. All people were voters and he loved all people and he loved all voters. No hard feelings. No hard feelings anywhere.

"Let me be explicit," Moretti said, "and tell you what I mean by belief. It's a faith. I'm a Catholic. I have to believe. If I say I believe in Mary the mother of God—which I do— it's not because I can reason it out or win an argument from you about is the Virgin the mother of God. No. The belief is part of me. I can't exist without it. It doesn't make me good or bad, it's just something I have to have. Now this lady, Barbara Lavette, she has to believe. That's why she breaks her back with her peace movement. What she has is either grace or an affliction. I don't know. When I retire, I'm taking a trip to Italy, and I'm going to put that to the Pope. No, not really." He smiled. He had a good smile. "You see what I'm getting at, Boyd?"

"She believes. What then?"

"Do you know what a free election is, Boyd? It's one of the most beautiful things man ever invented. I'm not talking about the turkeys we put in office. I'm talking about the process. Let me tell you what we'll give your Barbara Lavette if she agrees to be our candidate. First of all, we'll help her raise money from our sources, aside from what she might decide to raise on her own. She'll have a sound truck, posters, at least ten hours of radio time, and this is a radio city. We'll make sure she can buy some TV time, and she'll have some free TV coverage, the equal-time privilege, and the party behind her for two large mass meetings. Furthermore, we'll put her on the platform with our other candidates. I can't be specific now, but believe me, she'll talk to millions. And she can say her piece. No one is going to censor her or interfere. That's what the process means, an opportunity to say your piece."

Boyd had come to her to repeat Tony Moretti's proposal, and to add, "Before you agree or disagree with this, Barbara, I have to tell you how I feel about it."

"Shouldn't that wait until you hear how I feel about it?"

"No—for one reason. I know the Forty-eighth Congressional District and you don't. I also know you. I'm not going to wait until you grab on to this with all your enthusiasm and then try to talk you out of it. You're too damn stubborn for that."

"I'm stubborn? Oh, I like that, Mr. Kimmelman—I certainly do like that."

"Good. When you're really hating me, I become Mr. Kimmelman. Well, I know how your mind works. Know the truth and the truth will make you or your constituents free. Baloney. You can deliver the truth as passionately as only Barbara Lavette can. You can evoke the whole dirty stink of this war in Vietnam, and it will not win you a vote. But halfway into the campaign, you will come to believe that you can win, and when you don't, it will break your heart.

And in the Forty-eighth C.D., there is no way you can garner even a respectable losing number."

"You're a dear man," Barbara said.

"Yes. Which means that in spite of what I said or might say, you're going to run."

"You can bet your sweet patooties."

"Yes, I suppose I can."

"Now you're peeved with me," Barbara said. "Don't you even want to know why?"

"I know why."

"Not really, because you're a lawyer, and no matter how cynical or horrified you may become, you still see yourself living in a land that is ruled by the law."

"Sort of. Don't you?"

"No. I see my country ruled by nincompoops, governed by pompous fools, driven witlessly into a terrible war—and we'll pay the price of that war for years to come. And I don't like it, and if your friend Moretti will give me TV time and radio time and a sound truck to boot—well, Boyd, I'm going to shout my head off."

"All right. And who knows, miracles happen."

The miracle did not happen, but Barbara lost the election by only three thousand votes, whereas the general pattern was for a Democrat to come in at least twenty thousand votes behind his Republican opponent. She spoke, pleaded, unrolled facts and figures, and drew applause from those who would not vote for her as well as from those who would. It was a catharsis she needed desperately, and in the course of lashing out against a war she hated, as she hated all war, she came to know Tony Moretti. A half-dozen times during the course of the campaign, Moretti turned up to sit and watch her and listen to her speak. He never had a comment. He never spoke of approving or disapproving of anything she said, but he always chatted with Barbara for a few minutes, mostly about the old times and the people he had known in the twenties and the thirties.

The day after the election, Wednesday evening, Moretti asked Barbara and Boyd to join him for dinner at Gino's place. Gino was dead these many years, but the place had not changed, defying the freeways that laced the city and the hordes of tourists that had invaded the city during the sixties. It was still an old-fashioned Italian restaurant, with straw-bottomed bentwood chairs and checked tablecloths, maintained by one family for over seventy-five years—a long, long time in San Francisco. Barbara wondered whether it was as filled with memories for Moretti as it was for her.

After they had been greeted effusively by Gino's son, Alfred, escorted to the best table, and there ordered their dinner, Moretti nodded at Barbara and said, "Now we'll talk about it."

"While I was banging my head against the wall," Barbara said, "I thought you might tell me to stop, or shift my position and let the bloody side dry up."

"No, you had to do it your own way. You made the best race of anyone in the party. I didn't think there was any way you could win, and neither did Boyd here, but maybe you could have won. I've been thinking about that."

"Oh?"

"Did you think you might win?"

"Yes, I guess I did."

"Ah—"

The spaghetti came. Moretti had ordered, and without emphasis he had included a Higate Cabernet Sauvignon 1968, their very best year. Barbara took note of this. It was as if the man knew everyone in San Francisco who was worth knowing, and perhaps he did, and their ways as well.

They finished the spaghetti, and Barbara asked him what she had done wrong.

"I don't like the question," Boyd said. "You knew who she was. I told her she was being set up."

"I wasn't set up!" Barbara exclaimed. "And if you don't mind, this is between Mr. Moretti and myself. I want to know."

"I don't like the question so much either," Moretti said, "because it wasn't what you did wrong. You're a political person, Barbara, but you're not a politician. What do I mean by that? First, let me say something about a political person. I remember you when you were a young woman. I can remember once, right here at Gino's place, must have been just before the end of the war and you had been writing for the *Chronicle* in the Far East and you were having dinner here with your father, and I came over to wish him the best, and he introduced us."

Barbara knitted her brows and closed her eyes, and then, "Oh, yes. Of course. But your hair was black—"

"And I weighed sixty pounds less. Well, thirty years is a long time. But I recalled that, Barbara, because there was a beautiful young woman, richly endowed, and like fifty million other young women, you could have settled for a family, for kids, or for a job or a career—the way this new women's movement puts it."

"I had a family and a son," Barbara reminded him.

"Yes, but you know what I mean. You started way back with the longshore strike, when you went into the soup kitchen, and then you ran your car right into Bloody Thursday and set up a first-aid station. Guilt, I suppose. You know, three men from my family were on strike there, and Limey—Harry Bridges—well, we still see each other about once a year. A lot of threads in my life. But it wasn't only guilt. You were a political animal—and I mean that in the best way. One of our Stanford sociologists would say you had developed a social conscience, and when the oppressed bled, you bled. Maybe so, but to me, you became political—

in the best way again. You were connected. That's one part of politics, the best part. You follow me?"

Barbara nodded, smiling slightly. "I think so, Tony, and now you're going to tell me why I'm a rotten politician."

"No. Leave out the rotten part. You're not a politician, good or bad, and the fact that you and your friends organized Mothers for Peace, maybe the biggest headache Nixon has with this lousy, stupid war of his, doesn't change it. You're a damn good organizer."

"But not a politician."

"No. Now listen to me carefully, Barbara. I'm pretty long in the tooth. Now maybe you're thinking that I don't call you a politician because a politician has to be elected, and that's the only way he can work at his job. No. That's not the crux of it. I'll admit that maybe ninety percent of politicians will jump to sell their souls just to be elected, but we still got the other ten percent. The core of the matter is that the politician, if he's a good man and not an asshole like Nixon, studies where his constituency stands, and then he tries to give them one small push. He accepts the world the way it is because he knows he can't change it. All he can do is push in the right direction without losing his people. And sometimes that little push pays off."

Barbara nodded. "I see what you mean."

"Now if you want it, this district is yours. Go in there two years from now, and the party will put everything it has behind you. What do you say?"

"A political animal," Barbara reflected. "Perhaps so, perhaps not. I've tried to understand why I do what I do, but that's just as hard as trying to find out who I am. I'm fifty-six years old, Tony, and you want me to become a politician."

"You know who you are," Moretti said.

"Yes," Boyd said sourly, "you make your party's points

with a woman candidate, but we both know there's no way in the world Barbara can get elected in that district."

"Come on, Boyd, let her talk for herself."

"I don't think I want to be a politician," Barbara said. "I live in a demented world hanging on the brink of destruction in an atomic holocaust, fighting absurd and hideous wars, killing without end while a parcel of strange people put heart and soul into calling for an end to abortion, to the killing of the unborn. But these same pious folk pour their money and their sons into an unending killing of those born eighteen or twenty years before. One small push, Tony? No way. I am going to shout my head off. Your Congress would bore me to distraction."

"Suppose we talk about it in two years," Moretti said.

But two years later, in the fall of 1972, Barbara and Boyd were in Scotland, attending an international lawyers' meeting in Edinburgh. Barbara sent Tony Moretti a postcard, on which she wrote, "Scotland is the most beautiful country on earth, except for Northern California, and please forgive me and raise the subject in 1974." But in April of 1974, Boyd Kimmelman died.

Tony Moretti came to the funeral. He came to Barbara and kissed her cheek. He held her hand, a huge, fat mountain of a man, topped by a thatch of thick white hair. Sam, standing with his arm around his mother, looked strangely at Tony Moretti. Barbara, listening to the keening chant of the rabbi, watched the plain pine coffin, raw unfinished wood, being lowered into the earth. Boyd, who in all the years they were together had hardly mentioned the fact that he was Jewish and had never entered a synagogue, had left specific instructions as to his burial. A plain pine coffin—as Jewish custom had it—and a rabbi officiating.

Later, at Barbara's house on Green Street, Moretti talked to Sam about Sam's father, dead these twenty-six years. As Moretti left, he said to Barbara, "It would be good at this bitter time, Barbara. To involve yourself in an election campaign would take your mind off your grief."

Barbara shook her head. "It's meaningless without Boyd."

"Think about it," Moretti said.

Barbara thought about it, but it remained meaningless without Boyd. A week or so later, Sam asked her about Moretti.

"He's the head of the party here."

"You mean the Democrats?"

"Yes."

"He said he knew Pop. How did he know him?"

Barbara always felt awkward when her son brought up the subject of his father. He had been less than two years old when his father was killed; he had no memory of the man, but an insatiable curiosity, and through the years, he had questioned Barbara persistently.

"A man like Moretti—well, people are his thing, Sam; knowing people, remembering them, influencing them. Your father was a man other men valued."

"What does that mean? Brains, skill?"

"I think you know what I mean. Men have said that in a tight or dangerous situation, there's no one they'd rather have had with them than your father."

Switching abruptly, Sam asked, "Why didn't you marry Boyd?"

Taken totally aback, Barbara stared at her son. She realized that he was exercising with her, his mother, that curious prerogative of physicians, the right to ask any question of anyone, no matter how intimate the question: Have you moved your bowels? Was the stool soft or hard? How many times a week do you have intercourse? Even of the Queen of England, any question was permissible.

She always answered his questions. "I'm not much good at marriage."

"Not even with my father?"

"I loved him. He was an extraordinary man. But the marriage wasn't much good. He walked out on the marriage. And you're old enough to remember how it was with Carson."

"What does Moretti want of us?" Sam asked, after a long moment.

"Us?"

"You're my mother."

When it pleases you to remember, Barbara thought, and said aloud, "He wants me to run for Congress again."

"Just like that? He wants you to? Does he appoint candidates? I thought there were supposed to be primaries and that kind of thing."

So angry, she thought. At me? At Boyd for dying? Or because his mother is becoming an old woman and there's no one to take care of her? No. That's not Sam. At least he knows me that well. No one will ever have to take care of me. The anger belongs somewhere else, and he uses me because I'm here and I'm his mother.

"Mr. Moretti does not appoint candidates. The Democrats have never won an election in the Forty-eighth C.D. There are no primaries, because no one wants the headache of running a hopeless campaign."

"Except you?"

"That's nasty, Sam, and I won't have it. There are things you don't know. I don't want to talk to you anymore. Not when you're like this."

"I'm sorry," he burst out. "I'm so damn sorry. My own world stinks, and I bring it here to you."

Barbara put her arms around him and held him close. It was her first hint that Sam's marriage was going to pieces.

In the weeks after that incident, the weeks after Boyd's death, she brooded over the election invitation, but finally she wrote a note to Moretti that it was impossible.

Moretti came to see her soon after the birthday party at Higate, and he said to her, "In two years, we will discuss it again." And Barbara realized that they would, that in 1976 the sharp edge of the pain would be gone. Long, long ago, in France, in Paris of the nineteen thirties, she had fallen in love with a journalist whose name was Marcel Duboise, and who died of a wound during the Spanish Civil War. Then she believed that time would never erase the agony, but time took away the pain, just as time took away the pain of her husband's death. All things give way to time—ideas, causes, nations. Her life had been passionate, filled with belief and trust and love, but that was long ago.

She had always thought that Sam might understand.

"No," he said. "No, I can't understand why you do what you do, why you went to prison, why you couldn't just give the committee the names they wanted. Nothing would have happened to the people you were protecting. The McCarthy era wasn't Hitler Germany."

"What might have happened to the people who gave us the money to buy medicine and send it to the Spanish Republicans, I don't know. Perhaps they would have suffered, perhaps not. For me, it was a matter of honor."

But honor, too, had gone on down the road. What conceivable meaning could honor have during the administration of Richard Nixon? He had not seized power at the point of a gun; he had been elected and re-elected by the people of the United States, people who knew his values and accepted them, and here was her own son handling the word *honor* and trying to relate it to reality. Nor was Sam one of those doctors who rooted in every grubby hole for a buck, who robbed the government through Medicare, who handed their patients a warning never to be sick on Wednesday, our golf day. He gave hundreds of hours to a charity clinic, and he cared very little about becoming a millionaire, a condition with which many of his colleagues replaced the caduceus. But why his mother went to prison as a matter of honor, that was hard to grasp.

Slowly, the pain went away and the loss receded into the background. It was a very slow process, like the emptying, grain by grain, of some enormous hourglass. Through her years, she had slept alone too many times for it to be something that had to be learned, and if, in the dark hours of the night, she reached out for warm flesh, that too had happened before. The two men who had been the true and deep loves of her life died violent deaths. Death was a stranger then; now as Barbara passed her sixtieth year, death was no longer the dark stranger who came from a place unknowable. Days passed and days became weeks, and the weeks stretched into months. She sat in the park on a warm, sunny day and she noticed other women who sat in the park. The men died and the women were alone. That was the way it was in America. There were few families where the old were cherished. Sam tried to call every few days and to take her to lunch at least once a week. That was pleasant. He didn't take her to dinner because of his own disintegrating marriage. He was still trying to save it.

There were hours now when no thought of Boyd crossed her mind, and this filled her with guilt; but on the other hand, she realized that she could hardly remember the face and speech of her first love, Marcel Duboise. Almost forty years had passed, and to save the mind from madness, time obliterates. She was invited to a party in one of those gigantic and improbable highrises that had sprung up on Russian Hill, and she accepted. More than a year had passed since Boyd's death. To her utter amazement, she found herself the center of attention by admiring men, and this embarrassed her and even frightened her a bit. She told herself it was the result of notoriety, yet she knew that her thinking of herself as a notorious woman was rather ridiculous; and she even dared to think that she, Barbara Lavette, was still a very lovely woman. An older man, at least ten years older than herself, used the word *regal*. "Regal," he said. "I remember your mother very well. She was a regal woman—no other word to describe her—and when she and Dan Lavette entered a room, believe me, the conversation stopped."

Barbara got rid of her slump. She straightened her back, recalling her dance teacher at Sarah Lawrence. "Your back, ladies, and hold your damn heads as if each of you had a jug of water sitting there." The younger men there knew that she was someone of consequence. Here was a tall, handsome older woman, whose wide blue-gray eyes suggested both wisdom and sadness. Barbara had never fully understood why an older woman should attract the eager interest of young men half her age. She wondered whether they were homosexuals. She had never been troubled by the accusation that San Francisco, her city, her beloved wonderful city that was like no other city in the world, had become a national center for homosexuals. She argued that it only gave the city more style, which it already had in excess of any other city in America.

"The devil with it," she said to herself. "I am enjoying myself, and if I'm not happy, I'm not unhappy, and that's a change."

They had read her books. Boyd once suggested that the work of an interesting good-looking woman sells better than the writing of her opposite; and Barbara smiled now at the recollection, recalling her annoyance with Boyd and her retort that he wore his male chauvinism on his sleeve. Dear, sweet man—yet always he faced her with the attitude that Barbara Lavette could do no wrong, which was perhaps the main reason she had never married him. To be tied to a cruel bastard was a bondage from which escape was at least possible; but to be married to a man who worshiped you—well, that was something else.

"I read your last book," the young man was saying. "I mean, my friends steer clear of this whole rash of new feminist books—no, I'm not gay, if that's what you're thinking."

"No, I was simply listening."

"I read them. I love women, but you're different. When I heard you would—no, might—when I heard you might be here tonight, I was terribly excited. I read what your life has been and I expected an older woman—"

"I am an older woman," Barbara said cheerfully.

"No way. I'm not coming on—I'd like to—I don't know how—" Then he added, "Have I offended you?"

"Good heavens, no."

Moments later, a young woman, mid twenties, darkly good-looking and very intense, told her, "I voted for you— the first time I ever voted. I mean, I wanted so much to be like you—oh, from the first time I read something you had written, the book about France, I wanted to do the things you had done, to be just like you. And then when you ran for Congress—you don't remember me, do you?"

"I think I do, yes," knowing how dismal it was not to be remembered. "Leaflets?" It was a shot in the dark.

"Yes, oh, yes, and one wonderful day when we did the fences with your poster, my boyfriend and myself, and both of us convinced that the cops were one jump behind us. Of course, they weren't. And you will run again, won't you?"

"Perhaps, if you help me."

The hostess at the apartment, Birdie MacGelsie, whose husband had made many millions out of a uranium discovery, and whose own guilts had made her an eager partner of Barbara's in Mothers for Peace, overheard the young woman's enthusiastic political endorsement of Barbara, and got Barbara aside a while later to ask her if it was indeed true.

"Is what true?"

Small and bright-eyed, like a perky bird, Birdie whispered, "Congress. Will you be a candidate again?"

"I don't know. Until tonight, I wasn't thinking about it very seriously. I suppose I was carried away by her enthusiasm. By the way, what is her name?"

"Carol Eberhardt."

"Eberhardt?"

"Same one. The child is his daughter."

"You have to be kidding. The same Jim Eberhardt, the one who heads up the Republican organization here?"

"Absolutely."

"Why?"

"A perfectly proper rebellion," Birdie said. "You ought to know about rebellion, Barbara. If I remember—"

"We both remember," Barbara said shortly.

"You see, Barbara, when you ran the last time, you weren't a bit sure of anything. All of a sudden, there you were. When you do it again, and you must, we're going to be in the act."

"Oh?"

"Now don't get your ass up, my love. I'm not talking about giving you directions or cutting in on your independence. I am talking about money, pure and simple. I know Tony Moretti staked you to something, but what the party gives you won't get you elected dog catcher. I am talking about real money and real publicity, which means television and more television. How do you think our late but not lamented governor got in there?"

"Yes. Still, I must want it. If you don't want it, then it's not much good even trying."

"Of course you want it," Birdie said. "How else can you stand up down there in Washington and tell them what a bunch of hopeless idiots they are?"

But did she want it? It might be an antidote to loneliness and to a purposeless existence, or it might not; and why, she wondered, was she so hooked on the notion that her existence must include purpose? Most people lived without purpose. She had begun a new book, a book about Boyd; not actually about him, but a novel to be based on his life. That was purpose enough, but the book went slowly and painfully, more slowly and more painfully than anything else she had written. Her writing had never come easily, but this writing about a man she had lived with in her years of maturity was most difficult, as if each of the many threads that bound them had to picked apart, investigated, thoroughly studied. Surely this gave her a purpose.

But not enough. She had taken to long walks again, miles each day, along the Embarcadero from Berry Street to Fisherman's Wharf, and in the course of these walks, touching at each block some deep memory, she came to realize that the memories were an illusion. In the same way, the writing of her memories plucked at strings of illusion. That was all very well, and it was the writer's business to try to create reality out of illusions, but for her there had to be more; and one day in July, walking down Jones Street to the Bay, she saw ahead of her, standing large and wide, looking over the water, the heavyset figure of old Tony Moretti. She made her way across the Embarcadero and joined him.

For a while, he said nothing. He glanced at her and offered a nod of recognition, but said nothing, and neither did she. And then, perhaps a few minutes after she had joined him, he pointed across the sparkling waters of the Bay and remembered, "Way over there, Barbara, we picked up the garbage. Oakland garbage. Nineteen twelve, I think. Anyway, I was twelve years old and I got my first job on one of Dan Lavette's garbage ships."

"Oh, no. Garbage ships?"

"Big scows. Pick up the garbage, dump it in the ocean. We didn't know a damn thing about ecology then. He sold them a few years later. Never knew that, did you?"

"I think I did. I'm not sure."

He pointed down the street. "Over there—Pat Salvo's

crab stand. We're old friends, and his crabs are fresh, believe me. I said to him, When will Miss Lavette be coming along? He tells me, Any time now."

"No. I can't believe that, Tony. You mean I've become some sort of ridiculous fixture here?"

"I wouldn't say that. People who know you see you and remember you. After all, your father put his mark on Fisherman's Wharf. Everyone knew him. A lot of people know you."

"Oh!"

"Shouldn't surprise you. Lived here all your life. You write books. You worked for the *Chronicle* on and off."

"Tony," she said, "when I ran for Congress back in nineteen seventy, no one brought up the fact that I had spent six months in prison."

"No, they didn't."

"Why?"

"Why? Because they knew you couldn't win, so they got themselves some points by treating you with class. But they didn't know how close you came to it, and this time, they'll bring it up all right, and I think we can turn it around and make some points for us."

"This time!" Barbara exclaimed. "What do you mean, this time?"

"Things have cleared up. It's two years since Boyd died, and I don't like the thought of Barbara Lavette sitting over her knitting and pretending she's an old lady."

"Which I am."

"My dear girl, if I were not almost seventy-six years old and seventy-five pounds overweight and carrying four different colored pills which I take three times a day, I wouldn't be able to keep my hands off you."

"Tony, that's the nicest thing I've heard in months, and I don't believe a word of it."

"We had a meeting the other night, Barbara, and the

question of the forsaken Forty-eighth came up. That's what
we call it. You lost by three thousand votes. Murray Henig,
who we put in there two years ago, lost by thirty-two thousand votes. This year, no one wants to touch it. Even Al
Ruddy's nephew, who's been working in Ruddy's district
and who's so eager politically that he begins to sweat if a
designation is even mentioned—even he doesn't want the
Forty-eighth, because he says the political career he doesn't
even have would be ruined. Sort of true. Nobody wants
Henig after the beating he took in the Forty-eighth. But I
said I got someone."

"Me," Barbara said. "Thank you."

"That's right. You can thank me, because you're going to
win and you're going to Congress."

"And how do you do it?"

"We do it. You and me, we run the campaign together."

"Only you haven't even asked me whether I want it,"
Barbara said.

"Do you want it? Not just a platform to say your piece,
but a seat down there in that pesthole they call Washington?"

"I think I do," Barbara said.

"All right." He put out his hand, and she took it. "Now
we'll have some lunch at Gino's."

After she left Tony Moretti, Barbara felt that she had to
sound off about her decision with someone. Her two closest
friends were both sisters-in-law of a sort: Sally, who was
Clair's daughter and who had married Barbara's brother
Joe, and Eloise, who had married Barbara's other brother,
Tom Seldon Lavette, and had then divorced him to marry
Adam Levy. Sally was brilliant, but she could not properly
listen. Eloise listened and adored, and Barbara felt that at
this moment in her life, she needed a lot of listening, not to
mention at least a thimbleful of adoration.

It was past six in the evening when Barbara turned her

car off Route Twenty-nine onto the winding oiled dirt road that led to Higate. Old Jake had never permitted the road to be modernized, but now that he was dead, Adam was making arrangements for a macadam surface. The evening was stuffily warm, not a trace of a breeze, and the mountains appeared to be undulating gently in the heat.

But only Joshua was at Eloise's house, sitting in the den, his face expressionless as he stared at the television set. Long ago, before he had joined the marines, before he had been sent to Vietnam, Joshua had been a round-faced, sound-limbed boy, chubby if not fat, his straw-colored thatch of hair standing straight up from his head. Eloise's other son, Frederick, had come of her marriage to Tom. Joshua was her son with Adam, and as a small child, he had had the same golden locks and blue eyes as his mother—which led him to be petted and cuddled in a manner he always remembered as distasteful. Barbara had noticed his anger at the showing of pictures of himself as a child. Asked about his resentment, he once told Barbara that they might as well have been pictures of a little girl as of a small boy.

His face remained expressionless as he opened the door for Barbara and explained, tonelessly, "They're all having dinner with Grandma Clair, over at the big house."

"Oh? I thought I'd find your mother."

"She's there." He was no round-faced boy with a thatch of yellow hair. He kept his hair clipped close; his face was tightly drawn over the bones; and there was a nervous tic under one eye. Now twenty-eight years old, there was nothing left of the gentle, chubby boy whom Barbara remembered. His bleak tone dismissed her and said that he wanted to be alone, and he turned back to the room where the television was blaring before Barbara could think of any way to continue the conversation. She left, nervous—and feeling that she should stay and talk to him.

It was still light outside, still before seven o'clock, when

Barbara opened the door to Clair's house and went in. The door was never locked. It was a door you passed through without ever thinking too much about it, and everyone passed through it, the Chicano and Mexican workers on the place, their children, the family and their children, delivery men, salesmen. The door led directly into the huge kitchen, twenty by thirty-five feet, equipped with a coal stove, a gas stove, a walk-in refrigerator and a fourteen-foot-long refectory table made of polished oak. The kitchen being the natural core of the house, most of the family meals were taken there; and since this was a farm, dinner was eaten early. They were already at the table when Barbara entered, Clair and Eloise and Adam and Freddie and May Ling, who had acceded to Freddie's desire to have a second child. Freddie's house, while on the Higate property, was about four hundred yards from the main house, and after her first experience at giving birth, May Ling was in no mood to leave her child—seven months old now—with a nurse. The new baby was a boy, plump and perfect, with ten fingers and ten toes, all that May Ling could have desired, and now he slept peacefully in a crib in the corner of the kitchen.

At seventy-six, Clair was still strong and energetic, but unhappy in hours of being alone. At least twice a week, she persuaded some or all of her family at the winery to eat at her house, and tonight, when Barbara entered, there were sounds of pleasant greeting around the board. Clair got up to embrace her and beg her to eat with them. Barbara insisted that she was not hungry, and Clair protested that this was not a real dinner, only a pickup of roast lamb, chile beans, and red onion and cucumber. Hard liquor was rarely served at Higate, but there was no meal without half a dozen bottles of wine on the table, and always three of them were the Cabernet Sauvignon, the red wine that Jake had loved so and about which he had boasted—about Higate's red being the best that California offered. By Jake's measure, there was no other good wine, only California.

Even though Jake had been dead a good many years now, to Clair the wine on the table was more than a candle. As far as white wine was concerned, Jake had no strong preference. The market demanded white wine, but to Jake, only red wine was real wine.

Barbara joined the table and indicated the Cabernet, which Freddie poured for her. A small ceremony, but old enough for her to have developed a true preference. The two Mexican women, both of them illegals, passed around the table with platters of sliced leg of lamb and bowls of chile beans, and Barbara, who had given no thought to dinner, found her appetite in the delicious aroma of the food, helped herself and considered how much of the food served here had the flavor of Mexico in it. There was much of Mexico at Higate, and old Jake, from the time he and Clair bought the place, well over half a century ago, had made a point of hiring a certain number of illegals. Barbara could remember his argument that the land was theirs and we had taken it from them. To give back a little had eased his conscience.

"I'm so glad you decided to come," Eloise told her. "I mean, just on the spur of the moment. You hardly ever do, you know—it takes such pleading to get you here."

"I treasure my welcome—and guard it. I don't want to waste it."

"What nonsense!" Clair snorted.

"Aunt Barbara comes when the sky is falling down—she props it up. Right?" Freddie said.

"Wrong," his wife informed him.

"Oh, I wish I were propping it up," Barbara said. "But—well, sort of."

"We want a toast," Adam said, raising his glass. "Barbara?"

"Just peace—and a few grains of happiness, wherever we may find them."

"Good enough," Clair said.

Barbara realized that there was no way she could lure Eloise away and say to her, "Darling, I have lost my mind, but I must tell you all about it." Instead, she paused in her dinner, chewed a mouthful of lamb, and said, "Dear ones, I'm running for Congress again. I had to tell someone."

All the eating stopped, and they stared at her. May Ling said it was great and she was sure Barbara would make it. Clair thought she had lost her mind. "Oh, I have. I certainly have," Barbara agreed. "But I think every candidate is a little bit insane, don't you?"

"A little bit?" Freddie asked.

Adam said, "Stop being a damn smartass, and let Barbara talk."

"I don't want to talk," Barbara protested. "I've said my piece. I was walking down at the Embarcadero, and it occurred to me that walking along the Embarcadero each day is hardly the most interesting way to spend the rest of my life. I am bored to death with looking at crabs, watching sea gulls and watching the tourists watch sea gulls and watching the film companies film the tourists watching the sea gulls— good Lord, listen to me—and then I saw Tony Moretti standing there on the street. I walked over to him, and he said, How about this time? And I said yes."

"Just like that?" Eloise asked softly.

"Just like that."

"Does Sam know?" Adam wondered.

"No, I'm afraid to tell him."

"What nonsense!" Clair exclaimed, forgetting that she had already disposed of Barbara's mind and judgment. "What does he expect you to do? Sit by the fire and knit?"

"Something of the sort. You know, being a doctor doesn't mean you're wise or bright. Well, Sam's bright enough, but not overequipped with common sense. He constantly asks me to rest. Rest, take it easy, Mother, haven't you done enough?"

"The first time," Eloise said, "you were after something else. You wanted a platform. Oh, I've felt like that so many times—just to stand up and shout that we must do something about our agony—about their stupidity and our tears, their cruelty and idiocy—"

It's Joshua's absence from this table. That's what she's saying, Barbara thought. No simple absence, either.

"But I'm not Barbara." Eloise sighed. "You do know, Barbara," tentatively speaking yet apologizing for having the temerity to speak, "you will be elected this time. Do you really want that?"

"Why do you say I'll win this time? No Democrat has ever won in the Forty-eighth."

"Because it's not six years ago," Eloise said. "We've been so deep in the women's movement that we never really got outside to look at it. We've ended that horror in Vietnam and Nixon's gone and no woman in this country will ever be quite the same again, and even if the Forty-eighth is slightly to the right of Pasadena, you'll still win, Barbara."

"It's different," Clair said. "A few months ago, Gerald L. K. Smith died down in Glendale, and it hardly made the papers."

"Who was he?" May Ling asked.

"There you are—only the most notorious anti-Semite and public native fascist of our time, my time, darling, not yours. I can't applaud what you're doing, Barbara—Washington is an unhappy place—and I know you a little. But—oh, hell, why not?"

After dinner, May Ling's baby had to be taken home, and Adam had to go over things with Clair. Freddie said to Eloise, "Mom, I want a half hour with Barbara."

Eloise looked at him curiously, and then nodded. "I'll wait here with your father."

"We'll be in the living room," Freddie said.

All very odd, Barbara thought. At this point, she hardly knew whether to be depressed or pleased by her decision. There had been a time when the decision would have been hers, entirely hers—perhaps tested on Boyd, but still entirely hers, regardless of Boyd's agreement or protest—but now, after the conversation at the dinner table, she felt neither enthusiasm nor any real approval from the only family she had. Of course, Eloise's calm certainty that she would win the contest surprised her, but Eloise always surprised her when it came to a matter of importance. The same might be said of Freddie. At age thirty-four, Freddie was knowledgeable, sometimes brilliant, and usually iconoclastic. He had always adored Barbara, and he underlined that now.

"You know," he said, sitting opposite her, his long, good-looking face, the Seldon face, set seriously, "I do feel like a horse's ass, Aunt Barbara, and I have no damn right to say what I'm saying—"

"For heaven's sake, Freddie, stop apologizing and get to it."

"All right, and you can put me down and walk out of here, but I'm saying it anyway. You're being used by a pack of bums, and that includes that benign old gentleman Tony Moretti. Where was he when they tossed you in jail? Same party, same head—do you want me to stop?"

"No, Freddie. I want you to say exactly what you want to say, and I won't take offense. You are very dear to me."

"All right, I'll go on. There's a notion around that because Nixon behaved like a complete turd, the Democrats have come up smelling like roses. Not to me. The crazy time of terror that sent you and a lot of others to jail was called McCarthyism, and the Democrats loved that. It made people forget that Truman started the whole thing with his Executive Order on the Loyalty Oath, and let me add something else. When we drove down to Mississippi to help in the registration drive, back in the sixties, and they whipped us and tortured us and they murdered Bert Jones and Herbie Katz—you remember that, I think?"

"Yes, I do," Barbara said softly, recalling how she found him after the incident in the hospital at Jackson, Mississippi.

"Well, who was in the White House then? Brave Jack Kennedy and brave brother Bobby, and they knew what was happening down south, they knew—"

"Freddie," Barbara said gently, "what are you trying to tell me?"

"That they'll break your heart, and it will hurt. Of course, you'll win. Aunt Barbara, I know you. You're the last real romantic, and you've always been your own person—and down there in Washington—"

"Still," Barbara said, "I may be able to change something —just a little. Wouldn't that be worth it?"

"I don't know. I just haven't said anything the way I wanted to—I mean, what I was trying to say—and it's none of my business, is it?"

He had been trying to say, Barbara realized, what Boyd would have said, that Congress was no place for a lady Don Quixote to go tilting at windmills—or was it the best place in the world?

Adam was still huddled with his mother, papers and ledgers spread on the kitchen table. This was the material of thirty years ago, reminders of a time before computers— only a sample of the boxes of material that Adam wanted to be rid of and that Clair could not bring herself to destroy.

"We'll work something out tonight," Adam said. "Another hour or so."

"Oh, go on home," Clair said to Eloise.

"A half hour more, Mom." He turned to Eloise. "Go ahead with Barbara."

Eloise didn't protest. She knew that Barbara had come to talk to her, and she wanted some time for the two of them to be alone.

"I'm going your way," Freddie said. "If you don't mind, I'll pop in and say a good word to Josh."

"How is he?" Barbara asked, as they walked toward Eloise's house.

Eloise shook her head hopelessly, and Freddie said, "Too much depression, too many memories. He'll come out of it, but it takes time. If I could only get him interested in something. Trouble is, he's so full of hate—he hates everything, the Pentagon, the government, the army. Well, a lot of the vets are that way. He feels that they turned him into a murderer. He killed two little kids, Aunt Barbara—"

"No!" Eloise exclaimed. "I don't want to hear that!"

"You have to face it, because it's eating his guts out. Oh, not anything he did purposely. They were hiding in the high grass, and he saw the grass move and let go with his rapid fire—"

"Freddie!"

"No. He has to talk about it, Mom. You have to. Aunt Barbara has to."

"Freddie," Barbara said, "for heaven's sake, stop it. We'll talk about it, but not now. Josh needs help. I know someone who can help him."

"I've pleaded with him," Eloise said. "He won't—no, it's not much use. I've almost given up."

Freddie opened the door and held it while they entered. No doors were locked on the winery grounds. Lights were on in the living room and the den, but both rooms were empty.

"I'll have a look in his room," Freddie said, going up the stairs and down the hall to the big room they had shared when they were kids. The room was lit but empty, the floor was wet, and there was a sound of running water from the connecting bathroom. Freddie went into the bathroom. Naked, Josh lay in a tub filled with blood-red water. He had cut the veins in both wrists. His face was icy cold under Freddie's touch, his blue eyes wide open and fixed.

It took a minute or two for Freddie to get control of himself and to feel in his brother's neck for a pulse beat, knowing all the while that Josh was dead and had been dead for at least an hour. He turned off the water, and then he dried his hands. He was crying without knowing that he was crying. He was trying to think of a way to go downstairs and tell his mother and Barbara what had happened.

Three

She put down the date first: "July 23, 1976."

She was at home in her house on Green Street, sitting in her tiny study.

"This is the first time in seven days, except to change clothes for the funeral of Joshua Levy, that I have been back to my house in Green Street. I note with some surprise that nothing here has changed, but why I should be surprised, I don't know. Nothing here changes. I suppose that I expected change because I saw a vibrant and wonderful young man change into a corpse. No one will ever say that. We surround death with euphemisms. They will say he passed away. No one will mention or even think of the fact that he cut his wrists in a bathtub, where he lay naked in the running water—naked, I think, so that he could stare with grief and anger at the stump of his left leg—and the water running to wash away his sin and the blood. If, indeed, any of this is true, because what he thought we will never know.

"I revise that. I think that his mother knew. Freddie tried to keep both of us out, but Eloise said something to the effect of, Freddie, damn you, get out of my way—and she said it in a way that he could not face down. When he put out an arm to stop her, he seemed to know that he could not stop her; and then she walked into the bathroom and I came after her. She didn't faint and she didn't become hysterical. She looked at her son for a long, terrible moment, and then she said to me, almost wistfully, 'Is he dead, Barbara?' I told her that he was. Then she bent over, slid down on her knees, and kissed his face. She didn't weep—not until later, not until the funeral. Joshua's father, Adam, wept. He pretty well went to pieces that first night. He clung to Eloise, not she to him.

"How little we know about people! Last night, Eloise couldn't sleep. After the first two days, Dr. Milton Kellman, who has taken care of Seldons and Lavettes and Levys for a lifetime and who is practically the last family practitioner left in San Francisco, gave her pills, but last night she threw them away, telling me that the dreams were worse than the reality. Eloise and I sat up for most of the night, and we talked. I put down the conversation here mostly because I want to remember what she said. Eloise is an extraordinary woman, but I have come to the conclusion that to be a woman in this world is an extraordinary thing. Eloise said to me:

" 'Do you know, Barbara, that in certain Arab countries, they sew up the vagina of a woman who has committed adultery?'

"Apropos of what? I wondered. I simply stared at her.

" 'I mentioned that,' Eloise went on, 'because the cruelty that men display toward women is beyond my understanding. You may think I am being very cold and restrained about the death of my son. I loved Josh more than anything on earth—'

" 'I know that,' I said.

" 'And in return, Josh did to me—and to Adam too—the

most terrible thing that a son can do. My wonderful Joshua is dead, but I'll live with this pain all the rest of my life.'

" 'He didn't do it to cause you pain!' I cried.

" 'Oh, but he did, he did. He knew what he was doing. I know that life had become unbearable for him, but life is unbearable for many people and they go on living. He did it because he blames me and he blames Adam—because we brought him into a world where Vietnam happened. We can never understand that. We weren't there, and only those who were there understand it!' "

Barbara stared at the paper and at what she had written. Since she was a writer, it was entirely proper to put words on paper, and she had often found that when something was confused in her own mind, it clarified matters to spell it out on paper. Now it was on paper. Barbara recalled the time when Eloise had married her brother Tom—thirty-six years ago—and she remembered Eloise as she was then, a slender, baby-faced upper-middle-class girl, with blue eyes and golden locks. She was Eloise Clawson then, and the Clawsons were very rich, almost as rich as the Lavettes, and Barbara had characterized her at that moment as a brainless bit of fluff.

Barbara wept more easily than Eloise, and after she dried her eyes now, she telephoned Tony Moretti.

"I would like to see you," she said.

"Of course. I know what a terrible time you had. Your nephew, wasn't it?"

"No, but very close to me."

"We still bleed for that stupid war, don't we?"

"I suppose you could put it that way."

"All right, Barbara. Tomorrow we have lunch at Gino's, and we talk."

"Not tomorrow. Tonight," Barbara said evenly.

"It can wait. I'm an old man, Barbara, but what do I tell

my wife—almost ten o'clock and I'm going to meet a beautiful lady? She'll believe that?"

"Tony," Barbara said coldly, "don't ever patronize me again and don't ever tell me that I'm a beautiful lady. I am sixty-two years old; you said what you said because I'm a woman. There's no man of sixty-two years in the world to whom you would talk like that."

"Barbara, Barbara," he said mollifyingly. "I talk to you like you're my daughter."

"I know. I'm not angry with you, Tony. But if I wait until tomorrow, I'll forget everything I mean to say, and it's important."

"Important?"

"Yes."

"All right. I know what you been through."

His car drew up in front of her house about twenty minutes later. He had a long, sleek stretch Cadillac and a chauffeur, and that eased her sense of guilt at dragging him over to her place at night. She had been very angry before, but anger was not an easy emotion for Barbara to cling to. She tried to maintain it now—anger and objectivity.

She took his coat and sat him down on the single large, comfortable leather chair that invaded the black horsehair delicacy of her Victorian parlor. Moretti nodded his gratitude, looking suspiciously at the frail sofa and side chairs. "It's the kind of chair Bernie, my first husband, liked so much, a chair for men of substance." She couldn't help smiling.

"He was a man of courage and distinction. You suffer a lot, Barbara. I know you're not a Catholic, but you're half Italian. Try to accept God's will."

"Oh? Can I give you a drink, Tony?"

"My drinking days are over. A little red wine with my meals."

"I have tea?"

"Good."

Barbara poured the tea, and said, "If I didn't love you, Tony, I might get very bitter about this communication with God. Was it God's will that Kennedy should take time off from screwing his dozen women for the day and start that horror in Vietnam? Don't be shocked by my language, Tony. I was a correspondent in World War Two and lived with the army. Was it God's will that a son of a bitch named Johnson should continue that crazy war until seventy-five thousand American boys were dead and another half a million wounded and crazy? Was it God's will that this pissant, Nixon, should be voted in to go on with that horror? Don't ever mention God's will to me. We blaspheme every time the words pass our lips."

"You got no right to talk to me like that, Barbara," the old man said tiredly. "You brought me over here to tell me that you don't want the designation. All right. I understand."

"No. You don't. I didn't ask you over here for that. Not at all. I want the designation."

"Then why in God's earth are you cutting me up? I know what happened. I make allowances. The world is the world. You want to call the Kennedys a pack of Irish bums—your opinion. Johnson, you want language—an iron rod up his asshole, but he tried to be a President. You think anyone can govern this country? The people decide. Nixon was what they wanted."

"All right, Tony. You see it your way. I told you I want the designation. But the conditions have changed, and if you want to give it to me, these are the new conditions. You people walk away from the war. I won't. I'll live the rest of my life with that image of a beautiful young man dead in a bathtub of bloody water, with a stump where his leg once was and with his wrists slit. I'm going to talk about that war, because the past is also the future. I learned that. There is a big Democratic contingent out of California in the House of Representatives, and if I join them, they won't love me. I want you to know that too. There are enough atomic weapons to kill the human race ten times over. I intend to raise all hell about that—and about the treatment of the illegals and offshore drilling and our brotherhood with every filthy dictatorship on earth—all of it, Tony."

He sipped at his tea and nodded. "That's a lot, Barbara."

"You're damn right."

"I got a feeling you're practicing on me," he complained.

"Oh, Tony—no. Tonight is one of my crazier moments, but I had to say it to you."

"All right. Now listen to me for a little while. These young men in the party, thirty, thirty-five, they live in a world of computers and polls and multinational corporations, and they say, How long before that old dumb Italian gives up? Soon, but when I go a lot of things go that they never knew or understood. They don't know their history, and that's a sad thing. We learned about it. We learned ward politics but we also learned history, because we were the children of the immigrants, and we loved this land. A different way than they talk now about loving it. So we learned. We read, we studied. We learned that there was once a President of these United States whose name was John Quincy Adams, a farmer from Massachusetts. He lived before the Civil War, so the Southern states were slave states. Adams was elected President in eighteen twenty-four. He served four years and fought the slave-owners every inch of the way. Then Andrew Jackson was elected, and John Quincy Adams went home to his farm in Massachusetts. Well, his neighbors came to him and they said to him, Adams, we want you to run for Congress. He did. Never happened before and it never happened again, but John Quincy Adams went back to Washington as a congressman after he'd been President. But before he took the designation, he said to his neighbors, You want me, you can vote for me. But I'm my own man, and I vote my conscience."

"Did he?"

"Oh, he did, Barbara, he did. And he died there, in the halls of Congress, fighting the slave-owners."

A long silence as Barbara stared at the old man. He sipped his tea. Then he said, "You want the designation, you can have it. Only because we can't find anybody else to go through the motions. But you can have it. You mind now if I go home, Barbara?"

He stood up, and Barbara threw her arms around him. She was crying, not unusual for her. After Moretti had left, Barbara went up to her bedroom and observed herself in a full-length mirror. A tall woman, five feet eight inches. Her features had always been just a bit too prominent for people to call her beautiful; she was better described as a handsome woman. And while there were wrinkles around her eyes and her mouth, she could still on occasion notice heads turning. Her hair was streaked with gray. She would not interfere with it. Her belly was flat, her breasts still round and shapely. Lucky, she thought. I've been lucky, all things considered. No more tears—not for the moment.

The telephone rang. Sam's voice, asking her how she was. "I'm all right."

"I was worried. I know how you feel about Aunt Eloise."

"More to the point, you know how I feel about Josh."

"Josh is dead. Eloise is alive. It makes a difference."

"You could have been more attentive, Sam. They wanted you there. They needed whatever there is of the family."

"Mom, please stop scolding me!"

Scolding him? Was she scolding him? He was thirty years old.

"Then don't shout at me," she said with annoyance.

"Mother, Mother," he said, gently now. "Don't you understand this? I stayed as long as I could after the funeral. It wasn't easy. I had a knockdown, drag-out fight with Josh when he decided to enlist in the marines. So did Freddie. We were rotten to him. I understood later, the beautiful fat little boy with the big blue eyes and that same strawberry blond hair that Eloise had, with Freddie and me lording it over him and pushing him around, and the only thing he could do that was more than we had done. As he saw it, the only thing that would give him that damn macho that has killed kids since time began—well, the only thing was Vietnam, and he did it. I tried to stay there after the funeral—"

"Sammy, I'm not blaming you."

"The divorce came through today," his voice flat and miserable.

"Oh, I'm sorry. Poor Sam."

"Poor Carla, poor both of us."

"How is she?"

"She feels free, kicking up her heels. You can have your friendly divorce."

"Sam, have you eaten tonight?"

"Mom, don't worry about me."

"I haven't eaten all day, and now I'm very hungry. Will you take me to dinner? Late, late dinner at some silly place —the Fairmont? Yes?"

"You're on."

She dressed carefully for the evening. There is death and there is life, and if the one takes over the other, then there is nothing left, absolutely nothing. She was not ready for nothing. For the first time since Boyd's death, she felt intensely alive.

It was not until the end of the summer that Barbara's campaign for Congress actually began. During the weeks following the end of July, she did her homework, studied the newspapers, read books on the recent history of her country, and watched the Carter-Mondale team with the greatest of interest. This was not, as far as she was concerned, a reprise of 1970. The Vietnam War was over. Watergate had happened, and the mean, snarling visage of Richard Nixon had passed from the scene. She was a candidate, and she intended to win. When she appeared before the party's subcommittee on new candidates, they asked her a few cursory questions, generalized questions about her response to the principles that the party stood for, and then they were ready to congratulate her and dismiss her.

"I'm sorry," Barbara said. "I can't leave it this way."

"What way, Miss Lavette?" the committee chairman asked. "Have we missed anything of importance?"

"Everything," Barbara answered flatly. "Either you're ready to accept me on this flimsy basis because I'm a woman or because you're convinced that I don't have the chance of a snowball in hell of carrying the Forty-eighth C.D. One reason is as distasteful as the other. Don't you think you ought to know how I feel about specific issues? Suppose you felt I could win in the Forty-eighth?"

The chairman was a patient man. "It is true, Miss Lavette, that six years ago you rolled up the highest number we ever had in the Forty-eighth, but then you were running against a nonentity who was already on the carpet for a matter of unreported income. He finished out his term, made a deal, paid off Internal Revenue, and bowed out. In 'seventy-two, our candidate scored thirty-two hundred votes. That was not the difference between his vote and his opponent's. That was his total vote. In 'seventy-four, we ran a name. He barely set foot in the district. We had other fish to fry, and the man the Republicans put up in 'seventy-two was still on the ticket. Let me tell you about him."

"You don't have to," Barbara said coldly. "I know Alexander Holt. He was part of the law firm that represents my brother Thomas Lavette." She noticed how they quickened when she mentioned Tom. He was one of the half-dozen wealthiest men in San Francisco. "Mr. Holt is very good-looking and very bright. A widower. You see, I do my homework. From your attitude, I gather you'd be perfectly satisfied if I telephoned my campaign to the Forty-eighth."

That brought a laugh where Barbara had intended no humor. Al Ruddy, whom she had met through Moretti and who was one of the old man's protégés and whom, she remembered, Boyd had disliked intensely, spread his hands and said, soothingly, "I don't think Miss Lavette is trying to be humorous. Tony has only the highest respect for her, and if anyone in the Bay Area could make a reasonable showing in the Forty-eighth, she could."

More meaningless words followed. When Moretti asked her how it had gone, she answered, "Very well indeed. From what I heard there, if I lived in the Forty-eighth, I'd make sure not to vote Democrat. And by the way, they regard me as a silly old lady whom you're encouraging to exercise her vanity."

Moretti shook his head and sighed. Barbara realized that there was nothing very much that he could say.

She was a good walker; thank God for that and for the fact that a tall woman is forgiven for wearing sensible shoes. In Maine Trotters, a plaid skirt and a white blouse, Barbara decided that she transcended the various social layers of the Forty-eighth C.D. There was a lot to do, an office headquarters to be rented and furnished, a plan of action to be worked out, fund-raising—a successful fund-raising committee could make all the difference—media time, leaflets, posters. She had been through a sort of trial run six years before; now she had to rethink it and do it better, and, as she was determined, differently.

It was still August, mostly a cool and pleasant month in the Bay Area, and Barbara decided to do parts of the district on foot. Six years ago, she had driven through most of it, but then six years was a long time, and there is much you miss in car that you can see clearly when walking.

The area called the Palisades she knew very well indeed, and she could point to at least a dozen fine houses where she had once dined or danced. That was a long time ago, so long ago that two of the houses lay in her memories as places where she had attended sweet-sixteen parties. The houses, layered on terraces gouged out of the hillside, offered a splendid view of the Bay, and in the present market would command prices up to a million dollars. Back from there, pleasant streets, shaded with live oak and massive pines, were lined with houses less grand than those which faced the Bay, but still expensive, with close-cropped lawns, beautiful and expensive plantings, and back yards—to call them by so mundane a title—sporting tennis courts or swimming pools and very often both. Here, reality was pressed back and away from this California land-island that reminded her of Beverly Hills.

Two of those improbable California shopping centers marked this part of the district. They were done in California–Spanish Colonial and whatever-money-will-buy style, red tile roofs, great redwood timbers, a supermarket like something dreamed up by imaginative and underfed children as a centerpiece, and then a selection of somewhat less magnificent stores to provide whatever the heart might desire, the best of men's and women's clothes, furniture, drugs, household appliances and whatever else was needed to save the residents of the area any need to cross the path of the less rich. But beyond this inner island, there were rows and rows of tract houses, most of them bare and naked of fancy shrubbery or shade trees, young people fighting desperately to meet monthly payments, lots of kids and a good many unsmiling mothers. One still needed sixty or seventy thousand dollars to buy such a tract house, and as upwardly mobile as the owners might be, they still had huge mortgage payments and children to feed and clothe and wives who either worked to meet the bills or chewed an eternal cud of discontent.

And then, beyond the tract houses but still in the district, a barrio to house the servants, the cooks and gardeners, the brown-skinned men and women who worked the fields, driving out of the district in trucks that took them to the orchards and vineyards and then brought them back, and their children and the mini-gangs, imitative of the larger urban areas. And on the edge of the barrio, the houses of the black community, small cottages, some of them neat and well cared for, others with paint peeling, surrounded by dead shrubbery, kids playing in the unpaved streets, the men gone to jobs in Oakland or Berkeley or some other Bay area or to the fields. It was not simple; it was very puzzling and complex indeed, and this was only one of a number of small communities in the district. As day after day passed, Barbara parking her car in one part or another of the district, trudging on by foot, a tall lady with a leather pouch slung over her shoulder, the problem of the Forty-eighth Congressional District became even more puzzling and troubling.

Obviously, the poor, the working people and the young professionals in the district outnumbered the rich, yet the district was solidly, unshakably Republican—except that she had shaken it a good deal six years ago. Apparently most of the Chicanos and blacks did not vote, and apparently they were positioned to provide a threat to the rest of the district. There were hardly enough of them to make her win, yet possibly enough to swing the margin if she could do what she had done six years ago. But could she, she wondered? Six years ago, she took on the Republican Party at a most peculiar historical moment. Nixon was in the White House, an affront to any person of decent sensibilities. The country was bleeding from the horror of Vietnam, and her opponent was sleazy, dishonest and on the verge of being indicted. Now, it was a presidential year; Jerry Ford was at least an upstanding and photogenic citizen, and her own opponent was an attorney of distinction, a man of experience, and handsome enough to be a middle-aged star in a soap opera. Barbara felt demeaned by brooding over the question of good looks, but the media had turned that into one of the prime requisites for office. It was hard for her to tell herself that she was as attractive as Alexander Holt—or to believe it.

Well, be that as it may, she still had a race to run, and if Alexander Holt were Paul Newman himself, he nevertheless could be beaten. She had studied his record carefully, and it asked for such care, since it was an uncommonly careful record. He was one of those Republicans who early on had recognized the awful stupidity and hopelessness of the war with Vietnam, and during his four years in the House, his record on that score was near perfect—according to Barbara's point of view. He balanced this opposition to the war with a firm stand against abortion—to a point where he was the first representative to ask that foreign aid be withdrawn from nations that permitted legal abortion. It was an untenable and idiotic position, but it put him firmly in the conservative ranks. He was for the strictest of immigration laws, thereby writing off the whole Mexican community, and he was a close old friend of Ronald Reagan and had served in Reagan's administration when Reagan was governor of California. He had pressed for a larger share for private industry in development of federal lands, and while he did not come out solidly against the entitlement programs, he fudged on any vote that favored such programs.

Barbara thought about Alexander Holt as she explored the Forty-eighth Congressional District. In California, a congressional district can be as large as or even larger than certain Eastern states, and while the Forty-eighth was not the largest, it was by no means the smallest. It contained four separate independent towns, not to mention stretches of unincorporated area; and moving away from what she had thought of as the Forty-eighth, Barbara was surprised and somewhat chagrined to discover how much of the district she had not set foot in, how much of it she hardly knew existed. In the course of her exploration, she came to an area even more wretched than the barrio on the Bay side. A yellow dirt road ran between a line of ancient shacks constructed out of whatever might be put together to keep out the night and the rain and wind and cold—tin, old plywood, boards, corrugated paper, tar paper. There were about thirty of these shacks, skinny kids playing in the road, women washing clothes in an old horse trough, a few teen-agers lounging around, smoking, and an absence of men—which meant that they were doing something to survive, even if it was for only fifty cents an hour in the fields. A second glance told Barbara that they were not Mexicans, and when she stopped to talk to an old lady who sat smoking a corncob pipe in front of one of the shacks, she discovered that this was a community of people from El Salvador.

"That's right," the old lady said in Spanish, since Barbara had addressed her question in Spanish. "El Salvador. You speak good Spanish for an Anglo. Do you understand me? I have no teeth left, so I garble my words." She tapped her head. "But the mind is all right."

"I understand you perfectly."

"Thank you. God bless you. You are very elegant."

"But why don't you have your mouth fitted for false teeth?"

"Bless your heart! I have no money, no family; all dead. They give me food, my neighbors, my friends. So where would I find the money for teeth?"

"But the state pays for it."

"Lady, lady," the old woman said, "you are kind. We are illegals."

Barbara nodded unhappily, thinking of the long, almost impassable distance, through Guatemala and Mexico. "Still, perhaps something can be done."

The old lady puffed on her pipe and looked sidewise at Barbara. By now, others had noticed Barbara, and a small crowd of children and women had gathered around her, listening to the conversation.

"Who are you?" someone asked.

"Don't talk to her, you old fool," another woman said to the old lady. "She could be from Immigration. Hear the way she speaks."

"I'm not from Immigration," Barbara said. "I'm the Democratic candidate for Congress in the Forty-eighth Congressional District."

"What's the Forty-eighth Congressional District?"

"Where you live, here."

"Oh!"

"You speak Spanish."

"I've always spoken Spanish," Barbara said. "Since I was a kid." And to the old lady with the pipe, "If you'll give me your name, I'll see what I can do about the false teeth."

"Never mind her name."

"Oh, shut up, you fool. My name is Rosa Hernando," she said to Barbara. "You write it down, yes? I would like to eat an ear of maize before I die."

Walking back to where she had parked her car, Barbara thought about people so desperate that they would come from El Salvador to slip across the Rio Grande River to live in such shacks and in such poverty. Another part of her mind said, Illegals. No votes there.

"I suppose," she said to herself, "that's what Tony Moretti would call thinking politically."

That evening, Barbara called her son and told him about the old woman and her teeth.

"It's a tricky business," Sam said. "As an illegal, she

could run into trouble, and I don't think there's any program that fits her."

"There must be."

"Is she a voter, Mom? No, that's a dumb question. If she's an illegal, she's not a voter, and I don't know why you're knocking yourself out. Anyway, I'm all for you making this race, so don't feel I'm making snotty remarks about voters. It just crossed my mind, and I love you, and I think you'll walk all over this Holt character."

"Thank you, Sam." She put down the telephone, thinking that Sam was one of the most sensitive and caring persons she had ever known—yet he could treat his mother as if she were a rather superior idiot and had treated his wife as if she did not exist. Strangely, or perhaps not so strangely, Barbara had become much closer to Carla since the divorce. The day Barbara's candidacy was announced in the press, Carla had called and begged to be allowed to help. "Barbara, I need this kind of thing. I can talk to Chicanos. I swear I'll bring you a thousand votes!"

Barbara had accepted on condition that she pay Carla a salary. Carla had refused alimony or a cash settlement of any kind from Sam, and she had found a job selling cosmetics at Macy's in San Francisco. That was *until:* all the jobs Carla had held were until something turned up in the theater. The reviews of her work in Ford's *'Tis Pity She's a Whore* were excellent, but after six weeks the play had closed and the reviews faded from everyone's memory. Now Carla dumped the job at Macy's without a tear.

Freddie did almost the same thing. He turned up at the house on Green Street two days after Barbara's public announcement and informed her that he had worked out with his stepfather, Adam Levy, a leave of absence to extend until the first Tuesday after the first Monday in November. It was then the third week in August, which meant that he would be away from the winery for more than two months.

"But you're running the winery now," Barbara protested.

"No, oh, no. I try to give that impression, just as Pop tries to give the impression that he runs it, but the truth is that Grandma Clair runs the works. She always did, you know, even though Grandpa Jake established the image of the tough old man in charge. Well, sure he was in charge, but every important decision was made with Grandma. Pop can get along without me for two months, and if he needs me, I can run out there. On the other hand, your campaign needs a manager."

"And you're that?" Barbara asked, smiling.

"Better than anything you can hire for the money."

"And how much is that?"

"Pay me a dollar a week," Freddie said.

"Oh, no. You work for me, you work for pay."

Freddie shrugged. "All right, if that's the way you want it. Thing is, you need me. You need someone who is cold and calculating and not taken in by the bullshit that thickens the blood of politicians."

"Freddie, why do you hate them so?"

"Look around you."

"But it can be changed. Believe me, it can be changed. If I didn't think it could be changed, I couldn't go on living. You came to your manhood in the sixties and there was some hope then, and I suppose you feel that there's none left now, none at all."

"Only one hope, Aunt Barbara—that we're not all blown to hell and gone by their bombs. Anyway"—he took out his wallet—"here are the first campaign contributions, the beginning of that quarter million we're going to raise. Grandma's check for two hundred dollars and Pop's for five hundred."

Barbara took the two checks, telling herself that she must not refuse because they were family and she must feel no guilt. It was the beginning. Others would give her money;

there was no other way. "Thank them," she told Freddie. "How is your father?"

"Glum. Miserable. I'll never really get over Josh's death, but I'm young and a brother isn't a son. Pop won't get over it. Funny thing, Mom is stronger. No matter how she hurts inside, she faces up to the world. Pop is wounded too deeply. Don't forget, his brother, Joshua, was killed in World War Two. Two Joshuas to their stinking wars, and this Vietnam thing is like a curse that won't end. You want to know why I hate politicians? You excepted."

Telling May Ling about the meeting with Barbara, his son, Danny, on his lap, Freddie made a point of not excluding his wife. "No way are you out of it," he said. "The damn idiocy of a congressional campaign is that it takes two months of backbreaking, heartbreaking effort, not to mention the money involved—and believe me, May Ling, she needs all the help she can get."

"But can she make it?" May Ling wanted to know.

"She thinks she can."

"Do you?"

"God knows. I'm tempted to say that she'll get a worse pasting than she got six years ago, but miracles have happened. The point is that Moretti and the others are using her to bring in women voters all over the state. You know, what great guys we are—running this distinguished old woman—"

"She's not an old woman."

"Not to us—all right. This guy she's up against, Alexander Holt, is smooth as silk. Looks like John Forsythe—you know, we've seen him on the tube maybe fifty times: fine Waspy elegance, gray hair, square face, good features—"

"You're describing Barbara's brother Tom, who just happens to be your father."

"Leave that end out of it. Adam's been my father for as

long as I care to remember, but I suppose you're right. He does resemble Thomas Lavette, except that Holt's only fifty-nine years old, a widower, and the secret love of every rich broad in the district."

"How do you know so much?"

"Studying. Are you serious about working with us?"

"You're damn right I am," May Ling said.

"Good. I'm used to having you around."

"You're being very generous today."

"I have to be. Who else is going to look after that crazy aunt of ours? Sam says she has to get it out of her system. That's because he doesn't know one damn thing about her system. Aunt Barbara doesn't get anything out of her system. It just adds up inside."

"Do you know something else?" May Ling said. "The way you and Sam talk about her disgusts me. She's wonderful. She reminds me of Mrs. Roosevelt. And you talk about her—"

"No!" Freddie protested. "I'm crazy about her. You know I'm a male chauvinist pig."

"You are indeed," May Ling said. "Why do you cultivate it?"

"They're related—I mean also married but related some way, aren't they?" Tony Moretti asked Barbara the following week. It was his first visit to the campaign headquarters Freddie had set up at Sunnyside Plaza, the largest shopping center in Sunnyside, which was the part of the Forty-eighth C.D. that fronted on the Bay. He had just been introduced to Freddie and May Ling. "Is she Chinese?"

"Her father's half Chinese. She's the daughter of my brother Joe and Sally Levy. Joe is Pop's son through May Ling, and that beautiful kid was named after Pop's May Ling."

"Half cousins."

"Something of the sort."

"Doesn't seem to like me much," Moretti said, his glance moving around. "He put this place together?"

"What makes you say that?"

"He's the type who takes charge. You got eleven people here. How many are on payroll?"

"Three."

"That's good, Barbara. Try to keep it that way. Volunteers are better anyway. They're dedicated. What about money?"

"We sent out one mailing. That was only three days ago. Not too much yet."

"Don't depend on mailings. Functions, and the conscience of the rich. I'd like to meet that young fellow who thinks I'm a ward heeler and an old bum."

"Oh, he doesn't think that," Barbara protested.

But Freddie regarded Moretti coolly for a long moment before he shook hands, and Moretti said, "I know your generation as little as you know mine, Lavette, but I've known a few Lavettes, and when they're good, they're good."

Freddie smiled and shook his head. "I don't know what that's supposed to mean."

"Not much. You think your aunt's being set up, don't you?"

Moretti waited. Freddie didn't answer.

"Nobody sets her up," Moretti said softly. "She's too smart."

Then Moretti went to her and kissed her cheek. "I'll be going and I'll be back. I'll be back a good deal. We're going to win this one."

She knew that money was the mother's milk of politics, but six years earlier she'd made out with whatever she had, and if she didn't talk on television, she talked from a sound truck or on the street at a shopping center. It amazed her now to reflect that in that earlier election, spending less than thirty thousand dollars, she had almost taken the impregnable Forty-eighth. Of course those were other circumstances, other times. She still talked at shopping centers; May Ling, tall, slender, with a face that drew the attention even of women, was her partner at the shopping centers. She would stop women not too overburdened with children and packages, and ask whether they wouldn't like to meet the candidate, Barbara Lavette. Barbara never used a platform. Standing on their own level, she found she could talk to women very easily and intimately. It didn't matter if she talked to only a handful; they would remember her and repeat what she said and take it to others. Here, she was a new incarnation, and the younger women she spoke to had little knowledge of her past. Most of them had not read her books, and if they knew her at all, it was as the candidate who had shaken up the district six years earlier.

But Freddie insisted on television and radio, and that took money. "It's the new politics and soon it will be the only politics," Freddie told her. "Believe me, Aunt Barbara, from here on the candidate won't exist; the only thing that will exist is his image on the glass tit."

"The what?"

"The box, the glass tit that America sucks morning, noon and night, and the candidate will be whatever image they want to put on that box. You don't make points by talking to a dozen people at a shopping center—whatever May Ling says."

"What does she say?"

"She says you make points," he admitted.

Barbara couldn't be angry at him. Freddie was the physical image of her brother—as he would put it, his natural father—six feet and one inch, large bones but lean, a long head and sandy hair, altogether very handsome, which made him trouble with women. Yet he was bright enough not to confuse his good looks with other parts of himself. He was ingratiating without reaching, a quality Barbara envied.

"Come with me and see for yourself."

Freddie came to a shopping center and watched and listened.

"Nobody ever asked me what I thought." A young woman, dragged apart by three children. "How do I know what I think?"

An older woman, her arms full of packages. "Just let me put these in the car, Miss Lavette. But we don't think. It's not in style for ladies."

"They say Ford's wife is a dancer. I'm a dancer who doesn't dance. In Europe the government supports the dance."

"My mother's fifty-one with cancer. We don't eat much. Every nickel goes to the doctors and the hospital. I'd like you to look at my kids' shoes."

"She can't do anything about that."

"She can't do anything about anything!"

"Who can?"

"I vote for nobody. My kid died in Vietnam."

"But she's here, isn't she? How many congressmen have you seen at Sunnyside Plaza?"

"The thing nobody ever told me is exactly what can a congressman do."

"What does he do?"

"It beats me."

"There's a spot behind our house that oozes. The smell is sickening. A friend of ours from the university at Berkeley says it's an old chemical dump. He tested the stuff. He says sell our house and move. With that smell, who'll buy it?"

"I'm on the same block."

"You know what happens when you write your congressman?"

"Who is our congressman?"

"Alexander something."

"He's beautiful."

"You vote for him because he's beautiful?"

"Why not? What other reason is there to vote for him?"

"The plain truth is that it's wonderful to have a woman running for Congress, but what can you do about things? We're not cynical. We're just hopeless."

"I see what you mean," Freddie said to Barbara. "But we still have to buy television, and that costs money."

Everything cost money. The pretty girl who was hired to sing the song from *Cabaret,* "Money Makes the World Go Round," was paid three hundred dollars. She sang the song four times, and Barbara thought it was more than enough, but Birdie MacGelsie, at whose home the party was being given, said to Barbara, "You can't raise money and be a lady too. No way. Money makes the world go round, and you've got to beat it into people with a stick."

Birdie's husband, Mac, climbed onto a chair and called for silence. Greeted with hoots, he said, "The next one who hoots gets his ass broken by me, personally." Since he was over six feet and weighed three hundred pounds, it was not an empty threat. He went on to point out to them that he had not asked them here tonight, drinking his booze and gobbling his sandwiches, for the pleasure of their company.

"This is not one of those hotshot Republican thousand-dollar-a-plate dinners. We don't deal with such people. This is a poor little party to honor a great lady, Barbara Lavette, old Dan Lavette's daughter, who has taken upon herself the task of reclaiming the Bay Area from the political sewage that has been flooding it." He took out a roll of bills and began to peel off hundred-dollar notes. Birdie came out of the kitchen with an enormous aluminum pot. "So here's my five hundred in the pot, and I want every one of you free-loaders to match it. There are no welfare cases here, and none of you was invited for his talent. And couples to me are two people, not one. So keep the pot boiling."

Voices called for Barbara, and she had to stand up and thank them and tell them that she would try to do an honest and decent job.

After the party, Freddie, who was driving her home, said to her, "Don't feel the way you do—please, Aunt Barbara—or we'll have to wash it up right here."

"And how do I feel?"

"Sick and disgusted, and there's no reason to feel that way. We picked up seventeen thousand, five hundred dollars tonight, and we got a pledge of ten thousand from a guy called Lars Swenson, who said his father sold Grandpa the *Ocean Queen* or something of the sort."

"The *Oregon Queen*," Barbara said. "Good heavens! Which one was he?"

"I think it must have been his grandfather. Tall feller, about forty, blond hair going white. He had that beautiful red-headed gal with him. I heard about him. Swenson Explorers—three big cruise ships that sail out of Long Beach. Who's this Carol Eberhardt? Skinny, good-looking kid about twenty-eight or thirty?"

"Why?"

"She wants to come in as a volunteer. Very earnest."

"Yes, we met at Birdie's place before. She helped out the first time. Her father's Jim Eberhardt, top of the local Republicans. I think he's the Republican whip at the State House. A lot of inherited money. None of the Eberhardts have to work for a living."

They were at Green Street now, and after Barbara had climbed out of the car, Freddie said, "Just a moment. Look at this. I thought of tearing it up, but now I'll deposit it—if you think it's real." He handed Barbara a check, and peering at it in the light of a street lamp, she saw that it was a check for a thousand dollars, drawn on the Crocker Bank and signed by Carol Eberhardt. On the line given to *Memo,* she had written: "Republican—one grand."

"It's real."

"I can understand that," Freddie said.

"Yes, I thought you might."

But at home with May Ling, who would have no part of fund-raisers, it was not that easily explained.

"Why?" May Ling insisted.

"Isn't it obvious? She probably feels about her father the way I feel about mine."

"Adam!"

"Not Adam. Thomas Lavette."

"You mean you'd toss off a thousand dollars just to let the world know how much you hate your real father?"

"Twice a day, if I had the money to spare. I don't think of him as my real father. There's a genetic connection, but since I can remember, I've thought of Adam as my father. In fact, I have no memory of Thomas Lavette as my father. I was a very small kid when Mom married Adam."

"Why do you hate him so?" May Ling wondered. "How can you go on with that kind of hate?"

"I don't know. I'm not even sure I hate him or how I feel about him. I just don't care."

"And do you think this Eberhardt woman feels the same way about her father? I remember seeing pictures of the family—she's very pretty. They all are; no half-breed Chinese-Italian-Jews like me."

"Of all the damn nonsense! Why do you keep putting yourself down?"

"Don't shout at me."

"I'm not shouting at you—only God help me if I should dare to say that another woman is pretty."

"Because I'm ugly, and every woman who looks at you—"

"You're one of the loveliest women I've ever laid eyes or hands on, and you keep on and on with this 'ugly' crap."

May Ling was crying. She had no more defenses. Freddie took her in his arms and said, "Let's go to bed and make love all night."

The baby began to howl.

"Still, it's the sweetest thing you've said to me in a long time," May Ling told him through her tears as she went to pick up their baby.

The next day, Freddie said to Barbara, "We need a pollster."

"Why?"

"Because that's the way it goes these days. Alex Holt will have his pollster. We have to check it and we must know how we're doing, where we're weak and where we're strong. Just as we have to have radio and TV. That's the way it is."

"How much will it cost?"

"Too much. Look, Aunt Barbara, I've been thinking about this. I used to think I'd die before I'd do it, but I think I'd do it for you."

"What on earth are you talking about?"

"Thomas Lavette, my father, your brother. He has more money than God."

"And you'd ask him?"

"Yes. But he's your brother, so it's up to you."

"Over my dead body. It's very sweet of you and very gallant, but leave the tilting at windmills to me. Yours is the practical end of this business."

"All right. Then let me suggest something else—with great temerity."

"Great temerity. I shudder to think of what's coming."

"Carson Devron," Freddie said quickly, talking very fast and not permitting Barbara to get a word in until he had finished. "He runs the *L.A. Morning World* and they have their own pollster and if they took on your campaign as a matter of statewide interest, I mean intensively, they would run their own polls and save us a bundle—" He stopped suddenly and waited.

There was no explosion. Barbara stared at him thoughtfully for a long moment, and then she asked him, "Why statewide interest? This is the Bay Area. Southern California's another world." She had been thinking of Carson lately. It seemed impossible that fifteen years had passed since their divorce.

Freddie handed her two clippings. "Op ed page, one of them. What you keep forgetting is that you're Barbara Lavette, and that you put together one of the most successful peace movements this country ever saw, and that you stuck in Lyndon Johnson's craw like an oversized fish bone."

"A beautiful image," Barbara murmured, reading a clipping, which said, "The decision by Barbara Lavette to challenge the incumbent in California's 48th C.D. is one of the most interesting developments of the current campaign. Credit must go to the local Democratic organization for this choice, the choice of a brilliant and principled woman, an advocate of peace and women's rights, but one who has lived her life apart from the body politic—" Barbara paused, confused. "This is an editorial, isn't it?"

"Absolutely. Which means that Devron either wrote it or approved it. You're still on good terms, aren't you?"

"Yes. We're friends."

"You don't seem very certain."

"Freddie, I haven't seen him in years, and I have no intention of seeing him now. I suppose it would be helpful to have his polling machine as a gift, but why would he do it?"

"Because he respects you."

Barbara shrugged.

"Would you mind if I went down there and talked to him?"

She didn't know. Would she mind or wouldn't she mind? Six years ago, her campaign had been so easy. Boyd had taken care of everything, and it was all very simple, direct and successful, because she didn't care whether she won or lost. However, two years later, Alexander Holt gave his Democratic opponent a few thousand votes, and two years after that, the Democrats polled a total of four thousand, six hundred votes.

"Another ball game entirely," everyone said to her. "There's a new pitcher in the game."

How she resented people turning everything into games. Games were the mindless passion of America, games and money. Freddie and Moretti kept talking about money—always money. Everything depended on money. If Freddie spoke to Carson Devron, it would save money. If she would talk personally to twelve people whose names they had given her, she might raise as much as fifty thousand dollars.

"Aunt Barbara?"

"Do you know," she said to Freddie, "we're going to drop the aunt. You're thirty-four and running this campaign. When we're alone, Barbara. Other situations, Miss Lavette. Now, about Mr. Devron, I suppose I must be practical, as practical as I could ever hope to be because, believe me, Freddie, I would not hesitate to nominate myself as the most innocent or witless character in this politics business. Do you know that in nineteen seventy I never gave a thought to money? Oh, Boyd raised a few thousand dollars—Now what on earth are you shaking your head about?"

"I hate to say this to you, but in 'seventy, they were voting against that silly little ass who opposed you. That's the way it is. Half the voters in this country never voted for a candidate; they vote against a candidate. Think about it."

She thought about it and nodded. "I suppose you're right."

"And Devron?"

"No reason why you shouldn't talk to him." She didn't hide from herself the fact that she wanted a connection, and that Freddie would make the connection. You lived your life and you loved men, and of all the men she had loved, only Carson Devron was still alive. When she was a schoolgirl, it had seemed impossible, if not somewhat unnatural, that love and passion and sex could continue into one's old age; and now, almost sixty-two, she felt reluctant to admit, even to herself, that she so desperately wanted a man's arms around her, the warmth of his body in bed and the surging, incredible climax of sex. Carson was younger. He would still be in the full vigor of manhood.

Her bed was icy cold. It was August, and San Francisco was the coldest place on the face of the earth. She lay curled under the covers, shivering, trying to warm herself after standing naked in the cold room, like some sentimental child of thirteen, and trying to remember the name of the Arctic explorer—was it Stefansson, or something like that?—who had remarked that he'd never felt so cold in the Arctic as he had in San Francisco.

She couldn't manage indifference when Freddie returned from his errand to Carson Devron in Los Angeles. When Barbara saw the small store at Sunnyside Shopping Plaza that Freddie had rented for their headquarters, she realized that the campaign was beginning in earnest and that it should have been twice or even three times as large. The furniture consisted of two long sawhorse tables for the mailing operation, two old desks for Barbara and Freddie, an ancient kitchen table and two dozen folding chairs. With a stream of eager volunteers, mostly under twenty, who were going to remake the world in the Forty-eighth with Barbara Lavette as their Joan of Arc, and now five others on staff, with and without pay, and crates of material arriving daily from the printer, and Carla sitting at the kitchen table, sign overhead specifying *Talk Spanish to Me*, the place was a bedlam of chaotic energy. When Freddie showed up, Barbara grabbed him and steered him outside to Daisy's Delicious Lunch, on the other side of Gelson's Supermarket. At the same time, telling herself, You, Barbara Lavette, are acting like some idiot teen-ager, about to make contact with a lost love who is a running back on the varsity team. A proper level of comparison, she decided.

"I'm starving," Freddie said.

"Then order before you say another word," Barbara told him. "I've been talking to Tony Moretti about polling, and, you know, the party has their own pollster, but believe me, they are not going to waste him on the accursed Forty-eighth. They may give us a smidgen, whatever that is in polling terms. Tony thinks it would be wonderful if the *L.A. World* took us on."

Freddie ordered ham and eggs and fried potatoes.

"We got it," he then announced.

"Oh? Come on. How? You're charming, nephew, but that charming?"

"You're looking at it. He thinks that your contest in the Forty-eighth is symbolic of the post-Watergate era. You know, his paper supports Carter, but with no great enthusiasm, and I think he's trying to shift the emphasis to statewide events."

"We're not statewide."

"Well, Brown's not up for re-election—you know, he likes Brown enormously, but some of that must be reaction to Reagan. He froths at the mouth when he speaks about Reagan."

Barbara smiled. "Oh, yes, he detested Reagan. You know, he grew up in Los Angeles, side by side with that whole film crowd."

"Anyway, he'll have one of his political reporters up here —of course covering the whole Bay Area, but with specific emphasis on the Forty-eighth, and he's going to poll the district week by week. You know he's still in love with you, don't you?"

"Freddie, middle-aged men don't remain in love for fifteen years. I admire Carson and I think he admires me. That's it. Tell me, how does he look?"

"He looks great. In fact, he looks like Alexander Holt, in a way. Total Wasp elegance and good breeding. I thought I was smooth, but he could walk circles around me. Didn't he win the decathlon or something at some long-forgotten Olympics?"

"Or something. He remembered you?"

"Says he did. Kept asking about you and about the campaign and what you were doing otherwise and how you'd taken Boyd's death."

"He has a lovely wife, three children, and the best newspaper in California. So turn your sneaky thoughts elsewhere."

"Sneaky—oh, no. No, indeed. I'm realistic, dear aunt. I'm working up to calling you Barbara."

She did a record for a sound truck, and she found that she disliked more and more of what a candidate had to do. Upstairs in her own house, preparing for a television interview at home, she heard Freddie, sotto voce, telling May Ling, "I warned her about it. Knee-deep in crap, and it gets worse and worse. It's not for people. In England maybe, but not the way we do politics in this country, and you take someone like Aunt Barbara, with her beauty and dignity, and throw her into this lousy rat race where everything is P.R. and media beauty contest—everything that isn't pure bullshit."

Aunt Barbara decided that she would put up signs to let people know that in this house, sound carried through the heating system. It was the sound of a Watergate generation that believed in nothing, and she was not going to let this get under her skin when she had just completed a listing of issues that she intended to refer to in the upcoming television interview. Regardless of what else was cosmetic, the issues were real.

"Thank God she's beautiful," Freddie was saying.

"Freddie, will you shut up," she shouted. "This house lets me hear everything you say. Suppose you do your thing and let me do mine."

The issues were not cosmetic. Immigration—Mexicans moving across the border by the thousand, facing starvation at home. Welfare, constructive, not destructive; foreign policy, get rid of the bombs before they get rid of us; energy, we must learn how to harness the power of the sun, the tides. That was the one Freddie was afraid of. "Puts us in the camp of the nuts." Gays; ah, there was one for a candidate in the Bay Area.

She closed her notebook and said, "The hell with it," and went downstairs to be interviewed for the first time on television.

Sam tracked her down to her headquarters in the Forty-eighth. "I've canceled three operations," he said, and seeing the look of alarm on her face, added, "Elective surgery. Which still doesn't change the fact that I feel like a motherless child."

"Yes, that will be the day. Go over and be decent to Carla."

"I did and I was decent. While you were taken over by three nuns."

"Nuns vote," Barbara said. "Anyway, they're good people. They've just come back from El Salvador. Some of the things they've seen—"

"I want to take you to lunch. Do you hear me? I want to take my mother, whom I haven't seen or spoken to in three months, to lunch. You're losing weight again. I can imagine the junk food you're living on. What's in there?" pointing to a brown bag on her desk.

"Corned beef on rye, mustard, pickle and coffee. I'm not losing weight. I am gaining weight, and Sammy, darling, I love you, but don't practice medicine every time we meet. I can't have lunch with you, because in thirty minutes I have to tell the senior class at Fremont High School why I'm running for Congress."

"High school seniors don't vote."

"You'd be surprised. Some of them do, and others have parents who vote. Be a dear and settle for half of my sandwich."

He sat across the desk from her, eating half of a corned beef sandwich and studying his mother, until she asked him, "Do you approve?"

"I've always been delighted with the way you looked. Sure, I approve. Still taking Premarin? How much was it? Three tenths of a milligram daily? Well, it's a small dose and I think it's safe enough, but you've been taking it for some years now, haven't you? You should be checked every six months. Are you?"

Barbara burst out laughing. "Sammy, you are impossible —utterly impossible."

Freddie, who had entered the store and picked up Barbara's remark, said, "Always has been. We were friends once."

Sam hugged him.

"Never mind the display. Come around and stuff some envelopes."

"You two are serious about this, aren't you?"

"Look around you," Freddie said. "Does it look like a joke?"

"You really think you can win?"

"We know we can win."

"Nobody else does."

"For Christ's sake, Sam!" Freddie exclaimed. "Which side are you on?"

"I try to be objective."

Somewhat later, driving Barbara across the district to Fremont High School, Freddie said, "I shouldn't have shot my mouth off at Sam."

"That's all right," Barbara said. "He can use a kick in his backside. On the other hand, I think you're angry about his leaving Carla."

"I won't deny that. I like Carla—always have."

"Talk to him about it. It was a mutual thing. Don't keep things inside of you. Talk to me. You didn't like that TV interview one damn bit, did you?"

"Not much, since you put it that way."

"Why?"

"Because you're way out ahead. You can't do that. You talk about an atomic exchange that will end life on earth— all life. People just don't believe that."

"Three scientists I spoke to, over at Stanford, do."

"Then they have to say it. You talk about what's going on in Central America and how we knocked over the democratic government of Guatemala in 'fifty-two and how Kissinger did the same thing with the CIA in Chile three years ago, and that's all right if people read the *L.A. Times* carefully and balance it with other things. But the average voter doesn't, and in your district he probably never sees the *L.A. Times* unless he's a teacher or some other similar type, who'll vote for you anyway, and if you're going to mention the *L.A. World,* the same thing applies. That stuff went over all right when the Vietnam War was running, because that was such a pile of deceit and bloody crap that the public was ready to believe anything about the CIA antics. But what matters here are the bread-and-butter issues, the price of food and gasoline, the Social Security mess, the ERA, unemployment, energy, things they can see and touch, a federal day care program, crime—these are the nitty-gritty. Now I think Carter's going to get elected, because I think most people are beginning to believe what Johnson said about Jerry Ford, that he can't walk and chew gum at the same time, and Carter's made a top priority thing out of dumping on Washington. It's popular. Blame the nonproducing bums down there. Whip the hell out of them. Call up Watergate. It doesn't make much sense, but the citizens love it because they're always on the short end while Washington eats steak every day—" He stopped suddenly and took a deep breath. "I've said too much, haven't I? I wouldn't blame you if you kicked me out on my butt right now."

That was her first impulse. She was heartsick and filled with anger. How did he dare talk to her like this, a kid whose nose was hardly dry? But as she listened to him, she realized that he made sense, that he was not such a kid and that he had been around and paid his dues and seen things and places. When he finished, instead of bursting out, Barbara closed her eyes and sat quietly and thought about what he had said.

When she didn't speak, Freddie said hopelessly, "I never wanted to see you in this position. I love you. We all love you. But now you're in it."

"That's right. I'm in it. What you say is true. Thank you, Freddie."

She had gotten it out. I think I'm growing up, she said to herself. And it's about time.

Four

They had hired, on Moretti's recommendation, a young man named Mort Gilpin as fund-raiser. He was a well set-up fellow, with a beard; he wore three-piece suits and he came off as knowing everyone in the Bay Area who had a bit of extra money to put into a political campaign. The first week, he brought in twelve thousand dollars. He told Freddie that this was only a token of what he would do, and Freddie was impressed.

"I like her," Gilpin said to Freddie. "That's why I'm in this, believe me. For an old girl like her to sound off and get around the way she does—"

"Just hold it," Freddie told him. "You don't talk about her like that, and don't push anything when you talk to her."

"As long as I bring it in."

"Work through me," Freddie said.

But it was on the basis of what Gilpin did that Freddie went out on a limb and bought eleven thirty-second spots, prime time, on the local independent TV station, for a hundred thousand dollars. It was a tremendous bargain, as he told Barbara, because while this independent station did mostly reruns, they had picked up some worthy stuff from Thames TV in London and at least six of the spots would frame the imported TV shows.

"But we don't have a hundred thousand dollars," Barbara said worriedly. "Or do we?"

"I put down ten percent, which nearly cleans us out, but it's coming in. Gilpin is doing a fabulous job."

"He's like so many of the young men around the party," Barbara said. "Talks very fast, keeps quoting statistics and graphs and demographics and appears to be absolutely unaware that the voters we deal with are living people."

"The wave of the future," Freddie said.

"Heaven help us."

"But don't underestimate Mort. He's good."

The advertising agency that prepared the commercial spots depressed Barbara even more. The script called for her to be talking to a group of students, six male, four female, seated as for a seminar around a long table. "Which, of course, will be in our studio. But the effect will be absolutely valid." Like Gilpin, they talked fast, quoted figures and suggested that she take a half hour with the script. "No great study," they assured her. "We know how busy you are, Miss Lavette. We do a tiny piece at a time—for a total of thirty seconds, including establishment and close-up. So there's really nothing to memorize."

They handed her the script. They had asked that she wear a gray suit, if she had one, with a white blouse. She had one. She sat in her gray suit in the cold, smelly, air-conditioned studio and read the script:

MALE STUDENT: I'm graduating this semester, Miss Lavette. I'm getting married and I have tuition debts. Will you vote to raise taxes?

LAVETTE: I see no necessity to.

FEMALE STUDENT: Are you for the ERA?

LAVETTE: Absolutely. I was a pioneer in the fight for women's rights.

MALE STUDENT: Offshore drilling. Are you for or against it?

LAVETTE: Our beaches and ocean water are gifts from God.

FEMALE STUDENT: Abortion? What is your position?

LAVETTE: I abhor the thought of abortion, but if the law says the government must support abortion, I will support the law.

ANNOUNCER: A candidate of integrity and truth. Vote Barbara Lavette for Congress.

Watching her, a copy of the script in his hand, Freddie said nothing. The two men from the agency waited. When Barbara remained silent, one of the agency men said, "Of course, it's flat in a script. You'll be amazed how it will come to life under the camera. We have four excellent actors lined up—"

"It's nonsense," Barbara interrupted, wondering how she had gotten to this point, why she was sitting here, trying to make some sense out of a puerile bit of scribbling. Was it all to be downhill, all her vows and principles reduced to nothing, the arena in which she chose to battle lions reduced to a cheap electronic trick? Was this all that was left of the noble dream of Democracy that had come into being two hundred years ago?

"Nonsense? Oh, come on, Miss Lavette."

"Tell me where you got this rubbish."

"From your position paper."

"Really? I find no resemblance. There's not a word of truth here. The whole thing is ridiculous"—her anger mounting, her patience finally stretched to the breaking point—"and I want no part of it, and I do not intend to answer questions as fraudulent as the answers."

Freddie held up his hands and said, "Suppose you leave Miss Lavette and me alone for a few minutes."

"It's your play."

When they had gone, she said to Freddie, trying not to sound severe or petulant, "Did you see this?" holding up the script. "Did you see it before we got here?"

"No. And I don't know what to say. I've been rushing things too much, and the days slip away. You're not angry with me?"

"No. I'm annoyed with myself."

"What do you want to do?"

"I don't want actors. I know how necessary TV is. Get me a pencil and paper and I'll scribble thirty seconds of something."

"Just straight on? You mean, reading a statement?"

"No, I won't read it. If I make a few notes, I can do thirty seconds without reading it. Do you think that's bad— wrong?"

"Aunt Barbara, I don't know what's right and what's wrong anymore. Maybe you should fire me. Sometimes I feel I'm stumbling around in the dark. Sure, do it your way."

"You fight it out with them, Freddie."

"Right."

So in the end, she simply stood in front of the camera and said, "Good evening. I'm Barbara Lavette, Democratic candidate for Congress, and some of you will recall that I ran on the same ticket here six years ago. I lost by a few thousand votes then, but this time I hope to win. What do I stand for? I want our air to be pure, our beaches undefiled by offshore drilling. I am wholly for the Equal Rights Amendment, and I want federal support for child care. I believe that even as a man's body is his own, so a woman's body is her own, and her right to abortion is sacrosanct. Above all, I am for peace."

It was not easy. There had been other things in there, other positions, but it had to be chopped down to thirty seconds, and she said to Freddie, "This is only just all right. When we do the other nine, I'll deal with one issue in each."

Freddie felt her performance had been nothing short of remarkable, and even the agency people grudgingly admitted that it might do. Relieved that the day was over, but feeling no better about the campaign, Barbara sat glumly while Freddie drove her back to the shopping center, where she had left her car. It was past five, and the storefront was empty.

"I told them they could bug out at five," Freddie said. "No meetings tonight and they've been working hard."

"I'll see you tomorrow," Barbara said. "I have a few things to do inside. Thanks for your patience."

"I know I'm a pain in the rump. I don't know any other way to do this."

"Neither do I," Barbara admitted.

It gave her an odd feeling to stand alone in the store they had rented. Outside, the shadows were lengthening and the air chilled suddenly. The store was half dark, and on the long tables, as always, piles of envelopes waited to be stuffed with orange-colored inserts. Barbara picked up one and read, "A woman for all seasons—this is Barbara Lavette. She comes to us not simply as a candidate for a seat in the House of Representatives, but as a person with a lifelong dedication to civil rights and—"

"And nothing," Barbara said. "Who could have written that? I'll never be myself again. Why did I ever get into this thing?"

She sat at the old desk Freddie had rented for five dollars a month and stared at the long shadows that swept across the shopping center. It was the best time of the day, the air cool, the sun-and-shade-patterned breadth of the shopping center washed with the smell of the Douglas firs that were planted around the place. She really had no work there tonight, only the desire to be alone for a while, and her being alone was reinforced by the emptiness of the big plaza. Shopping was over for the moment, and it was still too early for diners at the two restaurants or moviegoers at the twin film house. Not a soul was in sight, and Barbara experienced the fanciful notion that comes to people at such moments, that she was alone in the whole world. She closed her eyes, and when she opened them a few moments later, she was no longer alone. A man stood in front of the store, his hands in his pockets, staring at the storefront and at Barbara. He was a tall, slender man, graying hair, wearing a flannel shirt and gray flannel trousers. He was about sixty, Barbara decided, give or take a year or two, good-looking as such things go, and with a face that was oddly familiar.

He tried the door, which Barbara had locked, and at that moment she realized that this was Alexander Holt, whom she had seen in film and still photographs but never before in the flesh. He now came back to the window to face her at her desk and made motions to indicate that he would like to come in. His grin was pleasant and natural, and in any case Barbara had looked forward to meeting him. She unlocked the door and said, "Come on in, Mr. Holt."

"Good. Then I don't have to introduce myself. And you're Barbara Lavette."

"So it says on the door."

"Except that you're younger and so much prettier. No, beautiful. You should not be called pretty."

"Good heavens! Do you always come on like that?"

"Have I offended you?"

Barbara couldn't help smiling. "Flattery rarely offends anyone. Anyway, do pull up a chair and sit down. What brings you into the enemy camp, Mr. Holt?"

"The enemy."

"Oh? Then you're on a scouting mission—or a spy mission?"

"We're both open up front, so let's call it a scouting mission. No, no—truth is I was dying of curiosity. All my life, I've come across odds and ends of Barbara Lavette. You can't live in San Francisco and be unaware of the Lavettes, and here's the lady who gave away a fortune, who was neck-deep in the longshore strike in the thirties, who covered World War Two for the *Chronicle,* who twisted the nose of the Un-American Committee and went to jail with a banner as white as Joan of Arc's—"

"Enough!" Barbara cried. "Any more of that, Mr. Holt, and you talk your way right out of my door. What on earth are you up to?"

"Too much?"

"Much too much. I do hope that you debate better than you flatter."

"Well, that's just it," he said, ingenuous and accepting defeat without argument. "You named it the enemy camp, and like some dumb kid, I'm trying to prove something."

"What?"

"That I'm not the enemy, I guess. Hey, look, are you waiting for someone?"

"No." It was twilight now; the store was becoming dark, and in the half light Alexander Holt was very attractive indeed. "No." She felt a need to talk. His mawkishness—well, she had seen that in other men who didn't know where to put their feet when they spoke to a woman who was on their level, and this man was certainly trying to put an attractive woman and a congressperson together. Barbara had enough self-confidence to specify herself as an attractive woman, and now she went on to say that she was waiting for no one, only trying to get the bad taste of making a commercial out of her mouth. "I thought it might be a relief to sit here alone for a while without a crowd of loud-voiced and very clever young men and women."

"I'm sure they're cleverer than my loud-voiced young men and women, but I do know what you mean. What about dinner?"

"What about dinner?"

"I mean," he said, "do you have an evening filled with at-home groups or radio interviews or newspaper people or whatever?"

"Not tonight. No. I'm free tonight." She could have added that it was the first free evening in three weeks, and she had made no plans because no one had invited her, because everyone knew that she was too busy now to do anything. She had also decided that it would be interesting, at least, to have dinner with Alexander Holt, and a relief to talk to someone close to her own age.

"Great. All I have is a session with a group of young computer wizards in Chesley. That's the south corner of the district, but I'm sure you know. It's no Silicon Valley yet, but it's getting there. I can push it into another night if I may use your phone?"

She pointed to the telephone and turned on her desklight. She liked the way he was dressed and the way he wore his casual clothes, but he was not dressed for dinner in any fashionable restaurant. She had no clear idea of where he lived, but something she had heard or read suggested Pacific Heights, and if that was the case, it was a long drive from the Forty-eighth C.D. She heard him make his arrangements with his office, and then he said to her, rather unexpectedly, "Can you tolerate Mexican food?"

"I like it."

"I did ask you whether you would have dinner with me—or did I?"

"Sort of, yes."

"And will you?"

"Yes."

"No fear of consorting with the enemy?"

"No. Absolutely none. Of course, we're not enemies."

"No? What then, Miss Lavette?"

"Two very lonely people, I think. According to the profile your committee put out, it's six years since your wife died. You have three children, one in school in Florida and two of them working in Massachusetts. Your wife was from Florida. Someone mentioned that you have no family here, but then you do have your work and the people who make up your staff—sixteen, I believe—and you dine at least twice a week at the Redwood Club."

"Well, you have done your homework. What else?"

She locked the door of the store behind them, and they started across the shopping center. "Where are we going?"

"At the other end of the plaza, under the big Dalton bookstore, there's a Mexican restaurant call Don Demos. The name sort of enticed me. The food is simple and good, and the college kids drive miles to eat here. I'm afraid I'm not dressed for anything more posh. You don't mind?"

"Not at all."

"And you're through with my dossier?"

"Through with what's printed. You don't want me to recite your voting record?"

"My word, do you know it by heart?"

"Just about."

"Two very lonely people. Is that what you said? My own case I can understand. I was born in Springfield, Massachusetts, only child, which narrows the family. Nothing left now but my kids, and they're far away. And Miss Lavette, associates are associates, no more, no less. On the other hand, San Francisco and the Bay Area are your nest, your place of nurturing. Did you know that I was on the committee that renamed that short street that turns off Pacific Avenue and used to be called Fritz Street and now is Lavette

Place? And aren't you connected through family with one of the big wineries in the Napa Valley? Gateway or something?"

"Higate."

"Yes, the best Cabernet Sauvignon in California, and also the red mountain wine with their own native label. Good wine. My word, if I had that kind of backup—"

"You still go to bed alone and wake up alone, and when you pick up a smooth stranger, like the one I'm with, and decide to have dinner with him, no one worries about where you are and whether something might happen to you."

"I picked you up."

"Oh? Yes, of course."

"I knew Boyd Kimmelman," Holt said. "As a matter of fact, at the end of World War Two, I took my discharge in California and went to school and passed the bar here. I worked in Benchly's old firm one summer, and I met Boyd there. He helped me along."

What a small, strange world, Barbara thought, remembering the Boyd who had entered her life at the beginning, the stocky, cocky young lawyer, with his bristling thatch of sandy hair and his bright blue eyes and his eagerness to grasp whatever piece of life presented itself. The world evoked by Alexander Holt's words glowed with memories of sunshine and excitement and hope. What had happened? What had happened to everything?

No answer to that. One dealt with simpler things. Holt knew the owner of the restaurant, a short, mustached Mexican, Don Demos. Smiling and bowing, he selected their table. "For the congressman and his lovely companion."

"Who is a contender for my job on the Democratic ticket, this same lovely companion."

"No!" It came out as a sigh of wonder without disapproval. Don Demos did not engage in disapproval.

"Good evening," Barbara said in Spanish. "What a very pleasant place. Do you vote, Don Demos?"

"Absolutely. I am not an illegal and I am not a green card holder. I am a citizen, married, three kids, and sole owner of this restaurant—for which I paid with blood and tears."

Holt listened, open-mouthed.

"Then of course you vote."

"Of course."

"Republican?"

"Señora, this is most embarrassing."

Smiling sweetly, Barbara said, "He can't follow when we speak this rapidly. I want you to vote for me. I need your vote. He doesn't."

"Señora." Then in English, "A bottle of wine, on the house. Please?" He paused, glancing worriedly at Holt. "Your choice?"

Holt was still struggling with what had just happened. "Higate Cabernet," Barbara said soothingly. "And it must not be a gift, please understand."

As Don Demos turned away, Holt finally burst out, "You were telling him not to vote for me. You were telling him to vote for you."

"Asking," Barbara said gently.

"I'll be damned."

Barbara smiled. "Do you know," she said, "you must call me Barbara, and I will call you Alex. We are going to be much too close for the next few weeks to address each other formally."

"Where did you learn to speak Spanish like that?"

"Just around. You pick it up. They say if you love Spanish, it will speak for itself. Oh, I studied a bit at Miss Leonard's Classes and at Sarah Lawrence College; and at Higate where they make the wine you admire so, they speak as much Spanish as they do English. Everyone speaks Spanish there."

"You won't be offended, Barbara, if I say that you are remarkably possessed of slender, invisible knives."

"It's a bit nasty, but others have said as much. Shall we be friends?"

"Someone mentioned that you described me as being slightly to the right of Genghis Khan."

"Oh, no. No indeed. When Reagan was governor, I did put that into a piece I wrote for the *Nation*, but about you, oh, no, never."

Don Demos appeared and opened the Cabernet Sauvignon, and took their order for red snapper, Vera Cruz style, with a side order of refried beans, and Holt poured the wine and offered a toast:

"May the best man—"

"Not quite," Barbara interrupted.

"Amended. May the best person win!"

"That I'll drink to."

Holt drank and then regarded her thoughtfully. "You are nothing like what I imagined you would be. I did meet you once before, but I am sure you've forgotten completely. Somewhere around twenty years ago, at a party given for you in Beverly Hills."

"I remember the party," Barbara said. It was the place and time that she had met Carson Devron, something she was not likely to forget.

"You don't remember me, of course. I was there with my wife. She was an actress then, had a bit part in a film. They were making one of your books into a film, as I recall, and there must have been a hundred people packed into the place—" His voice trailed off. "Too many crossed paths to be proper enemies. Politics is not nice. I wish there were some other way to run things, but there isn't, you know. But of course you believe in sanctity of purpose."

"No, I don't. I think, Alex, that it's time you took a good look at me. What you see across the table from you is a woman to whom most of the things have happened that could happen to anyone. So don't spare your punches. I will give what I receive."

"Hear, hear."

"And now that we understand each other, let's eat."

"I'm with you there."

"And incidentally, before we set politics aside, I would like to pick a date for a debate—say, in one of the larger high school auditoriums."

"A what?" Holt asked incredulously.

"Debate."

"You mean you're asking me to debate the issues with you?"

"Exactly."

He leaned back, clasped his hands and nodded at her. "My dear Barbara, I may not be the brightest fellow in the world, but neither am I an idiot. No debate—no way, ever."

"But why?"

"Why? You know, there must have been a period of great innocence in your life. But now it's simply a ploy. Can you picture the two of us on a platform? I'm sure you can—the saintly crusader and the slick politician. Come on, my dear."

He walked with her to her car after they ate, shook hands warmly and said, "I enjoyed this evening beyond words."

Barbara nodded. "It's been fun."

"And now, each back to his corner and come out slugging."

"As you say, sir."

Barbara felt youthful and heady as she drove home, telling herself with some wonder, I've had a date; I've actually had a date. And it was a very nice date, as she contemplated it: two civilized adults, each with a sense of humor, opponents in a political contest, but sensible enough to realize that it was just that, a political contest.

Would I see him again? she asked herself. I wonder. She had to admit that it would be pleasant. He was a nice man, low key and a good listener, as few men were.

Freddie had worked out a plan for door-to-door canvassing. He had made inquiries and had learned what he expected to learn, that no one had ever canvassed the Forty-eighth. There had been no need to. Aside from Barbara's run of six years before, the Republicans had never been even modestly threatened, and when Alexander Holt replaced the incumbent, the Republicans had no fear of being seriously threatened again. Freddie knew that he could round up at least two dozen couples, but before he sent them off on their mission, he felt that he ought to go out himself and get a sense of the process. He asked Carla to join him.

"Why? Why me?" Carla wanted to know.

"Two reasons. First, your Spanish is better than mine. Secondly, I like a man and a woman combination. A man alone tends to alarm people who come to the door. A woman alone makes me nervous. She could go into the wrong house—you know what I mean. So we put the couples together."

"You and me?"

"It's a good combination."

"Where's May Ling today?"

"She has the baby and other things," Freddie said, a note of annoyance in his voice. "What gives with you, Carla? Do I bother you?"

"These days everything bothers me. All right. Let's start."

"I'll take my car. We'll do five houses at the cliffs, five in the tracts, five in the barrio. Then we'll move out of Chesley into Valley City—if we're still capable of walking at all."

They sat down with Barbara, who freed herself momentarily from the questions, demands and complaints that were being flung at her. Barbara knew that she should have provided for some kind of office in the storefront, but it was too late now to find a carpenter to do the partitioning, and in any case the money could not be spared. Freddie tried to talk to her, and then gave up. Finally they went outside and found a bench in the shade.

"Let Carla be your point person," Barbara said. "They'll respond more easily, but if you see a woman looking at you, Freddie, the way a lot of women do, pick up and make some points. Not complicated, not too many issues. ERA—first and always. The woman doesn't live who won't respond to it, even if she snorts at first. Federal child care. Education and the cops are local, but you can suggest that people with jobs don't commit crimes. Don't bore anyone. A person bored becomes annoyed. So make it short and sincere."

"You've changed," Freddie said. "You never talked like this."

"Like a pro? Well, I'm trying. So onward and upward."

It was like nothing they had imagined, even in the wealthiest part of the district. They avoided the out-and-out mansions. They wanted voters who answered doorbells, not butlers or maids. "Still, they might be voters," Carla said pointedly. "A lot of them are my people." They saw two gardeners, Mexicans, to whom Carla spoke. "Naturalized," she told Freddie. "They can vote." They tried a large house. The maid who answered the door was a Chicana, and after a few words with Carla, she called in the upstairs maid and the cook. Great excitement. She had not registered, the upstairs maid had not, the cook had not, her husband had not. The people who lived there were out. Freddie stood back, listening to the flood of eager Spanish that poured out of Carla and the three servants.

"I like this," Carla said.

Back, away from the wealthiest homes, four women were playing bridge. This was upper middle, houses that were better than tract houses, yet by no means mansions. The four women were in their forties, attractive, and when the hostess ushered Freddie and Carla in, they put down their cards. Carla let Freddie take the lead position, and after ten minutes, they had to drag themselves away. Freddie let the main issues go by the board and dwelled on one thing: a society that takes adult human beings of wit and beauty and condemns them to days of playing bridge—not that bridge was not exciting and highly intellectual, but there were businesses to be run, bridges to be built, slums to be cleared and a hundred other things that these women were more than capable of. As Freddie's rhetoric soared, Carla thought they would be angry and put off. Unexpectedly, they were charmed and delighted with Freddie and his pitch.

"But exactly what can your Barbara Lavette do for us? We've missed the boat. It's way down the river now."

"She can stand as surrogate for you, and believe me, fight with all her strength for the ERA and all that goes with it."

Two blocks away, the door of a stately half-timbered house of the 1930s was opened by a buxom redhead who burst into laughter when Freddie began his pitch. "Sweetheart," she said, "this is a massage parlor."

Carla let out a squeal of surprise and delight, but Freddie, unperturbed, nodded and said that masseuses vote, even as beautiful redheads vote.

"That will get you the jackpot, sonny," the redhead said. "Come on in. Eleven o'clock in the morning is not prime time in this line of work."

Noontime, they were in the barrio, and at an open shed, hungry by now, they filled their bellies with tacos and burritos, washed down with Mexican beer. Freddie, lying shamelessly, informed all who cared to listen that Carla was a famous star of stage and screen, which increased the numbers of the crowd as word spread. Carla made no demur. The sun had put a flush on her cheeks, her face glowed. She smiled upon all as she spelled out the specifications for registration and said a few words about Barbara.

"You didn't push one damn issue," Freddie said later. "My Spanish is lousy, but I could follow enough to see that."

"And your brains are mushy," Carla said. "Star of stage and screen! What a liar! Issues? Dumbbell, they'll vote Democrat. They're Chicanos and Mexicans. You go and find a Chicano votes Republican. The point is, they don't register and they don't vote, and they say screw the Anglo and his lies and all his garbage about voting, because voting never got anyone anywhere. But they see a pretty Mexican girl, and she tells them a beautiful, good woman is a candidate—maybe they'll register and vote. Who knows?"

Door by door, they went on into the area of the cheap tract houses—as the song says, made out of ticky-tacky and all looking just the same.

"Excuse me, ma'am. Can I tell you a few words about our congressional candidate on the Democratic line? Her name is Barbara Lavette—yes, ma'am, the same Lavette family. This little brochure spells out what she stands for, but if you have time, I mean like a few minutes, I'd like to tell you something about her and why we feel that a woman must represent this district—"

The burning California sun moved slowly across the sky; the temperature rose to a hundred degrees in the shade; and Freddie and Carla doggedly pursued their specified route, made notations in their notebooks, walked a circle of about a mile each time, bringing them back to where they had parked, drove on to the next neighborhood or town or barrio or slum, walked again, rang bells, knocked at doors, made notations.

The afternoon lengthened. It was half past five when they decided to call it a day. They pulled into the parking lot of a Little League playing field, and Freddie went to a cold-drink dispenser under the grandstand, returning with two Coca-Colas. The car was parked in the shade of a big live oak, and at this time of the day, the field was deserted.

"Want to talk about our notes?" Carla asked him.

"Not right this minute. Right this minute I want to drink this bottle of Coke and luxuriate under this tree. Talking about Coke, Aunt Barbara told me an odd story—oh, way back, maybe ten years ago. She was in Assam during World War Two, up at the Tenth Air Force base, and she saw a patrol come out of the jungle. They hadn't met up with any Japanese, according to Aunt Barbara, but they were exhausted, clothes ripped, dehydrated and miserable. Well, there was a Coca-Cola machine at the base, and she put in all the dimes she had and began to distribute Cokes to the kids, and one of them put the cold bottle up against his cheek and began to cry. Can you beat that? What an ad for Coke."

"Freddie, you have such a weakness for bullshit," Carla said, leaning her head against his shoulder. "But I love you. I certainly love you. I always loved you," she continued matter-of-factly. "You were the first man I ever went to bed with—"

"The first kid. Dumb kid. We were kids."

"Did you ever tell May Ling?"

"No—good heavens, no. I always felt it was like incest. We grew up together. You know, I can't remember a time when you weren't there."

"I don't feel like your sister. Not a bit." She drew his head down toward her, and then he kissed her and she clung to him with an explosive passion, her mouth open to devour him.

"*Podría amarte,* damn you, Freddie!"

"Jesus God, we're making out in the seat of a car! Carla, we're not kids."

"Freddie, I'm starving, I'm eating myself up. Don't push

me away, you bastard. I got a prior claim. I thought I was pregnant, that time when we were kids, and my father beat the shit out of me. You owe me."

They moved to the back seat. Afterward, untangling their intertwined knot of passion, they looked at each other in amazement. Freddie kissed her gently. "Maybe—" he began, but Carla cut him off.

"Come on, Freddie. Don't talk about maybe if you had married me. It wouldn't be any better than it was with Sam. Worse. We'd tear each other to shreds."

Five

The *Morning World* took its first poll of the Forty-eighth C.D. The paper's first edition arrived in San Francisco early in the morning and was on the stands by eight o'clock. Barbara picked up half a dozen copies on her way to the Forty-eighth, but when she walked into the storefront at Sunnyside, Freddie was standing on his desk, calling for silence from the dozen or so people already there.

"The *Los Angeles Morning World*," Freddie said, holding up the paper, "today, Wednesday, front page: 'One of the most interesting congressional contests in the state is playing out in the 48th C.D., where maverick feminist Barbara Lavette is pitted against the Republican incumbent, Alexander Holt. The 48th is traditionally a Republican stronghold, where, it is said, the Republican candidate can phone in his campaign. The only time this very large Republican majority was even shaken was six years ago, when Miss Lavette first accepted the Democratic designation. The then incumbent was subsequently indicted for taking bribes, and the seat went to San Francisco lawyer Alexander Holt. In 1974, Mr. Holt received 87 percent of the votes cast. In the telephone poll taken by this paper yesterday, Mr. Holt received 61 percent. Miss Lavette received 29 percent, with 10 percent undecided. The district will be polled by this paper every Wednesday until Election Day, and we look forward to following this very important race.' Unquote," Freddie finished.

Applause. Shouts of delight. Friends kissing Barbara. Birdie MacGelsie assuring her, "Pure gold, darling. Next fund-raiser, it's worth a thousand dollars for every percentage point." And around noontime, a long black limousine containing Tony Moretti, older, heavier, but still with the same deep, comforting voice. He waddled over to Barbara's desk and allowed his bulk to descend carefully onto the frail folding chair.

"Barbara, you got the whole party talking," he said. "The bookies were making three to one on Holt. They tell me it's slipped to two to one. You've been going to Mass?"

"Almost as good. We've been canvassing. Freddie and Carla have worked out a system, and if we had enough volunteers, we could cover every home in the district. As it is, we hope to reach at least thirty percent. I think it may make the difference, when you add it to the sound trucks, the local advertising and the street meetings. Would you believe that there are three regular weekly newspapers in the Forty-eighth and four more giveaway sheets? We convinced one supermarket to allow us to lay a pile of program broadsides on the bench with the newspapers. I say we, us—but it's the kids who come in on their own who do it."

"How many volunteers do you have?" Moretti asked.

"We've signed on over a hundred, most of them students, high school and college."

"No, you're kidding."

"The truth, Tony. Well, you know, some of them come in for an hour now and then, some give us day a week, some come in once and don't come back. Tony, we're going to beat Mr. Alexander Holt. We're going to beat him to a frazzle."

"I hope so, Barbara, I sure hope so. On the other hand, watch him. He's smart and he's ambitious. Have you met him yet?"

"He took me to dinner," Barbara said, explaining how it had come about. And when Moretti frowned, Barbara put her hand on his and said, "Trust me."

"He's a charming man, Barbara."

"Agreed."

"All right, enough of that. I like what else you're doing—it's the way we used to do it. Know every man, woman and child and what you can do for them, and when the time comes, you have their vote. It's bigger today, too big, but the principle holds."

"I wish I could do that, Tony. But we don't have enough people and the district's too big. If you could help us—"

"I'm coming to that. It's no secret that the committee has written off the Forty-eighth. They're still writing it off, and when it comes to getting money out of the party, it's squeezing blood from a stone. But after this morning's *World* came up, I called a few members, and they're relenting. I went out on a limb. I told them you're going to win."

"You really believe that?"

"Barbara, I'm putting sixty years of being a political animal on the line."

"You're also dropping a big burden on me, Tony. I don't know if I can win. I don't know if I can keep this pace up until Election Day. It's worse than anything I had imagined."

"You'll keep it up."

"You said they're relenting. How much is relenting?"

"Ten thousand dollars to start the ball rolling, and that's a nice round sum, Barbara. We don't have money to throw away. I saw your TV commercials. They're straightforward and good. Try to buy some more time. We'll have a check for you tomorrow."

Astonished by Moretti's gift, Freddie said that they must have seen the light. "It's nothing to write home about but a fat chunk for the party to hand over. They're impressed and they should be. Until now, they haven't come near us."

"Tony has."

"You like Tony," Freddie said, "but don't get confused. They've put him out to pasture. They let him talk and feel that he's got some influence, but it's all fading away."

"We all fade away, Freddie. Time does that."

Time was creeping up on them. Another Wednesday, and the *Los Angeles Morning World* published its second poll taken in the Forty-eighth C.D. This time, Alexander Holt's share had shrunk to fifty-two percent. Barbara Lavette's share had increased from twenty-nine percent to thirty-seven percent, leaving eleven percent undecided. Freddie waved the newspaper from his desktop and spurred them on to greater efforts. He had completely forgotten his cynical attitude toward politics.

Sam showed up at the storefront for a second time, making the point that he had canceled an elective surgery case simply to put an afternoon into the campaign.

"Darling, there was no need to," Barbara told him.

"I can't let you think I'm not interested, and I couldn't tell you that I'm kind of frightened about your being so far away there in Washington, alone."

"Sam, that's sweet of you."

"I can't see myself stuffing envelopes and I'm no good for canvassing. Let me drive you around this afternoon. We can talk."

"Carla was going to drive. I suppose I can change that."

"I changed it. I'm taking her to dinner tonight. Would you like to join us?"

"No. Absolutely not. You want to be alone with her."

"Do I? I'm not sure."

"Then why the dinner date?" Barbara asked.

"I'm not sure of that either. When she agreed to have dinner with me, I got so damn excited. We can't get along married—You know, Mother, it's confusing. It's damn confusing."

"Most things are," Barbara agreed. "No one ever arranged things in this world to make much sense." She handed Sam a folded map. "Street map of the district. Today is church day, and fortunately all the churches are marked on the map. Since you don't know the district and I don't know it much better, we'll have to work it out as we go along. I'm off for the day!" she called to Freddie. "Sam's driving."

"Heaven help you."

"We'll manage. It's Carla who really knows the district. You're sure we shouldn't bring her along?"

"I'd rather be alone with you for a few hours. I've been neglecting you." He steered her to his car, a sleek new Cadillac. "I got it last week," he explained. "It's par for the profession."

Barbara studied him as he drove. People had changed since she was Sam's age; doctors had changed; Sam had mentioned a single day when four operations brought him seven thousand dollars, hastening to add that it was balanced by his work in the clinic. She said nothing. The leather upholstery in Sam's car was as smooth as a baby's cheek.

"Nice, isn't it?" Sam observed. "What do you mean by church day?"

"It's an idea Freddie had. He found seven churches and two synagogues and one tiny Buddhist temple to cooperate in hearing the candidates on one day. Holt and I have ten minutes each—"

"Debating, do you mean?"

"Oh, no. Alex won't debate. We're scheduled, supposedly to avoid crossing paths. The audience will be mostly women. Some of the pastors and one of the rabbis said they couldn't count on attendance of more than a dozen or so, but I feel that won't matter. The point is to meet people who would never come to rallies. We have a very tight schedule, and we begin at eleven o'clock at Holy Trinity. That's Catholic."

"Yes, I might have guessed." He handed the map to Barbara. "You steer me." After a moment, uneasily, Sam said, "This Alexander Holt, do you know him?"

"Slightly."

"What's he like?"

"A very elegant and charming gentleman, about my age."

"Oh? High praise, coming from you. Freddie's doing a good job, isn't he?" A note of envy there.

"Yes, he's awfully good."

"Well, I wish I could do more. You understand that a surgeon's in a different position. Freddie has all kinds of backup at the winery, but I can't just walk away from my work."

"Oh, of course not."

"I left a check for five hundred with Carla."

"Sammy, that's not necessary."

"It is. It certainly is. Guilt money. I have a lot of guilt."

Guilt for what, Barbara wondered? Guilt for not helping her in the campaign? Guilt for the fees he charged? Why did she always feel such a wide separation between them?

Barbara did not believe in hard-hitting political speeches; it was not her style, and at Holy Trinity she very gently told the story of Rubio Truaz, Carla's brother, who had died in Vietnam. A fragment from a Vietcong mortar had ignited a phosphorus grenade at his belt, enveloping him in flames. The ultimate horror was that a CBS photographer kept his camera on Truaz, recording every bit of the boy's agony. "That alone," Barbara concluded, "would have been enough to make me an enemy of war, but I was a correspondent during World War Two and war was not new to me. If you vote for me and elect me, I will do what I can to keep our country out of war, and I will do it with all my heart and strength."

As they drove on to the next church, Sam said, "You were wonderful, you know. Not like any political speaker I ever heard."

"I can't do it their way. I don't know whether my way is any good, Sam, but it's the only way I have."

Late afternoon, coming out of their last scheduled stop, a tiny Methodist church, built like a miniature Spanish mission, they finally encountered Alexander Holt. He had just gotten out of his parked car, and he grinned with pleasure when he saw Barbara.

"Greetings, lovely enemy. I've been chasing along after you all day."

Barbara took his hand and then introduced Sam: "Dr. Samuel Cohen, my son."

Holt shook hands warmly. "Of course, you kept your father's name. Making quite a reputation for yourself, I understand. Would you mind if I had just a word with your mother?"

"Not at all."

Holt drew Barbara aside and whispered, "Dinner tonight? Please don't say no."

"It needn't be a secret, Alex. I don't mind if the whole world knows I dine with you—so long as they vote for me."

"Good. Then I'll pick you up at your house—say at eight? Will that give you enough time?"

"Certainly. But don't expect wit and charm. This church circuit has exhausted me. But I would like it."

Driving back to the campaign headquarters, Sam said to her, "What was that all about? Unless I'm prying—"

"Not at all. He asked me to have dinner with him tonight."

"And you agreed?"

"Sam, my morality is securely in place. Why shouldn't I have dinner with him?"

"Well, you are putting him down. He's the enemy, the competition."

"Sam, he's a Republican candidate. He's not my enemy, and if you listened to my speeches, you'd know that I do not put him down. I do my own thing. He's nice and he's charming, and I'm a very lonely widow, and don't dare offer yourself as an escort. I don't want an escort. I want a son who lives his own life, because I'm still quite capable of living mine."

"Now you're angry with me," Sam said.

"No, dear. A little angry with myself, perhaps, but that's all, believe me. And thank you for being a faithful and patient chauffeur."

At the storefront, waiting for Carla to finish up, Sam said to Freddie, "Do you know who my mother's having dinner with tonight?"

"Should I know?"

"I think you should. She's having dinner with Alexander Holt."

"So?"

"Doesn't bother you?"

"Sam, if it doesn't bother her, why should it bother me?"

"I didn't think that was the way the game was played."

"Sam, forget it. It doesn't really matter."

Freddie watched Sam walk out of the place with Carla, telling himself that he, Freddie, was a worthless louse, going to bed with Sam's wife, and even though Sam and Carla had been divorced a goodly time now, she was still Sam's wife, and he, Frederick Lavette, would lie to Sam and lie to May

Ling and lie to himself as well, and Sam was the best friend he had in the world, more like a brother than a friend.

Driving back to her house in San Francisco, Barbara brooded over her use of the term *lonely widow*. It was a new thing. She had never used the term before, never thought of herself as a lonely widow before, and rarely scolded Sam. Was a plea for sympathy encased in the scolding, or was it a cry of terror, or was the outburst or scolding or whatever she might call it simply an excuse to dangle her pain in front of her son? Again and again, she told herself that she was a strong and independent woman, that just about everything had happened to her that could happen, and that come what may, she would never whine or whimper. Even that last day in the hospital with Boyd, when both of them knew that it was the end, when he lay there white and ghastly, tubes in his nostrils, she, who would dissolve in tears watching a third-rate sentimental film, did not cry or whimper, and was able to say "You've given me the best love of my life. It won't die. It will always be there." She was sitting beside the bed, holding his hand, talking gently about the best of times they had known together.

And tonight she was having dinner with Alexander Holt. That was all right, she assured herself. Life belongs to the living, not to the dead, and endless mourning was a corrosive indulgence. She smiled at the thought of how Sam had reacted, and her spirits perked up as she assured herself that now, as always, she would damn well do as she pleased and as she thought right.

At home on Green Street, Barbara changed her dress three times, and she was still not entirely ready when Holt rang her bell. She ran down the stairs, opened the door, told him to make himself comfortable in her parlor, and then went back upstairs to finish dressing. When she finally came down, wearing a thin woollen lilac-tinted challis and a single strand of pearls that her father had given her on her fifteenth birthday, Alexander Holt stared at her in undisguised admiration.

"You do me honor," he said.

She burst out laughing. "Bless you! Do you want a drink?"

"We'll have wine at dinner. That's about my speed these days." He kept glancing about the room and then back at Barbara. "I wonder whether there's another parlor just like this in San Francisco? It looks like nothing has been changed since the house was built."

"Nineteen hundred and two—before the earthquake, or around then. Sam Goldberg, my father's lawyer, built it for his bride, and after she died, he lived here alone. But none of this is the original parlor. When the house burned down ten years ago, I tried to put it together the way it had been—or almost the way it had been. Furnishings as well as building."

"But why?"

"I don't know. I suppose it was some desperate sentimental need at the time. I wanted something to survive from my schoolgirl days."

"Yes, I can understand that. It's lovely—but I forgot myself. Didn't you want a drink?"

"No. Why don't we eat? Where?"

"The most obvious place. I've reserved a table at the Fairmont. The food is decent, and they'll treat us like Oriental potentates. I mean, I do want to impress you tonight. You're laughing at me."

"Oh, no. Only my son took me there recently. He thought of it as a sort of therapy."

"The last person in need of therapy, I think. Shall I call a cab, or would you like to walk?"

"Not in these shoes," Barbara said.

At the Fairmont, Holt's thoughts were still engaged with her house. "Those old wooden San Francisco houses are probably the most uncomfortable places imaginable. The rooms are too narrow, everything is up and down, and they are firetraps. I should think you would have been happy to be rid of it and have a valid excuse to move into one of those new highrises. I live in that new one on Jones Street, and believe me, it's a pleasure."

He had never mentioned where he lived. "No, I don't think I could live in a highrise," Barbara said. "I love my house, discomfort and all."

Champagne appeared, and Holt said, "I know it's French, but Higate doesn't bottle champagne. Just for a toast." He smiled at Barbara. He could be very charming.

"To victory?" Barbara asked him.

"For one of us, anyway."

She drank, and then stared at the glass. A long moment of silence followed, and then the head waiter appeared, adroitly self-effacing as he placed two menus on the table.

"Later," Holt said to him.

"Of course, Mr. Holt." He disappeared.

Holt looked at her, smiling slightly—with approval, Barbara thought—and waiting for her to speak. Barbara was thinking of how much surface manners come to mean once one passed the middle years.

"Then a single glass of champagne does that to you," Holt said finally.

"No, not the champagne. After the second poll, I didn't think we'd see each other again, except in the arena with swords drawn."

"You feel that it dealt me a mortal blow?"

"Oh, no. Not mortal." Barbara smiled. "A wound at best, and believe me, Alex, I feel guilty. I think, perhaps, that we should have shunned each other. I like you. I'll have to comfort you when you lose, and that will be the oddest election aftermath, won't it?"

"If I were ten years younger, I would be madly in love

with you, and I would resign. Now, I'm only normally in love with you, which means that I must win and save you the horror of two years in Washington."

"That's a joke," Barbara said, pulling back. "You're not telling me that you're in love with me. We're not kids, Alex. I hardly know you, so I'll put it down as a conversation piece."

"Good heavens, it threw you."

"No, it didn't throw me. It's too damn important, and too damn casual at the same time. I don't appreciate a throw-away line like that. I've had too much joy and too much agony from men I loved. I know that a long time ago *I love you* was a game kids played. As I said, we're not kids."

"You're angry."

"No. It's just that after Boyd died, I gave up. I met no one I cared to spend a long evening with, much less be with. I said, All right, Barbara. You've had a great full basket of life, and now you can sit back and find whatever sustenance you can in being an old woman."

"You're not an old woman!"

"No. I had dinner with a man who was my opponent, and I felt like a young woman, damn it."

Holt reached across the table and took her hand. "What are you trying to say to me, Barbara?"

"I'm not sure I know. It's complicated. Suppose I win?"

"Then you win. Suppose I win?"

"All right. What's sauce for the goose is sauce for the gander. But I'm going to win."

"You want it so damn badly. Why? How does it fit in with everything I know about Barbara Lavette? You think you're going to play a part in stopping war. That's a delusion, Barbara. You'll stop nothing and you'll break your heart. ERA—another delusion. All your dreams, all your tilts at all the windmills of misery and injustice—nothing, Barbara. It's hopeless. They'll laugh at you. They'll tie you up in rules and procedures. They'll feed you frustration every day of your life, because that's the nature of the beast. I know. I'm one of them. I've had four years of it, and if you're in it for the honors and the perks, which are more than you ever dreamed of—well, if that's the way you're in it, and that's the way I'm in it, you can take it. Otherwise, they'll flay you alive. They'll block you and isolate you, and nothing will change."

Barbara was silent for a few moments, and then she asked softly, "Is that why you're in it, Alex? For the honors and the perks?"

"Do you want me to lie to you, Barbara?"

"No, Alex, I never want you to lie to me. And you know what—suppose we put a freeze on anything political? We've each of us found someone we can talk to, and that's rare enough."

After dinner, they walked to Green Street, slowly, in tribute to Barbara's high heels. It was a fine, cool evening, no fog for a change and just a taste of the sea in the air. At the door to her house, Barbara asked, "Do you want to come in for a nightcap, Alex?"

"If I did, it would be hard to leave, and you don't want that, do you?"

"Not tonight, no."

He moved to embrace her, and Barbara didn't resist. It was good to have a man's strong arms around her, to feel his lips on hers.

Tony Moretti pulled himself out of his stretch Cadillac and lumbered into the Barbara Lavette campaign headquarters and eased his bulk carefully into the folding chair in front of her desk. "It's not easy," he said to Barbara. "I never calculated how many pounds of pasta and how many quarts of good red California Zinfandel brought me to this pass, but maybe it's worth it. You got time for a small lecture?"

"I always have time for anything you want to tell me, Tony."

"Nice. You're the nicest lady I know. You won't hate me if I jump on you."

"Only a little," smiling.

"All right, a little. We got a word here in San Francisco—*gunsel.* It's local slang, or was in my time. I don't know where it comes from. Hammett used it in one of his books, and then people back east and writers in Hollywood decided it was a local name for a hit man and they began to use it for that. But gunsel doesn't mean that at all, and some people think it's a gutter word for gay, but that's not it either. There's a certain kind of man who would eat—no, that's not something I can say to a lady."

"Tony," Barbara said, "I know what a gunsel is. I was born and brought up in shouting distance of the old Coast, and I know what you're going to tell me."

"All right, here in a local Mexican place you can have dinner with him—not in the Fairmont!"

She had never heard that hard, sharp edge in his voice before, a memory of the Tony Moretti who had ruled a political world that was no more.

"Why?" she demanded angrily.

"Because people saw you and they saw who sat at the table with you, and if you sit a table with someone in the Fairmont, it speaks to the whole city."

Controlling herself, she said softly, "Tony, it's not earth-shaking for a Democrat and a Republican to dine together, even if they're both running for the same office. Why are you so upset?"

"Because that son of a bitch is going to put a knife into you. He's a damn gunsel!"

"Tony, you're in my place!"

"All right. I said what I have to say, and if I hurt you, I'm sorry. I'm also licking my lips, because you're going to win this one and we're both going to prove to these young smartass new-breed politicians, who don't have the patience to wait for me to die, that maybe Moretti knows something they don't."

The following Wednesday underlined his words. The *Los Angeles Morning World* ran a two-column head on page one: UPSET IN BAY AREA.

The story went on to say that the most interesting post-Watergate turnaround was taking place in the Forty-eighth Congressional District, "where the Democrats gave the designation to a political neophyte and maverick, Barbara Lavette, sending her out into a solid, traditional Republican stronghold like a lamb to slaughter. But Miss Lavette refused to be slaughtered. She attacked on the issues with a fury that left incumbent Alexander Holt dazed and frustrated. One week ago, our telephone poll in the 48th showed Miss Lavette to have increased her position from 29 percent the week before to 37 percent, while Mr. Holt's lead had dwindled from 61 percent to 52 percent. Our latest poll shows Miss Lavette and Mr. Holt running neck and neck, each with 42 percent of the vote, leaving 16 percent undecided.

"In our initial decision to poll the 48th Congressional District, we looked upon it as a sort of weathervane, pointing to the effect of Watergate and Mr. Ford's subsequent stewardship on a local Republican district. But we are told by leaders in both parties that the 48th can no longer be so regarded. Miss Lavette has apparently introduced a unique quality."

Barbara knew, as did many of those working in the campaign with her, that she had changed. She had the ability to look at herself and, at least to some degree, recognize what was happening to her. For the first weeks of the campaign, she had hardly spoken to Mort Gilpin, the fund-raiser Freddie had hired. Now she sat down with him for a full review of the financial end of being a candidate. He and Freddie met with her one morning at the Green Street house, and over rolls and coffee discussed money. Barbara knew what was happening to her: she had to win now. It was no longer a good fight to win; she had to win.

Gilpin was increasingly impressed with Barbara, but he also felt that he was doing a good job, and he pointed out that they had raised more money than most of the congressional candidates in California.

"I know that," Barbara said. "You've worked wonders, Mort—and I'm still afraid that the whole thing will slip away."

"Why?"

"Carla was talking to one of Holt's workers. The people working with him are worried sick about the polls. But he isn't."

"So he's confident. That doesn't mean a damn thing, Miss Lavette, believe me. The odds in the city are even now. A dollar brings you a dollar that you'll win."

"Mort, we haven't had a network commercial yet."

Freddie, listening to all this, put in, "They cost a bundle, and they don't make that much difference. The independents cover the same area."

"But at prime time, they're watching the networks," Barbara said.

"I'll try, but, Miss Lavette, I think I've squeezed the stone dry. But I'll try. I'll try."

Freddie went home early that night, apologizing to Barbara for taking a night off so close to the wire. "We're having dinner with Mom," he told her. "I've hardly seen her since we started. I had to—"

"Freddie, it's all right."

"But why on earth didn't you ask Barbara to come?" Eloise wanted to know.

"Because she wouldn't come."

May Ling and Freddie were at the table with Eloise and Adam, Freddie's stepfather, and Adam's sister, Sally, and Sally's husband, Joe. They all laid claim to Barbara.

"I don't believe she wouldn't come."

Eloise was closest to her, and Eloise said simply that Barbara had changed. People don't stay the same.

"She's speaking tomorrow," Freddie said, "to a meeting of most of the primary and secondary school teachers in the district. It was a damn hard thing to put together, and Mort Gilpin and I have been working on it for weeks. Why Aunt Barbara wanted it, I don't know, because it won't change enough votes to make up for the time. We may get five hundred teachers, and at least four hundred and ninety would have voted for Aunt Barbara anyway. Right now, you ask me, she's sitting at her desk there in the shopping center, working over her notes for tomorrow. She's become totally obsessive about this election."

"I don't think it's obsessive," May Ling said. "That's a lousy thing to say."

"I'm not putting her down. I'm trying to explain what's happening to her."

"It's perfectly normal," Joe said. "She's always been a trifle obsessive. There's nothing wrong with being a bit obsessive."

"It's not obsession. It's something else," Eloise said. She knew something about deep wounds. "She's trying to heal herself." Eloise knew about healing, "It's not easy."

Her husband looked at her curiously. After Joshua's suicide, he had come to realize that he had been married more than thirty years to a woman who at times was a total stranger to him.

Freddie shrugged. "Maybe. There's also a thing called candidatitis. It's a mental condition that grips a candidate. The win or lose factor becomes the driving force—"

"You're so damn glib," May Ling said testily. "You have an answer for everything."

"I'm only trying to explain."

"Something that you don't have enough sensitivity to understand."

"Stop it!" Sally said sharply. "You're both acting like a couple of kids."

"I wonder," Adam said. "What is this thing with Alexander Holt? I saw an item in the *Chronicle* about her being seen dining at the Fairmont with Holt."

"I never thought I'd see the day when we'd be gossiping about Barbara," Eloise said.

"Come on," Freddie put in, "he's not the devil. He's a pretty decent guy."

"Not according to Tony Moretti," May Ling said.

"Well, he stopped by at the store one evening and Barbara met him and they struck it off. It's no sin."

Later, at their home that night, Freddie said to May Ling, "What's gotten into you? You've been snapping at me all evening."

"Carla."

"Carla what? What are you talking about?"

"Carla's gotten into me, Carla, Carla, Carla."

"You'll never believe that I love you, will you?"

"How can I? You're a damn jack rabbit. You always have been."

"That's rotten. That's the rottenest thing you've ever said to me."

"I feel rotten," May Ling said. "I feel very rotten."

At the Jack London Intermediate School, about three hundred and fifty teachers had assembled to hear Barbara speak. She spoke simply and directly. In part, she said, "I began life as a rich girl, perhaps in our Western terms as the epitome of a rich girl. My mother was Jean Seldon, of the banking house, and my father was Dan Lavette, one of the largest ship operators on the West Coast. My first face-to-face confrontation with injustice came during the great longshore strike of the nineteen thirties. I was involved, first as a volunteer in the soup kitchen and then as a sort of untrained paramedic. It taught me lessons in injustice and it taught me a great deal about the gulf between the rich and the poor. After that, I was a foreign correspondent, first for a New York magazine and afterward for the *Chronicle,* and my sense of injustice was fueled. I've lived my life in a world torn by senseless war and unnecessary suffering. Other people, perhaps more fortunate, have lived in this same world and managed to be untouched or at least only slightly touched by the same events that made my life an agony. I am being very frank with you. Perhaps I can do only a little, but it is my wonderful opportunity and may well be my last."

"It was absolutely the damnedest thing," Mort Gilpin told Freddie the following day. He had gone with Barbara and had taken up a collection afterward, expecting perhaps a hundred dollars, a token tribute to Barbara if she carried it off nicely. "No, sir, Frederick. Eight hundred and twenty-two dollars from some three hundred and fifty underpaid teachers. I never heard a politician put himself forward the way she does. She doesn't talk politics at all; she talks like a preacher for some kind of religion that nobody's thought of yet."

"Aunt Barbara's a sort of Episcopalian," Freddie said, grinning. "They thought of that a long time ago. You falling in love with her, Morty?"

"If she were twenty years younger—sure. Why not?"

"You'd answer to me."

"Enough bullshit. We need ideas, Frederick, not bullshit. Where does the money come from? You know, your father's maybe the richest man in California. And she's his sister, right?"

"Wrong. They don't appreciate each other, to put it in its mildest form. Also, legally, he's not my father. Adam Levy adopted me. He's my father, period."

"O.K. I just thought it worth mentioning."

"What do we need for the commercials she wants?"

"We can get thirty seconds for fifteen thousand—maybe. It doesn't make sense."

"What time?"

"Eight-thirty. That's almost prime time. They consider it prime time."

"That's a damn stiff price for thirty seconds."

"I'm not sure of prices. We don't want network exposure. We want it on the network channel but as a local segment. Miss Lavette's right. Today, TV is the absolute determining factor. And I've plucked my chickens."

"Then find more chickens."

"Freddie," Gilpin said softly, "suppose I go to your father —you don't even know about it."

"I'd kick your ass across the bridge. I told you he's not my father."

"What burns your ass if I talk to the man? Maybe he's not your father; he's her brother."

"No!"

"What do I do—print the money?"

"You tell her she can't have it. She's my aunt, and she is like no one I've ever known. But right now, she's a little crazy."

"Because she has to win? Can't you understand that? She has to win."

"Suddenly, you're a damn psychologist."

"I'm a fund-raiser, Freddie. I'm a political fund-raiser, and I'm a damn good one. I went into this because I read her books when I was twelve years old. I learned about war from her, and I learned something about living and dying, and I learned something about women."

"That's enough."

"What's enough?"

"The hell with it. Do anything you want to do."

Gilpin decided to do it. There were all sorts of families, and the condition was more or less generic in the human race. A family this ridden with money, guilt, love and hatred was not entirely unfamiliar to him, but having been San Francisco born and bred, he had come to regard the Seldons and the Lavettes as a New Yorker might regard the Harrimans and the Rockefellers, except that here big money was more recent than in the East, and here there was an ethnic jigsaw puzzle and a tangled history that was difficult if not impossible to follow. Nevertheless, he went to the seat of the mighty, which in this case was a thirty-six-story tower of glass and steel and concrete, a piece of arrogant insanity in a city that had once before half perished in an earthquake and that was now and forever perched on top of that same uneasy continental flaw. The elevator marked EXECUTIVE OFFICES took him to the thirty-fifth floor, where he emerged into a severely formal foyer, decorated in a style that was a cross between a British ducal establishment and a proper millionaire's den. The walls were oak, the floors pegged walnut, the carpets expensive Persian, the furniture English-club style, soft leather, and on the paneled walls, oversized nonobjective modern paintings.

At the reception desk, a young man in his thirties, wearing horn-rimmed glasses and a properly stolid look on his handsome face, asked what he could do for the gentleman who faced him.

"I'd like to see Mr. Lavette."

"And you are?"

"Mort Gilpin."

"Do you have an appointment?"

"No."

"Then I'm afraid you can't see Mr. Lavette. No one does without an appointment."

"I understand that. I'm a fund-raiser, engaged by Mr. Lavette's son to raise money for Mr. Lavette's sister's congressional campaign. His sister's name is Barbara Lavette." Gilpin took out his card. "Here's my card. The telephone number on there is a storefront at Sunnyside, which Miss Lavette uses as her campaign headquarters. If you wish to verify my identity, you can call this number and talk to Miss Lavette or her nephew Frederick. No tricks. Everything aboveboard. Suppose you send some kind of word to Mr. Lavette, and if he won't see me, I leave. O.K.?"

The good-looking young man picked up his desk phone and said, "Willie, step out here for a moment." The raised arm revealed a bulge. When Willie came through the door, thirtyish and also good-looking, his jacket bulged slightly, too. Gilpin had not realized how nervous the seats of the mighty were.

"Take over a moment. I have to speak to Mr. Lavette." And then to Mort Gilpin, "Sit down. I'll be back in a few moments."

It was closer to five minutes, and then the man with the horn-rimmed glasses returned and asked Mort Gilpin to follow him. They went through an inner reception room, where a pretty blond young woman sat at a desk and smiled pleasantly, and then down a hallway, to a door Gilpin's guide opened for him, allowing him to enter, but not following him. No ducal pretensions here; this was a tasteful modern office with an enormous picture window that overlooked San Francisco Bay.

There was no greeting from Thomas Lavette. He sat behind his desk, stared bleakly at Mort Gilpin and then motioned for him to sit down alongside the desk. "You work for my son?" he asked quietly.

"Yes."

"He's running the campaign?"

"Yes, he is."

"Does he know you're here?"

"No."

"Is he any good?" Lavette's voice was low and rasping. Gilpin could see a resemblance to Barbara, but Thomas Lavette looked older than his sixty-four years. His thin hair was white, and the nest of wrinkles around his pale blue eyes belied the puffy youthfulness of his cheeks and chin.

"Damn good, sir. Fred's brilliant."

"I see. What does he pay you?"

"Two hundred a week, plus five percent of whatever I raise."

"So if I give you money, you take five percent?"

"No, sir. To come to Miss Lavette's brother for money— well, that's not my idea of fund-raising. That's family. I wouldn't take a nickel out of that."

"Then why the hell are you here?"

"Because I want her to win. I've been doing this kind of political fund-raising for five years now—I never ran into anyone like her."

"Can she win?"

"I think so. I think we have a winning edge already."

"Of course, you have to figure that if you admitted to a very unlikely shot, I'd pull back. Nobody bets on a lost cause."

"Well, sir, tomorrow the *L.A. World* prints the results of its latest poll, the Forty-eighth C.D. among others. I think we'll have an edge tomorrow. I can come back."

"You're here now. How much do you need?"

"Whatever I can get. If you ask a figure, I'd like fifty thousand." It took something for Gilpin to say that. He kept his hands in his pockets. When he took them out, he had to concentrate to keep them from shaking.

Lavette opened a checkbook on his desk, wrote a check, tore it out and handed it to Gilpin. "Fifty thousand. Cash." He took the check back and endorsed it. "I'll call my bank. You take this down there and turn it into cashier's checks or cash or any way you need it. But nobody else knows where this money comes from. I don't know whether it's legal or not and I don't give a damn. If my friends can do it, I can damn well do it. But two things—if I ever find out that you've blabbed to anyone, my son, my sister, your wife, if you have one, I'll break your back, and if you know me, you know I can do it. And secondly, don't dip into this money. I'll know about that too."

"I'm not honest," Gilpin said, "but I keep my word. I told you I'm not dipping into this. That holds." He had expected Lavette to offer his hand, but Lavette didn't move.

"You can go now," Lavette said.

The fourth poll, with Election Day still thirteen days away, showed Alexander Holt with forty percent of the vote in terms of the people polled, Barbara with forty-six percent, and fourteen percent still undecided. In the midst of the uproar at her headquarters, Freddie answered the telephone and then, after a brief exchange, covered the telephone and shouted, "Will all you characters please shut up for a moment!" He then motioned to Barbara and said softly, "Believe it or not, Alexander Holt. Wants to talk. I think he's going to concede."

"Freddie, don't be a fool."

"You want to talk?"

"Yes. Freddie, create some quiet and give me a corner by myself."

She picked up the telephone. "Alex?"

"I heard that," he said. "It would certainly set a precedent. Holt concedes before the election."

"Alex, I don't know what to say. Would it be too awful to say I feel rather sorry for you?"

"Not at all. I treasure a lovely woman's sympathy. But I still have a trick or two up my sleeve."

"I'm sure you have."

"Dinner tonight—to celebrate your temporary victory?"

"No, not until after the election, Alex."

"Busy? Or have you been warned off?"

"Some of both. Win or lose, we shouldn't feel too different Wednesday after next."

"I'm a rotten loser."

Later, having lunch in the Mexican restaurant behind the plaza, sitting with Freddie and Mort Gilpin, Barbara said, "No, he didn't sound disturbed. Very bright and confident."

"That I find damn disturbing," Gilpin said. "I hate to say this, Miss Lavette, but he isn't admired in the circles where I live."

"I'd rather not push that," Barbara said, rather primly. "It's only natural that this election means a great deal to him."

"On the other hand," Freddie said, "I want to know where that money came from."

"No way," Gilpin told him. "I picked it up from a circle of my own last resort. They live and give anonymously, period."

"No, sir. I want to know."

"What the devil gives with you, Freddie? Don't you want the money?"

"I want to know whether it came from Thomas Lavette."

"You're sick on that subject. No. No, it did not come from your father. Furthermore, it's committed. I made a fantastic deal, and we have four thirty-second local spots on national network prime time."

"I never agreed to that!" Freddie snapped.

Barbara said gently, "Come on, I did it. I have become

greedy and inhuman and I want those spots. You agreed that if Mort raised the money, we could buy them, and if it was Tom—" She shook her head. "No, I wish it were. But it isn't. It couldn't be. He's sworn to Alexander Holt's camp, he's Mister Republican, cheek to cheek with Ronald Reagan, and let's not put any more pressure on Mort. He's worked miracles."

Sam brought his new *relationship* to meet his mother. That's how he described it. "We have a relationship." "Well, we didn't have them," Barbara said. "We had other things." Sam was not very long on humor; in that, he was like his father, and since he was beginning to achieve a reputation beyond the Bay Area for his surgical skill and thereby earning very large sums of money, he found himself searching for a life style that would accommodate to it, without leaving all his principles by the wayside. To this end, he spent long hours in the surgical clinic, and it was there that he met Mary Lou Constable, who was also assuaging guilt, and exercising what some called the conscience of the rich, as a volunteer in Emergency, but in all truth as a cleaning woman to keep on top of the blood and debris—a low and unpleasant station. It was this, combined with her very real beauty, that grabbed Sam's attention, and the attention did not slacken when he learned that she was the daughter of Leonard Constable, who was possibly as wealthy and powerful as Thomas Lavette. The fact that Sam was part Seldon resided in a special section of his mind. He felt that there he had put it to rest, since he had always kept his father's name. The very first time he bought Mary Lou coffee and apple pie in the hospital cafeteria, he made a point of being Jewish. Mary Lou Constable, a tall, slender girl, dark, black hair and deep-set dark eyes, a narrow nose and full lips— altogether firmly beautiful—was far from being a fool. She knew who Sam was, and if he preferred to be Jewish, that only served to make him a bit more exciting, particularly so since she came from a virulently anti-Semitic family. Not only was Sam tall, and quite handsome, with his long head, his sandy hair and his very pale blue eyes; he was also financially substantial, as she saw it.

Barbara asked Sam to bring her to the house on Green Street between the daytime chaos at Sunnyside Plaza and the commercial she had to do live at eight o'clock that evening. While San Francisco had great pretensions toward being the New York of the Pacific Coast, it was in all truth a small city with less than a million in population; and in the area of importance that old money brings, everyone knew the money of everyone else—in the world of money. In this case, of course, old money was any fortune put together more than a generation ago. Barbara knew Mary Lou Constable. Originally, the Constables derived from Missouri, enough south for them to cling to Southern affectations, such as the double name for girl children and certain prejudices covering a wide spectrum of dark-skinned people. The fact that Sam, half Jewish, had been married to a Chicana would make him even a more unsuitable object in their eyes, Carla's people having lived in California for five generations notwithstanding.

Barbara, on the other hand, greeted Sam's new passion as evidence of a failure on her part. Like his mother, he was fiercely principled, dedicated to his profession, to healing, to the sacredness of life, and was possessed of a number of attitudes that, like those listed, could have no existence in a place like the home and environs of Leonard Constable. Yet despite all this, he had selected Mary Lou with a passion he had never revealed toward Carla. Barbara always tried to balance her reactions, remembering her feelings about Carla when Sam had decided to marry her, rooting out her own prejudice and trying to face it. She felt that she had tried, that she had always tried; and here was another woman evoking another side of her prejudice, her dislike of inherited wealth, her distaste for people of wealth, her scorn for the self-styled San Francisco *society*, and her muted dream that Sam might find and marry someone who could be the daughter she had never had.

At home in Green Street, tired as she always was after a day at the madhouse called her campaign headquarters, wanting no more than to lie down and watch the news on television after a hot bath and then dress leisurely for the commercial appearance, she nevertheless went about doing something in the way of canapés. She put out olives, nuts and a tray of cheese and crackers, all of it bought on the way home, since after two months of campaigning, her own cupboard was as bare as Mother Hubbard's. She also whispered vows to herself that she would not condemn until she had learned something to condemn, and that she would try her best to view the girl sympathetically—accepting the fact that this meeting might be much more of a trial for Mary Lou Constable than for her.

Mary Lou was beautiful and charming, and after the introduction and a bit of small talk, she said to Barbara, "I love my father and mother, but please try to see me as my own person. I tried very hard to be my own person and I feel that I succeeded in some ways and less well in others."

Taken somewhat aback, Barbara said, "I'm sure you are your own person."

"No, not the way you are, Miss Lavette." She actually blushed as she went on to say, "This dreadful world—and believe me, when you work in Emergency, it can be very dreadful—well, I mean it can also be wonderful. I mean, I grew up reading your books and watching your career and wanting more than anything to be like you, and even if Sam is Jewish, he's a special kind, isn't he?"

Barbara stared in speechless dismay.

"I mean, not like—you know what I mean."

Somehow, Sam got her out of the house before she could say any more, and when he reached Barbara on the telephone, he pleaded, "Mom, will you give her a chance, please?"

"Yes—yes, of course."

"She doesn't mean the things she says. Please, believe me."

"I believe you, Sam," Barbara said, not knowing what else to say.

The final poll, six days before Election Day, gave Barbara fifty-two percent, Holt forty-three percent, with only six percent undecided. Freddie rented the hall at the Sunnyside Elks for an election night party, and word went out to at least a hundred and fifty people, among them the people at Higate Winery. Even Al Ruddy sent her a telegram of congratulations, and Moretti turned up in his big black limousine to take Barbara to a luncheon at Le Trianon on O'Farrell Street, where they would be joined by half a dozen top party people. "Just our own small celebration prior to the fact," Moretti said. "I chose Le Trianon for symbolic reasons, if you will forgive me a little sentiment and what you may regard as superstition. The chef, Mr. Verdon, was chef at the White House during the Kennedy years. I find the situation appropriate. Do you agree with me?"

"I am scared," Barbara said. "I'm frightened. I feel like a kid who's been found out. After the poll appeared yesterday —I didn't sleep last night, Tony. Not a wink."

"That's only natural. You've poured your heart and your soul into this. Now the reaction begins. That's only to be expected."

"We still have to face the election, Tony. People are acting as if it's all over."

"It's not all over, this election," Tony said as he proposed a toast at the luncheon table. "I've played this game too long to toast the next and first Democratic congressman—or woman, I should say—in the Forty-eighth. Tuesday night, we'll know and drink to it. But meanwhile, to a fine lady. It has been my privilege to know her."

Barbara was at home alone that Thursday evening. Since the campaign started, she had almost never been alone, and an evening at home by herself with no schedule and no one to address, lecture or contend with was a rare treat. She had time for a leisurely bath and hairwash; and brushing out her hair as she dried it, she speculated on whether it might not have been better to have colored her hair before the campaign began. She had toyed with the idea and had wondered whether she would not be using the election as an excuse for the coloring, but there was so much gray in the honey-colored hair that people would have been certain to note and comment on the change. Her hairdresser had disagreed with this. "You don't look that old," he had told her. "What I mean is, you're making yourself older than you are, because you walk young and you carry yourself young."

She had shaken his suggestions aside. She was going gray and she'd go gray, and that was that. Her peers were doing the face lifts and breast lifts and buttock lifts in a desperate race to bring the Beverly Hills syndrome here to the Bay Area, which left her cold and increasingly aware of the ravages of mortality. She was brooding a bit over the fact that Alexander Holt had not called, not for a week, and somehow in her mind the hair coloring connected with Holt. You did such things if you thought of a man, and she thought of men. God knows how many times she filled her mind with thoughts of men. Clair had once said to her that old age is a land never visited; one enters it as a resident, casually and thoughtlessly. No one had ever told her it would be like this, strange, lonely, threatening, but this was America, youth eternal. The truth was, she realized, that no one ever thinks of growing old. Youth looks at a world where the young are young and the old are old, and nothing ever changes.

She tried not to think about Holt. She had found him gracious and charming, yet she knew almost no one who trusted him. What did she know about him—except for the few hours of their two dinner dates, facing each other across restaurant tables? And if she won this contest, as everyone around her was certain she would, what then? How would she deal with it? How would Alexander Holt deal with it?

When Sunday arrived, the Sunday before the Monday before Election Day, Freddie and Barbara decided to close down the storefront for the first time since the campaign started and have a day in the country. Clair was baking a fresh ham whole, and everyone was meeting for Sunday dinner in Clair's kitchen in the old stone house at Higate. The huge kitchen, with Mexican terra cotta tiles on the floor, and on the walls the blue and white tiles from Pueblo, was used as a dining room because it held an oak table fourteen feet long. Sam came with Mary Lou, and therefore Carla had to be left out, which bothered both Barbara and May Ling. Barbara watched Sam and Mary Lou worriedly, relieved finally when she began to realize that today Mary Lou would open her mouth only to eat or say thank you and yes and no. Apparently, Sam had coached her properly.

Freddie was present with May Ling, and Clair's daughter, Sally, wife to Barbara's brother Dr. Joseph Lavette. With them was their son, Daniel, twenty-one, a junior at Princeton. Freddie had invited Mort Gilpin to join them, and Freddie's father, Adam Levy, and Eloise, Adam's wife, completed the group around the table.

The warmth and pleasure Barbara felt whenever she came together with this small group, which was all the family she had, was muted by a sense of empty places. Death had taken its full measure. Why should she think of death, not only the death of others, but death intimately connected with herself? A cold, desolate feeling swept across her like a wave of icy nausea. Fortunately, it did not last. It went and she was smiling with pleasure, sharing their delight at the results of the latest poll. When Sally struck up "For she's a jolly good fellow," Barbara wanted to cry out for them to stop. But that would have cooled the evening. Freddie took her hand and said, "Nothing can stop the trend. We're going to make it."

"We're not in," Barbara said. "No one's in until Tuesday night."

Driving home that evening, she was detached from all the warmth and excitement of the evening. Something had shattered the passionate desire, the feeling that a whole life of supporting lost causes and tilting at windmills would culminate in the House of Representatives, where she would finally face those who inflicted pain, who lied and looted and made a mockery of justice. All the nasty and envious names that people had attached to her through the years came into her mind, *Girl Scout, Joan of Arc, Goody Two-Shoes, Lady Don Quixote from San Francisco, parlor pink,* threading through her whole life. When she had sorted out the memories and lined them up, they lay on her like a crushing weight. Why had she ever started this thing? Why did she deceive herself with the feeling that she was not old? When did a man last come on to her, and when would a man ever come on to her again? She had toyed with the notion of Alexander Holt. Could it be that he was at least a little bit in love with her?

At home, in bed, Barbara pressed her face into the pillow and wept. Alone in the darkness, she pleaded for her mother and father to come to her. She was sixty-two, but more than that, she was a motherless child and the years made no difference.

* * *

Barbara's last salute, as she thought of it, was a luncheon at the Mark Hopkins Hotel, where she addressed five hundred members of the Northern California branch of the National Organization of Women. It was well outside the Forty-eighth C.D., nor was it likely that more than a dozen or two of the diners would be from the Forty-eighth, but it would have large coverage from the media, and for this reason Barbara had accepted the invitation two months ago. Her subject was "Women and War," and she spoke gently, without passion, her voice rising only when she read: "I was the mother of brave sons. They were not ordinary children, but the pride of Phrygia, beautiful children. No Trojan or Greek or Barbarian mother could boast such children. All these I have seen killed by the spears of the Greeks; I wept on their coffins and cut my hair to its roots. Before my eyes, my beloved husband, Priam, was murdered, butchered in his own house. My city was captured. This I saw and watched. My daughters, whom I loved and raised for good marriage, they were taken from me to be whores for strangers. No hope ever to see them again, no hope, and myself—to crown my misery, I shall be taken in bondage to Greece, a slave in my old age, to die a slave."

Barbara paused. Her voice had turned into a plea of agony and sorrow. She let it drop, and it was again gentle and unemotional. "What has changed?" she asked. "Those words I just read were written by the Greek playwright Euripides, almost two and a half thousand years ago—spoken by the Trojan woman Hecuba after the Greeks sacked Troy. When since then have women not wept over the obscenity men call war, the murder they call glory, and the death of our sons? Now, if it happens, with the terrible weapons we have built, we will have only the awful comfort of dying with our children. It must stop. Perhaps I can help stop it. I can try."

There was great applause and a standing ovation. Freddie, at the back of the hall with Mort Gilpin, remarked, "This does it."

"I think so. If I had read the text, I would have said it's political suicide. But that woman gets away with things. How the hell does she do it?"

"She joined the Girl Scouts and never turned in her badge."

"You're kidding."

"I'm kidding. The truth is, my Aunt Barbara just doesn't live in this world. Maybe people like the place where she lives."

"I don't know. If she makes it, the animals in Washington will tear her to pieces."

"Maybe not. She's a romantic but she's not a fool. She's tough."

"And by the way," Gilpin said, "my spy at a certain network tells me that Mr. Holt has sprung for three three-minute spots, day after tomorrow, Monday night, seven-thirty, eight-thirty and nine-thirty. That's how to get a message through. His money doesn't know when to quit. I wonder where it comes from."

"Does your spy know what he's going to say?"

"No, but he hears it's a bombshell."

"There's no use worrying Barbara. We'll listen on Monday night. He needs more than a bombshell to turn this thing around."

Monday evening, Barbara and Freddie and May Ling and Carla and Mort Gilpin and a handful of volunteers were at the storefront in Sunnyside, seated around one of the long tables and eating sandwiches and drinking coffee out of paper containers. They were staying late to finish and nail up a large corrugated scoreboard, divided into voting districts, so that they could keep track of the incoming vote. It had an additional strip for Jimmy Carter, tracking the national election as well. One of the volunteers was an art student who had spent two full days on the enormous board. Carol Eberhardt had gone out, unasked, to return with two large bags of sandwiches and coffee. While Carla and May Ling were passing out the food, dealing with those who preferred ham and cheese to corned beef or liverwurst and Russian dressing, Carol Eberhardt had taken Freddie aside and whispered to him, "You know, Freddie, my father's head of the Republican organization here in the Bay Area?"

"I know that. Yes."

"Well, Dad said I could stay home today. It's all over."

"He knows you're working here?"

"Oh, yes. It's a great joke around his pals. He never took anything I did seriously."

"Well, you know, it is just about over," Freddie said. "You've worked hard. You could have stayed home."

"No, that isn't what he meant."

"Freddie, come and eat!" May Ling called to him.

"What did he mean?"

"He meant that what Holt says tonight will be devastating."

Freddie nodded. At the table, Freddie said to Barbara, "Holt's doing his three-minute commercial in about a half hour. Do you know about it?"

"I know he's running something tonight."

"Three minutes, seven-thirty, and then twice more on the half hour. It's network. Very big money. I hear the organization can't face losing the Forty-eighth."

"Well, come out with it, Freddie. What are you trying to say to me?"

"I've heard from two or three places that it's very dirty pool."

Barbara shook her head. "No, he's run a clean fight until now. He's not that kind of a person."

Freddie shrugged. "We'll see."

They had a small black and white set at the storefront, and Carla set it up on the other table and moved the rabbit ears until the reception was fairly clear, if not perfect. She got it in place and tuned in a few minutes before the station break. When the commercial began, Alexander Holt was photographed sitting behind his desk, an American flag to his right, a wall of books behind him. Barbara guessed that the commercial had been made at his law office in San Francisco. He wore a tweed jacket, light shirt and striped tie, and as he began to speak, he had the comfortable smile of a person completely at his ease.

"My friends," he began, "I'm no stranger to those of you who live in the Forty-eighth Congressional District. You know my past. The lady who is my opponent is very charming and very persuasive, but what of her past? What do you know about it? They say the child is the father of the man. Then the past is the father of the present. Let me tell you about the past of Barbara Lavette. In nineteen thirty-four a great longshore strike was directed against the shipping of her stepfather. Barbara Lavette was neck-deep in that strike —on the side of the strikers. After that, she turned up in France, where she involved herself in the Spanish Civil War, on the side of the Communists. Her lover was killed there, but this did not deter Miss Lavette, who went on to carry papers from the Communist Party of France into Germany. When she returned to America, she set up an organization whose purpose, ostensibly, was to buy medical supplies for the Spanish anti-Franco survivors. When a committee of Congress, investigating subversive activities in America, reasonably enough, asked her to name the people who gave money to support her organization, she refused and was cited for contempt of Congress. She was subsequently tried and sent to prison for six months. So we have a dossier for one Barbara Lavette. In recent years, we have tended to regard the behavior of those who resisted congressional committees inquiring into subversive activities as heroic. I do not regard it as such. Aside from her contempt of the same Congress she aspires to be elected to, Barbara Lavette has done nothing illegal. Fortunately, she lives in a free country. At the same time, when she presents herself as a candidate, voters have a right to know who they vote for."

He finished. The signature was a plea for a vote for Alexander Holt. He finished, and there was a stunned silence around the table. Barbara tried to remember all the words he had spoken. Ice inside her heart, and a quiet, cold voice that said to her, Here you do not cry. All of these people have given their heart to you, and you will show them how to receive this with grace and courage.

But she was bereft of courage and grace; like so much else in her life, this was an effort thrown away and useless—all for nothing.

"That lousy bastard," Freddie said.

"It isn't true!" Gilpin shouted. "We got that bastard on the biggest libel suit of the century."

Freddie stared at him.

"Is it?"

"It's true and it isn't true," Barbara said, fighting to control her voice. "Everything he mentioned happened, and he turned it on its head." She closed her eyes and shook her head hopelessly.

"Do you know why she went into Hitler Germany?" May Ling demanded shrilly. "To see if there was any resistance left—any organization left to fight for freedom."

"Easy, easy," Freddie said.

Carla was weeping. The telephone rang, and Carol Eberhardt ran to answer it, thankful to be delivered from the circle of sick faces. "It's Mr. Moretti," she called out to Barbara. The others became silent, watching Barbara as she picked up the telephone.

"You saw it, of course?" Moretti said.

"Yes."

"How are you?"

"All right."

"I want to talk to you."

She didn't want to talk to anyone; still, she couldn't say no to the old man. "I'll be home by nine," she said.

She was putting on her coat.

"We have to talk about this," Freddie said. "We have to do something."

"There's nothing to talk about and nothing to do. Let go of it, Freddie."

"Shall I drive you home?"

"No, I'm all right."

Moretti was waiting for her when she got to Green Street, his black car parked in front of her house. He went inside after her and dropped into the one large chair in the parlor.

"Tired?" Barbara asked him.

"After seventy, you're tired. When you're as fat as I am, you're always tired. You look all right. I was worried."

"I'm all right. It's almost a relief."

"You think it's over?"

"Yes."

"Wrong," Moretti said. "It's not over until the last vote is counted."

Barbara shrugged.

"The man's a whore," Moretti growled. "But don't think the whole world was listening, not even in the Forty-eighth. Jimmy Carter's speaking and so is Ford. It's a presidential year. So just don't be so sure the game's up." He hugged her as he was ready to leave. "You're a fine woman, Barbara, a fine woman. An honor to work with you." The smell of him, the mixed odor of aftershave lotion and cigars, lingered after he left. Her father had smoked cigars, and she couldn't help smiling at the thought of what Big Dan Lavette's reaction to Alexander Holt would have been.

She felt a deep sense of relief. She was sensitive enough, tuned outward sufficiently, to accept the fact that it was over. Regardless of what Moretti said, it was over. A miracle might happen, except that miracles did not happen, and now what she wanted was a hot bath, perfume and a large, soft robe, a glass of brandy and a good book.

The telephone began to ring.

Her first thought was to let it ring. Right now, she wanted to talk to no one, but when she considered that it would likely be a worried Sam or Freddie, she picked it up. The voice at the other end said, "Please don't hang up, Barbara."

"Oh?"—taken aback for just a moment. "And why not, Alex?"

"Because you have to understand."

"But I do. Completely."

"No, no, you don't understand. In your eyes, I'm a bastard. But just let me say this, Barbara. If I lose tomorrow, I'm nothing. I was nothing until I became a congressman. I'd be nothing again. I'm not like you. You're Barbara Lavette. You're a famous writer. You have people who love you and admire you. I have nothing. Nothing! I can't face losing the only thing in the world that made people respect me. I can't go back to the law firm and have them despise me. I can't face my kids. I can't face the world. It's all I've got. Can't you understand that?"

"I can understand it, Alex," Barbara said without anger. "But that doesn't make you less loathsome in my eyes. I can be provoked at myself for not sensing it sooner, but as for you—yes, I do understand. You did what you had to do. Everyone does, I suppose."

"Damn it, you can't feel that way. You don't understand—"

This time she hung up, put down the telephone, stared at it for a long moment and then went upstairs to draw her bath.

The following day, the first Tuesday after the first Monday in November of 1976, the returns in the Forty-eighth were very close. Alexander Holt won by 872 votes. Freddie and Mort Gilpin wanted a recount, but Barbara refused. A lot of tears were shed that night in the storefront at the Sunnyside Shopping Plaza, but Barbara's were not among them. She was dry-eyed.

Six

She was so relieved. That was the astonishing part of it, that relief enveloped her like a benediction. Thank God, thank God, thank God—but why? This is what she tried so desperately to understand, something she had put such a price on, and now worthless. It filled her with guilt. People were plying her with sympathy and understanding, and this brought on additional guilt. They were so sincerely sorry and she was so sincerely delighted. For more than two long months, she had been a ravenous, pitiless beast. Yes, pitiless, she said to herself. You, Barbara Lavette, savage with that disease called candidatitis. It couldn't happen to decent, knowledgeable Barbara Lavette; and then it had happened, and she had let it happen and had taken refuge finally in the indecency of Alexander Holt's performance; and now she could look at herself and ask herself whether she wouldn't have done the same thing—had she had the kind of dossier on Holt that Holt had on her. She tried to convince herself that if she had done the same thing, she would at least have been truthful; she would not have twisted and slanted the facts as Holt had.

But what did Alexander Holt believe, if indeed he had
any beliefs beyond self-preservation? He was fighting for his
life. Think of it, she told herself—the key to existence there
in Washington in a hall where several hundred representatives of the people watched the world go spinning down to
an atomic holocaust—and did nothing because there was
absolutely nothing that they could do beyond the posturing
and pretending that took up their endless hours of debate.
You didn't have to believe or dream or hope; you only had
to get the votes and magic would commence. All kinds of
magic. Importance. Desirability. Youth! In addition to everything else, it was a fountain of youth, because so much of
youth is the ecstasy of being desired by others, and down
there in Washington, where all aspects of government had
turned into a lobby, to be desired and wined and dined by
others was the name of the game. But wisdom sucked out of
the marrow of defeat and humiliation is no halo. Barbara
was not proud.

Tony Moretti sent her a great bouquet, and the note that
accompanied the flowers said: "For a gallant lady, as gentle
as she is lovely." This brought tears, and Barbara wept over
the note and the knowledge that Tony Moretti was dying of
cancer. It was only after Election Day that she learned this.
Al Ruddy told her, "He's got six months, maybe a year.
And when he goes, there's no more like him. The damn
computers have taken over." Moretti reminded her of her
father. You had to have someone in your life who would at
least touch off a memory of Father or Mother. If Dan
Lavette were alive, he would have been eighty-seven, and
Barbara could close her eyes and see him, smell the odor of
cigar smoke around him. He could have been alive. There
are people who live to see eighty-seven years, but there are
people of eighty-seven years who are poor suffering imita-
tions of life. Would she want Dan Lavette that way? Or was
it that the proud die young? Boyd was young. A hundred

planned specifics of what they intended to do in the years left to them had been worked out, all the journeys and strange places. It would have been the best of times.

Sam took her to dinner. He wanted to be festive, to drive away her sorrows.

"But, dear Sam, I am not in pain, I don't weep, and I've adjusted very nicely to losing the election."

He took her to Fleur de Lys on Sutter Street and, with what Barbara felt was excessive sophistication, ordered canard aux figues and urged her to have the same. For the wine, he ordered a Pinot Blanc, an imported white Burgundy with a château label. The head waiter took his order but glanced at Barbara rather oddly. She shook her head just the slightest bit.

Sam sighed. "Yes, I know, Mother, I've violated the code. I've ordered a French wine."

"That's silly, Sam. There's no code to violate. It's just that Emile knows me. Most French restaurants sneer at our wines. He doesn't. He carries a full line of our wine. You know, Eloise and I lunch here whenever she's in town—or almost so."

"Our wine! Good heavens, Mother, I'm not wedded to Higate."

"Of course not. It was silly of me even to mention it."

"You're not pleased with me," Sam said. "You're not pleased with me at all. You don't like Mary Lou and you've decided that she's an anti-Semite."

"No—"

"Mother, you're not Jewish, yet you're more sensitive than any Jew I know—and I know a lot of Jews. This is not the nineteen thirties, when you met my father. This is nineteen seventy-six."

"Yes, I've been given to understand that." In spite of herself, her voice had become flat and cold, causing Sam to protest that he loved her and that the last thing he wanted to do was to make her unhappy.

"Forgive me," he begged her.

She smiled, kissed the tips of her fingers and pressed them to the back of her son's hand. "You couldn't do anything that would require forgiveness."

"How little you know me."

"Or vice versa, and I think it's time we both knew each other better. Alexander Holt accused me of being a Communist tool and courier."

"It was a damn lie."

"Somewhat, but not entirely. I never told you about my time in France—except that I met your father there."

"No, but I think there's a great deal you never told me."

The food came, the wine was poured. She wasn't hungry. She felt that she was on the edge of something important to both of them. "I was in my middle twenties," she said. "I went to France without finishing college, to Paris, the old Paris before World War Two, and there I fell in love with a French journalist whose name was Marcel Duboise. We lived together. And then he was given an assignment in Spain, to cover the Spanish Civil War for his newspaper. He was badly wounded in Spain, and later he died in a hospital in Toulouse. Yes, of his wounds. They amputated his leg, but it was too late. There were no antibiotics then."

"You don't have to tell me this," Sam said. "It's disturbing you."

"I'm all right. You see, when Marcel was wounded, your father carried him back to the aid station. Your father was with the Abraham Lincoln Brigade. But I've told you that."

"Yes, you told me, Mother."

"What I didn't tell you, or anyone, for that matter, was how I felt in my time of grief. The first love is a sort of sacred thing. I think you know that."

"I know it, yes."

"I was depressed and lonely—very lonely. Marcel had introduced me to a number of his friends. Some of them were Communists, which in France did not make outcasts of people. They were trying desperately to find out whether any organization or resistance still existed in Germany. They had sent in several couriers, all of whom had disappeared and were presumed dead. Well, they came to me and asked me to go. I was not a Communist, so I would not be arrested as one in Germany. I was an American. I came from a wealthy background and I was a journalist, which gave me a legitimate reason for a trip to Berlin. I got in touch with my editor in New York—I was doing a Paris Letter for *Manhattan* magazine—and he was so absolutely delighted that I might get an interview with Hitler or Goering that I had to go through with it, no matter how I regretted it. It would take too long to tell you all that happened, but at the end I was arrested by the Gestapo."

"You never told me that."

"No. It wasn't something I wanted to remember. But now I want to tell you exactly how it happened. I was walking on a street in Berlin—Berlin before the war—and I saw a group of elderly people cleaning a street. Well—elderly—I would guess in their fifties and sixties, decently dressed, you would look at the men and say, A doctor, a college professor; that specific European intellectual look. They were sweeping offal into piles. A sewer must have overflowed. The street was unbelievably filthy. Then, as I watched, one of the SS men or Gestapo or whatever they were—he ordered this elderly man, a man with pince-nez and a beard, to pick up the filth with his bare hands and put it in a can. The old man was confused by this. I could see him spreading his hands, as to ask for some kind of tool. In response, the Gestapo man struck him, knocked him down, and then he and another Gestapo man began to kick this poor man lying on the street, and I lost my head and began to strike at them with my purse—and, well, that's how I ended up in a German police station. But that's not the point. The point is that these elderly people were Jews, degraded and dehumanized, used as slaves by those dreadful creatures of Hitler.

"You see, Sam, up until then I knew very little of Jews. Daddy's partner and best friend, Mark Levy, was Jewish, but I hardly knew the Levys when I was a young girl. Mother didn't like them, my poor, dear mother, who was full of the most wonderful set of prejudices, all of which she recognized and fought; and as for the people at Higate, I never actually thought of Jake Levy as being Jewish. The first person who came into my consciousness as a Jew was Sam Goldberg, Daddy's lawyer and a dear, dependable friend—and then, of course, I met your father in Paris, after Marcel died. But then again, one would not see Jews in any true historic sense simply by knowing your father. He was a splendid figure of a man, well over six feet, eyes like yours, that same pale blue—" Barbara's voice broke off; she closed her eyes and shook her head.

"Mom—Mom, you don't have to tell me all this."

"I'm all right. Just give me a moment."

"Mom, I think I know what you're trying to say."

"Do you? You were in Israel, Sam, but the Israelis are different. In my mind's eye, I always have the picture of those elderly people sweeping the filth from the street. I know about the camps and the rest of it, but this I saw with my own eyes—the final chapter of two thousand years of torture and humiliation. It made me at least try to understand something. It's not easy. I'm still trying."

"Mother," Sam said evenly, "I know what you've been through, and I think that all my life I've been trying to be something that you and a father I never knew would want me to be. I married a Mexican Catholic girl who grew up on a plantation—Yes, whatever you may think of Higate, it's a damn plantation, like every other big winery in the Valley. I know Jake paid his people the best wages in the Valley, but it's still a hacienda. Well, it couldn't work with Carla. I tried to make myself into a Jew. You know my Hebrew is almost as good as my English, and I suppose I became a sort of Israeli at medical school in Jerusalem, but that isn't being a Jew either. I wanted to find my father and maybe in the process find myself. It didn't work, not being in Israel, not keeping the name Cohen—none of it worked. Now I've found myself a woman whom I relate to. I don't think Mary Lou is an anti-Semite, and if she is, she can change. Grandma Jean changed. Your mother was something wonderful—you know that."

"Yes," Barbara admitted. "I know that."

She baked an apple pie and a pound cake. Barbara would win no medals as a cook. She was too indifferent to food, and she regarded with bewilderment the growing obsession with food and cooking that had overtaken America. Her editor had called from New York, full of an idea: Barbara should do a San Francisco cookbook. He was reluctant to accept her argument that she was the last person in the world to do a San Francisco cookbook. His idea had been born out of the notion that in some way she was connected with the Higate Winery, and that a profound knowledge of wine was somehow evidence of a profound knowledge of cookery. She managed to convince him otherwise, and perhaps it was in reaction to this that she was impelled to bake an apple pie and a pound cake, a project she managed by a meticulous following of the recipes. Since she was not too fond of sweets and since she couldn't bear for these two proofs of new creativity to be wasted, she invited Eloise to lunch at the Green Street house. Lunch would be simple: scrambled eggs with cheese, toasted English muffins, and coffee and pound cake and apple pie. Aside from Boyd, Eloise was the only one who approved of her cooking.

Through the years, Barbara had become very close to Eloise, and rarely did a week go by without Eloise coming into town to lunch. When Eloise first married Adam Levy, in 1946, her journey to Higate made her feel like someone taking residence in paradise. But much had happened since then, much pain and bitterness—to a point where escape to San Francisco was a necessary buffer against madness.

Eloise always dressed for town. A pink skirt of fine thin wool was topped with a white silk shirt and a pink silk scarf at her throat. She loved pink. Her hair was white, and she made no effort to color it, and her face, once the beautiful, round cherub face of the girl who wins small-town beauty contests, had become drawn and tight. She used almost no makeup, made no effort to conceal what time and pain had accomplished. Once, she heard another woman advising Barbara on the virtues of a face lift as a means of doing away with wrinkles, to which Barbara had replied that she earned each and every one of those wrinkles and they were not to be lightly discarded. So Eloise felt. But when it came to selecting clothes, she refused to accept any strictures of age. Barbara was always delighted with Eloise's clothes. "If I only dared to wear a pink skirt in February!"

"Why not?"

"Thirty years ago was a proper time. I didn't have the courage then."

"Courage? Courage to wear clothes? Barbara, I will never understand you."

Barbara poured two glasses of Lillet on ice. "Instead of sherry. Try it. We're both far enough from Napa to drink a French apéritif. Oh, I made such a fuss with Sam when he took me to Fleur de Lys for lunch and ordered a French wine."

"It's good," Eloise said approvingly, tasting the Lillet. "Freddie is the other side of the coin. He would walk out of the restaurant if I ordered French wine."

"No!"

"But he would."

"Freddie is my notion of the civilized man. Let me keep my illusions."

"Let's not get on to Freddie—but we are, aren't we? Well, I wasn't sworn to silence. He hasn't spoken to you at all?"

"About what?"

"The Forty-eighth C.D."

"I think he knows what my reaction would be. I will never again put myself through that—which may be selfish or may be proof that I'm finally growing up, a bit late, I will admit. No, I've had enough of politics. Tony Moretti telephoned last week, and he wanted to know whether I'd do it again next time. I told him no, never, very emphatically."

"Do you know why he called you?"

"I told you why."

"Not so, Barbara. He called because Freddie went to him and told him that if you didn't want the district, he'd like to have a try at it in nineteen seventy-eight."

After a long moment of digestive astonishment, Barbara burst into laughter. "Oh, no," she finally managed to say. "Poor Freddie! He caught it."

"Poor Adam, poor Eloise. Barbara, if he should win, it leaves that whole wretched winery on our backs. Clair is seventy-seven and not well. Oh, I hate to be selfish, but since Joshua's death I've wanted to get away for a time. We planned to take a year in the wine country of France and Hungary. It's been an old dream of Adam's to make a reasonable facsimile of the Imperial Tokay—and now—"

"Freddie won't make it. Holt is no pushover. No, I don't think Freddie could make it."

"You can't be sure."

"Pretty sure. So let's have lunch and talk about other things."

Both the apple pie and the pound cake were delicious, but

neither offered Barbara an inducement to delve deeper into the art of cooking. A visit from Eloise made her feel abandoned and lonely when she left. A new feeling for Barbara. Self-pity had never been a state she enjoyed. After Boyd's death, friends had been considerate and had tried to include her in dinner parties, and even to find her dinner partners. But Barbara soon enough discovered that in the world of people past sixty, single men possessed of a modicum of wit and wisdom were not abundant; single women were, and soon the dinner parties became fewer in number. On occasion, she would have a small party at her house, but she found no great satisfaction in the role of hostess. At best, writing is a lonely profession, and only the knowledge that there was someone close by who deeply cared for her and for what she wrote made writing tolerable.

She was a compassionate person, yet she had no desire to become a Gray Lady at Sam's hospital, as he had once suggested, or to fulfill some romantic notion of working in a soup kitchen for the poor. That wasn't what she had been trained for through all her years of living. She was a feminist; she could say that to herself proudly and without equivocating. She had loved men and married and borne a child, and she had never stepped back from what she thought of as *the good fight*. It meant, as it always had since the end of her sophomore year at Sarah Lawrence College, standing face to face and without whimpering against whatever forces of cruelty and oppression confronted her. It was a fight she had never avoided and that had become the fulcrum of existence, yet it was a fight that always ended in defeat; and in that, she knew, she was like all other women on earth.

When she thought about it in such terms, her eyes would brim with tears of frustration, and she would have to remind herself that she was healthy and strong. That was something time had not taken from her, nor would she surrender whatever years still remained to silence and defeat.

Sam's romance with Mary Lou Constable came to a curious pause, the details transmitted to Barbara by Freddie, who, while not sworn to silence, was certainly told the story in confidence. But Freddie's dislike for the Constable family was such that he could not forbear passing said details on to Barbara.

"The point is," Freddie told Barbara, "that I know a great deal about the Constables. They tried to buy Higate, and we told them to shove it. They offered eighty-five million, which is not hay, and when we turned them down, they moved up the Valley and made an offer to Templeton. I don't know why they wanted so desperately to get into the wine business, but I guess it's the in thing these days. Well, Jack Templeton hired an investigative service to work up a total background on the Constables. They came out here from New Orleans after the earthquake; from New Orleans, not from Saint Louis, and they'd like to forget all about the New Orleans connection, because Mary Lou's great-grandma ran the biggest whorehouse in the city. That's where their stake came from."

"And you had to rush off and give that to Sam."

"Absolutely not," Freddie protested. "I'm giving it to you as background material. Sam proposed to her and she accepted, and the family figured that the nephew of Thomas Lavette could hardly be all bad—"

"He never told me," Barbara said.

"He would have told you. He wanted the proper moment, and then he was going to take both you and Mary Lou to a festive dinner somewhere and make the announcement. But Mary Lou comes back with the news that her family is arranging for the wedding to be held in the chapel at Grace Cathedral, a special dispensation from the bishop, and Sam says to her, Come on, honey, I'm Jewish, and if you want a church wedding, it will have to be in a synagogue."

"You're inventing, Freddie. I don't think Sam ever set foot in a synagogue."

"Well, so it went, and one thing led to another, and Mary Lou, who is no shrinking flower, told Sam that he was as Jewish as the Pope, and that was all Sam had to hear."

Barbara kept her peace for the following few weeks, and then, at last, when Sam stopped by for a drink, she could not refrain from asking about Mary Lou.

"We had an amicable parting of the ways," Sam said.

"Is it over?"

"Maybe all over. Maybe not."

"By the way," Barbara asked, "did Freddie ever mention anything about Mary Lou's great-grandmother or something of the sort?"

"You mean about her being a hooker, Mom? First thing Mary Lou told me. She was proud as a peacock about it. You see, Annabelle Fitzroy was not just a hooker; she ran the biggest whorehouse in New Orleans."

"And Mary Lou?"

"She's a first-rate tennis player. That's high on the list for a doctor's wife."

There were times when Barbara was not fond of her son.

About a month after this, Birdie MacGelsie decided to give a small dinner party for Sam and Mary Lou. When Birdie telephoned Barbara to invite her, Barbara was reasonably surprised. "The marriage is off," Barbara said. "At least, that was my understanding. I'm only his mother."

"Darling, these days you don't get too many points for being anyone's mother. My spies tell me that the wedding is probably on again. Anyway, I felt an obligation to meet the young lady. Don't you like her?"

"I'm not sure I know her well enough to like or dislike.

She appears to have had a childhood resembling mine, and that's reason enough to be wary."

"But you will come?"

Barbara assured Birdie that she would come, but she did not look forward to it. Her distaste for social engagements that she had to fulfill without an escort was increasing; she felt uncomfortable as the widow lady, the odd woman out. It made her angry to surmise that people might be sorry for her; she would not be an object of pity. Yet she knew well enough that people spoke about poor Barbara, and of course we must do something, but find us a man over sixty who isn't simply deplorable—

Still, she could not become a hermit in the little wooden house on Green Street. Once it had been cute and delightful, a valid old Victorian San Francisco hill house. Now even Eloise, who had always admired the house, said, "No, Barbara, it's too dark. At our age we need light."

Once she had allowed Eloise to steer her into one of the new highrises being built on the hills. They looked at an apartment on the sixteenth floor that had a splendid view of the Bay and the Golden Gate Bridge, but it brought a flood of memories and a stab of apprehension to Barbara, who reminded Eloise that two of her grandparents had perished in the earthquake of 1906. "I would never draw an easy breath here," Barbara said.

In Birdie MacGelsie's thinking, eleven people constituted a small dinner party. Nor did her apartment high above the city arouse her apprehensions. Aside from Sam, Mary Lou and Barbara, there were three other couples, one of them Al Ruddy and his wife, Susan. Barbara had never met Susan Ruddy before. She was small, dark, with a sort of apologetic prettiness. A large, redheaded man of fifty or so was introduced as Bart Limber. His wife was very tall, very thin, blond hair and bony shoulders. She wore two strings of pearls and a heavy necklace of carved quartz beads. Limber subcontracted airplane parts, and he had been a classmate of MacGelsie's at Stanford. The third couple, Barbara met with some relief. They were old friends, Dr. Milton Kellman and his wife, Nell. Birdie was sensitive enough to feel that Barbara needed additional buttressing. Both Susan Ruddy and Alison Limber were, as they put it, absolutely thrilled to meet Barbara Lavette, whom Susan Ruddy specified as "the" Barbara Lavette. "I heard so much about you, so many things, and of course it was years ago—when you were young."

Her husband looked daggers at her, and her voice dried up. It was the last thing Susan Ruddy said that evening— that is, the last thing that might have had either an opinion or a question tied into it. But on the plus side it produced a deep, suppressed giggle in Barbara, who was certain that, if left alone, Susan would have plunged into a host of questions about how it felt to be in jail or a Communist courier. Well, why not? Certainly the evening promised nothing much more interesting.

"Of course I read your last book, loved it," Alison Limber said in a deep throaty voice. Barbara realized that the tall, thin and stylish lady said things for the sound of them, not for the content. Barbara counted the years since her last book. Too long to be remembered.

"Oh! Writer, are you?" Limber said. "Never actually understood about writers. Suppose you just sit down at a desk and write. Boggles the mind, doesn't it?"

"Oh, yes, indeed—sometimes," Barbara agreed. Drawing her aside, Birdie whispered into her ear, "Horse's ass, but Mac loves him."

Milton Kellman kissed her and Nell Kellman embraced her and began to apologize for the time elapsed since the last time. "But that's Milt, and I'm a doctor's wife, and unless I have the bad luck to get sick, I never see him either."

Mary Lou grinned at Barbara and said, "I'm not going to

say anything but hello. I open my mouth any wider, and in goes my foot."

It was an improvement, Barbara felt, and at least the lady had a sense of humor. Sam whispered, "Give her a chance, please, Mom. Her parents are Neanderthals. She has to work her way through several thousand years of history. Not easy."

Birdie seated Barbara between Milton Kellman and Sam; she faced Al Ruddy and Bart Limber, with Mary Lou sandwiched across the table from her, but taking it well and being charming to the men who flanked her. MacGelsie proposed a simple toast to the younger generation present. The big, heavyset man was more sensitive than Barbara had supposed. Alison Limber talked about the election. "If I had only lived in the Forty-eighth," she said, in her husky voice, "I would have voted for you at least twice."

"If we lived in the Forty-eighth," her husband countered, "we would have moved after two days, so you wouldn't have voted for Miss Lavette at all."

"Not if you lived in one of those million-dollar waterfront shacks," Birdie said. "You might just endure it."

"Outside the city? Never, never, never."

The asparagus vinaigrette appeared. The wine was poured.

"A time will come," Sam said, "when we'll dine at your house, Birdie, or at the home of some equally lovely and generous person, and our hostess will not feel the necessity of serving Higate wine."

"Oh, no, Sam. It's simply the best. I'm not tipping my hat to you and your mother. I'm simply defying the myth that no California wine is as good as the French."

"Some people don't regard it as a myth."

"In our house, it's a myth."

The soup came.

"Does all this mean that you own Higate Winery?" Alison Limber asked Barbara.

"Oh, no—no. It's just a tangled family thing, but we have no financial interest in Higate."

With the roast, Al Ruddy said, "I saw your brother the other day, Miss Lavette. Remarkable man."

"Oh, yes, Tom is remarkable."

"I came as an improbable petitioner, but he was quite pleasant. Oh, I had met him before, but only casually."

Certainly they all knew that she had not spoken to her brother in years. Why did they persist? Or was it that money was an icon that must be worshiped?

"It's one of the perks of the profession," Bart Limber said. "Everyone's nice to a congressman."

"It could have been my charm."

"I'm sure it was," Mary Lou said.

"More perks. Beautiful women tell you you're charming."

"Are you going to tell us about it?"

"Only if you pledge not to put your hands in your pockets. I abhor people who raise funds at a social gathering."

"The easiest pledge I ever had pushed at me," Limber said.

"Well, no great secret. We're trying to build a new library as a sort of monument to the memory of Harry Truman. A repository for books about the Korean War; you know, maps, news reports. They want it down at City College. I think it's an appropriate place for a Truman memorial."

"I could think of a more appropriate place," Barbara said.

"Oh? And where might that be?"

"A military cemetery."

There was a long moment of silence. Then Al Ruddy, as if he had missed Barbara's remark entirely or thought it unworthy of comment, went on to talk about her brother. "I do mean, to ask a rock-ribbed Republican like Thomas

Lavette to support a memorial to Truman—well, that's pushing it. But he didn't throw me out. Not at all. Simply said he'd like to have some time to think about it."

Limber would not drop it. "I was wondering what Miss Lavette meant. This isn't a gravestone. You don't put a library in a cemetery?"

"Why not, if it's dedicated to death. Appropriate? Well, when one considers it, no man in all of human history, except Adolf Hitler, ordained so much death at one stroke as Mr. Truman when he gave the order to destroy Hiroshima and Nagasaki. And since the library is to be devoted to his war, what better place than a cemetery?"

Was she serious? She could see that Ruddy was uncertain. Limber was not uncertain. Alison Limber had the slightest smirk of satisfaction on her face. She had known all along, it said. When the sky fell on Barbara, Alison would watch with pleasure. MacGelsie was fighting a grin, and Kellman's face was impassive. His wife nodded gently.

"You don't mean that," Ruddy said at last.

"Oh, I do."

"Then you're way off base, Miss Lavette," Limber said sharply. "It was not Truman's decision. The military decided it."

"I'm afraid not, Bart," MacGelsie said. "That's one little bit of history I was very close to. I was a colonel, stationed in Hawaii, and I was in on some private talk. The Joint Chiefs did not want to drop it on cities. They voted to hit the fleet or a concentration of Japanese troops. It was Truman who backed dropping the damn thing on the cities."

"And saved a hundred thousand American lives," Ruddy said.

"They were not far from surrender," Barbara said. "But I only made a suggestion. You needn't take it to heart. The military cemetery will survive without it."

"I suggest a more cheerful topic," Birdie MacGelsie said,

"as for instance the disintegration of our beloved city. We have become a Disneyland of the North, tied up in ribbons of concrete, with monstrous highrises, like the one we're sitting in right now, up all over the place like mushrooms or like candles in the whipped cream top of a rich kid's birthday cake."

Barbara would have preferred to walk home alone. It was not a happy evening, and it had dragged on and on; and then it was late and Sam held the car door open for her, and she had absolutely no desire to get into an argument with him. Sam had barely started the car when he could contain himself no longer and lashed out at her. "Mother, for Christ's sake, why must you always do it? Will you never grow up? That was a perfectly decent, pleasant dinner party until you brought up that old saw about Truman and the bombs. Why? It's done! It's over! Can't you stop—"

Possibly he had forgotten that Mary Lou was in the car in the back seat. He was sitting at the wheel, with Barbara beside him, her heart feeling like ice breaking into small shards.

Mary Lou's voice came hard and sharp. "Sam, will you shut up!"

"What?"

"You said enough, and you said it more stupidly than anything I ever heard you say. Your mother is right. She said what had to be said about that dreadful little man."

"This doesn't concern you!"

He had stopped the car now in front of Barbara's house, having covered the few blocks from Jones Street, and Mary Lou opened the door and said, "It concerns me! It damn well does." And then she got out and walked off without looking back.

Barbara, still held in a sick spell, turned to look at Sam. "Oh, Jesus, I'm sorry. I have to go after her."

Sam leaped out of the car on the gutter side, leaving Barbara sitting alone. After a moment, Barbara left the car and went into her house. She went to her bedroom and dropped onto her bed, lying on her back and staring at the ceiling.

About ten minutes later, the front doorbell rang—again and again. Barbara could not bring herself to get up and answer it; she felt a weight like a large stone across her chest. Then the doorbell stopped ringing. No more than a minute or two went by, and then the telephone next to Barbara's bed rang. It rang five times before she forced herself to pick it up. She knew before he spoke that it was Sam. He had a radio phone in his car.

"Please, Mom, please. I don't know what got into me."

"We'll talk about it tomorrow," Barbara said. "I'm very tired now and not thinking clearly at all."

"Just a few minutes. We're right outside."

"Tomorrow, Sam."

Mary Lou's voice came over the phone. "Please forgive him."

"I'm not angry, dear. Just tired," Barbara said.

"My dear Barbara," Alexander Holt wrote. "Over a year has gone by since we spoke, and believe me I am still blistered by what you said. You can also believe that I have thought about it constantly, by which I mean that it was hardly ever out of my mind. Nobody likes to look at himself and say, 'You're a bum'; and I'm not so sure that it would explain what I did. The thing is that nobody in my circle feels that my TV appearance the night before the election was foul or dishonorable. But also, I do not deceive myself by believing that there is much left in my circle that can be called a sense of honor. I don't know how I can make you understand what being defeated in the last election would have done to me. I am not whining, or maybe I am, but the truth is that the only reason I have for existence would have been taken away. I tried to say something like this the last time we spoke. But that didn't explain and I don't know of anything I can say to explain an empty man. That's the only description that fits: an empty man, a hollow man. It is not that I don't know what is right and what is wrong. The truth is that I don't care. Being in the House means more than questions of right and wrong. I try to make a decent record when it doesn't mean bucking the tide. So having said this, why should I care where I stand in your book of dunces? I'll try to answer that as straightforwardly as I can. Meeting you made me alive for a little while, and I remember what it felt like to be alive.

"Now all of this can be dismissed by you as some fancy footwork on my part, except that I've underwritten it, and that at least is one honest thing and maybe the only honest thing I ever did. But I'm doing it. I'm writing this letter, and if my gut is not strained too much, I'll send it to you. You will then have in your hand the same kind of instrument, more or less, that I used to win the election, and it will be up to you to decide whether or not to use it. You may think that, as little as I know you, I know that you would not do to me what I did to you. Well, I know it and I don't know it, but sending you this letter is something I have to do. I hear that your nephew Frederick Lavette may get the designation. I wish it could be you. If I have to be kicked out on my keester, I would prefer you do it." And he signed the letter simply ALEXANDER HOLT.

"I have received your letter," Barbara wrote to him. "I thought you might wish to be certain that it was received." Just that and no more, and then after she had sent off her letter, she reflected on the fact that she could be as calculating a bitch as anyone else. All her life, she had fulminated against such distortions of the human spirit as revenge. She tore Holt's letter into small pieces and flushed them down the toilet. "I will not tell him," she said aloud. "For once in your life, you, Barbara Lavette, will not act like a sentimental Girl Scout. You suffered. Let him suffer—let that bastard have second and third thoughts. You know enough about men to know that macho is a fleeting illusion. The nobler nature can survive a few hours, but then it crumbles, and by now, he would walk through the fires of hell to retrieve that letter."

But a few days later, her resolve crumbled. She asked herself how she could play such an idiot child's game. She had never done that, never in her life. She had never practiced revenge, and she had only pity for those who indulged it.

She put through a call to Washington. When Holt identified himself, she said stiffly, "This is Barbara Lavette."

"I thought it was you when they said it was a woman who would not give her name. I got your letter."

"Your letter," Barbara said coldly, "has been torn into small pieces and flushed down the toilet. I thought it was mawkish." Then she put down the phone and broke the connection. And then she burst into laughter. It was good to laugh this way. "Thank you, Alexander Holt!"

"I have it," Freddie told her. "Not that it's any kind of great achievement, because nobody's contesting it. As far as the party's concerned, it's still the impossible Forty-eighth, but they figure that I've endless sources of money, and nobody else wants to come up with twenty cents. Unless you've changed your mind?"

"Not a chance, darling. Oh, no. It's an illness I never want to contract again."

"Ah, well. You know, they didn't just give it to me. It was the word of Tony. He put in for me. You know, I think he likes me."

"I can't imagine why."

"It's mutual. You know, Aunt Barbara, I didn't like him at first. I'm not exactly Freddie Lavette, friend of the establishment. If you had told me a year ago that I'd put myself on the chopping block and make a run for what they euphemistically call the House of Representatives, I would have said you were crazy. I despise politicians, but Tony Moretti's something else. I don't know exactly what he is, but he's a breed that's gone."

"Don't romanticize him, Freddie. He's a politician and a very good one. How is he?"

"In a wheelchair, dying slowly."

Barbara shook her head, fighting against the tears that were welling into her eyes. Why did he have to come here and talk about Tony Moretti?

"You've never been to his house?"

She rose and went to the window, her back to Freddie. "No."

"A small old frame house in North Beach—a lot like this, only less grand."

"Less grand than this?" Barbara asked. They were sitting in her tiny parlor. "Hard to believe."

"His limbo's a lot more magnificent, believe me. He sits there in a wheelchair and he seems to have a lot of pain—"

"Freddie," she interrupted, "what does May Ling think about all this?"

"Well, she'll come around."

"What on earth does that mean?"

"I guess she's frightened."

"Of course she's frightened. She grew up in Napa. She's a small-town girl. Have you thought it through? If you win, do you leave her here and become a weekend husband? Or do you take her with you and make a life in that place they call Washington?"

Freddie shook his head. "I don't know. We'll work it out somehow."

"I hope so."

Rising to leave, Freddie paused to stare at a magnificent

bouquet of long-stemmed red roses. "Two dozen. Whoever it is, Aunt Barbara, he loves you truly."

"I hope so. They're a peace offering from Sam."

"Are you angry with him?"

"No, Freddie, and don't pry any further."

"Are you angry with me?"

"I could never be angry with you."

"Then you'll help me?"

"Yes, I'll help you."

And pray that he loses, she told herself after he had gone. If he won, the marriage would not stand up. In no way could it stand up. Freddie was too charming, too good-looking, and completely enchanted with women. There were so few men like him, men who loved women simply because they were women, men who understood women without ever truly understanding a woman.

Mary Lou telephoned and asked Barbara whether she might come by at four o'clock to talk and to have a cup of tea if that didn't put Barbara out too much.

"Tea? My dear, that's lovely but unusual these days. Of course, if you can tolerate a two-year-old. May Ling is in town and has parked young Daniel Lavette with me. He's in that area of life the young folk call the terrible twos. Actually, he's not terrible at all, but a great strain on the shoulder muscles."

"It can wait—"

"No, it shouldn't wait. If you want to come today, there must be a good reason."

She was stronger than Barbara would have suspected, one of those women whose large frames hide behind soft, round faces. She lifted the little boy and hugged him while he tugged at her hair.

"He should be ready for a nap. He's been up since dawn. I've had him for two hours, and believe me, I'm ready to drop."

"I read somewhere of an athlete who tried to keep pace with the motions of a two-year-old for a day of the kid's life."

"Poor athlete," Barbara agreed, putting Daniel down on the couch. He stared at the two women for a moment or two, then curled up and closed his eyes.

"As easy as that?"

"Once in a blue moon, I would guess. What happened to the athlete?"

"They took him to the hospital."

"Well, we won't try to pace Danny. You know, my brother has a boy named Daniel. Senior at Princeton. I wonder what Pop would have thought of his two namesakes."

"What was he like, Barbara? May I call you Barbara?"

"Of course."

"Dan Lavette. Not the boy at Princeton. Your father."

"Big, easygoing man. Very gentle, very sweet."

"Gentle?"

"I know what you're thinking. That was only once, and I suppose it was the worst moment in his life. He got into a fight in a saloon in the Tenderloin and broke up the place and the men who jumped him. That wasn't Daddy."

"How do you tell when it is or it isn't? Who is my father? All my life, he treated me like some damn incredible princess until he found out that I was working in an emergency room, pushing around a bloody mop and holding the edges of a slit gut together until the doctor gets to it. That made him crazy, and he got even crazier when he found out that I was sleeping with a divorced Jew-doctor, as he put it. Just tell me there's no anti-Semitism in America—no way, not a trace of it. At first he was going to go along with a wedding at Grace Cathedral, where a bronze plaque was loaded with the names of Lavettes and Seldons, but that was before I told him that Sam's name was Cohen and not either Lavette or Seldon. He really hadn't done his homework—" She was becoming very emotional, and Barbara disliked hysteria, in herself and in others.

"We're going to have that tea," Barbara said firmly. "I think it's the first time in years anyone invited herself to this house for tea. And if you don't think I'm flattered, I took myself down to Bonier's for their special cookies."

They left the child sleeping on the couch and had their tea in the kitchen, no great distance in the tiny house. Meanwhile, Mary Lou had caught hold of herself, and she was able to say, very quietly, "I have been cast out, like in those silly old stories I used to read."

"No, those things don't last," Barbara assured her. "Your father will come around."

"They won't come to a wedding. They won't even admit it can be. Well, I am just as strong and hardheaded as they are, and I think Sam loves me, and I love him more than I can say."

"They will come," Barbara assured her.

"Oh, no. You don't know Daddy. But Barbara, please, I want to be married right here. Right here in this house. And I want your permission and I want your blessing, and I want you to love me." Now the tears came, and Mary Lou stood up and they embraced each other.

"You thought I was horrible," Mary Lou said.

"Oh, no. No."

"I was horrible."

"Mary Lou," Barbara said, "you need no one's permission to marry my son. If you love each other, that should be enough. My son was married to a fine person and he divorced her. I think he has a penchant for fine people; I pray he has the same penchant for staying married. As for having a wedding in this house, it is impossible."

"Why?"

"Have you spoken to Sam about it?"

"Not yet."

"Mary Lou, my dear, even a very small wedding would bring too many people for this house to hold."

"Only people who love Sam."

"I don't see how it's possible."

"Will you try, will you think about it? Please?"

Barbara had always written about things she had seen with her own eyes. She had not stopped seeing, but the writing would no longer come. After Boyd's death, she had planned to write a book about him but had written nothing. At first, she had gone to the typewriter each day, as a religious primitive might go to his wooden god, always convinced that a time would come when the god would awaken and perform wonders. But the god did not awaken, and no wonders were performed. Time after time, she formed a sentence, a paragraph, now and then a page, and once almost forty pages; but it all ended up the same way, shredded and dropped into the wastepaper basket. When she sought for some answers inside herself, she found that she didn't care. There were deeper reaches that she visited in the darkness of her sleepless nights, tearing at herself to discover why she should be cursed with the inability to write unless she cared.

She roamed among the bookstores, buying books, loads of books, books by all the eager, bright, liberated young women, confessions of love life and loveless life. Orgasms detailed and counted, marriages installed and shattered, love and hate to a point where men and women harried each other like a pack of demented dogs. She had no scorn for this, none of the contempt she felt for the endless stream of books about spies, secret agents, supermen who saved the world, the killers and the killed; no, for the work of the young women she had only admiration, a certain degree of envy, and the frustration that came from trying to be one with a world so distant from the world she had known as her own young woman. But reading the books of others did not help.

She brooded over these things as she tried to solve the wedding problems of Mary Lou, wondering whether this was her destiny, a housewife aged, helpful and cheerful. She was being helpful—or was she? She paced through the little clapboard house. A wedding here? Did she really care? She couldn't write because she no longer cared. Did she care enough about a wedding to crowd all her family and friends into this place? The whole notion was ridiculous, and she felt a marvelous sense of relief because, ridiculous or not, it was obviously a delicious idea.

"I think maybe I'll make it," she said to no one in particular, and not referring to the wedding at all.

Tony Moretti died, and he was taken to his grave and buried on a cold, wet spring day. Freddie picked Barbara up, and they went to the funeral together. The church was packed.

"They're making sure he's dead," Freddie said bitterly. "There isn't a California Democrat left in Washington. They're all here to tell each other how great the old man was."

"Why so bitter?" Barbara asked him.

"Because I bowed out. Because he wasn't dead more than a few hours when good Al Ruddy informed me that a certain Nancy Kraft was having petitions signed in the Forty-eighth and that I'd have to go through a primary. It's a joke—go up against a woman in the Forty-eighth. I wouldn't get a hundred votes in a primary. So I told the little bastard to shove it and I bowed out."

"And how do you feel?"

"Lousy."

"Poor Freddie—I'm so sorry."

But they both knew it was her doing. She had established the legitimacy of a woman in the Forty-eighth C.D. And she had given Ruddy good reason to hate people who were named Lavette.

Seven

The wedding was put off until February 1979, and then, as Mary Lou had insisted, it took place in Barbara's house on Green Street. Forty-two people had crowded into the narrow parlor and downstairs dining room. The wedding ceremony was performed by Judge Albert Pelzer, and the only member of the Constable family who attended was Mary Lou's brother Andrew, who was sixteen years old. The hatred and anger that had taken hold of the Constables after Mary Lou had announced her determination to go ahead with the wedding was at first beyond Barbara's comprehension, but the matter was clarified somewhat when Barbara took Mary Lou's mother, Jo Anne, to lunch. Barbara considered that she should take the matter in hand and refused to believe that a talk between two adult women, where common sense and low key prevailed, would not soften the situation.

But Jo Anne Constable felt that nothing would be gained by sitting down with Mrs. Cohen. Since Barbara had behind her a decade of writing when she married her first husband, Bernie Cohen, she maintained her maiden name as a literary signature, and when, as a widow, she had married Carson Devron, she continued to write under the name of Barbara Lavette. Yet Jo Anne's specification of the name was obviously intended to be offensive. Barbara, however, went on quietly to say that even if nothing was gained, each could at least make her views plain to the other. Finally, she persuaded Mrs. Constable to meet with her.

Barbara reserved a table at the Fairmont. The Constables lived in San Mateo, and Barbara felt that her knowing the head waiter at the Fairmont would impress Mrs. Constable —even as the Fairmont itself would make an elegant and conservative setting. She tried to anticipate Mrs. Constable, having only a rather nasty telephone conversation to go by, yet found herself unprepared for the tall, well-dressed, dark-haired woman who was brought to her table. Barbara rose to greet her; they were of a height, both of them tall, good-looking women, but Mrs. Constable, in her forties, was taken aback confronting a woman in her middle sixties.

"Please sit down," Barbara said to her. "I'm glad you came."

"I'm afraid I can't say the same thing. I changed my mind, but when I tried to reach you, you had apparently left your home." Actually Barbara had not left her house; suspecting it was Mrs. Constable, she had not answered the telephone. "I tried to reach you," Mrs. Constable continued, "because I knew that if we did meet, I would have to talk frankly, and I know that frank talk is never pleasant."

"I wouldn't have it any other way. We must both talk frankly."

"Very well. My daughter, a very willful young woman, says that she is determined to marry your son. She has already made us quite unhappy by taking a job that amounts to no more than a cleaning woman, except that she deals with blood and with the offal of the human body. Now she has chosen a man who is totally unacceptable, and I have warned her that if she persists, her father will cut her out of his will and I will cut her out of my life."

"Isn't that terribly harsh?" Barbara asked. "I mean, today people look at things differently, don't you think?"

"I don't know what you mean by differently."

"And I don't know why you are so opposed to my son. He is young, quite attractive, healthy, very well regarded in his profession, making a decent living, already on the board of the hospital and destined for success, as such things are measured."

"We have our reasons."

"I'm sure you do."

The maître d' came to the table, and Barbara asked whether Mrs. Constable would have a drink. She consented to a martini, and Barbara asked for a glass of white wine and sand dabs and salad. Mrs. Constable ordered the salade Niçoise. Barbara then reminded her of their discussion—namely, why she so objected to Sam.

"You must know."

"I'm his mother," Barbara said quietly, controlling her mounting annoyance. "So it's not easy for me to imagine reasons why he might be unacceptable."

"Well, I don't think we'll have a comfortable lunch, but since you press me so—well, he's Jewish."

"A good many people are," Barbara said.

"Not in our circle."

"No, I suppose not, and I must admit that you're very forthright. A rare quality these days."

"Before you put me down as some outrageous anti-Semite, I must say there are other reasons. His first wife was a Mexican, an actress with a very unsavory reputation."

"And you feel that since he married a Mexican woman, it reveals a deplorable lack of character."

"I think you know exactly what I mean, Mrs. Cohen."

"I've lost touch," Barbara said tiredly. "I didn't think

there were people like you still around. His first wife, whom you call a Mexican, Carla Truaz, was born in the Napa Valley, but the Truaz family came to California in the eighteenth century, long before the Seldons or the Constables or any other modern Americans."

"I don't think there's any point in listening to any more of your tirades," Mrs. Constable said, rising and fumbling with her purse.

"Please don't bother about the bill," Barbara said gently. "The maître d' is Jewish, and we have a Zionist conspiracy about dinner checks. My meals here really cost nothing."

She stalked out in a fury, and the maître d' came to the table and said, "Mrs. Lavette, has she gone to the powder room or shall I cancel the salade Niçoise?"

"Better cancel."

"Yes, I thought so. She's very angry."

"Arnaud, are you Spanish?"

"I am not," he replied sternly. "I am a Basque."

"Oh. Are there any Jewish Basques?"

"Not that I know of."

"Oh. Ah, well, either a small white lie or an outrageous dark one. I'm not sure which."

It was after this aborted luncheon that Barbara agreed with Mary Lou that the wedding might be held in her house. Judge Pelzer performed very nicely, and Mary Lou was lovely in her white lace gown, a gift that Barbara had insisted on providing. Her brother stood by her side, and Freddie, somewhat bleak through the ceremony, stood with Sam. Young Dan had come in from college, and he stood with his father, Joe, his mother, Sally, and May Ling, his sister. Adam and Eloise, and Adam's mother, Clair—the whole of the family, all that remained, except for May Ling's small child, of the intermixed clan of Levy and Lavette. Death had clawed at them savagely. There were Seldons and Apthorns—her grandmother's family—back east somewhere, perhaps alive, perhaps dead, but the parting was over a hundred years ago, and the last contacts had been in the 1930s. The continent had once been too wide, and as in so many California families, there were no deep, ancient roots.

Barbara wept. But she was not weeping the customary and obligatory tears for a son's departure. Sam had departed too long ago. She was weeping for herself, as all the shards and fragments of her life came together in her small house on Green Street. Enough of tears. She dried her eyes and tried to assess Sam's colleagues. A half dozen of them were present, each with a proper and pretty wife, all of them between thirty and forty, handsome men and women, prosperous-looking men and women, the Mercedes and Cadillacs parked outside, the minks taken upstairs to a bedroom, the four-hundred-dollar three-piece suits bearing testimony to the urban and fashionable quality of San Francisco as compared, for instance, with Los Angeles. And all of these young, smart, distinguished surgeons delighted to meet her, the notorious or famous, as you will, Barbara Lavette, or Miss Lavette or Mrs. Cohen, since she was Sam's mother, or Mrs. Lavette, and there was even one man present who called her Mrs. Devron. Well, fair enough; she had been married to Carson Devron—only, only, who was she? Confused suddenly, she was filled with doubt and fear.

"Please, stay with me for a little while after this is over," she begged Eloise. "Don't run off."

Eloise agreed, concerned for Barbara, who was not taking it well at all. But Barbara knew something about fighting for composure, and most of the wedding party thought that she had comported herself, as always, with dignity and grace.

"Except," as one of the doctors' wives remarked to her husband, "that she would look ten years younger if she would only dye her hair and have a face lift."

* * *

The guests had gone. The caterer's people were lugging out the empty champagne bottles and boxes of glasses and dishes. Barbara, slumped in a chair, watched the cleaning process without any particular interest.

"I think we ought to get out of here," Eloise said. "Nothing is worse than the aftermath."

"I suppose not. Where shall we go?"

"It's still sunny outside. Let's walk down to the Embarcadero."

"D.H. doesn't bother you?" Barbara asked. D.H. was downhill, a specific San Francisco foot and knee affliction that resulted from downhill walking with bad shoes.

"Not yet. And you?"

"Let's walk. When I can't walk, I shall quietly get rid of myself."

Beyond the Golden Gate, the sun was dropping to the sea, and the Bay was a wild tangle of golden flags, a million golden flags riding the surface, tipping the water and dancing a mad celebration of their short existence. Twilight had driven the tourists back to their hotels. The crab boats were tied up and the seafood stands were dropping their shutters. Both women had wrapped themselves in woollen coats, and they walked quickly with long, firm strides. Thank God for Eloise. She had been absolutely right, and a brisk walk in the cold afternoon air was just what Barbara had needed. "Like some men," Barbara said, "this is what you love and hate and cannot break from. It's a magic city."

"I'm turned sixty-one," Eloise said. "Today's my birthday."

"I wish I had known."

"Do you reach a point where nothing makes sense? The madness in Vietnam and my son's death. Do other mothers feel this way? I would give them Vietnam and Korea and anything else they wanted if I could have Josh back. Oh—

God damn them for their wars. All this beauty, all this awful beauty, and he is gone. Forever. No more sunsets— Barbara, tell me to shut up! This is a wedding day. This is a birthday."

"Let's walk," Barbara said.

They reached Jones Street, and now they swung around to walk in the other direction.

"Did Adam take the car?" she asked Eloise.

"Yes. Freddie and May Ling are having dinner with Sam and Mary Lou. I should think they'd want to be alone. I can call them at the restaurant for a ride back."

"They've been alone," Barbara assured her. "They've been living together for over two years. Marriage is after the fact these days. Anyway, Sam's operating tomorrow at ten. No honeymoon. Look, let me call Sally and invite both of us to dinner. I'll drive you out to Napa."

"And leave Adam alone? He doesn't age well, poor dear. Men are afraid to die."

"We're all afraid to die, aren't we? But include Adam. Sally won't mind."

"I've stopped caring. Why Sally's house?"

"I have a need for a brother," Barbara said. She had a need for someone of her own flesh and blood. Someone to fill the emptiness that came when she had said goodbye to Sam.

Eloise agreed. "I'll telephone Adam and tell him to meet us at Sally's, and you call Sally and tell her she's having three unexpected guests for dinner."

Barbara's birthday was in November. In the old days, when on the West Coast astrology was becoming a sort of nuthouse religion, people would look at Barbara strangely when she told them her birth date. "Oh, Scorpio." As if she were an unwelcome visitor to earth. Little of it remained now in 1979. Barbara felt that America had no memory for anything—much less such nonsense as astrology. A nation that had forgotten its birth ten years after it happened and that fell victim to an endless succession of crazes and cults.

It was three days before Barbara's birthday that her brother Tom died, a victim of the same kind of massive coronary that had struck down his father. He was older than Barbara, and while the accumulated bitterness of years had made them less than loving brother and sister, they had never wholly lost contact with each other. Tom's wife, Lucy Sommers, was seventy-one, a stringy, vinegary woman, who hated everything named Lavette, including her husband, from whom she had been separated for ten years. She would not grant him a divorce, and such was the corporate complexity of Tom's empire, a tangled web of ownership, that he could not afford—according to his lights—to force a divorce. Barbara, who had avoided Lucy since long before her brother's separation, hardly recognized the skinny, thin-lipped old woman who came to the funeral but shed no tears. When he had first heard of his father's death, Freddie feigned indifference, but Barbara telephoned him and said firmly, "We'll go together, Freddie. And you must go. There can be no argument about this."

As for Barbara, she didn't know what her own response was; the death seemed so distant and meaningless, as if time beyond measure had drifted by since a word of affection had passed between her and her brother. At Grace Cathedral, over five hundred men and women turned out for the funeral service, no surprise to Barbara. As she sat there, with Sam and Freddie at one side of her and her brother Joe and his wife, Sally, on the other, listening to words spoken without meaning or truth, breathing in the musty smell of the church air, a smell she had come to associate more with death than with marriage or baptism, she felt an icy chill of hopelessness. It was all pointless and meaningless—all the funerary trappings—except for one incident that happened after they had left the cathedral.

Mort Gilpin fell into step alongside her. Barbara was surprised to see him. Why would he come to Tom Lavette's funeral service?

"Miss Lavette, I know this is the worst time, but can we have a word?"

Her mind did its own research. Thinking of how odd it was to see Mort Gilpin here in Grace Cathedral, she also thought of the strange business of a woman's name. A man had his identity. Even in death, he was still Thomas Seldon Lavette, but what would she be when she died? Who would she be? Barbara Lavette? Barbara Cohen? Barbara Devron? Ms. Lavette, Mrs. Lavette, Miss Lavette? You don't solve such things at a funeral. She struggled to fix her attention on Mort Gilpin.

"Please, Miss Lavette."

They were outside. "Wait for me at the car," she said to the others.

Freddie was studying Gilpin curiously. The rest of the family made their way through the crowd, and meanwhile a stream of people, most of whom she hardly knew, some of whom she did not know at all, stopped to offer their sympathy to Barbara. It was an ancient rite; you had to cast your sympathy, like bread, on the water, whether it lay there soggy wet or not.

Freddie received sympathy coldly. If he had at least the decency to refrain from stating that he couldn't care less whether his father was dead or not, he did not, on the other hand, pretend to even a polite indication of grief. Barbara's grief was a slow thing, building to pain; now, at last, grief for what might have been and for all the petty annoyances and angers.

"What the hell are you doing here?" Freddie whispered to Gilpin.

"Paying my respects," he said coldly.

May Ling was waiting for Freddie, who grabbed her hand and walked off with her. Mort Gilpin blocked Barbara's way.

"Can't it wait?" Barbara asked.

"No. Let's cross the street." They had a few moments alone on the other side of the street, and Mort Gilpin said, "I should have told you this yesterday, but I couldn't reach you. You remember the fifty thousand dollars for the TV spots?"

A stab of pain went through Barbara. Of course she remembered, and she not only remembered but knew what Gilpin was going to say.

"It's none of my damn business what went on between you Lavettes in the past. All I know about the rich is squeezing money out of them, but you can bet your sweet life that the process tells me something. The fifty grand came from your brother, the same Thomas Lavette who is being buried today, and I didn't have to get down on my knees and brown-nose him. He asked me how much you needed, and then he wrote out the check. I thought you should know. He swore me to silence, but the hell with that. You can tell Freddie if you want to. The hell with him too." And with that, he turned and walked off.

It made Tom Lavette no easier to understand, no more alive, no more real. Barbara tried to recall a time when they were children; Tom had been there. He was a part of her life that resided in her earliest memories, always a part of her life, Tom in his first pair of long pants at a time when long pants had some meaning, Tom defending her from a couple of tough kids down on North Point, Tom with his first pair of white flannels, Tom with his tennis racquet and white sweater, Tom at Princeton. Where did it stop? Where did it all begin to crumble? When did Tom stop being Tom? Was it when he married Eloise? But Freddie was only four or five when Tom divorced Eloise, and Freddie's store of hatred was all at second hand. Was it Tom against their father, Dan Lavette? But that was business. How does hatred begin? How is it nurtured? Boyd had told her many times that the secret of the successful practice of the law was communication. "You can talk to anyone," he had said, "and you can be pretty damn sure that anyone wants to talk to you." And she had always told herself that one day she would talk to her brother, a long, sincere talk that would move all the resentment and hatred out into the open.

Now he was dead. They would never talk to each other.

The reading of Tom's will was painful, uncomfortable. The interested parties, called to the offices of Tom's attorneys, consisted of Lucy, Eloise, Freddie, Tom's only child, Barbara, and Joe Lavette, physician, half brother to Tom and Barbara. Neither Sam nor any of Joe's children had been mentioned by the attorney, Seth Richardson, the member of the firm permanently assigned to the enormous Lavette interests. A younger member of the firm, Digby by name, was also present. His presence gave Richardson, a tall, sallow and unsmiling man, the opportunity to say Digby, give me this, Digby, give me that. Richardson opened the proceedings by ordering, "Digby, give me the codicil."

Digby handed it to him, and Richardson continued, "This is a codicil to the will which I am preparing to read. For reasons that will be obvious in a few minutes, I am going to tell you the contents of the codicil before the will is read. The codicil provides for a separate fund of two million dollars, to be held in escrow. This fund is earmarked to pay the legal expenses of my firm, retaining us to fight any contest of any part of Mr. Lavette's will by any legatee. If no part of the will is contested, the two million will go to Mercy Hospital to establish a free clinic. Of course, you will all receive copies of the codicil as well as of the will itself. I will now read the will. Digby, hand me the will."

As Richardson opened the folder containing the will, he looked unsmilingly from face to face, and Barbara couldn't help thinking that in such dismal neutrality, the State Department must have lost a great entry.

"This is my last will and testament," Richardson read, his voice a toneless drone. "To my wife," Richardson read, "I leave absolutely nothing, not even good will or a shred of love. I have lived in fear and hatred of this woman, but now I am beyond her reach. She is rich enough in her own right, but she is still a minority stockholder in the Lavette enterprises. I am placing the controlling stock in a trust, to be used for the endowment of the following—" But before he could read the list of charities, Lucy Lavette stood up and drove a skinny finger at Richardson.

"We shall see," she said. "We are not without legal defenders, Mr. Richardson." And with that, she stalked out of the room.

Now the room was very silent until Richardson said, "There are no more comments on the part of the deceased Mr. Lavette. I will simply read the list of bequests, yet taking the liberty to make my own observation about the bequest to Mr. Lavette's son. As Mr. Lavette felt that his son, Frederick, had betrayed no interest in the various Lavette enterprises, his bequest is entirely in cash. Now the will: To my son, Frederick, twelve million dollars; to my sister, Barbara, two million dollars in United States Government bearer bonds; to my half brother, Joseph Lavette, one million dollars in United States Government bearer bonds. Whatever funds remain in my estate shall go to San Francisco Medical Center to take whatever steps they may feel necessary for the study of heart disease, which has taken the life of my father and, presumably, myself."

The newspapers made a large front-page story out of the

contents of the will. Barbara felt an immense surge of sadness. Sally telephoned Barbara to tell her how happy Joe was—he was not the kind of a person who could have expressed it himself—with the bequest. "We'll have a real clinic now, a real, functioning clinic, which is something he's dreamed about for years."

Freddie, however, received the news in grim silence. He made no comment whatsoever at the reading of the will. A month then passed, during which Barbara had no word from either Freddie or Eloise. Then Freddie telephoned and said he was going to be in town, and could he drop in for a drink?

"You're always welcome," Barbara replied.

"At four o'clock, Aunt Barbara. I hope we can be alone."

"No one else will be here, Freddie."

"That's good. I'll see you in a few hours."

His voice was without spirit or energy, and when he appeared at Barbara's house, he looked pale and tired. Barbara had not seen him since the reading of the will, and she wondered that a month could produce so profound a change. When Freddie's father married Eloise, he had chosen someone very much like himself in coloring and general appearance, as much as a very pretty young woman can resemble a man without the woman being less feminine and the man less masculine. The result, in Freddie, was a man who frequently made Barbara feel that she was seeing her brother as she remembered him many years ago, a tall, slender man, pale eyes and hair that was still the color of cornsilk. As a younger man, Freddie had been as lighthearted and easygoing as her own son, Sam, had been grimly serious. The change had come slowly.

"What will you have?" Barbara asked him. "I have a pot of coffee warming, or you can have a drink."

"Coffee, please."

When she returned with a tray that held a plate of cookies

as well as the coffee, Freddie was very seriously studying his fingernails. He glanced up at her as she set down the tray and asked, "Did my father ever meet Uncle Joe? I mean, did he know him at all? Did he know that Uncle Joe was a physician?"

Barbara thought about his question before answering, and Freddie, before she could answer, went on to say "I mean, a million dollars is a million dollars. You don't give away a million to a total stranger, do you?"

"I suppose not."

"I mean, did they ever meet?"

"Why is that so important to you, Freddie?" Barbara wondered.

"Because it's important. Because it's damn important!"

"All right," Barbara said soothingly. "As far as I can remember, they never met. Joe was an illegitimate child, conceived while my father was still married to my mother. Of course, later, when he married May Ling, he took out formal adoption papers for Joe. I don't think Tom ever got over his anger at my mother and father for their divorce. I think that's understandable if not too sensible. You might think about your own feelings toward your father, and perhaps you'll understand why Tom felt the way he did."

"Yes, I've thought about it. Why do you suppose he left Uncle Joe a million dollars? Guilt?"

"If there's one thing I learned as a writer, it is that there are no simple answers to human action or motivation."

"You must have thought about his motivations."

"Yes—"

"Why in hell's name did he do it? I've learned something about Jewish guilt, but he wasn't Jewish."

"Neither are you. Freddie, forgive me, and you know that I love you as much as if you were my own son, but you talk more damn nonsense than anyone I know. The Jews have no monopoly on guilt, but I don't think Tom did anything out of guilt. Time passed and he changed; things changed him, things that brought him great unhappiness, and I would guess that he was one of the most tragically unhappy men I've ever known. Maybe dead he could do things he couldn't do when he was alive. I don't know."

"When I was a kid," Freddie said, "I felt that putting aside that huge lump of money that your grandfather left you and turning it into a foundation and not taking a nickel out of it for yourself—well, I thought that was maybe the classiest quixotic act I had ever come across. I felt so damn proud that you were my aunt. I used to wonder whether, if I were in that position, I'd do the same thing."

"What difference does it make? Why should you brood over it?"

"Because I'm not and because I'm nothing I ever dreamed of being. I gave half of the money to May Ling. I'm keeping the rest."

He had been eating cookies furiously, stuffing his mouth as he spoke. Barbara had never seen him so rapacious for sweets before, nor had she ever seen him this tense. She picked up the plate and started toward the kitchen to replenish it.

"It's your money. But why divide it? May Ling's your wife."

"I'm leaving May Ling," he said dully.

Barbara turned around, plate in hand, and stared at her nephew. Then she put down the plate, her hand shaking, and stared at him again. "When did this happen?"

"It's been happening for years. Haven't you noticed?"

"I've noticed. You fight, you squabble. Every couple does. But you don't break up."

"It happens. Divorce happens. It happened to you, it happened to my mother."

Barbara took a deep breath and then said, "Yes, it happens. It certainly does happen." She picked up the plate. "I was going to get more cookies. Do you want more cookies?" She didn't know what else to say.

"Jesus Christ, no! To hell with the goddamn cookies! I tell you I'm leaving my wife, and you ask me if I want cookies!" He was scolding her, snapping at her as a kid does at his mother.

Barbara controlled her mounting anger and tried to see him as she would have seen Sam; indeed, as she had seen Sam—to be flattered by his coming to her instead of going to another. She realized that in search of some relief for his agonies, there had been no one else for him to turn to. So she said nothing at all, and he apologized, begging her to forgive indefensible behavior.

"There's nothing to forgive."

They both waited now, measuring each other, Barbara trying to remember what she, Barbara, was in his eyes. At sixteen, he had been madly in love with her; at twenty-one, in his last year in college, he had gone south in the big civil rights registration drive and had been taken and whipped by a gang of rednecks, and she had come to him in a hospital in Mississippi, and that was when he had said to himself that he would never marry or be content until he found a woman like her. His idol remembered. She reached out and took his hand.

His defense and explanation were commonplace. How many tortured and frustrated men had pleaded that their wives did not understand them! He defended May Ling and called her an angel. What did he mean when he said that his wife was an angel? What, in human terms, is an angel? What is a bitch? We are demented because the world is demented. We use code words and names because we understand nothing.

"Yes, I could stay with her and live with her—sure I could. She's sweet and kind, and she's beautiful, and she makes me absolutely crazy. What on God's earth do I do,

Aunt Barbara? Do I piss my whole life away satisfying a woman who can't understand one damn idea I have in my head?"

"Come on, Freddie," Barbara said softly, "people don't divorce for a mismatch of intellect. May Ling is bright. Do you understand everything that's in her head?"

"I don't know. I can't be fair to her. Well, there it is—my father, whom I hated all my life, leaves me the money to make me free."

"That's an odd way to look at it. You were making enough money at Higate to divorce if you had to."

"It's not that simple."

"I didn't think it was. The bitter truth, as O'Casey once put it, is that a man doesn't tire of one woman unless he's in the process of becoming untired of another."

"I suppose O'Casey was right. I don't know—I can't go on at Higate."

"Why?"

For a long moment, Freddie stared at Barbara without answering. Then he shook his head hopelessly and said, "I may as well tell you, because if I don't tell someone I'll go out of my mind. I'm going to marry Carla. I was the one who deflowered Carla when we were both kids, and her father and Adam came close to killing me then because Carla thought she was pregnant, which she was not, and Cándido Truaz has never forgiven me, and on top of everything, Sam is not only my cousin, but he's my best friend, and how much more tangled do you want it?"

"It's tangled enough," Barbara said sadly. "Have you spoken to May Ling?"

Freddie nodded.

"Is she taking it very hard?"

"She's been taking it very hard for a long time, Aunt Barbara. It breaks my heart, and I know that's a kind of rotten, dishonest thing to say, because I'm breaking her heart and still it's true. Do you believe me?"

Barbara nodded.

"So by now—"

"Come on, Freddie, the world hasn't come to an end. Marriages do. There are people who know how to be married, and there are those who don't, and someone would have to be blind not to see that nothing's working out between you and May Ling. What will you do?"

"There's enough money for May Ling. She'll have custody of Danny. Carla and I, after we're married—well, I thought we'd go to France. I know the wine country there, but I've never been to Alsace or to the Rheingau district in Germany. I'd like to study the Moselles and the Rhine wines, and then I've been thinking of the north of France and learning more about champagne. Maybe a year, possibly two years. There's two hundred acres for sale in the Valley, a few miles to the north of Higate. I've put a binder on it. The price is very high, but I can afford it, and I couldn't live anywhere else in the world except in the Valley." He went on talking, almost compulsively.

Barbara realized that Freddie's small world was coming to an end. All worlds come to an end, all lives, all dreams, and then all the bits of paper that remain are pasted together into different dreams. Everywhere—and she remembered the barrios of the Forty-eighth Congressional District, where there were neither toilets nor running water and often enough no electricity either; yet even there dreams were shaped and reshaped.

He was talking about Carla. "You don't like her?" he had just said.

"When she was married to Sam," Barbara said, "things lost their shape. I liked her before that and after that. She has quality."

"I want you to like her."

"Want Eloise to like her. That's what really faces her. It faces both of them."

In the end, Freddie thanked her. "For being willing to listen to me. I had no one to listen to me, no one."

"It's easy for me, Freddie. It's going to be very tough for you. It's not hard to listen. To do it right—whatever it is—that's hard."

As the months passed, it was not easy for Barbara. When you are young and things become dislocated, there is time ahead to patch things up and put them together again. Now that endless river of time seemed to be drying up. Barbara began to fall prey to the belief that things were different from the way they had been when she was young, heartlessly different. She was beginning to forget youth's necessity to be heartless. Otherwise they would be trapped—as she felt trapped!

Self-pity disgusted Barbara, yet it was no more controllable than some tuberous growth on the skin, and she was vain enough to choose an inner pain, if such a choice had come to her. But the inner pain was there without notice. When Sam neither visited nor called for two weeks, her misery grew inside her like a tumor. It was only slightly helped by Mary Lou's explanation. "You mustn't feel neglected, Barbara dear, because Sam hasn't had time to breathe, and I'm afraid I see him almost as rarely as you. He's observing a series of eye operations—you know, cataracts and such. Not that he'll ever be an eye surgeon, but Sam's curiosity just can't be satisfied."

Barbara had accepted Mary Lou as a woman with a mind and a will to look at the world with open eyes, but now she found herself irritated and provoked. Why did they have to be condescending? Why did the confrontation of an older person turn an otherwise intelligent and attractive woman into a duty-directed machine fueled by guilt? And how much of it was her own fault? Why did she fall into Sam's trap? All her life, she had been her own responsibility. She told herself angrily that now this must not change.

She went to the telephone and dialed a number. This is the way she would have proceeded thirty years ago, and being alone in the world with no one depending upon her and no one to account to, she could turn the boredom into a sort of laughter. She could act out the fact that loneliness and aloneness were two very different things. The number she dialed belonged to Jim Bernhard, a film producer and an old friend of Boyd's and hers. Years ago, she and Boyd would travel south whenever their spirits needed refurbishing, and after Boyd's death Bernhard had called several times, trying to persuade her to come and stay with him and his wife.

Barbara had always rejected the notion of going alone to experience what she had experienced only with Boyd. But Boyd had been dead full six years and more by now, and time has a way of dealing with the past. It was almost seven o'clock when Barbara put through the call, certainly the best time to find Jim Bernhard at home; and indeed he answered the phone himself, delighted to hear from her after so long a time.

"Nothing bad, I hope," he said, after the salutations.

"Just enough to make me desperate to get out of this place, and I thought I'd drive down the coast road, nice and easy, and perhaps you and Joan could put me up for a night."

"All the nights you can spare. We'd love it."

"Bless you."

"When?"

"Tomorrow night too soon?"

"Perfect."

She was free. She owned a 1974 Volvo, an old, reliable workhorse, and it held two small suitcases, a bottle of cold beer, and two sandwiches of creamy chèvre and parsley. She drove off like a kid running away from home at six o'clock in the morning, when it was barely light. She had her coffee and toast in a little roadside place, where she sat at the counter and giggled to herself and savored the knowledge that at this moment no one in the world knew where she was and, except for the Bernhards, where she was going. She had invested in a telephone answering machine, a wonderful little gadget that told the world that Miss Lavette was not at home, but if you waited for the electronic beep, you could talk for two minutes and Miss Lavette would return your call as soon as she returned home. Since Sam might properly be worried, she mailed a note to him which informed him that she was off for a few days.

She drank her beer and ate her sandwiches at a place where the Pacific Coast Highway dropped to a level only twenty feet or so above the beach. She parked her car by the road and climbed down to the beach, and then up onto one of those amazing rocks that dot the Pacific shore. Then, sitting up high, dressed in her blue jeans and blue work shirt, she drank beer and munched away at her chèvre sandwiches. A young couple came walking along on the sand, and they stopped and the boy said, "You want some help off there, lady?"

"Why?" Barbara asked him.

He couldn't bring himself to reply, but the girl asked in some amazement how she'd got up there.

"Climbed," Barbara said.

"Well, you could hurt yourself," the girl scolded.

"Oh, bug off," Barbara said.

They departed, rejected and miffed. There was no one else on the beach, only the gulls swooping and screaming, so Barbara sat happily on the rock for at least a half hour, savoring her place and position, remembering how at the age of seven she had climbed to the top of a set of monkey bars for the first time and rejoiced. Small victories can be very important ones.

She was in no hurry, and it was early evening when she reached Santa Barbara. She parked her car at Pueblo Gardens, a Mexican place right off the Pacific Coast Highway, ordered Mexican beer and an enormous taco and tortillas on the side, and stuffed herself properly, meanwhile chattering away in Spanish with the waiter. She had a good ear for the accent, and the waiter was impressed. A tall, heavyset young Chicano, he said to her, "Lady, you are no Anglo, are you?"

"Sure I am."

"Your Spanish is pretty good for an Anglo."

"Thank you."

"You live around here?" Speaking in Spanish gave him a lead toward intimacy he would not otherwise have dared exercise, and that, together with Barbara's jeans and blue work shirt, allowed him to study her with a warm grin.

"Just passing through."

"You got time, I'm off at nine. If you're still here, suppose we have a drink—if you feel like it, I mean."

"Sonny," she said in English, "I'm not only old enough to be your mother, I'm old enough to be your grandmother."

"You're kidding?"

"Bless you, no."

Driving south from Santa Barbara, she giggled again with delight.

At the Malibu Colony, the Bernhards were waiting for her, and they were out to greet her as she parked her car. It made her feel welcome. They both embraced her, obviously delighted to see her. Jim Bernhard was a large, heavy man in his middle sixties, white-haired and possessed of abundant energy. Joan was fifteen years younger, a slender, handsome woman who had been an actress and had given it up to raise four children. Two were in college and two were out in the world. The Bernhards' marriage of twenty-eight years had overcome all hurdles, healed all the wounds inflicted upon each other, each by the other, and settled down into an easy and comfortable partnership. Jim was just about ready to give up film production. Like many old-timers in the film industry, he was not thrilled by either the industry's taste or the public's taste, and he was perfectly content to swim, walk on the beach, read books and play gin rummy and sometimes chess with his wife. Since she enjoyed the same things, it made for an easy and uncomplicated household. They shared the cooking, and tonight it was grilled lamb chops and pilaf and sliced tomatoes. Barbara had not the heart to confess to them that she had stuffed herself with Mexican food only a few hours before. She joined them at the dinner table, amazed at how her appetite adjusted to the situation.

It was over six years since she had seen them; the last time was when they came to Boyd's funeral. In the beginning, they had been Boyd's friends, not hers, and she had taken to them slowly, suspicious as she was of anyone connected with the film business. But in every such situation, there are those who reverse the role, who make of the cliché a pattern of what not to do or be. The Bernhards did not sniff coke, they drank moderately, they did not possess a hot tub or a Jacuzzi, they didn't engage in switching and they did not go in for wild parties. They lived at Malibu because they loved the ocean; and after Barbara got to know them, Bernhard had asked her to write a screenplay—but asked her tentatively, as if it were certainly too much to ask of someone who was a good writer in another medium. Barbara based the screenplay on an incident she had witnessed during World War Two, when she had been a correspondent and had come across the case of a young soldier, stationed in Arabia, who had sex with a willing Arab woman. He was accused, tried and found guilty of a rape he did not commit, and was sentenced unjustly as a sop to the Saudis. The film was a moderate success, and the fact that Bernhard had it filmed without asking Barbara to change a word, or degrade it in any manner, endeared him to her. Seeing them with Boyd had been very pleasant, and though it had taken her years to will herself to see them without him, she discovered that it could continue to be good.

At the dinner table she talked about her drive down the coast and the delight she had taken in the few commonplace incidents she had encountered. She had no desire to talk about serious matters, feeling that her present mood of guilty pleasure in her truancy might be as fragile as a spider's web. The Bernhards, on the other hand, were intrigued by an election campaign already four years in the past, and they insisted on discussing it.

"It was a brief aberration," Barbara said. "It was a fit of ego. The little child who can't have her own way kicks and screams, hoping that it will put her small world in order."

"Not a good comparison," Bernhard said.

"Just reading about it, I became terribly excited," Joan told her. "I mean, I've never been the great feminist, but I began to tell myself that if Barbara could do it, then we could all do it."

"There are women in Congress," Barbara pointed out.

"Oh? How many in the House—a dozen? No, not even that. And how many in the Senate? I began to think, Just suppose half of Congress were women—"

"There she goes," Bernhard said.

"Really? And why not? We happen to be half of the human race."

"I got a notion for a TV show once," Barbara said. "It happened when I was working here on my first screenplay. Twenty years ago. That is a long time, isn't it? Well, you know that wonderful little lady Norma Felson, who plays the quintessential Jewish mother? What would happen, I asked myself, if she were elected to Congress?"

"Great idea," Joan said.

"So I decided. I set up a situation where my little lady is watching TV and discovers that here in America, in Appalachia, children are starving. Outraged, she decides to run for Congress and change all this. Her son is a lawyer, her daughter a smooth professional woman. Son and daughter think she's crazy. However, she puts her bridge club onto it and they get her on the ballot as an Independent. The Republican candidate is indicted for fraud. The Democratic candidate is mixed up with the mob. So the Democrats go all out for our little lady, figuring they can control her after she's elected, and, of course, she makes it. I have two standing sets. One is her West Side apartment in New York. The other is a section of Congress where we see Norma Felson with a Southern racist on one side of her, a born-again Christian on the other, a tough old politician behind her and a young me-generation know-it-all in front of her."

"Absolutely fantastic!" Bernhard exclaimed. "They should have grabbed it."

"They did. CBS grabbed it, just as you say. And do you know what they did?"

"I can guess," Joan said.

"You'd never guess. They began by saying, No Jewish mother. That was twenty years ago. So they changed the mother to a Wasp, which let Norma out. They thought Jane Wyman would be fine for the role, if they could get her. Then they washed out Appalachia, the mob, the bridge club and the election. They decided that the Wasp lady's husband should die and she takes over his seat in Congress. They insisted that her secretary should be a two-hundred-and-twenty-pound football player. Funny. Comic relief. And they felt that obviously such a lady should be a Republican."

"You're kidding."

"And what happened?" Bernhard asked.

"What would have to happen. They trashed it and then they junked it and it was never done."

"At least they paid for it."

"Oh, yes. They're very good about that. But the point I was making is that essentially this reflects their opinion of a woman. A decent woman who can't bear to see suffering. This they couldn't go with. And yet we dream of a Congress that's half women."

"It's a local disease, the Hollywood concept of women."

"They've infected the whole nation," Barbara said. "Here I am, sound of limb and reasonably clear mentally, and most of the time I feel that I'm looking at a world that has ushered me out. Damn it, I'm not ready to be ushered out. They laughed and trashed that idea of mine out of existence because it challenged their notion of a woman. Tell me," she said to Bernhard, "would you think seriously about making a film where a woman in her sixties or even in her seventies was the protagonist? I'm not talking about those cutesy numbers that Helen Hayes and Ruth Gordon have been doing, and I'm not talking about the specter of youth that comes from a couple of face lifts and the art of the makeup man. I'm talking about a serious film about an old woman."

"Right now?" Bernhard shook his head. "I don't know. I'm tempted to say that if the screenplay is good enough, we can get anything on the screen, but that's not the bottom line either. Some day, sure. Perhaps not yet."

"Some day. You see, Jim, Joan put her finger on it, didn't she? We're half of the human race, and properly we should be half of the Congress of the United States."

"And," Joan added, "we could hardly mess things up worse than the men have."

The talk went on. They had all the missing years to fill in. Barbara, hardly able to keep her eyes open, was ready for bed at ten o'clock.

"Make no apology," Jim Bernhard said. "Off to bed."

"And tomorrow, what kind of a program?" Joan asked.

"Bare feet and wet sand. I want to walk on the beach and lie in the sun. That will be as close to paradise as I have any right to expect."

When a week had gone by and Sam had had no word from his mother, other than the note telling him she'd gone away, he said to Mary Lou, "What do I do now? I don't know where she is. No one has heard a word from her. What do I do? Do I call the cops and tell them that my mother wandered off seven days ago?"

"That would be real smart, wouldn't it? Your mother would love that."

"I don't suppose she would. What's your suggestion?"

"That you leave her alone. She's perfectly capable of taking care of herself."

"I can't just forget about her. She's my mother."

"You forget about her very nicely when she's here on Green Street," Mary Lou pointed out.

"That's different. Then I know where she is."

"Well, right now she knows where she is."

"What's that supposed to mean?"

Mary Lou sighed and shook her head. "Nothing much."

"I'm worried about her. Do you know, I have a tennis date at the club. I'm late and I will be lousy. I'm always lousy when I have something like this on my mind."

"And you know," Mary Lou said, "you can be a sweet and compassionate and wonderful person."

"All right," Sam said with annoyance. "But I've turned into a louse because I don't want to be late or rotten for a tennis game and because I'm worried about my mother."

But Mary Lou, understanding Sam a good deal better than Carla ever had, made no reply to this but kissed him and told him that she loved him.

Eight

Divorce, as Barbara told Boyd, somewhat defensively, was not a matter of ceasing to love a man, but of being unable to continue to live with him and share his life. At least, such was her perception, and when Boyd had pointed out to her that a great many divorces end in hatred far more intense than the original love, Barbara argued that there had been no real love to begin with, which simply stated that Barbara Lavette was as incapable of defining love as anyone else in America. Barbara had married twice and loved twice without marriage, and death had made short shrift of one marriage and both loves; but the marriage that had ended in divorce had never truly finished. If she had hated Carson Devron, it would have been over, but her love for him had never turned into hatred, and his love for her was not a part of the divorce.

Probably he had never understood the divorce. "We can't hack it anymore." That's no excuse and meaningless. "It's just not working." "We tried." "We gave it our best shot, didn't we?"

None of that meant anything. Tag words, code words.

Carson, divorced, stayed with her—remote but nevertheless with her. There were other things besides his giving the campaign a polling mechanism, other gifts through the years, but always gifts at arm's length. If someone had ever asked her, Barbara would have replied, "Did we ever make love again? The answer is no." Boyd had never asked her.

Joan Bernhard sort of asked her. "We do want to have at least one celebration of sorts while you're here. Nothing very large or splendid. Jim and I gave up the large and splendid years ago. I was thinking of a small dinner party. Perhaps eight or ten people."

"Joan, it's not necessary," Barbara said. "I came to be with you."

"Most things aren't absolutely necessary. But if you don't mind?"

"Of course not."

"Some of our friends, and some of yours."

"You're my friends down here. You know that."

"What about Carson Devron? Still friends?"

"I haven't seen him in years, but the cords are still there. He's a good man."

"Then why don't we have him?"

"Marriage and kids, for one thing. I hardly think it's a good idea. No—no, I don't think so."

"It's not the best of marriages. She's in Palm Springs. He's here."

"How do you know that?"

"Any cocktail party here at the Colony, and you know everything. But this time, it comes from Jim. Carson's been his partner in a film now and then, and they lunch together every few weeks or so."

"I didn't know you even knew Carson."

"No," Joan said, "it's not anything we'd have talked about in front of Boyd. He was fiercely jealous of you."

"I know, poor dear. But Joan, just stop thinking whatever you may be thinking."

"What? Tell me what I'm thinking," Joan said, smiling.

"Dear Barbara, no. I'm thinking that if you and Carson are good friends, it would be nice for you to see each other after all these years."

"Yes, I want to see Carson," Barbara admitted. "I want to touch something that used to be, something that was a part of my life that isn't dead or broken or soured or lost. But I don't want to hurt anyone, not Carson, not his wife."

"I think we're all past the age of hurting people that way."

So it was to be just a casual meeting of old friends, yet Barbara tried on every piece of clothing she had brought with her, not once but twice, and finally sighed hopelessly and settled for a white blouse, a pink cashmere sweater and a full gray skirt. It was not fashionable, but all she had with her were a few skirts and sweaters and blouses.

She was coming downstairs after dressing when the doorbell rang. It was too early for Carson. Jim Bernhard opened the door, still in his apron as self-appointed cook, and a policeman on the doorstep inquired whether the Bernhards had a guest, name of Barbara Lavette.

Her heart stopped when she heard this, and all her guilts and fears, so easily set aside, now swarmed over her. "What is it?" she asked, her voice high-pitched and anxious.

"You're Barbara Lavette?"

"Yes. For God's sake, tell me what happened!"

"Nothing to get upset about," the policeman said. "The way I understand it, your son, Dr. Cohen—your son?"

"Yes, my son."

"All right, lady. He put out a missing person on you with the San Francisco cops—"

"What on earth are you talking about?" Barbara demanded. "Who's missing? Is my son missing?"

"You are, Miss Lavette," the officer said stolidly. "If your son is a Dr. Samuel Cohen, then he decided that you are missing and his information sheet suggested that you might be at the Colony here, but he didn't have any name or address, so the San Francisco cops called here and asked us to do a house check—"

Relieved, laughing now, Barbara tried to assure the policeman that it was some kind of stupid joke.

"Well, if it is, ma'am, your son put us to a lot of trouble. If you'll give me the telephone here, I'll report it back to San Francisco."

When the policeman had left, both Bernhards—Joan having joined them at the door—turned to stare at Barbara.

"No, I did not tell him where I was going," Barbara said. The Bernhards still made no comment. "I ran away," Barbara said hopelessly. "I wanted to do it all my life. I finally did it."

Once Jim Bernhard had invited Carson, who said that he would be delighted to come but that he would be coming alone, both Bernhards felt that they would do best to have no other guests. "In fact," Jim had said to Barbara, "when Carson asked me who else would be here, aside from you, I told him just Joan and myself. I had a feeling that as much as he might want to see you, he would have bowed out if others were here."

Barbara decided that Bernhard had been quite right. As casually as she might take an evening with Carson, he on the other hand might look forward to it with great anticipation. The years that had passed did not matter, time did not matter—that well she knew him and understood. For men like Carson, the unfulfilled is always laced with golden webs of wonder. He would come tonight as he had come almost twenty-five years ago to a party given for Barbara by William Goldberg, her producer; and he had come then not because he liked parties—he hated them—but because he was already in love with the author of *Driftwood*, whom he had never met. And tonight, as his herald, a delivery boy appeared with two dozen long-stemmed roses.

It prompted Jim Bernhard to say to his wife, softly, in the confines of their bedroom, "I don't know which of them is more the idiot child or more the wonderful person. Why couldn't they stay married?"

"If we knew that, we could sell marriage prognoses and make us a bundle."

"Of course, it's pretty damn easy to love Carson."

"At his age?"

"I happen to be older than he is," Bernhard informed her.

"And how old would that make him?"

"I'm not sure. He's younger than Barbara."

At first, at the dinner table, the conversation was constrained. The Bernhards, doing their own cooking and serving, took turns in the kitchen. A maid came in the morning and left at noon, and for a large dinner party, they would have had help. But tonight there were only the four of them, and Jim Bernhard had poached salmon fillets for the main course and had wrapped Brie cheese in phylo to go with the salad, which in California precedes the main course. With an icy cold Sicilian wine, it made a meal that nobody could fault and a conversation piece as well.

But after exhausting the virtues of the food and the beauty of the Pacific, iridescent in the moonlight, and the pleasure of eating in sight of a boundless ocean, Carson Devron became strangely silent. He was a large, handsome man, his once blond hair turned white, his manner, for all of his very real diffidence, the manner of a man who has ordered other men and indeed ruled a substantial empire all of his adult life, the Devron holdings in Southern California being very much of an empire. Some years younger than Barbara, he lacked her ebullience. Barbara approached each day as if she had never actually experienced a day before. What was always new to her was old to Carson Devron, who appeared to exist in a rigid frame of depression.

On first entering the Bernhard house, he had smiled with pleasure and embraced Barbara as if she had conferred an ultimate favor upon him. He fussed over her appearance, repeated his observation that time had dealt so well with her, and treated her for all the world like an attractive young woman.

But now that brief spell of excitement had worn off, and he sat, mute and worried, at the dinner table. Barbara took up the slack with observations about the role of food in the current world of the middle class, recalling that in her youth there was no ideology of food.

"And is that what you'd call it, really—an ideology of food?" Joan wondered.

"Pick up any newspaper—pages devoted to food, cooking, spices, quick cooking, gourmet cooking—"

"Like mine," Bernhard said.

"Oh, absolutely. Or try a bookstore. Almost half is cookbooks. And this dinner—wonderful dinner. But thirty years ago, who would ever dream of serving this marvelous poached salmon, cooked by a man, no less." She went on chattering, a woman who rarely chattered, and at the same time reflecting on the fact that she was clinging to this nonsense because Devron sat opposite her like some damn Indian sachem, never saying a word.

Whatever the constraints within the Bernhard house, the weather outside was delightful, rather warm for a seaside evening, but nevertheless with a clean edge in the air that called for a heavy sweater. So when Barbara suggested a walk on the beach after dinner, Joan was quick to second the motion and provide sweaters—and at the same time to be greatly relieved that the grim attitude Devron had fallen into would not be encased for dreary hours by the walls of her living room. "You and Carson go ahead," Joan said. "We'll be with you as soon as we straighten up a bit."

"Shoes full of sand," Carson muttered, once they were out and walking on the beach. "I never did like the damn beach."

"You loved the beach," Barbara told him. "What happened, Carson? What awful thing happened to you?"

"No awful thing at all."

"Carson, I'm no stranger. We were married."

"Yes, we were."

"Could you smile once? Once. Just once, so that I'll know that somewhere inside that damn perfect decathlon body of yours a human being survives."

"Damn perfect decathlon body—" He began to laugh.

"There you are. Funny. You are still Carson."

"Hardly. I'm trying to diet my way out of a triple bypass, which is why Jim served salmon. I passed on that marvelous cheese dish. I just spent a month at the Pritikin Institute. Your perfect decathlon body leaves a hell of a lot to be desired."

"Oh, I'm sorry. I didn't know."

"Nothing to be sorry about. I live with it, and if I've been a pain in the ass tonight, it has nothing to do with my health. At least not with my physical health. My life stinks, Barbara. That's the long and short of it. Aside from my work, it's not worth a plugged nickel."

"I don't believe that," Barbara said. "I don't believe it for one moment."

"No," he said with annoyance, "no, you wouldn't believe that. You never did understand me. You never could figure out why I didn't dance through life the way you do, without one damn care in the world. Oh, no. No—"

Barbara stopped short, grasped his arm and pulled him around. "Just cut that out, because it's pure bullshit, and you know it is. If you want to talk, we'll talk and try to make some sense. Otherwise, let's go back."

"You're really mad," Carson said in astonishment. "You're really angry. I've never seen you so angry before."

"Sure I'm angry. I've been a widow for almost seven years. Try being a widow some time. Try looking at a telephone that stops ringing, that doesn't ring for a week at a time. Try being invited to a dinner party where you know damn well that it's poor Barbara, and it's just too long since we invited her, and try shopping around in a world that doesn't want you or need you! But I don't whine and whimper about it. I'm older than you. Damn you, Carson, I was so excited and delighted about seeing you again that I didn't sleep last night—not a wink—and what do I find—"

"You were? So excited you didn't sleep? Come on."

"Damn right I was. And there are the Bernhards coming out of their house, so do we walk or go back and tell them the evening's over?"

"Let's walk."

They walked on, the Bernhards making no effort to overtake them, and after a minute or so, Carson asked, "Is it true what you said before—you were that pleased to see me?"

"True. Good heavens, Carson, we were married, we slept with each other. We made love. We shared our dreams and our fears." She took his hand. "You don't forget that."

"No, you don't. I was whining?"

"I'm sorry I said that."

"I *was* whining. You're right. Absolutely right. I'm trapped. You may be suffering all the miseries of being a widow—which I don't believe for a minute, because you would beat the shit out of being a widow or anything else—but still you're not trapped. Not the way I am. There's something you can't really understand, which is a very beautiful woman who is stupid. But you meet such a woman, and her beauty spells out everything else, because that's the American doctrine, fed everywhere by Hollywood, and she has to be wonderful and understanding and kind and clever, and that's what I married, and so help me God she's as stupid as our Irish setter, who's also very beautiful and very stupid. Only the Irish setter can't talk, thank heavens. This one can talk. Would you believe it, she calls me Kit Carson in front of others? But she doesn't understand anything I say and never will. Do you know why she's in Palm Springs, which is, forgive me, the utter asshole of creation? Damn it, you're laughing at me!"

"Carson!" She threw her arms around him and kissed him. "Carson, Carson, I'm not laughing at you. I'm laughing at our ridiculous world. Don't be offended. Why is she in Palm Springs?"

"Because she thinks people like Sinatra and Hope and Jerry Ford and the Reagans and the Annenbergs are wonderful and bright and diverting and admirable, and she believes that to be in that hot desert pisshole is the summit of human achievement."

"You could divorce her."

"My dear lady, divorce is not something you make a profession of, not if you're a damn Devron, and we have three kids, and she's as decent as one can be with an IQ of about ninety, and she knows by now that I'm delighted for her to be in Palm Springs while I'm here in L.A. running the paper, and we haven't had sex in the three years since my heart attack, because if I'm going to pass out while screwing someone, it won't be my miserable wife. It'll be someone I care about." He stopped suddenly, and then, "Are you listening to me? Have you ever heard me talk like this before? What has gotten into me? Let's join the Bernhards before I say anything else."

Devron called the following day, just before noon, and asked Barbara to have dinner with him that evening, to which Barbara replied that she would love to, except that she was leaving today, having already overstayed and abused the hospitality of the Bernhards.

"Stay another day," Carson begged her.

"I simply can't."

"Well, where will you go from here?" Carson wanted to know.

"I don't know. I had thought of driving down to Tijuana, but I've lost the taste for it, and now I don't know where I want to go, except that I have no great desire to go home."

"Then listen to me, please," Carson pleaded. "I have an important meeting tonight, but I put it off until ten o'clock, thinking I could take you to dinner. Let me do that. If you feel that you must leave the Bernhards, then why not drive into town and spend a night at the Beverly Wilshire or some such place and then take off tomorrow?"

"Carson," she said, "is it so important to see me again?"

"Important for me—yes. Believe me. Seeing you after all these years is not something I can leave with an argument on Malibu Beach, which I concluded with the ravings of a lunatic. My God, we do enough clowning in the normal course of things. Don't leave me with this kind of memory of being with the one woman I have been able to love."

Poor Carson, she was thinking. What a mouthful of words! He'd never tolerate that in one of his editorials.

She couldn't refuse, and she said, "All right, Carson. The Beverly Wilshire."

"I'll pick you up at six-thirty. That's not too early, is it?"

"Six-thirty," Barbara agreed.

But when she told the Bernhards what she intended, their response was to be hurt and to spell that out. "You've been here ten days," Joan said, "and it's been a perfectly wonderful visit, and why you should feel for a moment that you've overstayed your welcome, I don't know. At least stay another night. Let Carson come here."

"No. I think he wants to stay in the city. He said something about an important meeting at ten o'clock. You've been wonderful, but no guest ever left too soon."

After Barbara had driven away, Joan Bernhard admitted to herself that she was somewhat relieved. "Even with someone you love," she said to her husband, "ten days is long enough. And Barbara—I love her, I do love her—but she makes me feel that nothing in the world is right. She won't leave it alone—the government, the bomb. Can't she just relax and live with it?"

"No. That's Barbara."

Barbara had her own sharp twinges of guilt. Her mother had long ago impressed upon her that in polite circles—which were the only circles a lady should ever seek—one did not discuss three subjects, namely, religion, money and politics, which as far as Barbara was concerned left very little of interest. She had learned long ago that dinner table discussion of art and letters was limited to very few, and while the partial liberation of women had made talk of sex possible, it was often less than enlightening. However, why annoy people who liked you? Why indeed?

After Barbara had greeted Carson in the hotel lobby and then seated herself in his car for the drive downtown to a restaurant of his choice, she said to him, "Do you find me boring when I dwell on things not very nice?"

"Most things are not very nice," Carson decided. "And boring? No indeed; I have never found you boring. But it's an odd question."

"I feel guilty. I like the Bernhards enormously, but I think I troubled them. You know, when I was a little girl and left food on my plate, our nanny would remind me that there was enough food left on my plate to save the life of some small child dying of hunger in China, after which I stuffed the food into my gullet, never inquiring how one could get what was left on my plate to China and save the life of the poor child."

"The curse of those rich enough to have a nanny."

"You're missing the point completely, and I've paid the price in guilt for being a rich kid."

"I don't think I've missed the point," Carson said. "I'm only needling your guilt. The fact is that the Bernhards live out there in one of the loveliest spots on earth, and they want to live pleasantly and quietly and forget about all the small starving kids, because they feel they can't do much about it and they've never really felt that they had to do much about it. You and I, Barbara love, are different. We are cursed with what Veblen called the conscience of the rich, and all our lives we've brooded over what a cesspool most of society is."

"That's not because of any such notion as the conscience of the rich," Barbara protested. "Most of the rich I've known don't have a shred of conscience—and as for Mr. Veblen, he wrote as much nonsense as anyone else who sets out to be a fancy philosopher, and you call me Barbara love and never even paused to give me a peck on the cheek there in the hotel lobby. I suppose you decided that there was no way you could walk into the hotel without half a dozen people saying, There goes Carson Devron, and if you bussed me, you'd be compromised."

"Exactly. Would you like me to kiss you now?"

"Too late. Tend to your driving. Anyway, if someone saw you kissing me, they'd think I was your mother—"

"You're nothing like my mother."

"Or your Aunt Becky from—wherever she comes from. For heaven's sake, Carson—"

"I love you," he said quietly. "I always have. I forget what desire is until I'm near you. Goddamn it, don't lament your age. It's a damn lie and a fraud you're using, and I've never known you to lie before!"

Barbara made no reply, only thinking about what he said, until they reached the parking area of an Italian restaurant on Washington Boulevard in Culver City. Neither had he spoken. When he got out of the car and opened the door for her, she said, "Thank you, Carson. That was a good thing you said to me."

"May I kiss you now?"

"If you still want to."

He took her in his arms and held her to him, his open lips against hers. It was the first time any man had done that since Boyd died.

The restaurant was called the Gondolier, and the proprietor, Vito Lucheno, knew Carson and welcomed him as if he were royalty, which perhaps he was as such things go in Los Angeles. The restaurant was dark, poorly lit, as are most restaurants in Los Angeles, as if each and every one of them recognizes the city as a place of countless assignations. When Barbara was with Carson, she had the feeling that everyone in the city knew him, even though, as he explained, he came to the Gondolier only two or three times a year.

"But why come here at all?" Barbara wondered. "It's so out of the way."

"That depends on one's destination. We're only a few blocks from the M-G-M Studios, so it's a good place to eat if you're seeing someone from Metro, and the food is good."

"Is that where you're going tonight—to the studio?"

"Oh, no. Not at all. There's a little enclave of people, mostly refugees and illegals, from El Salvador, and I promised to see some of them tonight, leading figures in the struggle against the government, and since it's not far from here, I decided this would be the best place to eat and squeeze out the last minute I can be with you."

Mr. Lucheno came to the table now to take their order himself, and after he had done so he opened a large bottle of red Italian wine and ceremoniously poured two glasses, to which Carson added, "To Barbara Lavette!"

After they had tasted the wine, Barbara asked, "Is this a deep secret, this thing with El Salvador?"

"Oh, no. Not at all. But as I said, they're illegals and nervous. They refused to meet at my office. Have you been reading about that poor damn place?"

"More than I want to, Carson. I was a correspondent during World War Two, as you know, but I don't think I ever encountered anything during those years that shook me as much as the incident of the Catholic nuns and the churchwoman who were murdered down there. It was only a month ago, and still when I think of it, I am cold and sick. I wasn't in Europe to see the liberation of the death camps where millions of Jews were murdered, but I saw enough of horror. I don't know why, but this was different."

"We're not used to the deliberate murder of nuns by soldiers who are supposed to be our allies. We used to believe that that brand of barbarity existed only in Hitler's Germany. And I suppose what makes it worse is Mr. Reagan's brushing it aside."

"Then they know—the government, the CIA?"

"Of course they know. The women were murdered and raped on orders of a creature called Luis Antonio Aleman. National Guard in El Salvador. Now where does the *L.A. World* come into it? The *New York Times* and the *Washington Post* both have their men in San Salvador. Of course, we have the United Press and the Associated Press and Reuters, but there's a difference in having your own man, who writes what he sees and who sees it from our point of view. We've been talking about it, and we have been pressured by this little group of political refugees, and I agreed to meet with them and let them convince me that Los Angeles needs a correspondent in El Salvador. I must say, I don't need much convincing—and there it is, on the one night that we have to be together. Anything else I could have ducked. But I have some deep feeling about this."

"Carson," Barbara said eagerly, "Carson, if I remember right, your Spanish is lousy."

"Oh, no, I wouldn't say that."

"Rotten."

"Come on, Barbara, I had eight years of Spanish in school."

"Carson, take me along. Then we have the whole evening together. The Central American Spanish isn't Castilian, not by a long shot. It isn't even Mexican. My Spanish is good. So take me with you tonight, and between us we'll make out."

"It's not a bad idea," Carson agreed. "I don't think they'd mind. Introduce you as a writer. They want to talk to writers. But why? I admit I'm enormously flattered, but this morning I had to go down on my knees to get you here."

"No, don't say that. Carson, I'm not young. A man comes on to me—"

"I'm not any man!"

"I know, I know, but I can't handle it anymore. I don't know how. What woman my age does know how? We're not supposed to. You know that. Inside, we feel no different. You're the only one in the world I could talk to like this. You want a man's arms around you so desperately you could cry out in pain. You want a man in bed next to you, and damn it, you want sex, and I look at you and I feel crazy, I want you so much."

He reached across the table and took her hands in his. "That's enough," he said softly. "I love you. I've always loved you. I am not going to apologize for that, and I don't want you to apologize for one damn thing. You don't have to go with me tonight or try to convince me that your Spanish is better than mine—which I am sure it is—or to give us another hour. I'll take you back to your hotel after dinner, and I'll meet you later."

"But I want to go with you," Barbara said.

"Why?"

"Carson, when I was campaigning for Congress up north in the Forty-eighth C.D., I found a corner of the place where a wretched barrio existed—Salvadoran illegals. I spoke to some of them, and something about the whole incident dug into my guts and stayed there. Then, when I read what happened to the nuns, I had my own hour of sickness and despair. I don't know why I haven't been able to live like other women, but I haven't, and all my life I've had this umbilical cord tying me to the horrors of this poor cursed planet. It's too late for me to alter my character and become content. Can you see me as a contented old lady, sitting by the fireplace and waiting for eternity?"

"No, I'm afraid not."

"Then let's eat, and bless you for listening to my rambling."

It was less than half a mile to the house where Carson's meeting had been scheduled, the type of house that had once been the face of Los Angeles and that had been called, in another era, a California bungalow. It was an oblong frame house, tile roof and a porch across the front. This particular bungalow sat in a weed-grown yard and cried out for paint and patching. The door was opened for them by a slight, brown-skinned, dark-eyed woman of about twenty years. Her English was hardly understandable as she asked what they wanted, and Carson hastened to assure her in Spanish that he was Carson Devron of the *Los Angeles Morning World,* and that he was there at the invitation of Professor Dante García and that the lady with him was Barbara Lavette, a writer and associate. He spoke in Spanish, and he was answered in Spanish.

"Yes, of course. We are expecting you. I am Lucía, Professor García's daughter." She led them through a small hallway into a living room, where three men stood up to greet them. The furniture in the room was old and decrepit, a broken-down couch, four kitchen chairs and a kitchen table. But the place was clean and neat, and to Barbara there was something woeful at the sight of a bottle of red wine, six plastic cups and a plate of packaged cookies on the table, the necessary hospitality of great poverty. One of the men, bearded and older than the others, at least in his mid sixties, wearing glasses over deep-set, pain-filled eyes, introduced himself as Professor Dante García. A man of about thirty, wiry, nervous, his hands locked in front of him, clenching and unclenching, a fierce mustache drooping down over his chin, was introduced as José Santiago, and the third man, slender, scholarly, a great scar, chin to ear, marring a pleasant face, was introduced as Brother Jesús Domingo; he was a Franciscan monk. He, like Santiago, wore blue jeans and a blue work shirt. Only the professor was carefully attired in a threadbare three-piece suit.

They all shook hands with Carson and Barbara; and Professor García, speaking in English, and apparently knowledgeable of American literature, recalled her novel *Driftwood,* and remarked that he had read it with interest and enlightenment.

Thanking him, Barbara explained that they both spoke Spanish and that it might be easier for everyone if they used that language. The professor thanked her, admitting that his two colleagues spoke almost no English.

"We are very anxious to talk to you," Professor García said, "very anxious, believe me, because people say you will help us."

"Help you, no," Carson said firmly. "Write about you— well, that's another matter. We come here to listen, to hear your side of this business in El Salvador. If it's a story, we will write it and print it as truthfully as we can, and if it merits someone on the scene, we'll send a correspondent down to El Salvador. I think my paper is open-minded and fair, as fair as any newspaper on this continent."

"That is all we ask," García said. "But before you hear our testimony, I would like to say a few words about my country, since until a few years ago, no one in the United States even knew we existed. A very small country, El Salvador, hardly as large as your state called Massachusetts, with a population of almost five million people—imagine, a country not much larger than Los Angeles County, and still half of it wild scrub and jungle and mountains. We are, I think, the most densely populated country in the world and possibly the poorest people in the world. My people are almost all mestizo, which means a mixture of Spanish and Indian blood, and maybe a few hundred thousand of Indian blood alone—"

"You say half the land is arable," Barbara broke in. "How do you live? How do you survive?"

"Very poorly, señora, very poorly indeed, because, you must understand, my people do not own the half of the land that is arable. Eighty percent of the land that can grow anything better than mesquite is in the hands of ten percent of my country's population. They operate great plantations, true latifundia, where they grow coffee and sugar cane and cotton. The men who labor in these plantations earn perhaps ten dollars a week, the women eight dollars, and the children—a dollar, two dollars. Seventy percent of the people cannot read or write, and perhaps ninety percent are functionally illiterate. For them, tiny plots of land, which they must work with love and care to grow their beans and melons—if they are lucky enough to have a plot of land. And a few dozen families live like princes, with great houses and servants. I read that you have here a large and powerful movement against abortion, but if they only came to Salvador, they would see that our children begin to die the moment they leave the womb. But the few families who own the plantations, the banks, and of course, the government, which means the country itself, their children are strong and healthy and they are sent here to the States to go to private schools and then to Stanford and Yale and Harvard. But the ordinary people, Señor Devron, I don't know whether in all the world there are people who suffer so."

"But you resist. You fight back."

"Even a mouse fights back when it is being destroyed."

"Tell him a little of our history," the man with the mustache said, the man whose name was Santiago. He had been watching the professor intently as he spoke, nodding his head, his hands never still. He fascinated Barbara; she felt him as a warped bundle of pain and anger, pain endured and anger controlled.

"A hundred years ago, the plain people, the peasants, owned most of the land. Much of it was held in common. Indians, mestizos—they cannot truly comprehend private ownership of the land. It is not in their culture to have a man say, I own the land. God creates the land. God gives it to the people. So when a few rich and powerful families banded together to take the land from the people, the people resisted."

"But tell them!" the man with the mustache interrupted. "No, I'll tell them. You say, fight back? In nineteen thirty-two, we fought back. My grandfather, Raoul Santiago, was one of the leaders. Thirty-two thousand of our people were killed by the soldiers of the rich. Among all of us, we had perhaps two hundred old guns, knives, clubs, sickles. They killed us until they could kill no more, until their fingers were too tired to pull a trigger, until the hand was too tired to slit a throat. My father was a little boy. He hid in a basket in the house, but through the basket he saw them come into the house. They murdered his mother. The new baby they killed by smashing his head against the doorpost. My father's two sisters, one nine and one twelve, they raped. A nine-year-old raped, and then they chopped off their heads with machetes. That's what happens when we fight them, and still we fight them. Last year alone, the death squads murdered fourteen thousand people."

"José, enough!" the professor cried.

"Enough? Why is it enough? I'm a revolutionary," he said to Barbara and Carson. "The professor here is not entirely sure that he approves of fighters. He feels there is a peaceful way. He still hopes for something from Duarte. Did I say before how many in nineteen thirty-two? No one counted. There is a ravine called Poco Colorado a few miles from San Salvador, maybe twenty feet deep, maybe ten feet wide. It was filled with bodies, women and children mostly —but who was to count?"

"José, enough!" García shouted.

"It touches him. He's a distant relative of the other García. No, I must go on—"

"Let him go on," Barbara said. "I want to hear it."

"I'll tell you something about Duarte," Santiago said. "He is a good, brave man whom I would trust if I did not know what happens to a man who falls into the hands of the rich and their death squads. First they stole the election of nineteen seventy-two from Duarte, and then the army officers arrested him, tortured him, beat him unmercifully, smashed his nose, his cheekbones—well, what happens to a man after that? I understand such things. They smashed my own nose, knocked out most of my teeth, put three bullets into me and then left me to die. Oh, Jesus Christ, you ask did we fight back?"

The third man, Brother Jesús Domingo, who had not spoken until now, put his arm around Santiago. "You must forgive José. He has suffered too much. I know how he has suffered. I know how we all suffer." He touched the scar on his face. "They did that with a branding iron. They like to play with a hot iron. I gave the last rites to a peasant they had shot. He wasn't a fighter. He wasn't part of the resistance. He was only a poor householder, whom they shot because, when the resistance leaves a village, it is their pleasure to shoot the villagers. Do you think we are Communists? I was called a Communist because I heard the confession of a dying man. He was called a Communist because he lived in the village. His wife, whom they raped and shot, was called by them a Marxist. Do you think anyone, any peasant, knows what Marxist means?"

"You're denying there are any Communists among the guerrillas? Is that what you're telling us?" Carson wanted to know.

"Oh, no," the professor said. "No. Santiago here is a Communist. He doesn't deny it. I am not. Brother Jesús is not. Santiago is a good Catholic; I am not. You North Americans never try to understand such things. You want everything black or white. If you had helped Castro to throw the Mafia and the dope kings and the pimps and the assorted bloodsuckers out of Cuba, he would have been your friend and ally. But always you are against us, against the people who want to live like human beings. So you create the Communists and you drove Castro into the arms of Russia. Duarte won in nineteen seventy-two. That is the truth, and your people knew it, but the landowners and the bankers in my country were against Duarte, and the army stole the election and you would not help him. You keep saying democracy, but you will not support real democracy, and so we did the only thing that was left to do—we listened to the Communists and the other radicals and we went into the mountains to fight. But what is my word? What is Santiago's word? What is Brother Jesús' word? Only if you send your own person down there will we be validated."

"How do you know he will write the truth?" Barbara asked.

"If he is not a politician, if he is not part of your government, he will look around him and see. Then he will write the truth, be assured. So with the people from the *New York Times* and the *Washington Post.* They are writing the truth."

They drove to Ocean Avenue in Santa Monica, where they parked and then walked on the footpath high above the beach and the glistening Pacific. The moon was full, and the cold current of air, flowing in from the sea, was sweet and clean and untainted with smog. They had spoken little in the car. Only now, Barbara wondered how Carson responded to what they had heard.

"You run a newspaper; well, it's almost like being a cop, without the intimacy with misery and horror. You look at it from a distance; nice things don't make news."

"Does this make news?"

"Oh, come on, Barbara, don't needle me. This is run of the mill—well, maybe a bit more. People are jaded. They've had Hiroshima and Vietnam. Do you think anyone really gives a damn about a pint-size banana dictatorship in Central America?"

"When I suggested that you drive to Santa Monica and that we walk on Ocean Avenue and breathe some clean air and get the nausea out of our systems, you agreed. I know you a long time, Carson. You felt something."

"I felt something. Sure. Damn it, Barbara, you're ready to weep over every motherless child on earth, every injustice. Every bit of horror. I'm not. I can't afford to."

"You can afford a good correspondent down there."

"I'll bring it up. We'll talk about it."

"I think I want to go back to the hotel," Barbara said.

"Now you're angry at me. If you want the truth, Barbara, that's where our marriage went straight to hell. I did what I had to do by my lights, and you couldn't stand that. It had to be by your lights or nothing at all."

"That's the way you saw it?"

"You're damn right!"

"Oh beautiful. Now we're having a fight—why? Why?" she demanded. "What have I said to make you so angry?"

"It's what you haven't said."

"Oh, yes. Of course. No, I'm just too tired and too old for that kind of kid stuff. Take me home."

It was almost midnight when they reached the Beverly Wilshire Hotel. Carson gave his car to the attendant and went into the hotel with Barbara, who told him that he didn't have to do that.

"I can't leave you this way. If we say goodbye like this, what are the chances that we'll ever see each other again?"

"Thin."

"Have a drink with me."

Barbara faced him, studying him thoughtfully. She had loved him so much. She loved men; she even felt at times that she understood them; and she had always been able to make a sort of compact with them. They valued her, apart from love or desire—two very different things, *value* and *love*. Perhaps she never thought of it in precisely those terms, yet she understood it.

"Sure," she said.

They went into the bar, and Barbara had a Scotch and soda. She drank very little and could count on one hand the times in her life when she had been drunk, but it was a social convention of great importance. It gave them both an opportunity to sit down and loosen the tightness that had enveloped them. Carson had a double bourbon on ice. They drank and looked at each other. Carson saw opposite him a tall woman, a good face, gray hair, lean in her figure and lifting her glass with a hand that did not shake. He remembered the same woman in bed in his arms, and he wondered how much he desired to have her in his arms and in bed again. Or was even the thought inappropriate? In any case, was it desire or need or what? And suppose he pushed it to that end? Would he be impotent? That could be the conclusion, likely as not, but even more important was the direction of his thoughts. Why should their bodies join? He had been scrapping with her over nothing at all, and now he was loosening. Why not just sit here and enjoy what was certainly a very remarkable woman? Why couldn't he break the cords?

"Shall we have another?" he asked Barbara.

"Yours was a double bourbon?"

"We're not married. If I get drunk, you can leave me here weeping into my cups."

She drained the rest of the Scotch and soda. "Simply stated, I don't like to sit in judgment on anyone."

"That will be the day," Carson said.

"Anyway, Devrons don't get drunk. One needs blood to get drunk. The blood was drained out of the Devrons and replaced with liquid money."

Carson ordered another double bourbon, and Barbara had another Scotch, this time on the rocks.

"That's a very colorful image. No such thing as liquid money," Carson assured her.

"I heard that your father gave a cool million to the Reagan campaign."

"He runs his shop. I run mine. I don't tell him what to do with his ill-gotten wealth, and he doesn't tell me what to put in my newspaper."

"Hurrah."

"What does that mean?"

"It means hurrah."

The drinks came, and Carson lifted his glass. "To all poor bastards like Carson Devron who live on the thin edge of desolation."

"I won't drink to that," Barbara said.

"Why not?"

"Self-pity. I don't like you when you get into self-pity. Here's mine: *L'chaim!*"

"What's that? No, don't tell me. That's a Jewish toast and it means *to life.*"

"Score ten."

"Probably got it from Boyd."

"Nope. My first husband, Bernie."

He finished his drink and signaled the waiter.

"Oh, come on, Carson, hold on," Barbara said. "You'll be drunk as a lord. I want to talk to you, and I don't want you sodden drunk."

"How drunk?"

"Just a tiny bit. Like me. What's gotten into you? You never used to drink."

"Make it a single," he told the waiter magnanimously. "I'm not drunk," he said to Barbara. "I love you. In fact, I adore you. We took on a kid and he did a sidebar for something on FDR, and he wrote that FDR adored his little dog. Love, I told him. You can love a dog, but you only adore a woman."

"Interesting point," Barbara admitted. "Last year you ran an editorial admitting that the right-to-life movement had valid aspects."

"They ran that while I was in Europe. It wasn't the end of the world. My wife is on the steering committee of the Southern California right-to-life organization. She does her thing. I do mine."

"You Devrons are a remarkable family, each unto his own. You know something, Carson, if men became pregnant and bore the children, there wouldn't be any right-to-life movement, would there?"

"My mother used to say, When steers sprout wings, it'll beef things up."

"I don't think that's so clever."

"Look," Carson said, "I tell you how much I love you,

and I sit here thinking about going to bed with you—and you put me down. I'm the publisher of the *Los Angeles Morning World,* and it's the damn best newspaper in the United States, except maybe the *Washington Post* and the *New York Times,* except that Washington isn't a city but a company asshole, so we'll settle on the *New York Times,* and I'm not so sure that they're so much better than we are, and nobody puts me down except you. Why do you do it?"

"I don't know. Maybe because I love you."

"Hell, you don't put down someone you love!"

"If you love him and you don't want to, because it's all so stinking impossible. Oh, Jesus, Carson, I don't know whether I love you. We toss that word around until it has no more shape or meaning, but I love to be with you, and I like you just the way you are right now, and no one who calls Washington, D.C., a company asshole can be all bad, and I think I'm a little drunk. You didn't tell him to make that a double Scotch on the rocks?"

"Never! Word of honor."

"Then I'm looped on two shots of Scotch—Dan Lavette's daughter. The family tree is withering fast. Do you remember that brilliant, crazy nephew of mine, Freddie Lavette?"

"Tom's son, the one who married that gorgeous part-Chinese kid?"

"Well, he divorced her. I don't know why I thought of that, except something about the family tree. No—one moment while I get my head on straight. I want to talk seriously to you, and then if you want to come up to my room and make love, I'm yours."

"Great. Go ahead. Seriously."

"Seriously. Try to feel a little less drunk and listen to me."

"Right."

"Good," Barbara said. "Now tell me, what was your real reaction to that meeting tonight? Did you believe them? Do they deserve your further investigation?"

"Barbara darling, I'm in no condition to go philosophic. They told us one side of the story. There's another side."

"I've heard the other side."

"Sure, and I've heard other witnesses on their side. Yes, I suppose I believe them. It's not a new story, south of us. A gang of the rich and powerful hire some Mussolini-type hoodlum, and he sets up his dictatorship and neutralizes the opposition, mostly with a bullet in the head, and then the poor bastards who make up the population are robbed blind, and in the process there's a lot of dollars and some hanky-panky by the CIA, and what are we going to do about it? It's a tradition, a way of life. Chile, Guatemala, Honduras, Colombia, Bolivia—you want El Salvador to be an exception? Come on, Barbara."

"No one has any big expectations, Carson. You light one little candle—"

Carson blinked at her and then closed his eyes. "It gets hazy. That's why you don't drive a car in my condition. Did we split a bottle of wine at dinner?"

"A whole bottle. We did."

"You should have told me. What little candle?"

"Carson, you have a paper. You send a correspondent down there to look at what's happening in Salvador and write about it. That's one little candle."

"You're kidding."

"No, my dear. I am not kidding. The truth is very damn powerful indeed."

"Barbara, take me up to bed, please. I'm not even hearing right."

"Five bourbons. You poor overgrown child."

"The wine did it. The bourbon on top of the wine."

Barbara signed the check, and then she helped Carson to his feet, thankful that he had a good stomach. She steered him to the elevator and then up to her room. There was a message waiting from her son, Sam. Having finally tracked her down to the Bernhards', he'd found out from them where she had gone, and had called in her absence to inform her that he was leaving for New York in an hour or so and that he would return in a few days. She allowed Carson to sprawl across the bed while she read the message.

"Who's it from?" he wanted to know.

"My son, Sam."

"Fine boy, fine boy. Good night, Barbara."

"So much for passion at twilight." Barbara sighed, beginning to undress him, and finally, after much tugging and heaving—Carson being neither a small nor a skinny man— got down to his underwear. She pulled his legs up onto the bed, straightened his body as close to the edge of the double bed as it was safe to park him, and then stared at him thoughtfully. Physically, at least, age had dealt kindly with this golden boy of Southern California. His once strong and shapely body still held its shape. Certainly he was no more than ten pounds heavier than he had been on their wedding day, and while his hair had turned white, it was almost all still there, covering his finely shaped head. Looking at him, not entirely sober herself, Barbara let her fancy roam, imagining herself married again to this handsome man who had always been more her child than her husband, a good, decent, intelligent man whose instincts put him on the side of the angels at least seventy-five percent of the time. He would have been her protector, even as he was still the protector of the beautiful, empty-headed woman he had married.

Why, then, had she kicked over the apple cart? True, there were reasons enough at the time, and she could even spell out the reasons today: his inability to connect with the boy who was her son, his decision to back Nixon, his indifference to her pained dislike of Los Angeles as a place to live and raise a child, his inability to take proper measure of her feminism. She could recall all of this, but now, standing by the bedside, watching him snore gently in alcoholic slumber, it all seemed so unimportant. Time had taken the strong colors of the moment and washed them into a translucent film of memories, just as time echoed her own intolerance of Carson, her impatience, her annoyance.

I am going to cry, she told herself. I cry at the most idiotic moments.

In the bathroom, the incipient tears disappeared. In his attempt to urinate, Carson had missed the bowl for the most part. Half provoked, half amused, Barbara mopped it up with a bath towel, did her own thing, got into her night-gown, switched off the lamps, and crawled into bed next to Carson. His body was warm. It was good to feel the touch and warmth of a man's body. She kissed his shoulder, and then pressed up against him and fell asleep.

She was an early riser. As the years passed, she found it was almost impossible to sleep past six or six-thirty. Carson was still asleep, and she let him go on sleeping. She dressed, went down to the hotel coffee shop, had juice and a cup of coffee, thinking that Carson might want a real breakfast later, and since it was still only a few minutes past seven, she decided to take a walk. It was a wonderful, cool, beautiful morning, the smog not yet apparent, the air still sweet with the touch of night-blooming jasmine, and, since it was Beverly Hills, the streets were utterly deserted. Barbara felt guilty at her sense of so much beauty and her feeling of so much real pleasure in a place she habitually detested. But she was not resident here, and she was able to whisper, remembering, "Though every prospect pleases, and only man is vile." She felt she was old enough to be less provoked at a place so totally dedicated to acquiring wealth and then spending it conspicuously. She walked along Rodeo Drive, remembering a time, long, long ago, when she bought a dress in one of these very shops at a price that would hardly buy a few handkerchiefs on Rodeo Drive today, and then she realized that she was turning into one of those old bores who kept recalling pre-inflation prices. Carson would have reminded her that, as the only daughter of Jean and Dan Lavette and the only granddaughter of the Seldons, she had at one time been richer than almost any of the ladies who would wander in and out of the Rodeo Drive shops as the day wore on.

Barbara was never very good at putting together the contradictions of her existence, nor was she ever untroubled by what she did, no matter how carefully she brooded and tried to justify herself.

It was almost eight o'clock. She went back to her hotel room, noting, as she put her key into the door, that the DO NOT DISTURB sign was properly undisturbed. Carson emerged from the bathroom as she came in, drying his face and apologizing for using her razor.

"How do you feel?" she asked him.

"Pretty good, all things considered." He regarded her curiously. "What happened last night?"

"Nothing much. We had a few drinks at the bar—"

"How many?"

"You had two double bourbons and then a single. They pour ample measure down there. Earlier, we split a bottle of wine at the restaurant. If you recall, you didn't eat much at dinner, and you never were a good drinker, Carson."

"Totally blotto?"

"Not totally. You walked up here. You didn't throw up. I undressed you and put you to bed."

"Oh." Then he added, "Where did you sleep?"

"In bed with you."

"Oh. Where's my tie. Did you see my tie?"

"In the closet. On one of the hooks."

He started for the closet, and then he stopped and turned to her, for all the world, as Barbara saw it, like an actor doing a silly, contrived double-take in a movie. "You say we slept together—right there?" pointing to the bed.

"Yes."

"Did—I mean—did we—?"

"Make love? No. I snuggled up to you for a bit, and that was nice, but you were too much out of it for anything to happen."

"Wouldn't you know it," he said bitterly.

Barbara put her arms around him and kissed him. "It's all right. We'll see each other again. Meanwhile, put your tie on and we'll have a good breakfast."

"Where were you?" he wondered.

"Just walking. I had to clear my head. Beverly Hills at seven A.M. Empty. Full of good air and sunshine, like a Hopper painting."

"Barbara darling," Carson said. "I can't go downstairs and have breakfast with you, not after spending the night in your room and in your bed."

"Why not? No one knows you were here."

"It's only eight-thirty. Everyone around here knows who I am. Good heavens!"

"Dear Carson, they'll see you eating with an elderly gray-haired lady who doesn't wear lipstick, and if you think that in this town anyone will imagine hanky-panky, you are out of your head. If an old buzzard like you fiddles around with anything over forty, he's thrown out of the club. You're seen here with me—obviously it's business. A writer in from out of town. Anyone comes by, I'm Barbara Smith."

"You really feel that way?"

"Carson, look at me."

"Barbara, I have an office and a newspaper and a home where there are servants, and if my wife calls—"

"Call home and explain. Call your office and explain. Carson, you own the damn newspaper. You can come in at six o'clock tonight, and no one will dare to say one word about it."

He made the calls, and they went down not to the coffee

shop—for, as Carson put it, anyone who saw him eating in a coffee shop would be instantly suspicious—but to the restaurant, and there the maître d' welcomed him expansively, telling him how delighted he was to see Mr. Devron again. In return, Carson said pointedly, "Mrs. Smith, here, and I would like a corner table where we can discuss what we have to discuss."

"I love to go to a restaurant with you," Barbara said, once they were seated.

"Why?" Carson asked suspiciously.

"Because you are the only man I know who can quietly give the impression that he owns the place and the head waiter is there by your leave."

"That's nonsense."

"You and my father. Only he always took me to an old Italian joint on Jones Street, where he could fill his belly with spaghetti and smoke one of his impossible cigars."

"You miss him."

"Every day of my life. Him and Marcel and Bernie and Boyd—all the stupid, beautiful men who only know how to die—and if you ever die on me, Carson Devron, I'll never forgive you, so help me. I'll stand at your grave and cuss you out instead of bringing flowers—"

"I'm to be cremated."

"I'll work that out too. Let's eat. I'm starved."

"You look twenty years younger than you have any right to look. Are you sure nothing happened last night?"

"Eggs, sausage and fried potatoes—home fried, not French fried. Croissant and coffee."

"My God," he whispered, "don't you gain weight?"

"No. I worry it off."

After the order had been taken, Barbara said, "Last night —what did you decide?"

"Decide? I was too stupidly drunk to decide anything."

"Before you took me here. Those men from the Salvador

resistance asked you to send a correspondent down there. It's important. We're the most Hispanic part of America, out here in California. You used to talk about the need to develop a Mexican readership. This fits in, doesn't it? We should not have to depend on the wire services and gleanings from the *New York Times*."

"What's all this leading up to?"

"Last night, those three men asked you to send a correspondent to Salvador. Will you? Yes or no?"

"I don't like anyone telling me how to run my newspaper."

"Oh, come on, Carson. This is Barbara."

"Who always knew better how a newspaper should be run."

"Carson, about the correspondent—yes or no?"

"I happen to have thought about it several weeks ago. I'll take it up at our meeting today."

"Then your answer is yes?"

"I suppose so," Carson agreed.

"Good. I want the job."

He stared at her. The food came, and he continued to stare. She dipped a piece of potato into the yellow of a fried egg and swallowed it.

"So that's it," Carson said finally. "That's why you trailed around and let me in—"

"Carson, for God's sake, I love you, I've always loved you, and one thing has nothing to do with the other. So get off that horse. I asked you something."

"The answer is no." He began to eat furiously, and then, mouth full, added, "I love you too. That's why the answer is no. No. No matter what you say, no!"

"You'll feel better after you've eaten something. I shouldn't have asked you to decide on an empty stomach."

He stopped eating and pointed his fork at her. "Do you see? It's exactly that kind of thing that broke up our marriage. No matter what it is or where it is, you have to be so goddamn superior!"

"Oh, Carson, I'm trying to be nice. But suddenly there's a chance to do what I do best and to stop decaying and disintegrating, and I think that if I went to the *New York Times* and asked them to give me the assignment for that beautiful Sunday magazine section they publish, they'd give it to me. I have a very good reputation in New York. A prophet is always without honor in his own place, and I realize you can't afford a Sunday section like that. Nevertheless—"

"You're doing it again," he interrupted. "You know, you're childish when you begin to plead and you think you can tease me into something. Not only are you totally transparent, but it comes off insulting."

"Carson, come on, I couldn't be insulting to you—"

"And furthermore, we don't have to copy the *New York Times,* and that magazine of theirs is not too expensive for us, but I'm not a damn bit sure that what's right for New York is right for L.A. We're unique, a place of our own, and don't tell me that L.A. is a great place to live if you're an orange."

"I like you when you're angry," Barbara said. "I wouldn't like it if you were my boss, because your eyes get very cold and nasty, and that would frighten me. Your food's getting cold."

"So is yours," he growled.

"That's because I'm excited about this assignment."

He continued to eat without further comment, and after a minute or two, Barbara said, "I did have an offer for an assignment from *Good Housekeeping* magazine."

"Oh?"

"To do a story on Demel."

"Who was Demel?"

"The father of Viennese pastry. Do you want that to happen to me?"

"I need more coffee," Carson said. "I'm dry and my head is beginning to split."

"Oh, no," Barbara said. "That won't get you anywhere with me, because I remember very well all the times I had to telephone someone you didn't want to talk to and tell him—"

"O.K. Now look at it sanely for a moment, Barbara. Last night wasn't my introduction to that mess called El Salvador. I've been reading the dispatches for months. The army's death squads murdered reporters and photographers, as well as Catholic nuns, as well as maybe thirty thousand men, women and children in the past few years. You want me to send you into that? You want me to be your executioner?"

"Carson, I'm not a fool, and I'm not an amateur. I have something of a track record, in case you've forgotten."

"I know your track record. Like mine, it was made a long time ago."

"Carson, the place is full of reporters. They're not going to kill me, and you simply don't know what it is to vegetate and have your friends tell you to take up knitting. Carson, I'm in good health and strong and possibly with more brains than I ever had in the past. Oh, I admit I sort of connived when I heard who you were going to see last night. So what? I want this. I need it. There are better ways to go than to dry into nothingness and become what they so euphemistically call a senior citizen. To hell with that! I need work, because if I don't work, I'm going to die—the wrong way. And there is a right and a wrong way to die. Stop protecting me, and give me the one thing you can give me."

He was silent for a while, and then he said, "You really want it that much?"

"Yes, I do."

"All right, it's yours." Then he added, "You know, Barbara, you don't need me or my paper. You could go down there on your own, and I couldn't do a thing about it."

"I know that. I want a newspaper behind me. There was a time when I diddled lions and alligators, but that was stupidity, not courage. I was never anything to shout about where courage was concerned. I may have some store of moral courage, but when it comes to physical courage, I'm as barren as most people. It's the gross stupidity that I feel I've overcome, and I like to have a press card from a big, fat, influential L.A. newspaper in my purse."

"You haven't asked about money."

"The hell with money. I'll take whatever you offer. It's the job I want."

"Not a job—assignment," Carson said carefully. "I've turned away too many damn good newspaper people. You can have the assignment, not a job. Three weeks. That's long enough to measure your background and dig out the story. When do you leave?"

"I'll go home and put things together. Then I'm yours."

Nine

Carla and Freddie had planned to spend a week in New York before going off to Paris; and Freddie, trying desperately to make each moment better than it actually was, had engaged a suite at the St. Regis Hotel on East Fifty-fifth Street. But not the hotel nor carriages in the park nor dinners at the best restaurants in town managed to shake either of them out of themselves—two gloomy selves who watched their uneasy romance begin to crumble around the edges. This mood had taken hold of them while they were still on the plane coming east, beginning, as Freddie recalled, with discussion about marriage. It was the first time he had unfolded any specifics of the future to Carla, and as he laid them out they consisted of marriage, possibly in New York, to be followed in due time by at least three children, the first, perhaps, to be born in France, symbolically in the wine country.

Concerning this, Carla had said nothing until after two days in the overfurnished suite at the St. Regis; and then one morning, refusing to make love, leaping out of bed angrily as a sleep-fogged Freddie began to run his hands over her body, stalking around the bedroom, naked and beautiful and very angry, Carla shouted at him, "Everything *you* decided, everything—where we go, where we live, children I must have and how many, and everything else, even what dresses I buy—because to you here in New York, you have decided that I look like one of them Puerto Rican hookers, and in this stinking city, anyone who hasn't yellow-dyed hair and a pasty skin is a hooker or what they call a Hispanic, and I say fuck the lot of them in this stinking place with that Hispanic shit, because my people were here in this country before you goddamn Anglos even learned to sail a boat so that you could come and take away everything that belonged to someone else!"

"Hey! You're really trashing the world!"

"And don't laugh at me!" Carla shouted. "I'll kill you if you laugh at me and try to show me how goddamn clever you are. I'm not clever! I'm a stupid Chicana."

Freddie got out of bed, spreading his arms to mollify her. Like Carla, he was naked. She shouted at him, "Put something on! I don't want to look at you naked!"

"You're naked," he protested weakly.

"That's different." Then she strode into the bathroom, slamming the door behind her. Freddie stared after her for a minute or so, still not entirely awake, trying to analyze and understand the explosion that had greeted him. He dressed without shaving, since Carla still held the bathroom, and then he ordered breakfast sent up. He had no idea whether Carla's anger had run its course, and he had no desire to share it with the guests in the dining room. However, and very much as usual, he had been unable to anticipate Carla's mood, and when he had finished ordering breakfast, she came out of the bathroom, wrapped in a charmeuse dressing gown of lemon yellow, her face shining. She needed no makeup. She had scrubbed her face with soap and water, and her skin glowed. Her mass of black hair fell to her shoulders, and Freddie, always astonished by her beauty, could picture her as the mistress of some great California hacienda in an era gone by. The sight of her melted him.

"Ah, my poor baby," she said, going to him and embracing him. "I make you so miserable. I am so rotten to you. I don't know why. I swear I don't know why. I pray to the Mother of God, she should make me like herself, sweet and loving and forgiving. I think I'm not one damn bit forgiving. Maybe I think of how you took my cherry when I was just a kid. Oh, that's a miserable thought, but sometimes nice. Don't look at me like that, sweetheart. I'm so crazy, but I love you so, and I don't want any kids in France. Fuck France. I want to go back to California."

"Why? You were delighted at the thought of living in France."

"That was when I was in California. Everything comes up roses when you're someplace where you're unhappy, and you think that anywhere else you could be happy. No way, darling. You speak French. I don't know one damn word of French. You know that in school when a Chicana picks a second language, if she's a dumbbell like me, she picks Spanish. Sure, I was speaking Spanish since the day I began to speak anything."

"All right. Maybe my own dream of France is crazy. When you go back to a place where you've been happy as a kid, it never works. Does it?"

"Maybe not, Freddie. Oh, the hell with all this talk. Take off your clothes and get back into bed with me."

She stepped away from him, grinning and opening her dressing gown. Freddie began to unbutton his shirt. "We'll have to make a lot of adjustments, but we'll get married in California, if that's what you want."

"No."

"No?" He stared at her for a long moment. "No? Not in California? Where, then? Here?" But he knew the answer.

"Freddie—oh, Jesus, what kind of a game are we playing? I keep telling you this, and you keep forgetting. What kind of marriage would we have? Freddie, I don't want kids and I will not have kids. There are enough poor cursed Chicanos in this world. And I don't want any children, period. Some women are mothers. They got to be knocked up every year to be happy. No, no. Not me. You know, you confuse everything, you don't think straight, and I go along with you. My papa is Cándido Truaz, foreman in the growing fields. In your winery—hold on, don't stop me—so it's Adam's winery and what did you just inherit, ten, twelve million dollars. You want to make a lady out of me—"

"Damn it, you're a lady! A great lady!"

"Take off your clothes, Freddie. I'm sick of talking." She dropped the robe and threw herself on the bed. "Come on. This is the only language we don't talk different."

Carla took an afternoon plane back to California, leaving Freddie too stunned to assess properly what was happening. He tried to force money on her, which she rejected, and managed to stuff only a few hundred dollars into her purse. She insisted that she would have no trouble finding a job in San Francisco, and Freddie went through the phases of her decision like a man in a trance. He embraced her and kissed her, and then watched hopelessly as she passed through the metal detector and down the passageway to the plane.

"Poor Freddie," she had said. "I love you so much, I don't want to louse up your life beyond any repair. As soon as I find a place, I'll call Barbara and tell her so you can find me."

Freddie went back to his hotel suite and tried to get drunk. It had never worked for him and it didn't work now. If you grow up in a winery, you build unshakable defenses against drunkenness or else become a hopeless alcoholic, and he was not an alcoholic. Freddie sat and brooded until four o'clock in the morning, and then he fell asleep.

The following morning, at nine o'clock, he telephoned Sam. Nine o'clock in New York is six A.M. in San Francisco, and Sam underlined that angrily. "Damn it, Freddie, do you know what time it is?"

"Nine o'clock," Freddie said miserably.

"No! No, you horse's ass, it's six o'clock in the morning out here."

Freddie could hear Mary Lou in the background, telling Sam to have a little compassion. "For heaven's sake, he's in trouble," Mary Lou was saying.

"Are you in trouble?" Sam asked him.

"My God, Sam, I'm on the short end of the worst mess of my life. No one ever fucked up the way I did, and I deserve it—goddamn it, I do deserve it for taking off with your wife—"

"Freddie, will you stop being a horse's ass and talk straight for one minute. You did not take off with my wife. I was divorced, and believe me I was thankful that Carla had someone like you to turn to, and you did me the favor of taking on my guilt. Now will you please tell me what happened."

"She took off. No marriage. She went back to the Coast. Tried not to take a dollar from me; just took off and left me here—and so help me God, I look at the window and think about what a pleasure it would be to jump out."

"Freddie, I never thought you were particularly bright, but that's stupid—high-class stupid! Did Carla tell you that I now pay her four hundred a week in alimony?"

"No, she didn't."

"It's no fortune, but it keeps the wolf away from the door. Freddie, where are you staying?"

"At the Saint Regis."

"O.K. Now today's Wednesday, when the medical profession hibernates. I was going to take Mary Lou to the beach, but that can wait. I'll get an early plane and we'll have dinner together. Unless you can change your plans about France and come back here?"

"No. Oh, no—no. I can never go back there, never!" Then he added, "It's cold and wet here, and it's beginning to snow. Oh, God, Sam, I feel so rotten. I broke May Ling's heart. I left my kid. Do you know I was going to France for two years? I wouldn't have seen him. I wouldn't even remember what he looked like. Sammy, I don't know what's happened to me—Jesus God, I feel so rotten I want to die."

"Can you get on a plane?"

"I can't go back. Sammy, I can never go back. I've just fucked up beyond repair."

"Stay right there at the hotel. Get some sleep. Watch TV. But stay there, and I'll be there about four o'clock your time. Please, Freddie, just don't do anything until I get there."

When Sam finished speaking, Mary Lou said to him, "Do you have to?"

"He's the closest thing I ever had to a brother. It's not that Freddie's my cousin—he's my friend. How many friends do you have in a lifetime?"

But more than that, Sam sensed the illness of a man close to the breaking point, and when he greeted Freddie in the hotel room in New York, he felt that his apprehensions had been fully justified. Unshaven, always very thin and even thinner now, his eyes bloodshot, his hand shaking as a result of two ashtrays filled with half-smoked butts of cigarettes, Freddie was a man distraught.

"Did you eat at all today?" Sam asked him.

"I don't know. I'm not sure."

"Suppose you shave and comb your hair, and then we'll go down to the dining room and have dinner and talk about this."

"I don't know how to thank you," Freddie said woefully.

"Don't. I'm starved. Wait a minute—give me your hand."

Freddie's pulse was seventy-six. Sam touched his brow, which was not too warm, and then pushed him into the bathroom. When Freddie emerged, shaven, hair combed, he looked less like a man at the edge of death. Sam, somewhat heavier in build than Freddie, two inches taller, a face dominated by a strong, high-bridged nose, had always looked upon Freddie, with his flaxen hair and his long, narrow head, as the quintessential Anglo. As a kid, he had envied him both his appearance and his easy flirtation with girls; as a man, he continued to admire and envy Freddie's wit, his bright intelligence, and the fact that most women were totally enchanted by him. Now, rejected, disposed of like an unwanted pet puppy, a new and vulnerable Freddie appeared. Sitting at the dinner table in the hotel dining room, he said hopelessly, "I don't know what to do with my life, Sam. I don't know what to do with it anymore."

"What do you want to do?"

"I've been thinking, brooding over that for hours, waiting for you—I swear, if I didn't know you were coming, I don't know what I would have done. I've finally painted myself into a corner, Sammy. The thought of going to France now, alone—it's senseless. It chills me, like locking myself into a cell for two years. What's the use of kidding myself? The only life I ever had that made sense is in Napa, and I can't go back there. And if I can't go back—" He shrugged.

"Why can't you go back?"

"Why? Face my father again? Face Carla's father every day?"

"Your father and mother would be two of the happiest people on earth. Your grandmother Clair is dying. You know that."

"I know."

"Freddie, you've been running that winery for the past ten years. I know Adam's the boss, but you've put it on the map. It's five times the size now. That's your doing. You could walk away from it—but to where? People like us, we're a part of that place, and there isn't any satisfaction for us anywhere else. Sure it's going to be a son-of-a-bitch thing to face up to Cándido, but we didn't do him in. His daughter shafted both of us, so to speak."

"Come on. We're big boys. If we were shafted, we asked for it."

"Freddie, we'll both defend Carla right down to the finish line, but the plain truth of the matter is that she used us. Maybe it was reciprocal—maybe we used each other. We're all too close, too damn incestuous, but maybe that's because there were so few of us to begin with, and death has chopped away at us so savagely."

"I love Carla."

"Oh, hell, Freddie. We go back a long time together. You've loved a lot of women. You loved May Ling. You were absolutely crazy about her."

"I still am."

"So you divorce her and take off with Carla."

"Sam," Freddie pleaded, "try to understand. For three years now, I couldn't get it up with her. I'm only thirty-eight. Do you know what it feels like to go to bed with a woman night after night and not be able to have an erection? I was impotent, plain, stinking impotent. I never believed it could happen to me."

"Why didn't you come to me? I'm a physician."

"Carla turned out to be all the medicine I needed. Oh, Christ, I don't know what I'm talking about anymore. May Ling moved in with Sally and Joe, but before I left, my mom persuaded her to come back. How do I face up to that? She's right there. Do I go back to work right under her nose?"

"Maybe it's the first real thing you've ever had to face up to, Freddie. We're the kids of the rich. We slide through life without ever facing up to anything. The money's a fucken waterbed, and it rocks us like a cradle wherever we turn.

I'm beginning not to like us. I don't like the people we see at the club, and most of my colleagues are milking the Feds and depending on Reagan to pour the money into their laps. I'm losing all my fondness for them too. Look at us. Did we ever fall down without a hand waiting to pick us up? We're so snotty sure of ourselves that it's beginning to turn my stomach. Do you know what I deal in? Two-thousand-dollar appendectomies, five-thousand-dollar hysterectomies—I'm a lousy highwayman. We all are. God bless us all and Medicare too. We make the Mafia look like a bunch of inept idiots, and none of us goes to jail. So suppose you cut out all the shit, and I'll try to match you at shedding crap and we'll both go back together."

"Sam, I just haven't got the guts."

"Make the guts, and if you talk to Cándido, tell him that you love and respect his daughter, but that it wouldn't work. I talked to him."

"No. You did?"

"I did. I went to him with Martí Pérez—Father Martí from Napa. You know him."

Freddie nodded.

"According to Cándido, his daughter had sinned beyond forgiveness. Father Martí convinced him that she could be forgiven and that she could find a place in the hereafter. Don't look at me like that. I don't edit what others believe. All I know is that I was able to shake hands with Cándido without feeling that he wanted to put a knife into me. If I could do it, you could do it."

"I deflowered her when she was just a kid," Freddie moaned. "He knew about it then. He wanted to kill me. Instead, he let Adam take over. It was the only time I ever saw Adam blow his top. This time, I swear to God Cándido will kill me."

"You'll die honorably," Sam said. "We still have time for the late plane."

* * *

The second day after she had returned to San Francisco, Barbara drove out to Higate. On her way to the winery, she stopped off at her brother Joe's house in Napa. Sally was at home. Joe was at the hospital, and young Daniel, out of college barely two years, was down in Silicon Valley, being a sort of genius and putting together, with two other sort-of-geniuses, a new computer company that would make them millionaires before Christmas. Or so Sally spelled it out after she had embraced Barbara.

"And May Ling?" Barbara asked her.

"She's wonderful. Barbara, I'm so proud of that lady. She's the one thing I did right. She's taking it all on her two feet, no weeping, no anger at Freddie. She won't hear a word said against him. She was with me here for a while, but then Eloise begged her to come back to the house at the winery. Well, it's her house. She moved back in with little Danny. Freddie came back to the winery a few days ago, got into words with Cándido, and Cándido decked him—"

"Decked him?" Barbara exclaimed. "What does that mean? Did Cándido hit him?"

"Cándido must be sixty-five if he's a day, but he has the strength of an ox and he clipped Freddie on the jaw and knocked him over. Thank heavens he didn't break Freddie's jaw. Then he helped Freddie up, and from what I hear did a lot of apologizing. Joe looked at Freddie and says it was a piece of luck his jaw wasn't broken. They shook hands. Adam doesn't know about it." As always, when she became excited, the words poured out of Sally, and again, as so often in the past, Barbara reflected on what a remarkable woman Sally was, one-time published poet, film star and other things, a tall, lean, sinewy woman, still beautiful in her middle fifties, still vibrant with a sense of the unexpected. "How can I be angry at Freddie? At first, I wanted to kill him, but I couldn't stay mad. Now it breaks my heart, the condition he's in. Barbara, have you ever thought about what a small family we are?"

"I certainly have."

"And that makes it even worse, doesn't it? I mean being so close. May Ling is out at Higate up the Valley, and it's like her refuge, her nest, her wall against the world. Her house sits between Grandma Clair and her Uncle Adam, and she is there with the child and perfectly content—or at least that's the way she appears to be. And Freddie's rented himself a house, the old Skagaway house—oh, you must have seen it a dozen times, because you can see it from the road, a silly stone house—and he drives to the winery every day and goes into his office there and does his work. You know, he installed a new computer system and apparently he's the only one who understands it, and Adam was trying to find someone to replace him but never did, so you can just imagine the confusion around the place when Freddie walked out without so much as a by-your-leave, and Adam doesn't speak to him."

"Not at all?"

"Not a word. Oh, I suppose it will ease up in time, but now no word passes between them, and Eloise is out of her mind with the situation."

"Does Freddie see the child?"

"Every day, and he and May Ling act perfectly civilized and cordial to each other, and where it goes from here, heaven only knows. But since it's Freddie, I can expect anything, and I do."

"And your mother?" Barbara asked her.

"Mom's dying. It just doesn't seem possible. I know she's past eighty, but it seems like only a moment ago that she was this strong, beautiful woman, with that great mop of red hair, and Pop was that indomitable tower of strength. Life can be so damn shitty. Pop's dead all these years, and she's dying. You know, Joe's her doctor, and we drive up there almost every evening now. She won't go to a hospital, and Joe doesn't want her to. But she won't have a nurse. She says she can't abide the thought of a nurse around the place. But she has María. You remember María, big, strong Mexican lady who's been with Mom over thirty years?"

"Is Clair in great pain?" Barbara asked. "I know how painful it can be."

"Joe keeps her sedated. She hasn't long, and you know Mom. If she's in pain, no one else is going to know it. She wants to see you, Barbara, so don't leave without seeing her."

"I wouldn't dream of it."

"I know how people are about a dying person. I don't mean you, but some people—some people can't bear to be with anyone who's dying."

Barbara had to stay for coffee and sandwiches, and for another hour she sat and listened to her sister-in-law. Sally, Barbara decided, was the ultimate sentimental romantic. If Barbara was a romantic, it was at least structured, and she could look at herself critically; but for Sally, the whole stretch of her life was like a film in which she was writer, director and star.

Out on the porch of the big, old-fashioned house, Sally clung to Barbara. "I just don't see you enough," Sally complained. "And I do love you so."

"Freddie's back." The first thing Eloise said to Barbara.

"I know."

"It's strange," Eloise said. "May Ling is living in their old house and Freddie has rented that weird stone château outside Napa. He had a fight with Cándido, but I really don't know what happened, because no one, Freddie included, will say word one about it, except that his face was swollen to twice its size. Adam's not speaking to him, and I'd hardly blame Freddie if he threw up everything here and got a job somewhere else—which heaven knows he doesn't need, after the inheritance. You haven't seen Mother yet?"

"No."

"Well, she wants you to have dinner with her—just the two of you. If you go off on that Salvador assignment—it is an assignment, isn't it? You wouldn't just go down there on your own. Is it Carson and the *L.A. World?* Are you seeing him again?"

"I saw him in Los Angeles, Eloise, yes."

"Well, you're both old enough to know what you're doing. I was thinking that if you go down there for how long? Two, three weeks?"

"About three weeks."

"Then you may not see Mother again. Joe says it's very near the end."

"Then I'm glad I came today."

At the door, Eloise took her hand and said, "Dear Barbara, listen to me. I know I'm nervous and neurotic, and I always have been. But we have three men here, pickers and ground men, who are from El Salvador. I've spoken to them. The stories they tell of the death squads are too terrible. They have been beaten and tortured beyond belief, so please, darling, be very careful."

"I won't mention it to Clair," Barbara told her. "I'm sure she has other more important things to talk about. You can tell her tomorrow if you think it's necessary."

Clair was in bed, in her room in the old stone house that she and Jake had lived in since they bought Higate in 1919. The room was spacious, the ceiling beamed, the walls hung with magnificent serapes and Clair herself propped up in an old Spanish four-poster bed—bringing to Barbara's mind a memory of her own mother, also propped up in bed and dying of the same cursed disease. They were alike in other ways, two women once tall, handsome, proud and purposeful.

María had brought up a tray for Barbara, setting it on a small table next to the bed, some chicken mole and saffron rice. Barbara went to Clair and kissed her, and Clair took Barbara's hand, clinging to it for a moment or two. "I want you to eat, darling. María made the mole for you. It's the best mole north of the Valley of Mexico."

"You must eat something."

Clair shrugged. "Why? I had a glass of milk. I eat very little, Barbara, and I don't enjoy people who make an impossible thing out of being with a dying woman. Believe me, it's bad enough to die, and so much worse to do it alone. So please eat, and we'll talk, and, María," she said to the square, stolid Mexican woman, who stood near the door like a Zúñiga sculpture, "bring us a bottle of wine. I have six bottles of our own Mountain White in the fridge. Bring us two of them. And a glass for me." When María had gone, Clair said to Barbara, "She is my rock. The full Indian blood. They understand about death. Now tell me about yourself. You were in Los Angeles?"

"Yes. Actually at Malibu, an odd place to look for something of myself."

"Writing? Were you looking for yourself or something to write? What are you working on?"

Barbara had to smile. "Always that question is asked a writer. All my life people ask me, and you know, Clair, I never know how to answer. No, I'm not doing anything. I try to write, but since Boyd's death all my attempts wash out."

"That's no good," Clair said, rather severely. "You must work, today, tomorrow, right up to the end, even if that's twenty years ahead of you. I get so angry when they try to cut me off from what's happening here at Higate. We have become an enormous institution. Would you believe that we do five million a year?"

María returned with the two bottles of wine and a silver

cooler. She opened one of the bottles and filled two glasses, large eight-ounce stem goblets. "Shall I stay?" she asked Clair in Spanish.

"No, señora. We must be alone to speak of things close to the heart."

How beautiful and proper it sounded in Spanish. You couldn't say such things in English without sounding mawkish.

"I understand," María said. "You will call me if you need me."

When she had left the room, Clair said, "Freddie was here before you came. I sent him away. Of course, I scolded him first."

"Poor Freddie. Everyone scolds him."

"We'll have a toast," picking up her glass. "This is our nineteen seventy-six Mountain White. No fancy French imitation—just our own name, Higate Mountain White. It is very dry with a sort of knife-edge cut to it, like the very best Sicilian. Well, my dear Barbara, this is to you, to the living. You have been a wonderful friend and companion on this short and somewhat silly journey we call life."

Barbara drank without demur. Her eyes had begun to brim with tears, and she fought it, wiping the tears and trying to pretend that she was simply wiping her mouth with her napkin.

"You like the wine?"

"It's beautiful," Barbara managed to say.

"Funny, how wine has become a sort of religion to all of us in Napa and Sonoma. Looking back, it seems like an odd way to spend one's life. You know, Barbara, as this cancer eats its way on, your brother Joe shoots more and more drugs into me to kill the pain. But it also messes with my mind. I hallucinate. I see Jake and we have long talks. Oh, I don't really see him. I know that. It's a kind of dreaming, except that he always has more sense about things than I do, which makes it a bit puzzling. Have you ever thought much about death?"

"Yes, when it touched those close to me, people I loved. But in terms of myself—well, not too much, no."

"God—or whatever it is that we call God. Do you ever wonder about it?"

"I'm afraid so," Barbara admitted. "I don't give him too many points."

"No? Well, when you think of this poor old gentleman sitting up there on a cloud and watching the lunatics he created kill each other—well, you can't give him many points, only a little sympathy. But when you lie here with a sore back, waiting for the drugs to wear off so that you can yell about the pain, and telling yourself that at age eighty, you've lived enough—well, under those circumstances you do brood over the mystery. It seems so damn pointless. Yet with all the misery, I've had such a good life—but that doesn't ease things. It makes going away so much worse."

Barbara felt that it was becoming increasingly difficult for Clair to carry on the conversation. Clair's hand groped for the switch that would summon María, and when the Mexican woman appeared, Clair whispered to Barbara, "I'm sorry, darling." She spoke with great effort. "It's all I can manage tonight."

Barbara bent over the bed and kissed her.

"God bless you," Clair said. "Thank you for coming."

Outside, in her car, Barbara sat at the wheel and wept.

The following morning, at about eleven o'clock, when Barbara was trying to put together a proper assortment of wearing apparel for El Salvador, Freddie and Sam appeared as a judgmental deputation. Barbara had already absorbed what information she could find about the climate, summed up in the *Encyclopedia Americana* as follows: "The year is divided into two seasons—the rainy months being those from May to October, the dry months from November to April. Low coast lands are hot and unhealthful; a comparatively cool and agreeable climate is to be found in the highlands of the interior." Since the dry season was almost over, this information made Barbara decide on two white cotton blouses, two blue denim shirts, two pairs of blue denim pants and two blue denim skirts. To these, she added a raincoat and sweater and a suit she would wear on the plane. Experience had taught her that for such an assignment she was best provided with a single small piece of luggage, which she could carry with ease. She was packing when the doorbell rang, and she went downstairs to greet her son and her nephew. She embraced both of them. "Too late for breakfast and too early for lunch. Coffee and toast?"

"Mother," Sam said firmly, "this isn't a social call. This time, thank heavens, we know where you intend to go. We have both taken time off from our work, which should mean something."

"You mean you don't want me to take this job," Barbara said. "That's very thoughtful of both of you, either an indication of love or a reflection of my increasing incompetence and furtive senility."

"Please, Mother, don't be angry."

"I don't know whether I'm angry, but I am provoked. The moment you use the word *Mother,* Sam, I raise my defenses. I am Mom until you suspect lesions in my mind. I find it just a bit insulting."

"Oh, no, no!" Freddie cried. "My God, Aunt Barbara, you have two people here who think you're the greatest woman we've ever known. Only, we do feel that you have a sense of invulnerability, and you're not—"

"Young?" Barbara asked. "Neither are either of you, so stop behaving like children, and suppose we all have a cup of coffee. And not another word on the subject."

"Mom," Sam said, "I am a doctor, and I know something about age and bodily resistance, so—"

"Not another word," Barbara said.

"Thin ice, Sammy," Freddie said. "Drop it. Can we have that cup of coffee, Aunt Barbara?"

"I don't see why not."

Carson rang her doorbell on Green Street at six-thirty that same evening. He had come up from Los Angeles on the commuter flight to have dinner with her, and he found her in a high mood of exhilaration.

"Carson, dear Carson," she said, "you have rescued me from a pit of despair. I don't know how or why, but I'm alive again—guilty, but alive."

"Guilty? Why guilty?"

"I'm having a tryst with a married man. My dear friend Clair Levy is dying of cancer. My nephew Freddie has messed up his life practically beyond repair, and my son thinks that I'm on my way to senility and should be put out to pasture, and I feel wonderful. Where shall we go for dinner?"

"Fourneau's? I made reservations there."

"Perfect. And now if you'll sit down and read a newspaper or a magazine or a book or whatever your heart desires, I'll go upstairs and do something with my hair, and I'll be with you in ten minutes."

In not much more than ten minutes, Barbara appeared and asked him, "How do I look?"

"Beautiful."

"Let's walk a little, and you'll tell me more. We'll walk downhill and then we'll find a cab to take us back uphill. Do you know something, Carson, it is the strangest damn thing in the world, but after talking to Clair, I opened my eyes and the world was like something I had never seen before. What on earth do you suppose has happened to me?"

"Last week, you happened to me. Would it be too egotistical for me to suggest that I happened to you?"

"No, it would not be too egotistical. To have a strong, handsome man who looks at you as a woman—that is so good, Carson, even when it can lead to nothing."

"Why? For heaven's sake, why?"

"Carson, I live from day to day, and if we can be friends, good, loving friends, that's all I could possibly ask."

After dinner, they walked down to the Embarcadero. The Bay shimmered, darkly shrouded with the first fog, the current sliding toward the Golden Gate. Barbara and Carson paused and stared across the darkening water, silent for a while.

"It's not that Clair is dying," Barbara said at last; "it's the opposite of that, a kind of triumphant life force that death can't touch. I cried for a time after I left her, but then the tears were over and I found myself smiling at the memory of her. Do you know what I'm trying to say, Carson?"

"I think so."

"It's the reason why I am and why I do what I do, if that makes a shred of sense. I hate all the killers—war, disease, poverty, hunger—because they're the enemies of life. That's the essence of those damn bombs they build. They're the toys of the death people, the power people."

"Some of us are on your side, Barbara, believe me, and it's cold down here by the water. On a night like this, there's no place as cold and wet as San Francisco, and I'm tired."

"Me too," Barbara said. "Me too. Enough talk of death."

He stayed with Barbara that night. Their lovemaking was easy and natural, with no sign of the impotence that had wreaked such misery in their marriage. In the morning, Carson took her to the airport. They were early. Barbara was always a half hour to an hour early at airports, always sure that if she was thirty seconds late, the plane would be gone. They had coffee at the airport restaurant, and Carson reminded her of Clifford Abrahams, the Reuters man in El Salvador. Carson had reached him by phone, and he had promised, with some pleasure, to meet Miss Lavette and to keep an eye on her.

"I don't even know whether you've jotted down his name," Carson said. "It's your damn independence that frightens me."

"Of course I jotted down his name. I'd remember it, anyway."

"Tall, skinny fellow—skin and bones, very British. He's a good writer and a good observer, and we use a lot of his stuff. But he tries too hard to hew a line down the middle. I'm sure you'll bend toward the guerrillas."

Barbara shrugged. "Maybe. I'm not really doctrinaire, Carson, even during my political campaigns; not like so many of the liberals I know. I see it and try to write about it."

"Three weeks. Not a day longer."

At the gate, Barbara embraced him and kissed him. "Bless you," she said. "You're the best thing that has happened to me in a long time."

"I hope to God I'm not the worst. Take care, please."

Ten

Barbara's ticket was routed from San Francisco to Los Angeles on United Airlines. At Los Angeles, she would change to Taca Airlines, which would take her to San Salvador. She had brought with her a copy of her first novel, *Driftwood*, feeling that any bit of status she could add to the accreditation the *Morning World* had given her would be useful. It was more than thirty years since she had written *Driftwood*, and she thought it would be interesting to look through it again.

She remembered very vividly the last time she had glanced at the book, twenty-five years ago, waiting in a hotel room in Beverly Hills for Carson to join her and take her to dinner. It was a winter day, the rain coming down in sheets, cold and damp enough to match her own mood. She had been informed that same day that the screenplay for the filming of *Driftwood*, over which she had labored so agonizingly, would be tossed aside, another writer having been hired to rewrite the screenplay. Result, a state of utter despair, from which Carson had rescued her.

She closed the book and lost herself in her thoughts as the

plane took off. A plump, pink-cheeked man, with gold-rimmed glasses, who was seated next to her, sighed and said, "I don't mind being up there or down here. It's the in-between that gets to me."

To which Barbara shrugged and murmured that she didn't think much about it either way. Carson, now and in the past, was in her thoughts. She had no desire to be jarred away from her memories. But a few minutes later, recalling the coldness of her response, Barbara turned to the plump man and said that she had flown so much that she had to assume an attitude of indifference.

"I've flown a lot of miles," the plump man said, "but I never could work up indifference. Name's Bill Donovan."

Barbara nodded, without giving her own name in response.

"If you want me to shut up, mention it. I'll shut up."

"No, I'm sorry if you took it that way." She pointed to the book on her lap. "My name—Lavette."

"Interesting. I'm sure the real Lavette won't mind."

"Not if we don't tell her."

"True enough. And what do you do, Miss Lavette—since I presume you don't write books. Or do you?"

"Well, as a senior citizen," Barbara reflected, "I'm not called upon to do much. As a matter of fact," she decided, "I peddle cosmetics." She was becoming bored. She did not want to talk to anyone, and specifically this plump man sitting beside her. She wanted to think, to reflect on where she was going and whether it made sense and about how she would put together what she might see in El Salvador.

"Cosmetics. Changes the look of things, doesn't it? In a way we're in the same line."

"Cosmetics?" Barbara asked indifferently.

"No, ma'am. Not cosmetics—guns. But you know, the end result can be the same. Changes the look of things."

"What did you say?"

"Gotcha! Come on, it's not so all-fired amazing. You peddle cosmetics. I peddle guns—large guns, small guns, ammunition, tanks, half-tracks. No planes. I stay away from planes. Another field entirely, and I'm not sure I'd like it."

"Forgive me," Barbara said. "I think a certain amount of astonishment is called for. I never met a munitions dealer before."

"Good heavens, there are lots of us. We don't advertise, true. We don't take commercials on TV, but there are over a dozen special trade journals devoted to our line of work. Now tell me something, Miss Lavette, taking the whole globe into consideration, not one nation or another but the world as a whole, just what would you say is the largest industry?"

"Agriculture, obviously."

"Obviously. And the second largest?"

"No. I can't believe that."

"You'd better believe it," Mr. Donovan said mildly. "Heavens to Betsy, have you ever considered how many guns there are, rifles, carbines, machine guns and hand guns, extant on this here planet Earth?"

"No, I never have."

"More than two billion—that's more than two thousand million—and they don't stay put, and thousands more come off the assembly line each and every day. Lord knows, I don't wish to frighten you, but don't it make plain horse sense that if there's so much of a product, it needs a few hands to move it around and buy and sell it?"

"Yes, I suppose that does make sense," Barbara admitted. "And what are you up to now? Buying or selling?"

"I can tell you, ma'am, I am mighty glad you're not one of them holier-than-thou citizens that throw up their hands in horror. You know, I don't make the things. I just move them around a bit, and as for your question, I'm selling. You don't travel south of the border of the good old USA to buy. No, sir. Only to sell."

Fascinated now, Barbara wanted to know whether it was not illegal.

"Nope. Not one bit. Oh, I suppose if I tried to run merchandise out of the country, the way the IRA does, I'd be breaking the law. But I don't sell to places like Northern Ireland, and I don't sell to the Afghans and I don't sell to guerrillas. No, ma'am. I do business with legal, established governments. Did it ever occur to you, ma'am, that when they do a big killing, like they do sometimes in Africa and sometimes down in South America, or sometimes in Vietnam or Indonesia or Cambodia, they pick up a hundred, maybe two hundred thousand pieces of small arms and what goes with it, and if it ain't uniform, they don't want it? Just the same as when a country brings in a new model. What do they do with the old? The New York City Police destroy maybe fifty thousand small arms each year. That's waste. That stuff could fetch a fine price. You know, I used to work for the Pentagon, same line of work, but it was too confining."

"Why on earth would the Pentagon sell arms?" Barbara asked. "Their yearly cry is that they don't have enough."

"That's their problem, isn't it? They want to poor-mouth, they got their reasons. All I know is that I sold maybe twenty, thirty million a year, and I was only one drummer. Lots of others."

"But to whom?"

"Anyone had good use for them—South Korea, Pakistan, Morocco, Chile, Bolivia—you name it. But there I was, doing millions on a wage of forty-seven thousand a year. That's why I put in for myself. Gives me an advantage, I'm not political. Of course, I don't mess with the IRA or the PLO—much too hot, much too hot. But aside from such very hot spots, I don't have political prejudice, and when push comes to shove, I can undersell the Pentagon if I have the goods. All I need is a three percent markup. That's thirty thousand on a million, and I've done as much as twenty million a year. That, miss, is real money."

For a few minutes, Barbara said nothing. Then, unable to resist the temptation, she asked, "Mr. Donovan, does your mother know what you do for a living?"

It made no impression. "My mama's been dead these fifteen years," Donovan replied, rather pleased that the lady sitting next to him took an interest in his mother.

In Los Angeles, Mr. Donovan disappeared, and Barbara changed over to Taca Airlines. They operated a fairly small plane, a 737, but very clean and apparently in good condition. She half-expected to see Mr. Donovan again, but he had gone his own way, intersecting Barbara's life like a strange, half-mocking omen. She would remember him with a chill of horror—a fat, humorless little man, determined to underline the mediocrity of evil.

The Taca official who looked at her credentials and passport was very polite, bending backward to be charming. "The first correspondent from the *Los Angeles Morning World*. That is very fine thing. We feel that of all the states, California is the closest to our beautiful country." He had stopped short of suggesting what she might write about his beautiful country.

On the plane, where she was the only woman, she found herself seated next to a well-groomed, good-looking man in his middle years, perhaps fifty, dark hair touched with gray, mustache, and a suit of brown Italian silk that must have cost upwards of a thousand dollars in one of the shops in Rodeo Drive. He introduced himself as Raoul Regana, remarking that he had four weeks of business here in Los Angeles, and was finally going home.

"To San Salvador?"

"Well, yes. I live in San Salvador, and eventually I will

arrive there. But the airport is sixty-five kilometers—well, say forty-one miles outside San Salvador. Built in nineteen seventy-eight—the old airport was a sorry mess—but built, as I said, a good distance from the city by men with fine visions of progress. In a way, these fine visions are the curse of our little land, a fervent desire for progress, sometimes so fervent that we are years ahead of practicality. The beaches are splendid near the airport, the water at least ten degrees warmer than Southern California, and some resort hotels have been built. Alas, they are not well occupied. As the Irish say, these are the times of the troubles. Are you possibly a part of the Red Cross?" he asked, in deference to her age.

"Oh, no. I'm a correspondent for the *L.A. Morning World.*"

"Really? I would think—"

He clipped the sentence, and Barbara said, "You would think they'd send someone younger."

"Forgive me. A thousand pardons."

"Not at all. One of the advantages of my age is that I can strike up a conversation with anyone, while a young and attractive woman, unfortunately, would do so at her own risk. I have been a writer and a correspondent for many years—indeed, my first assignment predates World War Two. My name is Barbara Lavette. I dislike long flights where one sits next to a stranger in grim silence."

"Then we shall have no grim silence." He motioned to the stewardess, who apparently knew him. "May I offer you champagne?"

"Some ordinary white wine."

"And I'll have a perfect Manhattan," he said, which Barbara translated in her mind as his statement that he was no ordinary inhabitant of an unhappy banana republic, but a very knowledgeable and sophisticated citizen of the international set.

"Do you have any trepidation about going home?" Barbara wondered.

"Ah, there speaks the voice of someone whose knowledge of my country comes from your media."

"Not entirely. I have read a good deal—Anderson and Penny Lernoux and Richard Millett—"

"Yes. Biased, very biased. The Maryknoll influence."

"Really?" Barbara never argued in such situations. Argument changed nothing, provided only a sop to the ego, and, worst of all, as she had learned long ago, cut off a source of information. "I never thought of it that way."

"But you must, if you are to write the truth. If you will forgive a most personal question—are you Catholic?"

"Well, that is getting right to the root of things, isn't it? I suppose you have a good reason for asking. More than curiosity, I trust?"

"Much more, Miss Lavette, believe me."

"No, I'm not a Catholic. I don't have very much religion, but I was born and raised an Episcopalian."

"I ask only because," he explained, "so many Catholics have very strange ideas and are not Catholic in any true sense. They have taken Communism into their bodies instead of the Host. Maryknoll. You will never see El Salvador as it is if you listen to the Maryknoll. They are not Catholics. They are an abortion—"

"Which was why the nuns were murdered," Barbara said softly. "Is that what you are saying?"

"Never, never so many lies as about that accident."

"Yes, and I imagine that the killing of Father Grande and taking over his church was also an accident."

"He was a spoiled priest, a Communist."

"Yes, I suppose so, but then they took his church in Aguilares and turned it into a pigsty. And Archbishop Romero tried to go to the church, and as much as he pleaded that he only desired to remove the Sacred host, they would not let him pass. Then he persuaded the National Guard chaplain to go and remove the Host, but the soldiers stopped the chaplain and dragged the priest into the church, and forced him to watch while they shot the tabernacle to pieces and then ground the Host into the filth on the floor."

"And you believe this?" Regana snorted.

"Should I?" Barbara asked. "I mean, one reads these things and one doesn't know whether to believe or not. Consider the murder of Archbishop Romero. Was it connected?"

Regana studied her shrewdly. He was no fool, Barbara decided; he was not taken in. He was indexing her for the future, and perhaps she had overplayed the fool simply by referring to the incident.

"To believe what the Communists say—" He shrugged. "You believe and you become their tool."

No more waves, Barbara told herself severely. She had made too many gaffes and she had said too much. Here was a man who obviously knew everything about his own land, and except for what she had read and heard, she knew nothing. He was equipped to play the devil's advocate; she was not equipped to prosecute.

"Would you like another drink?" he asked, still smoothly polite.

"That would be nice. Yes."

She made no more references to nuns raped or priests murdered, and gradually their small talk died away. All her indirect attempts to discover what kind of business had brought Mr. Regana to Los Angeles were of no avail, and she carefully refrained from pressing the point. Left to her own thoughts, she composed a story that would simply detail the essence of her two meetings on that same day, first with the arms dealer and now with this somewhat blood-chilling purveyor of a new kind of Catholicism, where priests and nuns were murdered, their death sentence based on their unwillingness to limit the practices of their religion to the rich. It would certainly be a most interesting story, and as yet she had not set foot on the soil of El Salvador. And as the story shaped itself, she felt a cold needle of fear. Until now, she had been on a sort of high, her spirits lifted hugely by the fact that she had been accepted back into the real world, where people work and are paid for their skills. It had partly returned her to youth, and the aches and pains were washed away in the excitement of the new project. Until now, she had not been afraid.

Now she was afraid, and this fear, like a sort of intestinal cramp, did not disappear when the plane landed and taxied up to the fanciful glass and white anodized-aluminum structure that proclaimed El Salvador's "fine visions" of the twenty-first century. It also did not escape Barbara's notice that this airport, so superior to so many tacky airports back home, was built with the tax dollars of the American people. Nightmarish, she told herself. I am Alice in Crazy Land, and I have not yet left this silly little airplane.

Regana said goodbye gallantly. "It has been a pleasure, señora. We will see each other again, I am sure."

Clifford Abrahams, briefed by Carson, was at the airport, waiting for her, instantly recognizable from Carson's description, a very tall, slender, almost cadaverous man, with a shock of brown hair and bright blue eyes, wearing a wrinkled tan cotton suit. He introduced himself with an impeccable upper-class British accent, took Barbara's suitcase— "No typewriter, Miss Lavette?"—and led her toward the immigration counter, where a cluster of unattractive men in camouflage uniforms, carrying submachine guns, bleakly and intently eyed each person who came off the plane. Other armed men in wrinkled uniforms were scattered around the airport terminal.

"Welcome and glad to see you," Abrahams continued. "Try not to make eye contact with the local hoodlums."

"If you weren't here to meet me, Mr. Abrahams," Barbara replied, "I think I would have turned around and leaped onto the next plane home. This place scares the hell out of me."

"Normal. Fear here is like smog in L.A. or fog in London, endemic."

"Oh? That's reassuring. No, I don't take a typewriter, since I'm not filing. I'll do a series of pieces when I return. I'll just make pencil notes. Why all the soldiers? Are they expecting something?"

"Oh, no. Normal—par for the course. I won't try to shield you, Miss Lavette. Carson tells me that you know your way around. Nothing very nice here. Let's do the credentials."

They studied her passport. No smiles, no note of welcome. After they stamped her credentials, they went through her suitcase, feeling their way through each piece of her clothing. Then they asked to look at her purse. Barbara glanced at Abrahams questioningly. He nodded. They emptied the purse, a large leather bag that she had purchased for this trip; then they went through the contents; then they returned the contents to the purse; and then slowly handed the purse to Barbara.

"Muchas gracias," she said sourly.

Away from the counter, Abrahams said, "Nice accent. Do you speak Spanish?"

"Yes."

"Good Spanish? Easily?"

"Pretty good. Why?"

"Don't. Not to any official. It gives you a priceless advantage. They'll talk to each other on the basis that you don't understand. I've been here too long to get away with it. But you can. And by the way, did you talk to brother Regana in Spanish? I saw you saying goodbye."

"He sat next to me on the plane. No, no Spanish. His English is remarkable."

"Good."

"Who is he? Do you know him?"

"No pal of mine, but I've interviewed him." Dropping his voice. "Bloody little bastard. They say he runs the death squads. In uniform he's Colonel Regana, and some say he has over a thousand notches on his gun, peasants, women, children, liberals, reformers—you name it. They call him the butcher of Morazán—guerrilla territory now. He was born there in poverty, out of which he fought his way up to this high position. A stirring example to the kids."

"I do pick them."

"You didn't say anything—like not approving of the rape and murder of nuns?"

"I did."

Abrahams sighed and said, "I think I'll call you Barbara. Call me Cliff."

"Instant intimacy before extinction, right?"

"Come on, love. I'm going to lead you through a fine three weeks. Carson said he'd hunt me down and destroy me if anything happened to you. And he would. By the way, I don't want to be pushy, but you and Carson were married once?"

"A long time ago."

"Forgive me for prying. Carson's a fine fellow, and I was curious to see the lady who'd been his wife. I suppose you'd rather we dropped that subject?"

"I would, yes."

The new road to San Salvador swung north from the ghost-like beach resorts, created and planned by the local bosses—or killers or tyrants, or revered leaders of the people, depending on the circumstances—to be competitive with the resorts of the Bahamas or Jamaica; but since El Salvador was the last place on earth a sane person would go for a vacation, they were for the most part deserted. The road went on inland and north, through dry hills, like the hills of a California summer. There were cars on the road, none of them pleasure vehicles, and most of them varieties of military transport: heavy station wagons with thick bulletproof side panels, the wagons fitted with machine gun mounts, small panel trucks, windowless and ominous, and once a heavy-duty United States Army half-track, its markings obliterated. There were also here and there soldiers by the roadside, sometimes squatting and eating and drinking, sometimes marching, sometimes just standing and watching the cars go by. And there were the bodies of two men, lying on the embankment and being torn to shreds by buzzards, so many buzzards and so hungry that they were jostling each other to get at the human flesh.

"I think I am going to be sick," Barbara said.

"Tell me in time. I'll pull over to the side of the road."

"I won't be sick. Absolutely not. I don't want to stop on this road."

They were riding in a small Toyota jeep, which Cliff Abrahams said he had bought a few months ago, at a very low price, from a San Salvador dealer. "They come here from Japan, and the local in-dealers buy them with US aid money. They want a quick turnover, so they sell cheap."

"How do car dealers get aid money?"

"They're not car dealers, love. Bless your heart, no. They're colonels and generals turning a quick buck, and making sure, as patriots, that none of the money goes to buy food for the kids, who might just grow up to be Communists. You didn't by any chance fetch a copy of *Alice in Wonderland* with you?"

"You don't believe in God, do you?"

"That is apropos of nothing—or are you making a point? You'll remember that Alice said a gent does not ask personal questions, and that's quite personal, isn't it? Well, sort of. I mean about God and such, I do give it some thought now and then. Not anything one talks about."

"No, but for a moment I had such a clear image of the old man up there with his head in his hands and weeping his heart out over the way his kids loused up all and everything, from worse to worse. I have been in this line of work since the nineteen thirties. We did think that when we finished Hitler, the bad guys had been done in."

"It would be a dull world without the bad guys."

"I suppose so," Barbara admitted. "It would be quite a problem to live without terror. Cliff, why do you suppose I'm so damn scared? I was arrested by the Gestapo in Germany in nineteen thirty-nine, and I wasn't as frightened as I am now. Is it being an old lady that changes things?"

"Drop the old lady line, Barbara. Even in Germany, one felt that one was living in the twentieth century and that certain niceties of civilization remained, at least if you weren't Jewish. They don't exist here. A civilized nation doesn't leave the bodies of dead men lying by the roadside, buzzards tearing them to pieces, while army lorries drive back and forth without so much as a glance. That touches the deepest and most vulnerable depths of our souls."

"But don't they know back home? Don't they have a notion?"

"It's your turf, love, not mine. I suppose they do and they don't, and they're a little crazy on the subject of Communism. They try to believe that these bloody murderers are fighting Communism. They're not, you know. They kill anyone who irritates them. It's as simple as that."

It's an instructive initiation, Barbara decided, and no one but herself to blame. She wanted to come here. She had used Carson and bullied him into sending her here. She argued with herself that even if she had bullied Carson, no one but herself had been hurt, but that made it no better.

"We're going to the San Salvador Sheraton. It's a new hotel, quite decent and quite clean. I engaged a suite for you," Abrahams said, a bit apologetically. "I mean, it's a few dollars more, but Carson can afford it, and you need a place to write."

"If Carson can't afford it, I can."

"Good. You'll be here just a few weeks, so buy every comfort you can."

"Are they available?"

"You bet your life they are. Like Saigon. When your troops were in Saigon you could buy anything from a Cadillac to a computer. Not too many Yankee troops are here yet, but the groceries and aftershave always come first."

It was dark by the time they reached San Salvador, and thus Barbara's first impressions were punctured by street lights and loud music from the houses, and what appeared to be, as well as she could make out in the darkness, large and impressive homes—a scene that for some reason recalled the single time she had been in Savannah, Georgia.

"The best part of town," Abrahams told her. "Tomorrow, we look elsewhere."

As the Sheraton Hotel rose out of the night, glassy, glistening, the first light rain of the season began to fall. There were people on the streets now, the sound of music from inside the hotel, music played very loud. The music reassured her. It chased away some of the imagined devils hidden by the night. They drove into the parking lot, where two young men raced for Barbara's single piece of luggage.

"Nothing doing, no way, no job here!" Abrahams snapped in bad Spanish, explaining to her, "They're not thieves. It's the utter hopeless poverty of the place. Better not chance losing your bag. Anyway, it weighs nothing."

But apparently poverty stopped at the Sheraton parking lot, for alongside Abrahams' jeep, two Mercedes, a Cadillac and a Rolls-Royce were parked. Going into the hotel, Barbara noticed two men in uniform, uniforms that fitted so perfectly that they reminded her of Hollywood film SS men in their fine-tailored costumes, covered with gold braid in this case. Obviously officers. One of them had a holstered pistol, the other carried a small submachine gun.

"Don't stare," Abrahams whispered to her. "For God's sake, Barbara, don't stare."

"Oh, yes, of course. They couldn't take me anywhere when I was a kid."

"Don't joke about this."

"Cliff, when you stop joking about anything—oh, the devil with it. When in hell, do as the imps do."

Abrahams shrugged. They stopped at the reception desk and suddenly the reception clerk, a skinny man with a pocked face, dropped his jaw and fairly dived through a door behind him. Cliff and Barbara both turned to see the cause of his curious behavior, and there, just past them, were the two army officers they had seen outside at the parking lot, this time led by a man in civilian clothes and followed by two soldiers, both of them carrying what Barbara discovered later were Ingram .45-caliber submachine guns. They moved at a steady pace to the room from which the music came, the main hotel restaurant, and then flung open the double doors that separated the restaurant from the lobby.

Without thinking, Barbara took a few long strides to keep them in sight. Cliff Abrahams caught up with her, and grabbed her arm. "Stay out of this, damn it!"

But they were in her line of vision now. They marched into the restaurant, paused by a table where three men were having dinner, and deliberately, without hesitation, without a word spoken, opened fire with the submachine guns and kept firing until the three men were riddled with bullets. Then, as calmly and deliberately as they had entered, they did an about-face and marched out of the hotel.

Cliff Abrahams grasped Barbara's arm tightly. "Steady, steady, old girl. Don't move quickly. Let's just ease ourselves away from any possible line of fire, and we'll see what happens."

Chaos happened. First, a mad scramble inside the dining room to get away from the blood-soaked table of the three murdered men. One of them sprawled across the top of the table; the two others lay on the floor; and this stark scene played to a background of screaming and shouting. Then people began to move in, carefully, to look at the carnage. The horror was dramatic and irresistible. At last, men in uniform poured into the hotel.

"Police," Abrahams said. "Calm. They may ask questions. If they do, you answer in English, not in Spanish. Do you understand? You don't speak Spanish—oh, maybe a word or two. We saw nothing. We don't know who went into the dining room and we don't know who came out, because we saw nothing, not yet. Later, when we get some of the picture we can amend our position. Right now, it's a bloody awful horror." He looked at her keenly. "You all right, old dear?"

Barbara nodded. "I'm all right."

"I know the desk clerk. I can get you your room now. Take a lie-down."

"Damn it, I'm fine. Now you do your thing. I'll trail along."

Following Abrahams, Barbara moved into the crowd around the bodies. It was increasing rapidly now, guests, hotel workers, police, some army officers, the hotel manager. From outside the hotel, Barbara heard the sound of sirens, men shouting, and a few scattered gunshots.

Abrahams moved out of the crowd. Barbara followed him. They walked across the dining room to where one of the waiters stood as if in shock, his back against the wall, his eyes staring straight ahead.

"Terrible. Just terrible," Abrahams said in Spanish. "A terrible business, Angelo."

"I saw nothing," Angelo replied. "Nothing. I was looking the other way."

"She's all right," Abrahams assured him. "I'd trust her with my life."

"She's Jewish?"

"Absolutely."

Angelo breathed deeply and said, "You know them, señor."

"Yes. But who was the civilian?"

"He eats here sometimes. His name is Fritz Oberman. He didn't do any shooting. He brought them to the table, and then just nodded his head like this, and then the shooting started."

A policeman turned toward them, and noticing this, Angelo raised his voice, and cried shrilly, "I told you I saw nothing. I was in the kitchen." He turned on his heel and walked into the kitchen. The policeman faced Abrahams and Barbara questioningly.

"I'm a correspondent; Reuters. She was here for the *Los Angeles World.*" Abrahams was not at his best with the tenses, and it came out somewhat mangled, but the policeman appeared to understand.

"It's very confused," he said. "I wouldn't write about it yet."

"Who are the dead men?"

The policeman shrugged. "Who knows?"

"The lady just arrived. I want to get her registered."

The policeman stared blankly, and Barbara said in English, "I must check in. I just arrived." Abrahams smiled and nodded and drew her away and then over to the desk.

"What on earth was that all about? I'm not Jewish."

"Angelo grew up in a little village in the hills where his father kept a small store. His father used to tell people that he was a Jew, because only a Jew can run a store properly. Angelo admired his father, who was killed by the soldiers in one of their purges. He thinks I'm Jewish because of my name and he seems to trust me for that reason. I'm not Jewish, in case you're wondering."

"I'm not wondering. Why are we staying here?"

"I wanted to get you registered, but that seems to be impossible. We'll do it later. Now I want to get over to the office. You might as well come with me. There's a chance we can clear a wire."

"You mean I could phone this in?"

"Possibly, but Carson could pick it up from our wire. Let's see what happens."

No one stopped them as they went out to the jeep, Abrahams carrying Barbara's suitcase, even though the parking lot was teeming with soldiers and civilians. An ambulance had just pulled up in front of the hotel, and an army vehicle with a bright search beam had parked itself in front of the hotel and was sweeping the sky with its powerful light. To compound the insanity, two runners in tight white shorts and undershirts were in the parking lot, interrupted in their late run by the commotion around the hotel, and curious enough to remain, jogging in circles. Catching a glimpse of them in the light, Barbara realized that they were wearing new, rockered North American running shoes. A man in khaki blew his whistle again and again as Abrahams carefully jockeyed his jeep out of the parking lot into the street.

"It's insane," Barbara said.

"Oh, yes indeed, but viciously insane. It's all mad, their lunatic army, their demented death squads, the way they go about getting rid of people they don't care for—oh, bloody well insane, like a world seen through one of those circus mirrors. Why ever did you come down here, Barbara?"

"I was dying up there—oh, not this kind of death, but

shriveling up, being pointless and useless. But never mind that. Who were those three men? You knew them, didn't you?"

"Yes, I know who they are—which makes it even more senseless. The youngest one of the lot is a chap called Alex Hellman, American, as was Pete Roberts. Roberts is a bit older, in his forties, if I recall correctly. I'll have to verify for my story. The third one was quite a decent chap, Carmen Luis. He was chief of the land reform agency. You know, the notion of splitting up the vast estates and dividing the land among the landless peasants—a sort of impossible dream project with this government in power, but very good political feed for the liberals in your Congress. This will be a bad mouthful for them, but the liberals seem quite capable of swallowing anything."

"And the Americans? Who are they?"

"That's the odd part of it. Both of them worked for the big labor combine in your country, the AFL–CIO. Specifically, a part of the labor union called the Institute for Free Labor Development. I've never really understood the workings of the labor movement in your country, but it appears that the AFL–CIO is a big supporter of all your wars. They were hot as hounds on the scent in Vietnam, and down here they've been staunch allies of what is euphemistically called the government. And that chap, the fat fellow with the brush hair, his name is Fritz Oberman, and he's cheek-by-jowl with the death squads and the government as well. All odd bedfellows. Pete Roberts made a nuisance of himself, going around as a sort of point man for the Reagan bunch, telling us all how good the local government was and how vicious and rotten the peasants in the resistance were; and the other one, Hellman, even defended lunatics like Fritz Oberman, and here Fritz Oberman leads in an assassination squad that blows the three of them into kingdom come. It's one of those unanswerable conundrums that haunt this place."

"Then why were they killed?" Barbara asked hopelessly.

"Ha, dear lady. Why indeed? I haven't spoken to either chap for some time. I don't take to these so-called trade union lads. For my money, they're as corrupt a lot as you'll find, but maybe these two saw the light. Maybe they were going to blow the whistle, as you Yankees say, and tell the world what a pen of pigs run this country. Such judgment is all right coming from chaps like me, but coming from the Reagan camp, it bespeaks trouble. Who knows? I'm just guessing. I'll name you in the dispatch. Barbara Lavette standing beside me as it happens. That ought to reassure Carson."

"I'd like to file my own story."

"Don't know. I do have a clear eyewitness beat—no other member of the press there as it happened. But let me brood over it."

The streets were quiet, deserted, lit by cold, impartial moonlight as they drove back to the hotel. Barbara had not been able to phone a story in, not because the wire service preempted her, but because, after Abrahams filed his story, there was no way to get through, either because the crush of demand had simply wiped out any free access or because the circuits had been deliberately blocked. By one o'clock in the morning, they gave up, and Abrahams took Barbara back to the hotel. Except for two bellboys and the desk clerk, the lobby was empty, although there was activity in the dining room. The glass doors were closed, but Barbara could make out the figures of several women, scrubbing the floor where the killing had taken place.

"Terrible, Señor Abrahams," the desk clerk said. "Such things should not take place in a fine hotel like this. If they must go about such business, one would think that they could find the proper place."

Abrahams voiced his agreement and introduced Barbara. The night clerk pushed a registration card toward her, shaking his head regretfully. "Please do not think that such things go on every day or every month. You will enjoy your stay with us."

"I am sure," Barbara said in Spanish.

Up finally in the two-room suite that Abrahams had promised, he asked Barbara why she had done that. He was plainly irritated.

"What?"

"Oh, you know damn well. Spanish."

Barbara dropped onto the bed, arms flung out, sighing with relief. "It's been a long day, Cliff. I've been thinking about what you said about language. My feminine wiles, considering I ever had any, have gone with time, and it's too late for me to learn how to punch. Language is the only weapon I have, and I'm pretty well lost without it. I know that you know what's best down here, but there's no way I can come out of this with anything worthwhile unless I use my language."

Abrahams thought about that for a while, and then he nodded. "Do it your own way, then, but for heaven's sake, be careful."

"Always."

"Tomorrow morning, I have to do a follow-up on tonight —if I can drag myself out of bed. It's two A.M., and I'm going to dash off in a moment. But about tomorrow—suppose I pick you up here for a late lunch, say about two o'clock. The whole schedule of meals runs late down here."

"Cliff, you've been lovely, but I can't monopolize your days."

"Barbara, you've been a godsend. I'll have none of that, and I can't think of anything more pleasant. In the morning, if you can't sleep, you might wander around the streets and get the smell of the place. Now, sleep well."

Abrahams left, and Barbara double-latched her door, managed somehow to crawl out of her clothes and got into bed. She was asleep almost instantly.

Eleven

The days passed, and Barbara realized that one could come to accept even San Salvador, the sweet, horrible stink of a dead body lying in a sewer culvert, the miasma of suspicion and fear, the submachine gun suddenly swung in your path, and children running and playing and laughing where other children had been murdered only days before. Abrahams seemed to appreciate her company, silencing her protests about taking up too much of his time. He made a point of rewards issuing from the company of an intelligent and sensitive woman. "I've been here too long," he told her. "Now I'm seeing things newly with your eyes." And indeed Barbara had a feeling that the streets were new to him because they were so new to her.

Underneath the fear and sometimes subtle and sometimes naked horror of the place, there was a thing that gripped her and, in a certain sense, fascinated her, scents other than the scent of death, a perfume of charcoal burning, food cooking, a night odor of jasmine. There was hunger among the men marooned there for women, even for a woman like herself. She made friends quickly. She spoke French and Spanish fluently, and the very fact of her age gave her entry into circles where a younger woman might well have been either excluded or received only in terms of her sex.

To some, she was a mother figure. She didn't resent that. A young captain in the American advisory force spoke to her as he never would have spoken to a male correspondent. "Why?" he pleaded, "why are we always on the side of the shitheads? Forgive me, I get carried away; but just once couldn't we team up with something different, something more human than these murderous bastards? I don't like to turn my back to them; believe me, Miss Lavette, I sure as hell don't."

The American senator, there on a junket, said, "He's right. But we can't choose our bedfellows."

"Suppose your wife said that to you?"

"What do you mean?"

"I mean, suppose your wife told you that she couldn't afford to choose her bedfellows."

"I find that remark rather strange."

"It's not a personal remark. I watch these killers and reflect that the guns they use to murder nuns and priests are bought by my tax dollars. It's not a nice thought."

There were no nice thoughts in the place. The gardener who took care of the plantings around the hotel would say good morning to her, and her reply, not a simple good morning, but a more gracious "Good morning and how are you today?" delivered with flawless pronunciation, induced further conversation and trust. One day, Barbara asked him about his past.

"I can tell you and trust you?"

"Yes. Absolutely."

"I believe you, señora. I'll tell you then, and if you want to write it for your newspaper, you will never mention my name."

"Never."

There was a small bench, the garden embracing it protectively. She sat on the bench, and he squatted alongside, his pruning clippers in his hand, not talking to her but speaking softly toward the shrubs in front of him. "I had a wife, a mother, four children. Three girls—one was eleven, one nine, one six. My boy is thirteen years old. We lived in a little village in Cabañas—oh, maybe sixty, seventy kilometers from here. The population of our village was about three hundred. A band of the guerrillas come through the village. We are not of the guerrillas, but we honor them and respect them. All the villagers do. They stayed for only an hour. We gave them food and water. Then they went on. The next morning, someone shouted that soldiers were coming. There is a narrow road up to our village, so we could see the soldiers when they were a kilometer away. In the floor of my house, I had dug a hole, for we knew that sooner or later the soldiers would come. I had not yet made a cave big enough for all of us, but under a wooden box in my house, there was a hole big enough for my son and myself. I knew they would kill my son and myself, and we didn't have time to run away. You know, señora, when they come into a village after the guerrillas pass through, they kill all the men and boys. Even if a little boy is only two years old, the government soldiers kill him, because they say someday he will grow up and go into the hills and join the guerrillas. But I felt that my wife and my mother and my little girls would be safe. I mean, what else could I do?

"So I hid in the hole with my son in my arms through all the terrible sounds that went on above us. And when there was no more screaming and the soldiers went away, we came out of our hole. They had killed all of them, my wife, my mother and my little girls, and all were raped, my six-year-old girl and my nine-year-old girl and my eleven-year-old girl, all raped and murdered, with their bodies lying on the floor in a pool of blood. The eleven-year-old girl was called Catherine, and she had heard stories from Father Paco about Saint Catherine, so she decided she would be a nun. That is all she dreamed of, to grow up and be a nun and help people, the way Sister Abigail, who is a nun from your country, helped us before this happened. Now she will not be a nun." He began to clip the grass, a few blades at a time. In El Salvador, there is no need for lawn mowers. Labor is cheap enough for the grass to be cut by hand, a blade at a time.

Forcing herself to speak calmly and quietly, Barbara asked him what had become of his son.

"Ah, señora, he is gone. At first he said nothing. He helped me to bury his mother and my mother and the three little girls, and then he said, Goodbye, Papa. I go to the guerrillas. That is how the guerrillas have an army. When such things happen, the brave young men go to them. I am not brave. I could not kill another man. I pray. I pray that in heaven God will be kind to my little girls. They were innocent children."

That evening, in the bar at the Sheraton, after she had put down a large martini, Barbara told the story to Cliff Abrahams. "I can't handle it," she said hopelessly. "You've been down here forever. How do you handle it?"

"I don't handle it. I write about it. That's my catharsis."

"Just like that?"

"Bless you, Barbara, not just like that. But how much blood does a chap have? If I bleed for every bloody incident down here, I'd soon be dry as a kipper. Do you know, I used to hear stories from the older members about the big fire bombing of London and the abattoirs where the Jews were murdered. I'd wonder how the silly clerics kept their faith in God after all of it. I still wonder, but my faith's washed out. I don't believe in one damn thing, because there's not one damn thing left that's worth believing in."

"Still, you come off as a nice guy. You wouldn't kick dogs."

"Only because they're a lot more decent than people."

"Let's get drunk," Barbara said.

"You don't get drunk. My money says you've never been decently drunk. Truth be told, you're a proper, upright Church of England lady who has eschewed sex and other worldly things to do good deeds in the parish."

"Bite your tongue and order another round. I'm not an easy drunk. I put your buddy Carson Devron under the table a few weeks back. How do you think I got down here?"

"I often wonder. What do you imagine you're going to get if you put me under the table?"

"An interview with one of the guerrilla leaders."

"No."

"I've learned nothing here except that if you're frightened enough, you must find a john or dirty your pants. I must talk to the other crowd, the resistance."

"You keep calling them the resistance. The resistance fought the Nazis. These poor buggers are fighting the death squads, which makes them commies, not heroes."

"Cliff," she said coldly, "I am not joking. Either you make this possible, or I'll go to someone else. But I prefer you. I know that you talk to them and that they trust you."

"How do you know that?"

"Word gets around."

It was three days later that Abrahams said to her, "I'll be by to pick you up tomorrow, seven o'clock, and you'll have your talk with the other side."

"You're an angel."

"I'm a bloody damn fool."

In the morning, a wet, steaming, nasty morning, ribbons of fog like snakes on the road, Barbara sat next to Abrahams in his jeep, excited, eager and reasonably frightened. During sleepless hours the night before, she had argued herself out of going. She would tell Abrahams that it was a dumb, dangerous notion, and she decided that, having heard this, he would be delighted and relieved. But when morning came, she realized that she would never forgive herself if she missed this opportunity, that her story would be fleshless, and that when all things added up, her whole journey to El Salvador would amount to no more than an aging lady's jaunt.

Thus it came about that she was seated next to Abrahams, cold, tired, her arms clasped, shivering partly from the damp cold and partly from fear. He assured her that if they got out of the city without being stopped by either police or soldiers, they would be all right. "They don't prowl outside the city, not at this hour."

"Why?"

"They're afraid. It's still not properly light. The guerrillas like the dark and they like to set an ambush in the dark."

"How do you know they won't ambush us?"

"An unarmed man and a lady in a jeep?"

"That's poor comfort. Where are we going?"

"Up in the hills." He pulled off the road onto a dirt track. "You can breathe easier now we're off the Pan-Am. No soldiers on this road. They don't like the narrow, unpaved roads. Too easy for the guerrillas to block, and anyway, another few weeks of the rainy season, and this road will be a muddy trap. We'll just go along nice and easy, no more than ten or fifteen miles an hour."

"Cliff, where are we going?"

"A little village called Isplán. No one lives there. It's been fought over and ravaged until there's nothing much left of it. It's only a few miles from here, and when we get there, someone will pick us up."

"What do you mean, pick us up?" Barbara demanded nervously.

"Love, you talked me into this, so either relax or I'll turn us around and push back to the city. Now look, I don't know my way around here. I know how to get to Isplán, because the government took us there on a junket to demonstrate how ruthless the other side is. But a burned-out house doesn't tell you who burned it. Anyway, there's to be some sort of chap waiting for us at Isplán, and he's to take us to Constanza María Gomez. I thought you'd prefer talking to a woman. Am I right?"

"It depends on the woman. Who is she?"

"She's a remarkable woman, depend on that. She's one of the top people in the FDR."

"Democratic Revolutionary Front."

"Right. If you're going to talk, they're the best lot to talk to. They're a combination of everyone who hates the death squads. The FDR are Christian Democrats, priests, anarchists, peasants who have no affiliation except revenge for the murder of family, intellectuals—a grab bag of every decent element in this society. Now let me tell you something about Constanza. She's twenty-nine years old, but she's lived through more hells than we can imagine. Seven years ago, the National Guard picked her up. She had slipped into San Salvador to see her mother, who was dying. They laid a trap for her, took her, beat her day and night to force her to divulge the location of her unit, raped her over and over, applied electric shock to her vulva—enough beating and torture to kill her. I got this from the confession of a National Guard soldier who was captured by the guerrillas. The confession finally got to Reuters. Well, somehow she recovered. She's a lawyer, a devout Catholic and an absolutely extraordinary woman."

Barbara nodded, unable to trust herself to speak.

"She's as good a story as you'll find."

"I'm not much good with any of this," Barbara whispered. "I have a chronic condition of wet eyes."

"I know the feeling."

An hour later they were in sight of what remained of Isplán: broken walls, blackened beams, and a roofless church. The place gave the impression of having been abandoned decades ago, but as Barbara learned, its destruction was only two years in the past. The broken and burned houses lined a single pitted street. The sun had burned off the mist, and with the wet heat there was a smell of mud drying, of sweet rot that Barbara would always remember as the smell of death, the scent of El Salvador.

Abrahams pulled up, almost to the church, and then cut his motor and the two of them sat in the jeep and waited. The sky had cleared, and the sun baked the wet road. A dog came out of one of the destroyed houses, paused to stare at the car and its occupants, and then ran off. A buzzard drifted down in slow circles and settled on the road, where it pecked at something in the mud. It pulled up the rotten flesh it had found, and then strutted stiffly to the side of the road, the bit of dead flesh hanging from its beak.

After a few minutes a bearded man in a ragged monk's robe came out of the ruined church, surveyed the street and then walked over to where they sat in the jeep.

"Abrahams?"

"Yes."

"And this," he said in accented but clear English, "is Señora Barbara Lavette, the writer."

"Yes," she replied in Spanish, "a very frightened Barbara Lavette."

"Your Spanish is very good. Shall we talk in Spanish?"

"I would prefer it. Yes."

"And you, Señor Abrahams?"

"Sure. She'll do most of the talking."

"Very good. I am Brother Pancho Campella. If my Spanish sounds strange and somewhat like your own, Señora Lavette, it is because I am Spanish, Madrid, Castilian, and even though I have been here a long time, one retains the accent. About fear, Señora Lavette," he continued as he climbed into the back seat of the jeep, "it is endemic in El Salvador, so we live with it as well as possible. But today, where we are going, there are no soldiers, no National Guard, so you can rest easy. We will be in our territory from here on. Drive straight ahead, Señor Abrahams."

Brother Pancho was a short, stocky man, his feet encased in thonged leather sandals, his arms muscular under the heavy sleeves of his coarsely woven robe, his round face encased in a curly black beard. Looking at him, Barbara was reminded of nothing so much as a figure out of the storybooks she read as a child, a Friar Tuck or a follower of St. Francis—and as if he had read her mind, he said, "Yes, if you are wondering, I am a Franciscan, one alone."

"You came here from Spain?"

"Eleven years ago, to seek for my soul, which indeed I found in this terrible suffering place."

She thought of his words: *our territory*. How was it their territory? They were a few hours' drive from San Salvador, and the guerrillas called this their territory. But how was it their territory? Again, as if in answer to her unspoken thought, the friar said, "Of course, when the soldiers come, unless we choose to fight them, we leave the land to them. The people mostly are with us, but they can't admit it. Otherwise, the soldiers would kill them. So some of the people must curse us when the soldiers come. But today, there are no soldiers here." And then, after a moment, he added, "Sometimes the people betray us. They are only human."

"You say, 'We fight.' Do you fight?" Barbara asked.

"No, señora. I am a Franciscan. I don't fight or carry a weapon. I help when I can."

"It's not that black and white," Abrahams said without enthusiasm.

"You take that track to the right," the friar said. "It's never black and white. People aren't made of two colors. It's always somewhere in between. This woman who risks so much to come here and write about us, what is she? Is she a saint or a devil? Are we the godless ones or do we worship God best? Everything is from a position. I never say, Come to my position."

Abrahams drove on, all of them silent for a while. Then Brother Pancho apologized for the road, admitting that it was hardly a road at all. Abrahams drove slowly, but still the jeep lurched and swayed. "Only another few miles," the friar consoled them.

It was a village even smaller than Isplán, and if it had a name, Barbara was not informed of it. There were no more than half a dozen mud houses, but there were people in residence, children playing in the muddy street, goats feeding, women who paused to stare at the jeep as it lumbered to a stop; and in front of one of the houses stood three young men in ragged trousers and old T-shirts, each of them with an automatic carbine of some sort, each of them with a bandolier of cartridges over his shoulder. They were very young, small in size; they couldn't have been more than sixteen or seventeen years old. At the same time, something about them gave Barbara the feeling that they were not new to this and that when the time came, they would handle themselves and their weapons proficiently.

When she climbed down from the jeep, it took a very conscious effort on her part to straighten up. Every muscle and every bone in her body ached, and as she carefully and gingerly forced her body to an erect position, Abrahams nodded.

"I know—feels like we've been bent into pretzels."

"Worse."

The friar was shaking hands with the soldiers. One of them said, "Bless me, please." The young man knelt and Brother Pancho made the sign of the cross over him. Barbara, watching, had the notion that this was for their benefit, and then felt wretched for even countenancing the thought. Nothing here was specific for their benefit. Who was she? They had only Abrahams' word for that, and he was by no means an uncritical supporter of the guerrillas. Certainly they had never heard of her, and certainly there was no specific position they could ascribe to the *Los Angeles World,* providing they had ever seen a copy.

Children were gathering around the jeep. They didn't come running, as American children would have, but slowly and cautiously, not laughing, not talking, but silent.

"Wait here—a small moment," the friar said to them, and he went into the house. A moment later, he returned and motioned for them to follow him. Barbara and Abrahams had to stoop through the low doorway; then they were in the single room of the cottage. The room had a hard dirt floor, for decoration a paper picture of the Virgin pasted or pinned to the wall, and for comfort a table and two benches. There was a bed against one wall and, at the other wall, a simple hearth where a small pile of charcoal burned, filling the room with its evocative scent. Two men, who had been sitting at the table, stood up as Barbara and Abrahams entered. Each had a bowl and a spoon on the table in front of him, and the woman at the hearth was filling two bowls with a sort of soup. She rose, the bowls in her hands, and carried them to the table. Barbara guessed that this was Constanza María Gomez.

She was not a tall woman, probably no more than five feet one or two inches, very thin, with a face cut so clean around the bones of her head that Barbara's first impression was of something carved from stone, so tightly was the skin stretched, and the resulting image was one of a woman wearing a beautiful but not quite human mask. Her hair, pulled tightly back and knotted in a ball at the back of her neck, increased the force of this first impression; yet when she looked directly at Barbara and smiled, the face instantly became warm, human and deeply sad.

"I am Constanza," she said simply. "It is very early, so you must have started without breakfast."

"We're not hungry."

"Of course you are. Who is not hungry? The dead are not hungry, and you are not dead."

"We are not dead," Barbara admitted.

"Then you must eat. And tell me where you learned to speak Spanish."

"At home. In California."

"Your accent is fine. I envy it. So we will speak in Spanish. Is that all right with you, Señor Abrahams?"

"Quite. I can follow. I listen better than I speak."

The bowls held bean soup flavored with onion, but Barbara was hungry, and she and Abrahams scraped the bottoms of their bowls and refused an additional helping.

"It's very good," Barbara said, "but you have too little food and we have too much."

"We have enough to survive on most of the time," Constanza said. "Food comes in from your country, but most of it is stolen by the army and the twenty families, and then it is sold in San Salvador and in San Miguel and Santa Ana. Sometimes we are able to intercept food trucks, and that helps. I know that you hear that the people feed us, but we try to give them food whenever we capture it, and we help with the crops and with the harvest. Our soldiers are not something apart from the people."

"In our country," Barbara said, "we read that you are controlled by the Russians."

"It would be very remote control, wouldn't it? I have never seen a Russian."

"We are also told that you have a pact with the Communists and that they control the guerrilla movement."

"The Communists fight our enemies, and they are brave and hard fighters. Shall we disown them because D'Aubuisson and his death squads want us to?"

"Our government says that if the guerrillas take control, the Communists will discard the FDR. You will be of no consequence."

Again, that soft smile stole over her face. "We are not easily discarded. I think we have proved that."

"Do you get arms from the Russians?" Barbara asked. "I know you may feel that these are foolish questions. But I must ask them."

The two men at the table chuckled at her question, and one of them took out his pistol and placed it on the table in front of her. It was a Colt .45-caliber automatic pistol.

"Not from the Russians, but from you," Constanza said. "Look at all the weapons we have here—all of them made in the USA. We take them from the dead National Guard on the battlefield. We pick them up when the soldiers run away and throw down their weapons. We take them from the National Guard soldiers we capture, and weapons are given to us by men who desert from the army. Still we have too few weapons. How could the Russians give us weapons? We have no seaport. We have no communication with Russians. You people think the Russians deal in magic. But we must deal with the facts of real life."

"I am a woman," Barbara said, "not a young woman, and I've seen so much war and suffering. Does it solve anything? I don't know. I see the way your people suffer, and I must tell myself that, in your place, what else could I do but what you do? But until when? Can you win militarily?"

"I'm glad to talk to a woman," Constanza said. "I talk to the men who are correspondents, even Señor Abrahams here. They are footloose. They don't understand what it is to have no home, no hearth, no growing things, no roof over a child's head, no school, no doctor, to be pregnant and watch the National Guard burn your home, to see your priest tortured and have to watch while his testicles are cut off. Yes, with my own eyes I have seen that. We are a deeply Catholic people, señora, perhaps the most Catholic in all of North America, and our priests and nuns are our own flesh and blood, father and mother—and they call us Communists! You ask me, can we win with guns? No, no, no—it would be such killing, and in truth we are fighting your whole giant country. Without your help, the death squads would not last a month. If your government would only leave us alone, we could finally build something good here; but as long as you arm these crazy monsters who kill us as if we were animals, as long as you support them, we must fight you. We can't win, but at least we live. If we lay down our arms, there will be such a slaughter as the continent has never seen, so we will fight until Duarte and his people destroy the death squads and join us to make a free country."

The friar guided them back to Isplán, and all three of them sat in silence in the jeep with never a word spoken. The sun was round and ruddy behind a slow gathering of clouds, the clouds becoming darker as they drove on. The endless chattering and chirping of birds died away, and the silence became as heavy as a blanket. After they dropped off the friar at the ruined hamlet of Isplán, Barbara could no longer control her tears. She didn't weep violently, but her eyes filled and the tears wet her cheeks—to which Abrahams said, with some irritation, "What in God's name are you crying about? You got your bloody interview."

"Did you see the children? They were starving. They were skin and bones."

"Christ, you Yanks give me a bloody pain! You shit on the whole world and then you weep your fucken tears over a hungry kid!"

The stinging slap she delivered across Abrahams' face came without thought or intent—and afterward she could not understand how or why she had struck him; but at the moment, all her frustration and anger and hopelessness boiled over, and she shouted, "Don't you dare! Don't you ever dare talk to me like that again! We are the best, the kindest, the most compassionate people! Is it our fault that we are ruled by lunatics? Will you show me a country that isn't ruled by lunatics? Is your country ruled by decent or sane people?"

Abrahams shook his head mutely, rubbed his cheek, and drove on without speaking.

Three, four minutes passed, and then Barbara said softly, "Sorry I hit you, Cliff. Please forgive me."

"You have a punch like a steam hammer."

"I only slapped you. I'm sorry. I don't know how I could do such a thing to a good person."

"You have a slap like a steam hammer."

"Oh, come on. You'll never forgive me. I think I should be forgiven."

"In any case, you stopped crying."

"I don't cry when I'm angry."

Again silence for a mile or so, and then he said, "You're a damn strange old girl."

"I suppose so. I'm no good for this kind of thing, Cliff, no good at all. I'm a tired old lady who doesn't have enough sense to know when to sit down by the fireplace and tend to her knitting."

"Can you knit?"

"No. No, I never learned. I tried once or twice, but I'm no good at it." He was rubbing his face, and Barbara said plaintively, "Come on. It can't still hurt."

"Why not?"

"Cliff, what should I do? If you'll stop the car, I'll get out and go down on my knees."

"That might help."

"Do you know, I'm less sorry. Until you apologize for what you said, there are no more apologies from me."

"I don't believe this. Here's a grown man and a grown woman snapping away like two silly kids. Maybe we should both of us shut up for a while."

"Thank you. The suggestion is well taken."

They drove on in silence. It was hot, wet, and uncomfortable, and Barbara had the damp, crawling feeling that her skin was raw, bitten, breaking out with nameless tropical abrasions. Her arms were covered with the sleeves of her blouse, protection against mosquitoes, her jeans down to her shoes. It gave her a sense of herself as a shapeless lump, peering out of a tangle of clothes from under a shapeless cloth hat. She had no good feelings about herself. Her slapping Abrahams was totally out of character; never before in her life had she done anything of the sort, and the subsequent quarrel was senseless.

Could it be that out of today they had both come to a point where civilization had to be viewed as a mockery, where the embrace of the murder machine in this tiny country by a presumably modern, civilized government was a swan song for everything either of them had ever believed in? Was it some crazy, doomed passion play that was being enacted here as a prelude to an atomic holocaust that would end life on this planet forever? Or was it simply a nightmare? Was she here at all? Didn't it make more sense to accept this moment as a dream from which she would awaken safe in her bedroom on Green Street?

"I am so bloody sorry," Abrahams said suddenly.

She didn't ask why. She was equally sorry, but it was tangled into so many knots that she knew no way to put it into words.

Whatever else was a dream, the heavy-duty Chevrolet four-wheel-drive wagon blocking the road in front of them was very real. They were about two miles from the slums on the outskirts of San Salvador. It was late in the afternoon. Three soldiers stood next to the wagon, which was painted in camouflage colors and bore the insignia of the National Guard. As they came up to the wagon and stopped, Barbara saw that one of the three was an officer. He was a fat, mustached man, sweating and wiping his face with a wet shirt sleeve.

"Get out of the car," the fat man said in Spanish.

Abrahams, in a deliberately cheery voice, speaking English, said, "Right-o, old chap. We're a couple of correspondents out for a look-see at the countryside—" Climbing out of the jeep, he whispered to Barbara, "Let me handle this, love."

"No English!" the officer said emphatically. "Out of the car!" pointing to Barbara.

As she got out of the car, Abrahams said, "My Spanish is rotten. Don't any of you speak English?"

One of the soldiers said, "She's an old crow."

"You unwrap an old crow, you find a fat chicken."

"Maybe."

"You two horny bastards shut up," the officer yelled. And to Abrahams, "You understand some Spanish?"

"Some."

"You come from the Communists? A big story, the Communists. You tell the whole world about them. You know something," he said, drawing his pistol, a heavy automatic, "I piss all over you filthy Yankee writers."

"I'm British."

"Worse. I shit on the British."

During this, one of the soldiers walked up to Barbara, grinned at her, and then with one quick motion tore open her blouse and brassiere, exposing her breasts. After that, things happened very quickly. As the soldier cried, "How about it? Look at those tits! Am I right, stupid?" Abrahams leaped defensively toward Barbara, and the officer hit Abrahams savagely across the face with his pistol. Abrahams went down on his knees, holding his bleeding face. Barbara shouted at the soldier who had ripped her shirt. "You filthy pig! You son of a sow! Don't you dare touch me again!"

"Hey, listen to that fancy Spanish!" the other soldier said. "She has a lisp, like a real, high-class pig."

His voice breaking with pain, Abrahams managed to shout, "You damn fools, she's the Spanish ambassador's wife!" The sentence was mangled. It came out indicating that the Spanish ambassador was Barbara's wife, and the two soldiers began to laugh. The officer looked at Barbara, who returned his gaze with utter contempt, so angry at this point that if she had had a gun, all her scruples would have disappeared, and she would have shot him. All the agony, fear and heartsickness at what she had seen during the past weeks took hold of her, and for the second time that day, and this time with all her strength, she struck a man, this time the National Guard officer. So unexpected was her action, so out of tune with anything the officer might have anticipated, that he was taken completely by surprise, both before the blow and after the blow. The slap was hard enough to rock him. The two soldiers froze, not moving, not speaking, and the officer raised his gun and pointed it at Barbara's breast.

"Go ahead," she said, speaking clearly but lisping, recalling how the Mexicans at the winery would mock Castilian Spanish, and using every bit of Castilian pronunciation she could call to mind. "Shoot me. Shoot the wife of the Spanish ambassador—and how long will you live then? You pig, there won't even be a trial. They'll terminate you and they won't even mark your grave. I am Señora Francesca Dolores d'Aragón Isabella"—and then, to herself, Oh, God, give me the name of the Spanish ambassador. She had met him, but right now, in this interval of seconds, in this matter of life and death, she could not recall his name. So having invented four given names, she topped them off with an equally desperate invention—"Castilla," which could be either a Christian name or a family name. "So," she continued haughtily, disdaining to cover her bare breasts, "if you desire an international incident that will end God only knows where, rape me and kill Señor Abrahams. If you dare. Not even your children will know where your corpses lie. No, the dogs will eat them!" With that, she ran out of ideas, names, notions and bravado as well, and simply stood still and straight, trying to look as arrogant as possible, and fighting with every ounce of determination she could muster to refrain from covering her breasts and bursting into tears.

Still the soldiers did not move, and the fat man stared at her thoughtfully. She was certain he was going to ask for her papers, and that would have ended everything, but he did not, and after a long, long moment, he said, brusquely, "I am sorry, but this happens. We are at war."

"I understand that," Barbara said gracefully.

"Can you drive?" he asked Abrahams, who was climbing painfully to his feet, his handkerchief pressed to the cut on his swollen cheek. "If not, I will give you one of my men to drive you."

"I will drive," Barbara said firmly, now pulling her blouse together.

"I am sorry for what my men did. They are pigs. But what can we do? We are pressed for recruits."

Abrahams had climbed into the jeep, Barbara getting in on the driver's side. "I will try to lighten your punishment," Barbara said, and Abrahams whispered to her, "Get us out of this bloody farce, and stop being Queen Isabella."

She turned on the ignition and put the car into gear. The soldiers were moving to get their car off the blocked road, but without waiting Barbara drove behind the wagon and then back on the road, resisting the impulse to go tearing away at top speed. But the road was so bad that she had to drive slowly and carefully.

A few moments later, she asked Abrahams, "Have they gone?"

"Off in the other direction. They're about out of sight."

She put the car into neutral, pulled up the hand brake, and burst into hysterical tears.

Abrahams watched her for a while, and then, rather impatiently, told her, "That's enough, Barbara."

"We're dead," she sobbed. "We're dead and buried."

"Not buried. I agree that we're dead, but you're not a nun and I'm not a priest."

"They only bury nuns and priests?"

"That's right. You and me, they leave us lying on the roadside in the rain. Now will you get this bloody car back to town before they remember that the ambassador's wife is in Madrid?"

"God Almighty, is she?"

"I think so."

Barbara slammed the jeep into gear and sent it hurtling and swaying down the road to San Salvador. Her hysteria disappeared, and when Abrahams pleaded that she would kill both of them, the way she was driving, she hissed, "I hope so, you limey bastard. You put me right into that. Oh, yes! Here's the Spanish ambassador's wife. Suppose they had looked at my papers? I would be raped and dead because some smartass limey was creative!"

"Creative, hell! That fat little bastard was going to kill me. So I took a chance. You know why I did it?"

"Tell me."

"Because I admire you. Because I think you're wonderful, because I think you can handle anything, and by God, you did. Oh, that was bloody wonderful! He wouldn't dare ask you for your papers. You know why? Because those National Guard creatures are the lowest form of human life. They could give points to the Nazis. Yes, they're bloody good when it comes to murdering nuns and unarmed men, but give them a proper tongue-lashing in a manner out of their own culture—if you can call it culture—and they'll crawl. Anyway, odds are he can't read, and every word I say is killing me, so please slow down and get me to a doctor."

But once in the city, Abrahams changed his mind. "No doctor," he said. "I don't trust any of them."

"Your office?"

"No. It's too late and they don't have anything there. I don't think my jaw or cheekbone is broken. Let's get to your place. Do you have anything?"

"I have a sort of Boy Scout first-aid kit."

In her suite, Barbara washed the cut with gin while Abrahams cried out in anguish. One whole side of his face was swollen, and the pain was so obvious that Barbara was filled with guilt. She had tongue-lashed him, her dear patient friend. She carefully squeezed antibiotic cream on the wound, which had now stopped bleeding, and she patched it together with two large Band-Aids. She assured him that it would hold through the night, but insisted that he see a doctor the following day. "There must be someone you can trust."

"Maybe Joe Felshun. He's the dentist in town."

"A dentist?"

"He's better than most of the doctors, and at least he has an x-ray machine."

"I suppose so. He can tell whether any bones are broken. Are you hungry?" Barbara asked. "It's almost seven, and we haven't eaten all day."

"I can't chew. Maybe some soup."

"I'm starved," Barbara said. "Room service is no good. I'll go downstairs and talk to your friend Angelo."

She decided to shower and change clothes. Her blouse was held together by the single button that had survived. It was incredible that she could stand here like this, washing, looking at her face in the mirror, reasonably calm, after having escaped death a few hours before through a childish ploy that was both improbable and ridiculous. Death without dignity was matched by escape without dignity, and both events had taken place in a sadistic, sweating madhouse of a country. Well, one brushed one's teeth and changed one's clothes and reflected on how very much the brushing of teeth had become a symbol of one's bringing-up and of the bringing-up of millions of others, not an exercise of brotherhood or sisterhood or compassion or charity, but simply the brushing of teeth.

After Barbara had changed her blouse and substituted a skirt for jeans, she remembered that she had aspirin, and brought out three tablets for Abrahams. He lay on the couch, his eyes closed, and when she asked in a whisper whether he was asleep, he said, "No—no indeed, love. I have been contemplating life and death. You saved my life, old girl. I can never properly thank you for that."

"What nonsense. You wouldn't have been out there if I hadn't talked you into it."

"No one actually talks anyone into anything. What do you have there, love?"

"Aspirin. Three. Can you take three?"

"Always do."

She gave him the aspirin and a glass of water. He grimaced as he opened his mouth.

"I'll go down now and pick up some food."

"Right-o."

"Just lie there and rest."

Downstairs, in the dining room, the *Times* man rose from a table where he was dining with three other men and intercepted Barbara. "I hear, Miss Lavette, that Cliff Abrahams has been badly beaten."

"We had a small accident in his jeep. Nothing very serious. I've patched him up and tomorrow we'll see a doctor."

"You're sure—nothing very serious? I heard his face had been badly mashed."

"Oh, no. Nothing like that."

"If I can be of any help?"

"Thank you."

Apparently there were no secrets in San Salvador, and the waiter Angelo said to her, "He's still alive, Señor Abrahams?"

"Very much alive. A small accident. His mouth was hurt. Do you have any soup?"

"Good black bean soup. Also, some mashed spiced avocado, soft and delicious. I'll bring it up to your room. He's there?"

"Yes."

"And for you?"

"Anything. Chicken. Whatever."

"I'll bring it."

Back in her suite, Abrahams sat with his hands pressed to his forehead. "But I'm all right," he said in response to her look of alarm. "Just a rotten headache."

When Angelo came with the food, Abrahams was at first unwilling to touch it, protesting that whatever appetite he might have had was now gone. Barbara insisted that he must taste the soup, and after the first mouthful, he continued to eat until the bowl was empty. He ate slowly and apparently painfully.

"I can't talk, old love," he said. "I mean, it hurts like the very devil. So forgive me if I simply shut up."

"I understand," Barbara said.

He refused her offer of the bed. Instead, he took the couch and chair cushions and laid them out on the floor. Barbara, more exhausted than she could remember ever having been, crawled into bed and fell asleep almost immediately. Sometime during the night she awakened, disoriented, her body warmed by the pressure of another body alongside. Reaching out, she felt the skinny chest of Abrahams. He lay beside her, unmoving, giving no clue as to whether he was asleep or awake; and Barbara did not test this, feeling that she understood only too well his loneliness and his need. She fell asleep again, and when she awakened, she was alone in her bed, and the door to the bedroom was closed. The night had done little to slake her weariness, a kind of fatigue that was as much mental as physical. She bathed and then dressed. In the tiny living room of her suite Abrahams was reading a copy of *La Prensa Gráfica* and muttering, half to himself, "Lies, bloody damn lies." He looked up at Barbara and attempted a smile, which made him wince. "Good sleep?"

"Utter exhaustion. You?"

He shrugged. He made no mention of being in her bed, nor did she bring it up. He pointed to a tray. "Pan dulcy and lousy coffee."

"Yes. They grow so much of it, you'd think they'd learn to brew it."

Again, he shrugged.

"I'll have just a mouthful, and then we'll find the dentist. What did you say his name was?"

"Joe Felshun."

"Good enough. Don't talk anymore. Your shirt's a sight, and I could wash it in the sink, but it would take hours to dry. No, don't bother telling me you don't give a damn. I seem to sense that you're very angry, which is all right if you're angry with me, but I think that to be angry down here invites trouble. Angry men are full of macho, and that never helps."

Joe Felshun was of the same mind. "Cool down, Abe. You're lucky." He was the only one she had ever heard call

Abrahams "Abe." "No bones broken. Who put on that weird bandage?"

They had found Felshun at his office, a small stucco building in Escalón, located modestly between two high-walled estates. There was no wall around the small, whitewashed house, and alongside the door a polished brass plate bore the legend DENTISTA AMERICANA. The office was clean and neat and very modern. Felshun x-rayed Abrahams' cheekbone, removed the bandage and replaced it with a more professional dressing.

"Looks good," he decided.

He was a small birdlike man, sharp-faced, an old resident of San Salvador, "who stays alive," he told Barbara, "because there's no replacement. I'm the only man in this whole benighted country who can do a proper root canal or a decent inlay. Believe it or not, I was born here. My folks got here in 'thirty-nine. Out of Germany and no other country they could get into. My English is rotten. Do you follow my Spanish?"

"I do indeed," Barbara said.

"How did this happen?"

Barbara hesitated, and Abrahams said, "You can trust him."

"Damn right!" Felshun said in English.

Barbara told him about their experience the day before.

"I don't believe it. You mean you carried off a charade like that?"

"We're here."

"You're here, but I'm afraid you haven't heard the end of this," he told Abrahams. "In your place I'd lay low a bit until the swelling goes down and it has a chance to heal. I'd say put a cold compress on it, but that's a nasty cut and I'd like it to have all the healing it needs. Use a compress if the pain doesn't stop." He turned to Barbara and regarded her thoughtfully. "You're a nice lady. What on earth are you doing here?"

"I've been asking myself the same question."

Abrahams drove her back to the hotel, dropped her off and said, "Call me tomorrow. I'll be at the office."

As she entered the hotel, the doorman said, "There's a gentleman here to see you," pointing to a tall, bearded man in a black jacket and striped trousers. Evidently, he recognized Barbara at the same time, and he approached her and introduced himself as Señor Raoul Domingo of the Spanish Embassy. "I am the ambassador's secretary, as you might say. Could we sit down somewhere and talk? Perhaps a coffee in the lounge."

When they were seated, he made some small talk about the weather and then complimented her on her use of Spanish. "Both the ambassador and I were astonished at the fact that your accent must have been letter-perfect."

Then they knew about it. "It's less my accent than the wretched Spanish of the soldiers."

His turn. She waited.

"Of course," he said, "the ambassador understands your action and the need for it. We both feel that it probably saved your lives, and we also admire the boldness and the wit that enabled you to carry it off. That pig of a National Guard officer was convinced that we would raise a frightful rumpus over his insult to the ambassador's wife, and he stupidly went straight to the colonel in command of his unit and pleaded his case. You must never underestimate the stupidity of the National Guard, and never underestimate their viciousness. You have placed them in an untenable position, and the plain and simple truth of it is that if you remain here, they will kill you."

"Oh, no! No! I can't believe that."

"Of course you can't. But what I say is absolutely true. You have never encountered men like those who officer the

National Guard. I have been here six years. I know. The ambassador knows. We both have great admiration for what you did. That is why I came here. You must leave immediately."

"I can't. I have an interview with the American ambassador tomorrow."

"Do you remember how they walked into this hotel and gunned down the two American labor people?"

"I saw it happen."

"The ambassador has reason to believe that the same thing will take place here tonight. It will be quite open. If the Englishman is with you, you will both die. If he is not, it will be you alone, while you are eating dinner. I am not trying to frighten you, señora. What is madness elsewhere is matter of fact here. I can only warn you. In your place, I would leave Salvador immediately."

He excused himself, bowed and left. Barbara sat where he had left her, unmoving, staring at a badly painted picture on the wall facing her. She sat unmoving for about ten minutes, and then she went to the desk and asked when the next plane for the States would leave.

"About three o'clock, señora. But that is schedule. It might leave an hour later."

She checked out, paid her bill and then went up to her room and called Abrahams' hotel. His room did not answer. With an increasing sense of panic, she called Reuters and drew a breath of deep relief when she was told that Abrahams was there. His pain must have lessened, because when he heard her voice, he said cheerfully, "Everything jolly at your end, love?"

She repeated what the Spaniard had said to her.

"Vastly exaggerated. On the other hand, you'd better get out of here. There's a plane this afternoon."

"I want you to come with me."

"Barbara, that's impossible. I can't just pack up and chuck my job. Believe me, love, I can take care of myself."

"No one can take care of himself in this place, and if you don't leave, I won't leave."

"Oh, that's lovely—all I need at this point is a female Don Quixote. Now look, Barbara, you've been on my back since you came here. Go home. I swear to God that if you don't, I'll never see you or talk to you again. Leave me alone! Just don't hang on and be a bloody pain in the ass to me!"

She put down the telephone, her eyes brimming with tears, and it was not until she was on the plane, on her way back to California, that she realized it was the only way he could have persuaded her to go.

Twelve

The house on Green Street in San Francisco was untouched and exactly as Barbara had left it. She was always surprised, after any length of time away, to come home and find everything just as it had been, and this time she walked slowly and thoughtfully through every corner of the house, touching things lovingly. At the very top of the narrow wooden house, there were two windows from which she could see San Francisco Bay and the Golden Gate. She could stand in front of one of the windows and watch the gulls swoop down to rest on rooftops just below her point of vantage.

She had stopped for a day in Los Angeles to see Carson, who embraced her with a fierce tenderness that almost crushed her ribs. Then he held her firmly by her shoulders, at arm's length, staring at her.

"Thank God," he said at last.

"It was a little hairy, Carson, but I'm back and I'm all right and I wish I could have stayed at least another week."

"Did you have anything to eat? Did they feed you on that lousy plane?"

"Nothing I wanted to eat."

"I have to talk to you, but not here. Do you want to check in a hotel? Or a late plane to San Francisco?"

"A hotel—at least to get cleaned up."

"I reserved a room at the Wilshire after you called. I'll take you there, and then we can have some dinner and talk."

"I'm not going to tell my story, Carson—not tonight."

"I understand."

"I mean, I want to think about it and brood for a few days and then write it. I'm not holding back. I have a hell of a story. I think I could do twenty thousand words and never have the reader pause to take a breath."

"Well, that's good. That's very good."

"I should think you'd be pleased."

"Of course I'm pleased. If you do twenty thousand words, we'll run it five days, give it the whole first column on page one, and finish it inside. But I don't want to talk about it right now. I want to talk about you."

"I've been going all day, and I'm dog tired."

"You're alive. That's all I care about."

It was after nine when they entered her room. Barbara went into the bathroom. Carson called his office. When she came out of the bathroom about ten minutes later, Carson was still on the telephone, talking very little, listening, nodding. Barbara dropped into a chair facing him, feeling deliciously lightheaded, still high with the wonderful exultation of someone who has escaped from an almost irretrievable situation.

"I'm ready for that dinner you promised."

"Barbara dear," Carson said without pleasure, "there's something I must tell you right now. I can't postpone it. This is something I discovered about an hour before your plane landed, and I've just had the facts fleshed out by Bill Hedley, my international editor. It's rotten news, but I don't know any other way to deal with it except to give it to you straight on. Cliff Abrahams is dead. He was murdered at about five P.M. today, while you were in flight. Thank God you were on that plane."

He waited, and for a few minutes Barbara did not speak. Her face crinkled, and now Carson could see every wrinkle, as if she had grown old instantaneously, very old. Her gray eyes filled with tears, and she put her bent forefinger in her mouth, clamping her teeth on it desperately. It took her minutes to manage to speak, as if she had to learn the art of speech all over again, while a wild protest, wordless, raged crazily in her brain. Then she felt that her heart had stopped beating, that the world had stopped turning, that all motion had ceased, and in this awful void where she was suddenly placed, she was able to talk again and to ask Carson where and how it had happened.

"The first news came to our office from the Reuters people by telephone. Two more detailed stories came in after I left to meet you, one from Reuters and the other from Associated Press. It appears he suffered some kind of facial injury the other day."

"Yes, I was with him," Barbara whispered. "He was pistol-whipped by a National Guard officer, bruised and cut around the face."

"Yes. This afternoon, at about four o'clock, he went to see a friend of his, fellow by the name of Joe Felson or Felron—anyway, something like that."

"Joe Felshun. Yes, he's a dentist. He bandaged Cliff's face properly. Cliff trusted him. That's why we went to a dentist instead of a doctor. There was no doctor he trusted."

"You were with him? You met Felshun?"

"Yes, I met him."

"Why did Cliff go to a dentist?"

"I told you. He didn't trust any of the doctors."

Carson shook his head hopelessly. "Barbara, the story that we have says that Cliff was coming out of this dentist's office, and the dentist had gone to the door to say goodbye to him. A car was standing at the curb, and when Cliff appeared, two National Guard soldiers stepped out of the car. They were carrying submachine guns and they opened fire and riddled both men with bullets. Then they tossed a hand grenade into the open door of the dentist's office. Cliff had been hit over thirty times. Both men died instantly. I don't like to put this to you so bluntly, but it's better than having you read it in the papers. I know Cliff became a good friend—" His voice wavered and choked. "He was a good friend of mine."

What should she say? The word *friend* was meaningless. When it came to the cords that knit one human being to another, the English language was empty. What had Clifford Abrahams been to her—friend, protector, companion, brother? No word fit. For a few days they had connected with each other in some mysterious manner. There was no sex involved—she was old enough to be his mother—yet the connections were strong and good. And now he was dead as a result of a process that she herself had set in motion. She couldn't have known what that day would bring; no one knows what tomorrow will bring, and in any case, once they had been stopped by the National Guard, their fate was sealed. Both she and Abrahams survived by their wits, but she, Barbara Lavette, was here in Los Angeles, and tonight Abrahams was dead.

Such was the news that greeted her in Los Angeles. And now, in her house in Green Street a few days later, she opened her front door and looked down the long sloping street and breathed the clean, cool air washing in from the same Pacific Ocean that lapped at the shores of El Salvador.

Sam and Mary Lou had been at the airport in San Francisco to meet Barbara when she came up from Los Angeles. Anticipating that the newspaper story about the death of Clifford Abrahams might mention her, she had called Sam immediately after hearing the facts from Carson Devron. She was right in her supposition that the stories would mention her, but it was only a passing reference to the effect that a writer from the *Los Angeles Morning World* had been with Abrahams earlier on the day of his death. Apparently, no one filing the story had picked up the business of the trip to meet Constanza, the interception by the National Guard and the incident of the Spanish ambassador's wife. The murder of Abrahams and Felshun remained, for the time being, a mystery.

During the short flight from Los Angeles to San Francisco, Barbara brooded over her relationship with her son. It was too easy an out to decide that he had disappointed her in some indefinable manner, and the truth of the matter was that it was her expectations much more than his failings that had created the gulf between them. In her deepest essence, Barbara Lavette was a product of the nineteen thirties. The thirties had shaped her thinking and turned her toward her father, Dan Lavette, a product of Fisherman's Wharf and the Tenderloin, rather than toward her mother, Jean, a product of one of the wealthiest families on Nob Hill. The great longshore strike of the thirties had put a stamp on her that would remain a part of her as long as she lived, just as her foray into Nazi Germany had given her a personal knowledge of fascism.

Yet the thirties was a time gone away and barely remembered, and why should Sam honor it any more than another would? The past was filled with things that made no sense to this generation. It was quite incredible to them that a person still alive and vigorous could have been a part of that past, the agony of the Great Depression, the rise of a man called Hitler, the postwar period of fear and intimidation that was called McCarthyism, and the slow growth of a mushroom-like cloud that had changed the world forever. Why must her son be more than he was, a decent, reasonable man, a good and honest physician, a man politically if vaguely on the side of the angels?

It's not too late to learn, she told herself. Listen to him. Don't make him listen to you.

She was ready to listen to him, but he offered no advice, simply embracing her in a bear hug. As tall as she was, he loomed over her, and then held her at arm's length, just as Carson had, studying her.

"My word," he said, "you look wonderful. You look absolutely wonderful," and in the manner of his saying it, there was an acknowledgment of his mother as a woman.

Mary Lou kissed her and said, "I'm glad you're back. I'm so glad you're back."

Barbara said nothing about Clifford Abrahams. It was of another world, and she needed no one to share her grief or offer sympathy. When they questioned her, she put off answers with the excuse that it was all very complex, and when she had finished writing they would be able to read thousands of words on the subject.

This was also her response to Freddie, who came the following day to pour out his problems. She told herself not to be upset by Freddie's being so totally immersed in his own frustrations; she must take it as a compliment, for Freddie, unlike Sam, looked upon her quite simply and childishly as a figure unconquerable and thoroughly unflappable. Freddie had his own difficulties with the world. He still lived apart, but he was now engaged in an exciting and rewarding affair with May Ling, his divorced wife.

"Then why don't you marry the poor child again, before she becomes pregnant out of wedlock?"

"She isn't a poor child. She's thirty-four years old, and she won't marry me. Our sex was rotten when we were married, and it's great now, but she says she'd have to have her head examined to marry someone like me twice. Everyone says, Oh, May Ling, the poor child. No one gives a damn about my situation. You haven't even the patience to listen to me, and right now you're thinking, Why doesn't this poor nut get out of here and leave me alone?"

If the truth be told, Barbara was thinking something of the kind, and she was upset at being caught with it, and it made her not a whit superior to lay Freddie's words against a recollection of hunger and fear in El Salvador—something that she had been engaged in, a kind of thinking that, in her youth, made her sneer, at least mentally, at the pastors who served the very rich congregants of Grace Cathedral in San Francisco. But years later, when she talked to Billy Clawson, Eloise's brother and an Episcopal minister, he made the point to her that the well-to-do were not without anguish, and that if there was a God, it was unlikely that he judged people purely by their economic status.

Barbara had never given too much thought to God, except to note that if he existed, he ran things poorly, and she had never accepted the validity of judgments; but Billy Clawson was so gentle and decent that his few words on the subject stayed with her, engraved even more deeply after his death in Korea, where he was serving as an army chaplain. All of this surfaced in her mind and memory, nudged by Freddie's statement, which she immediately denied.

"No, Freddie. I don't want you to leave and I don't think you're a nut. Do you love May Ling?"

"I've always loved her. She's wonderful and bright and witty. It all works, as long as I'm not married to her."

"Then don't worry about marrying her. Let it untangle itself. It will, you know."

"I hope so."

The following day, three cases of wine arrived from the Higate Winery, delivered directly to her front door and proclaiming Freddie's gratitude and love. There were twelve bottles of Mountain White, which Freddie always claimed was the best dry white wine made in California, twelve bottles of Higate Pinot Noir, that marvelous red that Higate, of all California wineries, had been exporting to France since 1938, and twelve bottles of Higate's Cabernet Sauvignon, which they so often drank on family occasions. Barbara sat and stared at the wine, remembering and remembering while her eyes filled with tears.

"The endless tears," she said aloud. "Tears and laughter. Thank God for the mix."

Thank God for Eloise. She could talk to Eloise. Without Eloise, there would be no one she could really talk to. Not Carson. How could she make Carson understand about Clifford Abrahams? "Could I tell Carson that I loved him?" she asked Eloise.

Eloise understood the bereavement of love.

She felt that Eloise had knowledge of something she, Barbara, had missed. They had shared pain, deep, awful pain; but Eloise had Adam, and Barbara was alone. Adam had been her husband for more than thirty years, and they had had the chance to grow old together and to learn in the process. Barbara grew old alone.

Yet Barbara felt that for herself, too, the men wrenched away from her time after time were like a single man. A curse had been placed upon her. But she fought the curse and overcame it, and found another man. He was a man gentle and soft under all the strength a man believes he must have, a man who could hear the lyric sweetness hidden in ordinary speech, somewhat like herself in man's flesh. All of her men were matched to that specific: Marcel, slender, gracious and very brave; Bernie, gentle and without violence, for all that he had lived half his life as a soldier, and very brave too. They were always brave men: Boyd, and then Carson Devron, whom she had left and come back to and who was the single man alive among all her ghosts.

"I sometimes wonder," she said to Eloise, "would I have lived better without all the sorrow that came from my loving?"

"Not you, Barbara. No. Not you."

"I suppose not. So many men I loved, and they loved me, and then I meet Clifford Abrahams."

"I read in the paper that you knew him."

"I knew him a little, yes. For a few weeks we were together, morning, evening, noon and night. It was a new experience for me, Eloise, being with a man day after day, with no flesh ever touching more than a handshake, and sex blown out the window, and he a handsome and delightful young man. It was such an odd relationship. I never even asked him whether he was married, and I didn't know until I read in the paper that he had been divorced and that he had two kids in England. My heart goes out to them. But, you see, he existed for me outside of those things, and as I grew so damn fond of him, I put away all those feelings that we are not supposed to have at our age, and which we damn well do have, like fires inside us that burn and mock at us and won't be doused. You know, this thing about Jews, which we all have whether we will admit it or not, and especially in our family, where it has been like a thread running through both our lives, ever since my father and Adam's grandfather became partners after the earthquake. Well, when I first met Cliff, I just took it for granted that he was Jewish, partly because of his name, which certainly sounds like a Jewish name, but also because of the way he was, which I don't understand at all, and certainly not because of his appearance. He was about six feet three inches tall, rather long, wavy hair—you know the way the British wear it—light brown hair, pale eyes, and he sort of shambled in that funny way some of the British have of walking. Well, it turned out that he wasn't Jewish at all. He explained that his people were Church of England and had been for the three hundred years or so that he knew about. No idea whatsoever where the name Abrahams had come from."

"He fell in love with you?" Eloise wondered.

"A very strange thing happened—" Barbara began. Her voice drifted away. How do you tell what makes no sense?

They took the long downhill walk from Green Street to the Bay, and once there they leaned against the sea rail, watching the gulls scream and swoop as they fought the gold-tinted wavelets for the fish. There, alone, yet with people all around them, in a place where no one carried submachine guns and where no murder squads roamed, Barbara poured out the story of that last few days in El Salvador. "And now it's like a dream," she said to Eloise, "but it wasn't a dream. I woke up in the middle of the night, and he was in bed with me, asleep, and Eloise, I think that never in all my life did I have a better moment than when I reached out and touched him and felt the warmth of his body—and that was all. I fell asleep, and in the morning I was alone in the bed, a foolish old lady."

"I think you're a remarkable lady, and I'm happy that I know you and that we have always been such dear friends. As for old, I don't know what old is, I don't know what time is. We've talked about that. We change, but when I think back to the first time I saw Adam, in that wonderful gallery your mother owned, it seems like only a moment ago. That was in 'forty-six, wasn't it? Why must we behave by the rules they make for us—at such and such a time, we must become old women and give up?"

"But that's what we become, old women, and we give up because we can't change what has happened. When we were young, we could sort of change it, choose another road, another style, but not anymore." After a moment, Barbara added, "I'm not down. I had my bad moments after I heard about Clifford's death, but I'm all right about that now. Not really all right—that never happens, as you know—but all right enough to keep things going."

They both thought about that, and then Barbara added, "We have to, I suppose."

"I suppose."

Clair was very close to the end. Dr. Kellman felt that she might have at least some additional weeks, perhaps months, if they put her in the hospital; yet after little persuasion, he agreed with Barbara's brother Joe that it would be less than an act of mercy. In any case, Sally would have fought against it.

"They do these awful things to people who are dying, and they go on breathing in a sort of semi-death. The fact that most things have become hideous doesn't mean that we should inflict a hideous end on those we love, and Mother would be the first one to fight it. She's had a long and good life, and most of it has been at Higate. Let her die there."

It was easier for Sally to talk about death than to face her mother's absence. There would be a yawning void. Of the three children that Clair had carried, she was the youngest. She was beautiful, brilliant, driven to taste everything—yet in the end drawn back to the Napa Valley. It was her cradle. The poems she had written and published were all of the Valley: memories, departure, return.

She was sentimental. She told Joe that she wanted to die when the time came to die. "When I'm dying, let me die here. Don't you dare put me into one of those crazy machines in the hospital."

Eloise begged Barbara not to put off coming to Higate. She recognized Barbara's need not to be pulled away from the story she was writing. At the same time, Joe had told her that Clair's death was near. Barbara put other things aside and drove out to the Napa Valley. It was hot, the Valley shimmering in the heat, the vines green and changed from rows of naked sticks to verdant necklaces that ringed the hillsides.

Joe was at the house when Barbara arrived. He was downstairs in the big kitchen, using the telephone, which he put down to hug Barbara desperately. It was the first time he had seen his sister since she returned from El Salvador. Joe looked haggard. He had lost weight. For years, Joe had been called the last country doctor. He sat and talked to his patients without counting the minutes. He doubled as internist and obstetrician and very often became the family's pediatrician. Sally was born in the Napa Valley, which made Joe very much of an insider with the odd assortment of folk who inhabited the valley. He still made house calls, but he had passed his sixty-fifth year, and day by day his routine became more difficult. Today, he appeared very tired, new lines on his face and heavy circles under his eyes. When Barbara remarked on his appearance, he explained that during the past week he had lost three patients. "It beats you down," he said to Barbara. "We grow old. It seems to happen so suddenly. Your patients are old and they go. Well, that's the way it is. I'm glad you're here. Clair is dying. She slips in and out of consciousness. I gave her an injection, so there's no pain now. But very soon she'll close her eyes and slip away."

"Is Danny here?" Barbara asked.

"He'll be here this evening. May Ling was here. She had to go home. Freddie is upstairs with Clair. I just spoke to Sam, and he'll be here tonight."

Eloise and Adam joined them in the kitchen. "She asked us to leave," Adam said uncertainly. "She asked to be alone with Freddie."

"Where's Sally?"

"In her old room," Adam said. "You know, Mother always kept it just as it was. Sally's in there, crying. She's taking it very hard."

On the other hand, Barbara thought, taking it very dramatically, with much histrionics, which Sally would do if she faced the end of the world.

"Mother wants to see you," Eloise said. "Why don't you go up now?"

"If she wanted to be with Freddie—"

"Don't worry. Go up. We'll join you in a few minutes."

In the bedroom where Clair lay in bed, her Mexican servant, María, stood by the door, a somber stone figure. She opened the door at the sound of Barbara's steps. Evidently, alone with Freddie did not mean María's absence. Freddie sat by Clair's bedside, holding her hand. Clair, her face bloodless, lay still, her eyes closed.

"Freddie?"

He read the question and shook his head. Then Clair opened her eyes and saw Barbara.

"Hello, my dear," she whispered. And then to Freddie, "Kiss me, dear, and then leave me with Barbara." She spoke with great effort.

Freddie bent and kissed her, and then he left the room. Barbara sat close to the bed, leaning over to hear Clair say, "Don't let this break us up, Barbara. We're a good family, and if we tug at each other, that's only natural."

"I know, Clair."

"I'm very tired, Barbara."

She appeared to doze off again. Barbara waited for a while, and then Adam came into the room. "I'll sit with Mom for a while, Barbara. Go downstairs and have something to eat."

At seven-twenty that evening, Clair Harvey Levy died. She was eighty-two years old, and her last wishes were observed, to be cremated and her ashes spread among the vine rows. "I want no grave," she had written. "No one lives in a grave. If I can leave a little nourishment for the fruit of the earth and some memories for those I love, that will be enough."

Adam had a simple stone cut, and fastened to it a bronze plaque with the words of his mother's wishes engraved on it. Two days after the cremation, they gathered together at Higate, the family and friends, for a sort of memorial service. Barbara, now the oldest surviving member of the family, knew that Clair had been born a Christian, but of which denomination and whether baptized or not, no one seemed to know. Neither she nor Jake had ever appeared to require or thirst for the comforts of religion, and when some religious ceremony was required at the winery, Father Gerry Mulligan would drive up from Napa and help out, since almost all of the workers at the winery were Catholic; and every year, a case of sacramental wine was sent to the Catholic church in Napa for Christmas service and a case of nonsacramental wine for Christmas cheer. So at this memorial service of sorts, Father Mulligan contributed a touch of a sacrament, more to please Eloise than the others. They gathered together in the big whitewashed hall of the old stone winery, once the aging room and now a sort of reception room for visitors, during the thirty days when Higate opened its doors to the public for tasting. In the room, along with the family and friends, were the families of the men who worked at the winery, some of them resident there and employed at Higate all of their lives.

Father Mulligan, a stout, small man, was helped onto the tasting counter, and standing there, he blessed the people assembled, the children and grandchildren of Clair Harvey Levy. "It's a pity the dear, lovely lady was not Catholic, since she would have honored our religion. But she was a grand, decent, generous and beautiful woman—oh, in her youth, she was something to see, with that great head of flaming red hair. Somewhere in back of her was Irish, believe me, so there was somewhere a bit of the Catholic, but it wouldn't matter. Whatever golden gates she faces, they'll open, rest assured."

After this, food and wine; and people wept and others laughed. Barbara found herself in a corner with Sally and May Ling and Freddie, Sally begging her to talk about Clair. "How did it begin?" Sally begged her. "Mother would never tell us. She loved her secrets."

Barbara felt like a storytelling teacher in a crowded classroom. Others were gathering around. It had become a mixture of a wake, a Jewish sitting-in-mourning, and a class in the history of San Francisco. Surely, the Easterners were right when they spoke of going back to the States from California. This whole place was a new thing.

"I only know what Pop told me," Barbara protested. "Clair's daddy, old Captain Jack Harvey, commanded one of those lumber freighters that ran up and down the California coast in the old days, and then things changed, most of the lumber ships were docked and so was Jack Harvey. Just for a place to live, he took the job of caretaker for a big iron lumber ship that was docked. He had Clair with him. I guess she was eight or nine. You know, my daddy and old Jake's daddy were partners. They decided to take a big step and buy this old iron ship. Harvey had been married to some pretty kid who became pregnant, delivered Clair, and then took off. Jack was father and mother to her. Jake was Mark Levy's kid, thirteen years old at that time, and he saw Clair, and that was it."

Sally burst into tears and made her way outside. Adam started to follow her, but Barbara stopped him and said she would go to Sally, and that tears at this time should not be interfered with. Outside, alongside the tasting room, the Mexicans had set up cook-fires in the stone remains of an old pressing tank. They were cooking steaming pots of beans, chicken mole, and fish and peppers, and on a slab of hot metal they were heating tortillas. Sally crossed the road and stood under a tree, her shoulders heaving. Barbara went to her, and Sally fell into her arms. The tears dried, Sally clung to Barbara, and finally Sally said, "The damn trouble is that I can't take a step anywhere here without seeing Mom and Pop. Do you know what she did, Barbara? She told Cándido Truaz that when she died, there was to be this kind of a memorial right here, and she even told María what kind of food they were to cook. Damn it, she was something."

A week later, Barbara had finished her piece on El Salvador. Reading it through, she regretted that she hadn't done better, but that was very much the case with everything she had ever written—and here at least she had achieved, she felt, a sense of that miasma of horror which pervaded that poor damned land. The report, over twenty thousand words, had been written as coldly and objectively as possible. She had always felt that her writing was most effective when she put down the facts and let them speak for themselves. Yet never before had she been involved in this manner, so deeply and emotionally and with such a sense of weariness and despair.

She addressed the envelope that contained the manuscript, brought it to the post office and sent it off to Carson without even a note. She disliked commenting on her own work.

That night, she dined with Sam. He had told Mary Lou that he had to talk to his mother, just the two of them alone, and when Mary Lou asked whether it was a medical matter, he said no, it was simply a question of relationship.

"That's very interesting," Barbara said after Sam spelled out his excuse to Mary Lou. "You were thinking of our relationship?"

"Mainly. There was a time, Mom, when we could talk

openly and frankly about a great many things." *Mom* was the soft, neutral ground.

"Yes," Barbara agreed. "There's a lot of that in our family, and it's one of the best things we have. I pity people who bottle up their angers and frustrations. They remain prisoners of themselves."

"On the other hand," Sam reminded her, "it has not been easy to be Barbara Lavette's son."

"I can go along with that."

"Or the son of my father. Do you know, when I was studying medicine in Israel, I was a curiosity. Cohen's son. Whenever they needed a figurehead or a hero, another Mickey Marcus, they trotted me out and recited the deeds of a father I never knew, how he flew the planes across the continent and across the ocean to Czechoslovakia to buy arms for the War of Independence, and I would stand on the platform like a total horse's ass, full of anger inside, screaming inside of myself, Who the devil needs a hero? The world is filled with dead heroes. I want a living father."

"And then you wanted a mother."

"No, it doesn't follow quite that way. I had a mother. I loved you so much it made me a little crazy. I still do. I look at you and nothing has changed for me. You are a great lady. I remember you telling me about the time you met Eleanor Roosevelt and your feeling that she was the most remarkable person you had ever known. I remember listening and thinking that there I was, sitting and facing the most remarkable person *I* had ever known. So I had a mother, and I still do. I was talking to Toby Fitzsimmons, who's chief of psychiatry at the hospital, and rambling about my two failed relationships—it's the word we use these days instead of love and fealty—the lovely Rachel in Israel and Carla here, both of them round, dark and beautiful women, and he pointed out that they were the absolute opposite of my mother. They were sweet as honey, but it didn't work. I finally made it work with Mary Lou, who is like you in more ways than you can imagine, with at least something of the same background that you had, and what it all adds up to, I don't know, but it seems to have smoothed away the hard edges. Do I made any sense at all?" he asked her. "Did I tell you Mary Lou is pregnant?"

"That makes the most sense of all."

"You know, I was talking to Toby Fitzsimmons because last week they made me chief of surgery. It's an honor, Mom."

"It's more than an honor. It's absolutely wonderful, and I am overwhelmed. Totally overwhelmed. Do you know how I feel, Sammy? I once met a Japanese Roshi who had experienced what they call *satori,* or enlightenment, and I asked him what it felt like, and he said not very different than he felt before, except that every step he took, his feet were two inches above the ground. And I am absolutely sure that when we leave here, every step I take will be at least six inches above the ground."

He stared at her lovingly and thoughtfully. "Do you mind it very much—being old?"

"I don't think so, Sammy. Sometimes it's tiresome, but mostly it's quite extraordinary."

"Would you be young again if you could?"

"You do ask the strangest questions tonight. The answer is, I don't think so, and please order a bottle of champagne, and when is the baby expected?"

Sam ordered the champagne and informed his mother that the baby was progressing nicely and would be born in November. "Scorpio," he said.

"If you believe that nonsense."

"Mom, when you are born and bred in California, there's an obligation to accept a certain amount of nonsense. Your birthday's in November."

"Good heavens, was I invited here to be instructed in

astrology? What would your learned colleagues at the hospital think of all this?"

"They have compartmentalized minds. It's a California affliction. No, Mom, I asked for the two of us here alone just to talk. I think I'm coming of age. I'd like to be your friend."

The champagne arrived and was opened. Sam poured two glasses.

"To you," Sam said.

"No. What will you call the child?"

"If it's a boy, we'll call him Bernie. If we have a girl, we'll call her Barbara. Mary Lou agrees."

"Then we'll drink to them, whosoever!"

Carson ran Barbara's story for five days in five parts, front page, column one. He brought the first issue up to San Francisco himself, hot off the press, appearing at her house slightly before midnight. Unable to talk him out of doing just that, she was expecting him. She had prepared a supper of cold cuts and salad, which Carson lit into hungrily while Barbara reread the first section of her report, experiencing the writer's pleasure of reading her finished product in type. When she had finished and Carson had washed down a plate of cold chicken and potato salad with half a bottle of Higate Mountain White, he said to her, "How do you like it?"

"Decent, objective journalism—wouldn't you agree?"

"A little less objective than it might have been, but what the hell. If it doesn't get a Pulitzer, it won't be the first really good story that they overlooked. It will be noticed, be sure."

"If you've come up here to turn me down personally when I ask you for another assignment—well, you can just forget it. I'm not asking."

"What the hell kind of a publisher would I be to come all the way up here at midnight, carrying a newspaper hot off the press, to turn down a request by you? You're scrambling your buttons, Barbara."

"It happens—sooner or later."

"You want an assignment, come down to my office in L.A. and ask. Make an appointment first."

"Hear! Hear! You're an old fussbudget, Devron." She put the newspaper aside, went over to Carson, and kissed the small bald spot on top of his head. Then she stood behind him, her palms against his cheeks. "I wish we had made it," she said. "I like you."

"I like you too."

"No more assignments, dear Carson. I shall sit in front of the fire for a while. I shall learn to knit."

He stood up and faced her. "You don't have a fireplace."

"No, I don't."

"Well, I did have an idea. How about a column twice a week? You're always in a royal rage over something. We'll put you on the op ed page, alongside Bill Buckley, so as to balance him, you might say."

"Carson!"

"Space rates."

"That's cheap—unworthy. I'm an old pro, and you offer me space rates."

"Take it or leave it."

"I'll take it!" she cried. "Bless your heart." She looked at the clock. "One-thirty. You'll stay overnight?"

"At the Fairmont. I reserved a room there. I'm not rejecting you, old girl—"

"Carson dear, you're wonderful. You're the ultimate of white Protestant respectability, just as I am. Our sinning is no less than anyone else's, but our self-deception is unbelievable. We are old folks. I know more about you than anyone else in the world. I was married to you, I loved you, I hated you, I divorced you, and like a dumbbell you never stopped loving me. We tried sex more times than you could shake a stick at and it hardly ever worked, did it? And I'll bet a fig that somewhere there's a lady that turns you into a horny old goat, but I'm not the lady, and I simply adore you, and I think you've been kinder to me than anyone in the world. Where's your wife?"

"Palm Springs."

"There you are. What a simple, harmless and dishonest affair we're having!"

"You know," he admitted, "what you said about self-deception is true. I left word at the hotel that I was not to be disturbed and that I would not take any calls."

"I have three bedrooms. You can crawl in with the old lady, or you can go it alone in one of the guest rooms."

"As you say, old dear. How about a nightcap?"

"You remember what happened the last time we did nightcaps?"

"I'll take my chances. We'll do it gently. Just a glass of sherry."

Barbara poured the sherry, and she and Carson sprawled on the chairs in her living room. "Do you know," Carson said to her, "it's a sort of relief to put sex aside and just sit and talk to a woman you're deeply fond of. All our lives, we're driven by this man-woman thing and the crazy macho that my sex has created and the wagon circle that you all had to build against it. It creates and destroys, and it's a blessing to reach a point where you can put it aside."

"But it's a wonderful game when you play it," Barbara said wistfully.

"Regrets?"

"Yes and no. I love men, no question about that. When Boyd died, I didn't know any way to live without a man. I had to learn, and it hasn't been easy. But I'm all right now."

"Because you found your way back to the windmills."

Barbara smiled fondly. "Dear Carson, you understand me, don't you? You know why I must tilt at the windmills."

"I've always known." He finished the glass of sherry. "Shall we turn in?"

"Sure." She took his arm. "Nighttime, this house turns cold as a witch's tit, and there's nothing in the world much better than a man's body next to yours."

"No question about that."

They went on up the stairs.

Two days later, Birdie MacGelsie telephoned and said to Barbara, "I'd like to bring some people around to talk to you."

"About what?" Barbara asked suspiciously.

"The freeze. The freeze on making those damn bombs."

"Who do you want to bring around?"

"Why are you so suspicious?" Birdie asked.

"Because I'm comfortable. I'm relaxed and I'm comfortable. I'm writing two columns a week for the *L.A. World* and I read books and I have cable, so I can watch a film when I want to, and every week I lunch with Eloise, and I'm normal and happy and content."

"What nonsense!" Birdie snorted. "You've never been normal and you've never been content. Happy, I don't know about."

"It may surprise you, but I happen to be quite content. Who do you want to bring around?"

"Just a few people—Father Gibbons, he'd be representing the Peace Fellowship; Terry Distan—"

"Gay rights?" Barbara interrupted.

"Yes."

"That's already an odd combination. Who else?"

"Your ex-daughter-in-law, Carla; she's become president of the Bay Area Chicano Union. And Abner Berman; he's the local NEA guy. Just the four of them for the moment."

"I shouldn't listen to you," Barbara said.

"Please, Barbara. You've never said no to anything like this."

There was an interval of silence, and then Barbara sighed. "All right."

"Two o'clock?"

"Make it three. I have a column to finish."

At three o'clock, she let them into her house and seated them in her living room, Carla, as vibrant as ever, Father Gibbons, a Jesuit priest, a slight man with a ferret face and a pair of black, accusing eyes, Terry Distan, a Montgomery Street type, tailored meticulously from head to foot, three-piece suit and properly clipped beard, and Abner Berman, jovial in tweeds and pipe and knit tie, and of course Birdie MacGelsie, swallowing her smile of triumph, deferring to Father Gibbons, who opened by asking, "Would you like me to make a short, convincing preachment to the effect that unless we rid ourselves of that cursed bomb, the good God will gaze upon a planet devoid of life?"

"No," Barbara said emphatically. "I am not friendly and I don't like sermons. I know what you're here for. There are other people in San Francisco. Why must you upset my life?"

"Ah, yes," Berman said gently. "But the plain ugly truth is that no one can do it the way you can. You have a track record that won't go away. You created Mothers for Peace, which was the smartest and most effective peace movement during Vietnam. We watched that. We watched your campaign for Congress—"

"You know our intentions," Father Gibbon broke in. "We intend to put a million people on Market Street. They'll be doing the same thing in New York, Chicago, Philadelphia, Boston—yes, in L.A."

"And you feel that will move Mr. Reagan?"

"Maybe not," Distan said. "But if we pull it off, the whole world will see it, and that means the Russians too."

"I agree with you," Barbara said. "If we pull it off, the whole world will look at it, and maybe Mr. Reagan too. But let me say this, Terry: if I let myself be talked into this, I don't want to have you telling me that you will deliver a hundred thousand gays if you can carry your own slogans for gay rights. If we march and assemble for the freeze, it is for the freeze, period. And that goes for you, Father—you don't push antiabortion here, and you too, Carla. For once the Chicanos are going to stop shouting about civil rights and talk peace. Either this is a single effort in one direction, or you go elsewhere for somebody to tie it up."

"I'll buy that," Distan said.

"And what makes you so sure I'm a right-to-life gent?" Father Gibbon asked. "Things change, Barbara. It's a fluid world we live in."

"The point is," Birdie said, "that this is the very beginning. We want to start the organizing pressure from here."

"What you mean," Barbara said, "is that you want to turn my home into a madhouse, and have a place rent-free, where you will install twenty telephone lines and stick me with the unpaid bills and store enough leaflets and pamphlets to make the halls impassable, and have every nut in the Bay Area aware that all this commie peace business comes from Barbara Lavette's house on Green Street."

"Sort of," Birdie admitted.

"We are not just talk," Berman insisted. "We will be with you every inch of the way. We understand your position and accept that you're not a young woman."

"You understand that?" Barbara said acidly.

"I'm sorry."

"Sorry, indeed! Now listen to me, all of you. If there were anyone around who loved me, he'd talk me out of it. Here, I'm alone against the lot of you. I'll base my response on two questions. First, has a date been chosen?"

"Three weeks from now. So the agony is at least terminal."

"And second, this: three weeks leaves small time for fundraising. How much money do we begin with?"

Birdie handed her a slip of paper. "Here's my check for five thousand. MacGelsie howled, but I won."

Terry Distan handed her a check for two thousand dollars. "It's a beginning," he said.

"We should have five thousand by Friday," Berman said.

"I don't know what," Carla said. "We'll do our best."

"What I can squeeze out of my lot, I don't know," Father Gibbon told them. "I have an appointment with the bishop for lunch tomorrow. I'll do my best."

"I will not touch the money thing," Barbara said. "We need a treasurer right now."

"I'm a lawyer," Distan told them. "I'll be glad to open the bank account and draw up the papers. We'll want two signatures on the checks. Suppose I say myself and Birdie?"

"So I guess I've done it again." Barbara sighed. "Ah, well, at least it's only three weeks. So let's get down to work."

That night, Barbara had dinner with Sam and Mary Lou, and she told them about the freeze demonstration plans. Sam said nothing. Mary Lou told Barbara that she had given up her job at the hospital. "But still and all, I don't see myself reading novels and watching the booby box for the next five months. Can I have a job, Barbara?"

"The pay is small—nonexistent, as a matter of fact."

"I'll be there tomorrow," Mary Lou agreed.

"Sam," Barbara said to her son, "don't be intimidated. Just say whatever you want to say."

"I don't know what I want to say."

"Ah, well, dear one, just don't see it as anything extraordinary. Some of us have to shout now and then, even if no one hears us."

"People hear you," Mary Lou said.

"I like to think so. Otherwise, I'd feel too absurd."

"You're never absurd."

"Oh, I have been, rest assured. One spits into the wind, you know. I like to think of such a label or requiem for my kind of person. Nothing pretentious, nothing like all the bad prose the other side lays on their cherished ones. I would leave it right there and call us the *wind-spitters*. It defines all the absurd qualities that we possess. It mocks at our impotence, yet it admits that we do stand up to the wind, that we face it and that we spit directly into it. I am not apologizing for anything tonight, Sammy; I am simply trying to explain your mother."

But having said that, Barbara was embarrassed. Regardless of chronology, she felt too young for requiems and thought that even to define herself as a *wind-spitter* was somehow pretentious.

The man and the woman sitting at the table with her were smiling affectionately.

"The hell with labels and explanations," she said. "I am just what I am, Barbara Lavette, and I intend to go on living with it and doing what I've always done. And that goes for the three of us, doesn't it? It's not easy to become the friend of someone you cherish, but we'll try."

"I'll buy that," Sam said.

"You wanted to say something before?"

"I think I said it, Mom."

"Then let's eat," Mary Lou decided. "I skipped lunch."

"You're eating for two, dear, and skipping lunch makes no sense. You see, whatever else changes, I'm still your mother, so call the waiter, Sam, and we'll order. That's the crux of it. Even the best of philosophy never filled an empty stomach."

"And I'll buy that too," Sam agreed.

THE LAVETTES

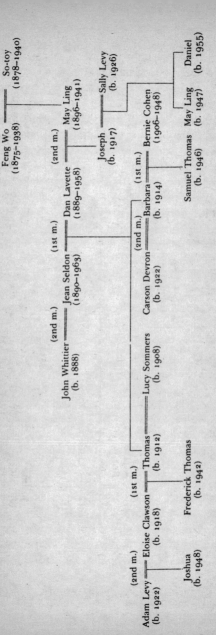

THE LEVYS

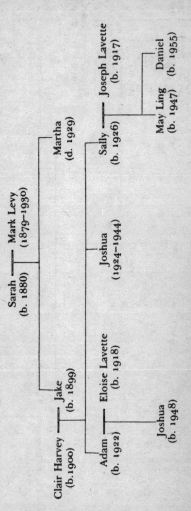

Sarah (b. 1880) ——— Mark Levy (1879–1930)

Clair Harvey (b. 1900) ——— Jake (b. 1899)

Martha (d. 1929)

Sally (b. 1926) ——— Joseph Lavette (b. 1917)

Adam (b. 1922) ——— Eloise Lavette (b. 1918)

Joshua (1924–1944)

Joshua (b. 1948)

May Ling (b. 1947)   Daniel (b. 1955)

Lose yourself in fabulous, old-fashioned storytelling— the triumphant *Lavette Family Saga*

_____	#1 THE IMMIGRANTS	14175-3	$4.50
_____	#2 SECOND GENERATION	17915-7	4.50
_____	#3 THE ESTABLISHMENT	12393-3	4.50
_____	#4 THE LEGACY	14720-4	4.50
_____	#5 THE IMMIGRANT'S DAUGHTER	13988-0	4.50

from HOWARD FAST